# THREE IN A BED

**ANDREW CROKER**

This edition first published in 2016

Unbound
6th Floor, Mutual House, 70 Conduit Street, London W1S 2GF
www.unbound.co.uk



Typeset by PDQ

Art direction by Mecob

A CIP record for this book
is available from the British Library

ISBN 978-1-78352-156-2 (trade hbk)
ISBN 978-1-78352-158-6 (ebook)
ISBN 978-1-78352-157-9 (limited edition)

Printed in Great Britain by Clays Ltd, St Ives Plc

1 3 5 7 9 8 6 4 2

*For Joanna, who let(s) me get on with it.*

Dear Reader,

The book you are holding came about in a rather different way to most others. It was funded directly by readers through a new website: Unbound.

Unbound is the creation of three writers. We started the company because we believed there had to be a better deal for both writers and readers. On the Unbound website, authors share the ideas for the books they want to write directly with readers. If enough of you support the book by pledging for it in advance, we produce a beautifully bound special subscribers' edition and distribute a regular edition and e-book wherever books are sold, in shops and online.

This new way of publishing is actually a very old idea (Samuel Johnson funded his dictionary this way). We're just using the internet to build each writer a network of patrons. Here, at the back of this book, you'll find the names of all the people who made it happen.

Publishing in this way means readers are no longer just passive consumers of the books they buy, and authors are free to write the books they really want. They get a much fairer return too – half the profits their books generate, rather than a tiny percentage of the cover price.

If you're not yet a subscriber, we hope that you'll want to join our publishing revolution and have your name listed in one of our books in the future. To get you started, here is a £5 discount on your first pledge. Just visit unbound.com, make your pledge and type threebed in the promo code box when you check out.

Thank you for your support,

Dan, Justin and John
Founders, Unbound

Andrew Croker has spent forty years in the front line of sports marketing and media. In the nineties he globetrotted for super-agent Mark McCormack, then tried and failed over lunch in New York to sell his doomed internet startup to Rupert Murdoch. Undaunted (right idea, wrong time) he went on to found the world's leading digital sports content business.

*Three in a Bed* is his first novel.

# THREE IN A BED

ANDREW CROKER

*People want to know that three things are going to happen. One: action will be taken to get to the bottom of these specific revelations and allegations – about police investigations and all the rest of it. Two: action will be taken to learn wider lessons for the future of the press in this country. And three: that there will be clarity, real clarity, about how all this has come to pass, and the responsibilities we all have for the future. That's what the country expects – and I want to make sure that everything that needs to be done will be done.*

**DAVID CAMERON**

*I only take Viagra when I'm with more than one woman.*

**JACK NICHOLSON**

# THE FRONT PAGE

*Three in a Bed* is entirely a work of fiction, though set against the background of real events. The newspaper headlines are genuine (and beyond parody anyway), and when real people do appear, their actions and words are entirely imagined – any similarity between them and the fictional characters is entirely coincidental, but it does add to the fun.

Vivienne Mather led me to Unbound, completely sidestepping the ritual humiliation of serial rejection, where Dan Kieran, John Mitchinson and their delightful team gave me this chance. Two of those in particular helped me with the heavy lifting: my wonderful editor Liz Garner – who was endlessly patient and skilful – and Mathew Clayton – who came up with countless good ideas, including the title.

I also want to thank those fourth estate insiders who read and commented on various drafts, including Mark Austin, Paul Kelso, Frances Coverdale, Tim Willcox, Tom Latchem, and others who, given the subject matter, must remain anonymous.

Finally, crowdfunding only works (the clue is there) with a crowd. I am indebted to all those who supported me – all listed here – and made this possible.

**Andrew Croker**
London, 2015

**Sunday 22nd June 2014**

***The Sunday Times*: BOSSES DAMN PM'S FAILURE TO CURB EU**

***Mail on Sunday*: I LEFT MY HUSBAND AND CHILDREN FOR OUR GAY AU PAIR**

***Sun on Sunday*: ENGLAND ACE LUKE BEGGED ME FOR THREESOME**

**Monday 23rd June 2014**

***The Daily Express*: HAYFEVER HELL AS BRITAIN HOTS UP**

***The Daily Mail*: DID THIS PREACHER GROOM JIHADI BRITONS?**

***Daily Star*: KEEP CALM AND HAVE SEX**

**Tuesday 24th June 2014**

***The Guardian*: JAILED: REPORTERS PAY PRICE FOR EGYPT'S CRACKDOWN**

***The Times*: QUEEN TO VISIT GAME OF THRONES SET**

***The Sun*: HEAD'S TWO-WEEK BRAZIL WORLD CUP BUNK-OFF**

**Wednesday 25th June 2014**

***The Independent*: COULSON GUILTY OF PHONE HACKING**

***The Sun*: GREAT DAY FOR RED TOPS. REBEKAH BROOKS NOT GUILTY**

***The Daily Star*: SUMMER PLAGUE OF FLEAS FROM HELL**

**Thursday 26th June 2014**

***The Times*: MET FORCED TO DEFEND ROLE IN £100m HACKING TRIAL**

***The Independent*: THE WONGA CONSPIRACY**

***The Daily Mirror*: WATSON CRASHES OUT OF WIMBLEDON**

**Friday 27th June 2014**

***The Daily Telegraph*: EU: FEARS OVER JUNCKER'S DRINKING**

***The Daily Mirror*: SHOCK NHS SAVILE REPORT: CHILD KILLER?**

***The Daily Star*: MONSTER RATS THE SIZE OF COWS**

# CHAPTER 1

## SATURDAY 28th June 2014 – DAY 1

***The Times*: BRITAIN NEARS EU EXIT**
***The Guardian*: CAN A FEMINIST GET MARRIED?**
***The Sun*: SCHOOL FURY AS BOY 7 DOES A SUAREZ**

One was standing, hands on hips, her toes curled over the end of the diving board. The other was lying on a sun-bed, her back arched, laughing. Bent over her in pink turtle-covered shorts, clutching a beer, the man was planting a raspberry on her flat stomach.

'Don't be daft.'

'I'm serious.'

'So am I.'

Frank leaned back in his chair, pushing his glasses up onto his forehead. 'Look at the contrast, the blue sky, the white villa, the little splash of colour from the umbrella, the olive trees. And Burke's shorts. And those bloody girls.' He spread his arms. 'I'm telling you, Sam, that is art.'

'Can I remind you we don't have a culture section? Last Sunday we gave *X-Men* five stars.'

Sam was standing at the sliding glass doors that could open to the terrace, looking out and back up the Thames. If it had been a normal summer's day he'd have been be able to see over the Eye and all the way to Heathrow. 'They're Vilebrequins.'

'Who's he?'

'His shorts are, Cameron wears them. Don't go all Brian Sewell, they're just pictures that tell a story.'

'But it's a classic, all four in focus, pin sharp.'

Sam came over, looking over Frank's shoulder at the layouts on his desk. 'How do you get four?'

'Nipples.'

'Very funny.' He leaned on the desk, thinking about all the options. He could see how each image could be cropped, what headline would work best. 'That one.' He pointed at the shot where Burke was on his back on the lounger this time, propped up, with the blonde one astride him, again in just the tiniest of bikini bottoms.

'Face?'

'Exactly. We need to see it is him.'

'But the big wobbly gut hanging over his shorts is good, and then I can't use the RASPBERRY NIPPLE headline,' said Frank.

'Exactly.'

Sam walked across the office, looking to his right through the long glass wall, past Mary, Frank's PA, typing away, and across the packed newsroom. At the horseshoe of sofas he sat down and looked up at the muted wall of TV monitors that showed what was happening in the world. 'Good job Wimbledon built that roof. Nadal's killing this guy now.'

Frank played with one of the remotes. 'Lost the first set. Football's on in a minute. But I'm still not sure you're right about this.'

'Give me strength.' Sam pushed himself up and went back. 'This is a serious story, Frank.' He stood next to him again. 'That one's going on five.' Looking at it all laid out, it was the best story they'd done for years.

'You sure we can use THREE IN A BED with it?'

'Housekeeper's affidavit. Says he did.'

'Lucky bastard.'

Through the glass Mary was now waving, two fingers raised, mouthing 'Lomax, line two.' Frank put him on speakerphone.

'Hi Carson, I'm with Sam. Where are you?'

'The boat's going back to Monaco, we're taking the jet to Nice in a minute.'

Sam resisted saying 'Of course you are' and said, 'Good trip?'

'Yeah, really good. But Caroline needs to get back. All under control?'

Frank said, 'Yes, fine, we're leading with your mate Lord Nigel Burke.'

'Good. Hi Sam. Anything new on it?'

Sam perched on the edge of the desk. 'No, we tried again today, it's still just no comment through his lawyers. No denial. There's nothing new on the story.'

'And guys, he isn't my mate.'

'Doesn't he come to your big summer party?'

'Hell, who doesn't?'

'Well, we don't,' said Sam.

'If you fellas came nobody else would.'

They exchanged a look, both imagining their owner, Carson Lomax, padding round the deck of his yacht with a cigar in one hand and the photos in the other, probably in similar shorts. Given his wealth, the *Hic Salta* was fairly modest at two hundred odd feet. As owners went he was fine, but he wasn't a newspaper man at heart. He was interested, helped when he could, but Sam reckoned most of the time he was just doing what he thought Rupert Murdoch would do.

'Anyway, there's more at stake than any friendship I might have. What's your intro? I haven't got that.'

Sam picked up the layout – 'MARRIED Tory Peer Lord Nigel Burke can today be exposed as a sleazy love-rat who took part in a tryst with a pair of stunning Ukrainian women a THIRD his age. As our shocking exclusive photos reveal, the 61-year-old dad of three was caught red-handed romping with two girls in their TWENTIES in a Black Sea love nest – behind the back of his loyal wife SARAH.'

'Love it,' said Lomax. 'What's the headline?'

Frank said it as if he was announcing a royal birth. 'It's RASPBERRY NIPPLED.'

'What?'

'Raspberry Ripple. It's ice cream,' said Sam, with no enthusiasm.

'I can't see any ice cream.'

'He's giving her a raspberry,' said Frank, looking at Sam for support, not getting it, and giving him a thumbs down.

'In what I'm looking at he's giving her a beer.'

'It's an English expression, blowing a raspberry.'

'Caroline, you have to listen to this, Frank's telling me that in England you blow raspberries.'

Sam suppressed a laugh, knowing that Caroline wouldn't.

'Oh, she says you do.'

Frank didn't want to give in. 'It's cockney rhyming slang, ripple nipple. As in she's got great raspberries. Which they have.'

'Stay there, Carson,' said Sam, putting Lomax on hold to talk to Frank. 'Actually that's wrong. Raspberry ripple is a cripple, not nipple... you berk.'

Frank went back, 'We also like YOU BURKE.'

'That even I get. Your choice of course. By the way, best photos we've had for ages – collector's items, like that German guy.'

'Helmut Newton,' said Sam.

'That's the guy. What else you got?'

'An eight page pull out on Scottish devolution.'

'Very funny, Sam. Birds and soccer then. This guy Sánchez really bite somebody?'

'Suarez. Oh yes. You supporting USA?'

'Hell no. Canadians don't do that, it'd be like you guys supporting the Welsh. OK, and how's your new boss doing?'

'Fine, good, great' said Frank, looking at Sam and shrugging as if to say, 'What am I supposed to say?'

'Listen guys, got to go, you know what's at stake, this is huge. Hold on.'

They could hear Lomax having some sort of discussion in the background. He came back on, 'Sam, Caroline says are you at the usual place later?'

'I will be. So you OK with it?'

'Guys, you two run the paper, you know I never make those calls, that's why I pay you the big bucks.'

Frank hung up and said, 'Thanks for that.'

'Come on, for years we worked for a chinless wonder trapped in the past, then you moaned about the aggressive venture capitalists, and now we've got a fairly laid back billionaire who basically lets us get on with it.'

'I know, I know. And I guess you can't dislike somebody who makes your soulmate Caroline happy.'

'True. But we have now got the boy wonder,' said Sam, pointing at the ceiling.

'One year making tea at the *Calgary Herald*, and he thinks he's Citizen Kane.'

'Anyway, what are we supposed to say to him? Carson, your son Jay's an irritating little shit and when he's not playing golf or out on the pull he's interfering, and trying to show he's in charge, while we put the paper to bed, yet again?'

'It's a small price to pay.'

Frank went out and asked Mary to fetch the new girl.

Mary gave him a filthy look. 'She does have a name.'

'Sorry.'

She waited.

'Remind me.'

'It's Justine. Walker. Try and remember.'

Sam looked at it all again. There really was a lot at stake here. For weeks they'd been running on empty. BGT, Bieber, Plebgate, lizard-face Farage, the World Cup, Murray mania, endless muslim scaremongering, royal babies. The irony was that the real political significance of nailing Burke would be lost on their readers. It annoyed him that the so-called serious newspapers would have the field day with the story.

Frank came back and sat on one of the sofas next to Sam, who had his feet up, scrolling through the shots on his laptop of the girls cavorting – maybe frolicking was better – by the pool.

'He's right. They are a bit Helmut,' said Sam.

'Gary will be flattered by the comparison. How did Boris describe the Olympic beach volleyball girls?'

'Glistening like wet otters.'

'Sure it wasn't beavers?'

'It wasn't.'

'Think that might be lost on our readers anyway,' said Frank, trying to get some volume on the football.

Sam switched to the website version of the Burke story. 'What do you think?'

Frank said, 'I can look at the paper and tell you what's wrong with it in five seconds. That? I've just got no idea, it's a mystery.'

'Well, this is the only place that this story will be real news.'

'Yes, but it's not a paper, is it?'

Sam looked around at Frank's time-warp office. Papers piled everywhere – the massive oak desk, the filing cabinets. Frank was old school. He admired his insistence on still coming to work in a suit, usually pinstriped, and a bright silk tie and cufflinks, his last defiant stand against the brave new digital world. Sam looked out into the newsroom where their senior crime writer was working away head to toe in lycra, a fluorescent yellow cycling jacket hanging on his chair, and thought maybe Frank had a point.

'The paper that drops on the doormat is about seven hours out of date, it might as well be seven days. It's reviews and previews.'

Frank looked at the web page. 'Who are all these women I've never heard of? Billi Mucklow. Iggy Azalea. Are they real people?'

'Sure are.' Sam scrolled down. 'Look at this.'

'Christ, that must be Photoshopped.'

'No, that's Kim Kardashian. Plan was that her arse would break the internet.'

'I like her already.'

*

They'd joined the paper on the same Monday in May 1980, both just twenty. At their Friday induction session the Sports Editor Rhod Boughton asked them to critique that day's *Sun* preview of the FA Cup Final where West Ham would play Arsenal.

Frank interrupted from the back row, 'That's bollocks.'

Boughton said, 'What? Who said that?'

Sam and everybody else in the room turned to look at Frank.

'That's not the team, Devonshire and Pearson will both play.' Sam tried desperately not to laugh.

'You don't know that, son.'

'Want to bet?'

Boughton, a notorious Welsh Fleet Street drinker and punter, said, 'Go on then.'

'If I get the West Ham starting eleven right then I start in sport for you on Monday.'

'OK, Billy big bollocks, you're on. But if you're fucking wrong you're fired.'

'You're on too, Rhod.'

Frank got up, marched to the front, and shook on it. Late the next night Sam found Frank in the pub. 'That was ballsy. How did you do that?'

'My cousin's in the youth team. Trevor Brooking told him, he cleans his boots.'

'You could have been fired before you were hired.'

'Exactly. A bet to nothing.'

And that was it, they were mates. And living proof that opposites attract. Sam was drawn to the front page, Frank to the back – though Frank had somehow completed the journey before Sam had even started. Sam took a little longer.

Frank outlasted most of the managers he knew on first name terms and became Sports Editor. From there it was a small step to be Editor twenty years later, helped by Sam telling the then chinless proprietor Viscount Woodbury that he couldn't see anyone else he could work for, and refusing to do it himself.

Sam knew that in theory it was simple now. They were too expensive to fire, and too good at what they did to replace. Sam had steered them clear of phone hacking and all the scandal that went with it. But he found himself increasingly wondering after all this time if this was all they'd ever know or do, or whether they were earning too much to do what they really wanted to, whatever that was. The last time they'd talked about it properly Frank had said, 'Cheer up, you make it sound like we're in the waiting room at Dignitas.'

Sam looked out across the office and something caught his eye. Way across the office, a girl was talking to somebody on magazines, both laughing. Then she turned and started heading their way. He didn't see a single person of either sex she walked past who didn't turn to look. And while she knew it, there wasn't a hint of self-consciousness. She seemed to be feeding off it, weaving through the desks. The way she moved reminded him of someone or something. No, he couldn't place it.

'Who's that?'

Frank looked up. 'Who?'

'Who do you think? The girl who looks like she's lost and looking for the Vogue offices.'

'That's the new girl. Justine, I think.'

'Bloody hell.'

*

Mary showed her in. Sam took his feet off the table, stood up, and slipped on his shoes.

Frank said 'Sam Plummer, this is Justine....'

She filled the gap, 'Walker.' He couldn't help thinking she

could hold her own with the two girls he'd just been looking at. Then he caught himself as he always did when he looked at a girl who he knew wasn't much older than his daughter.

'Justine's joined the legal team. She's on today,' said Frank.

'I thought Charlie was dealing with this?'

'I've been working for him, he's at a wedding today.'

Sam said, 'Are you new?' knowing she had to be. He would have noticed.

'Yes. I've been seconded, from the group.'

Sam turned to Frank. 'So where's the big white chief?'

'Donald? The Lomax's have got him in Canada, some huge group legal issue.'

'Has he signed off on Burke?'

'He told Charlie to deal with it. I hear he sorted the problem and Lomax told him to go fishing, so you know what Don's like, he'll be in some salmon river in the middle of nowhere.'

Way back when Sam had been in the front line he earned a reputation for being able to read people straight off, particularly women. He couldn't ever remember being wrong. She looked nervous but at the same time confident, determined even, and finally trying hard to look more businesslike than sexy – on that one Sam thought she was failing. Yes, she was in a suit but the skirt was cut just that bit tighter and shorter than most would try. He knew she was a lawyer, but if it had been his birthday he'd still not have been surprised if she'd turned out to be a strippergram. He tried hard not to stare.

They sat down. 'Has there been anything more?' she asked, looking at her notes.

Frank intimidated a lot of people, but Sam liked the way she was cool with him. He said, 'We've had this for nearly two weeks, we can't wait any longer. Burke's had his chance.'

Mary was now semaphoring and it was enough to get Frank out of the room.

Sam carried on, 'Not really. Been trying for a good follow up for next week, but it's a bit thin, no ex-boyfriends or pimps for the girls, they've never left Ukraine, I expect, and he's snow white – but that's why it's a good story. We do have more good pictures.'

'The one with the ice cubes is great,' she said with a straight face. He found the way she maintained eye contact interesting, almost unnerving.

'Isn't it likely somebody else he's slept with will come to us for a kiss and tell?' He was impressed she'd made an effort to understand the business.

'True. Our man on the ground, Damir, is still out in Odessa, babysitting the housekeeper. She's key. We've got her affidavit – saw all of it, him in bed with the two of them, cleared up the condoms. We paid her. More than she'd earn in a year.'

'Where is she now?'

'He's got her in a hotel, apparently she wants to go back to Kiev. It's one of those stories that unfolds very quickly – sometimes they take months – but it's watertight.'

'So what is the most likely follow up?'

'Burke will speak to somebody after this breaks. I'd like it to be us, but that's unlikely now. He'll use somebody, a fixer.'

'Like Max Clifford?'

'If he wasn't in jail, yes. What we can do is find the two girls – we've got a head start, and they'll be good value. Get the gory details, if we're lucky they took pictures.'

She smiled and said, 'Everybody seems to these days.'

He let that go. 'Burke has a huge amount of public support. All those years on TV, everybody likes him, sort of Michael Palin meets Jon Snow. But fatter.'

'But you don't.'

'Like him? No, we all hate him. What he's proposing, more regulation, is a disaster.'

She picked up the draft pages. 'That doesn't seem to be in here.'

'Our readers want sleaze, not politics.'

'So basically you're doing the heavy lifting for the broadsheets?'

She was impressing him more now than when she'd sashayed across the newsroom floor as if she was in a shampoo commercial.

'You don't know for a fact that he's actually had penetrative sex with either or both of them though, do you?'

She looked him in the eye as she said it, then crossed her legs. Sam was sure he blushed. She seemed awfully sure of herself.

'We don't actually say bonk or shag. All we say is "'love rat', love triangle, unfaithful, two-timing, usual stuff."

'If three in a bed is true, three-timing even. Well, he probably just wants a show, doesn't he? He is sixty-one after all.'

He let that go, too. 'Video is the best, but stuff like Colin Farrell and Paris Hilton ends up on line. And you get sued – and we don't often get pictures of actual sex acts, unless it's a honeytrap or blackmail – or you get very lucky with CCTV.'

He couldn't help hoping the Lomaxes would keep Donald waist-deep salmon fishing a bit longer. Don didn't come to meetings in Louboutins. Justine gave the impression she wouldn't be intimidated easily, not by men anyway. Frank had once said, 'Why have you got this pathetic weakness for strong intelligent women?'

Sam had said, 'Sorry, how would that be a weakness?'

She carried on. 'Have you seen the Tulisa video?'

'I have. Crazy. And it was the guy who took that.'

'That was fairly obvious. Doesn't justify what they did to her.'

'Mazher? That was another story, but I agree. Look, the media coverage of the last year or so paints us all as monsters, we're not. There are a lot of good people in our business.'

'Well, considering you write it, you get a pretty bad press.'

'If you only read the *Guardian* and *Private Eye*, that's true.'

'So where do you draw the line?'

'Well, I have some rules, but that comes down to values, judgement.'

'I'd like to hear the rules some time.'

Sam thought that was a toss-up between genuine interest, patronising him, or just taking the piss. He quite liked it.

And he hated being compared with Mazher Mahmood. The

Fake Sheikh had carried on at the *Sun* where he left off on the *News of the World*. As far as Sam was concerned, claiming a story was in the public interest simply didn't always wash. And he knew right now at the Old Bailey a judge was hopefully agreeing. Ironically, they just weren't allowed to write about it.

She said, 'So back to Burke. Why not just deny it, rather than just say "no comment"?'

'Because it's true, why else? You with us next week?' He hoped she was.

'Yes, I was seconded for a couple of months. I'm on this group fast-track programme.'

'Enjoying it?'

'Yes, very lively, rather fun. If you need to contact me here's my card.' She slid it across the table. As she leant forward he tried not to look down her shirt. 'My mobile's on all the time. Do you need help on the follow-up?'

He ran his thumb across the card. 'Hope so, we need a good one.'

'What will the Government do?'

'Drop him like a hot potato. Another really daft appointment.'

He thought they were done but she went over to the wall behind Frank's desk and said, 'So will this one go up there?'

He looked at the framed front pages, four rows of six, that covered nearly the whole wall.

'The Wall of Shame? Sure.'

'All yours?'

'All since Frank and I ran things, so about fifteen years' worth.'

She looked at them all, noticing how the masthead had subtly changed over the years, the acres of flesh and screaming headlines. SHAME was the most common word, closely followed by DRUGS and SEX.

'Will you start another row?'

'No, we keep it at twenty-four. Somebody will go. Probably the Hamiltons, fed up with them.'

'Which are your favourites?'

'I like the real ones. Politics is fun, Paddy Pantsdown, John Major. Mandelson, I loved doing him.'

'Not the showbiz?'

'The Hugh Grant one was good. Prescott, bought that off Max Clifford. We all called him Max Factor.'

'Why?'

'The make-up artist.'

She laughed. 'Any entrapment up there?'

Sam scanned them. 'No. Look, I've done it but I'm not a big fan.'

'Why not?'

'Well, if you get a hooker to tell some B-lister in a nightclub it's £500 for a quickie and you can snort coke off my tits and he goes for it, fine. But you can't say you'll give somebody a few million for a bit part in a movie, then badger them for sex and to score some drugs that you then supply.'

'Still naive to fall for it.'

'Staggering, but people do. And I simply don't believe it's real journalism. We're supposed to report stories, not create them.'

She stood looking up at them, with her back to him. The shirt was white, and looked new, cut narrow at the waist. The skirt could not have been a better fit. She was reading all the short punchy headlines, the photographs with acres of flesh. 'Dominant theme really.'

He was looking at her legs, not the stories. 'You can't have Watergate every week.'

She turned back. 'Do you put "gate" on everything now?'

'If we wrote Watergate now, our readers would think it actually was a story about water.'

She picked up the layout from Frank's desk, looking at the three pages. He went over and stood next to her.

'We call that a 1-4-5.'

'What's that?'

'Classic format, front page splash, double page spread on four and five.'

'Are you really allowed to put nipples on a front page?'

'No, we'd blank them out or cover them with text, that's easy. There's loads we can use though.'

'But you can show them inside?'

'Try not to, but in this case it's justified, so yes.'

She put it back down. 'With this story, these two Ukrainian girls look amazing, but isn't it just stereotypical to talk about them as bimbos? I read the notes – they seem pretty hard-working and well educated.'

Sam really was surprised and impressed that she'd read all the research behind the story. He sat down in Frank's chair.

'We don't call them bimbos. Nobody's used that word for a couple of years.'

'You know what I'm saying, sex objects.'

'I know one of them's at university, but then so's every girl in Ukraine, eying a way out, flirting with the escape committee, trading favours for a visa if they're good, and a black Amex if they're bad. They learn French and English so they can do the summer circuit in Monaco and winter in Courchevel.'

As she sat on the edge of the desk and looked down at him, he thought if she turned up in either place she could start a turf war.

'That's just cynical.'

She was right but he said, 'Unless incentivised, beautiful young women tend not to go to bed with middle-aged men.'

'If you say so.'

Before Sam had a chance to respond, Frank strode back in.

'How are you two getting along?'

'Emily Pankhurst is ahead on points.'

Justine laughed and stood up. 'Sam's been very helpful, yes. What would you like me to do?'

'You've not done much of this before?'

'A little in the group but to be honest we don't get many political sex scandals at *Auto Trader*.'

'Don't worry, we've done this a thousand times. It's just process. You'll need to stay until it's ready to go. Keep your phone on if you go out.'

Sam said, 'On-line is the issue. Once we put it up, it's out there. All over the world there are so-called journalists and all they do is look at social media and recycle it.'

'It's a joke,' said Frank.

'So what we often do, and we'll do tonight, is spoof the first edition with something else – that stops other papers getting it in their first editions. Frank, what are we using?'

'Nurses or Suarez.' Frank held up the layout, turning serious. 'Do you know why this is a great story, not just good, but great?'

She thought about it. 'Major political figure, sort of. Happily married, we think, or thought. Ukraine. Sex. Drugs. Exclusive?'

Frank signalled for Mary to come in, and he held up the front page mock-up. 'Mary Cheetham, your specialist subject is tabloid journalism. Your time starts now. What makes this a great story?'

'It's "c", Chris. The tits in focus. All of them.'

'Final answer?'

'Final answer.'

'You are funny, Mary, don't humour him,' said Sam.

She carried on, 'It's because Lord bloody Nigel Burke is the architect of the proposed bloody daft Tory media reforms, and for some bizarre reason Cameron and his cronies listen to him. But now it's another huge error of judgement, like Andy Coulson. If we nail him you two'll never have to buy another drink in Fleet Street or Wapping.'

'You're wasted out there, Mary, wasted.'

Justine said, 'Is that really what this is all about?'

Sam was on his feet, wanting it to finish on the right note. 'Yes, but not for our readers. They've mostly got double digit IQs and the attention span of Russell Brand. Both answers are actually right. If we ran that story with no pictures, you wouldn't believe it. It's like the Fergie toe-sucking, you just couldn't picture it yourself. It wouldn't have any credibility.'

'Anyway,' said Frank in closing, dropping the layout on his desk, 'you get Sam's point: it's irrefutable, the camera never lies.'

'Clearly,' said Justine, following Mary, closing the door on her way out.

*

Frank was looking at the story again. 'THREE IN A BED is a bit of a cliché, when did we last use it?'

Sam had to think. 'Couple of years ago, that darts player and the women, wasn't one a traffic warden? Or did we go with double top? Or double yellow?'

Frank leaned back. 'OK. Beautiful girl, that Justine.'

'One ugly flaw, sadly.'

'Really?' Frank seemed surprised.

'She was wearing an engagement ring.'

'Ah. Well, that never stopped you.'

'That's wedding rings.'

# CHAPTER 2

## SATURDAY

Sam worked his way across the newsroom, stopping and chatting as he went. While technically Frank's domain, everybody knew that the two of them worked in tandem. If Sam said something, they did it. He climbed one floor by the back stairs to his own department, using the keypad to get access.

The hot desks were half full. It had a different feel to the bustle of the newsroom downstairs – higher-spec furniture, more space, better hardware. He went into his corner office, which had the view up the river, turned on one TV to Sky News and the other to the tennis. The Royal Box was packed with sports stars: Becks taking selfies with volunteers, a bearded Sir Brad, Ian Poulter in a shocking checked suit.

He liked a simple office. Not much paper, no paintings, no framed front pages, just the screens, fridge, laptop and his desk phone.

It had been a slow week for news, Cameron having moved on from the hacking trial fallout to getting Britain out of Europe. And there was nothing on the horizon; it was as if everybody stopped during the World Cup. It was too good to be true – the quietest news week of the year and he was about to drop a bomb.

He did emails and went over a few stories, all knocked into shape by the subs and the back-bench. While he was at it he pushed a speed dial button. The one he always did when he needed to think out loud – Terry Thomas. He was really Henry Thomas, but he had the cigarette holder, the loud waistcoats. He was a rascal, so he was inevitably known as Terry, which he played to. He would pepper conversations with 'hard cheese' and 'how perfectly jolly.' Sam still used him as a sounding board, the voice of reason.

Terry was certainly at least sixty-five, but they'd all been lying about his age for so long nobody could remember exactly. Sam put the perma-tan down to growing up in India, which also explained his love of all things colonial. He'd once asked Terry about his odd career change. 'I was pigeonholed as a foreign expert. There was nowhere else to go at the *Observer*, they wanted me to go to Washington. My wife Grace had just died, we had no kids, I needed a change, and I'd never worked for a tab.'

So he'd arrived in '84, just after Sam's Paris adventures with Caroline had propelled him forward.

'Terry Thomas speaking.'

'Hi, Terry, can you talk?'

'Of course, dear boy.'

Terry was at home, retired for fifteen years since he had handed over early to Frank and Sam, but Sam kept him on a retainer. Sam put him on the speaker while he looked at his screen. 'I'm on my own. You knew Nigel Burke, didn't you?'

'Absolutely. Have you got him?'

'Splash tomorrow.'

'Crumpet trouble?'

'Exactly.'

'Proper swordsman, world-ranked, even worse than you. We've got him with two young girls.'

'Goodness me, Yewtree? I never figured him as one of those.'

'No no, not that. Legal, twentyish. Ukrainian.'

'*Filles de joi?*'

'Maybe semi-pro, we think. How do you know him?'

'I was at Reuters in Delhi, just before I joined the *Observer*. He was there with the BBC doing some documentary. Christmas 78, most Brits had gone home, but I lived there. Indira Gandhi got arrested and chucked in jail for a week.'

'I remember that.'

'He was the only person there, and they made him do live pieces for the news. He just knew nothing, still doesn't in my view. He was a 25-year-old researcher, so I wrote it for him, then the next day I helped him get a couple of interviews, told him what to ask. He came out of it really well. On TV he's a natural.'

'Fair enough.'

'Yes but at three in the morning I get a call from a senior police officer I had on retainer, saying he'd harassed some female guest at the Oberoi and had been arrested.'

'Don't tell me they took him to the same jail?'

'They did, Tahir. So that was locked down as you can imagine.'

'So what did you do?'

'India has the IB, the Central Intelligence Bureau, like our MI5 really. I knew the local Deputy Director. We went down there. Poor old Nigel was in a cell with three locals, crapping himself, literally and metaphorically. I got him out.'

'So you kick-started his TV career?'

'You might say that. Be rather neat if you can end it, old fruit.'

*

Sam made another coffee and walked over to the meeting room for the four o'clock. He knew that working for him was considered the main prize in tabloid land. The department had been known for a while as the 'School for Scandal'. People even put it on their CVs, but it was now generally referred to simply as 'The Plumbers'. He'd always preferred the 'Desert Hamsters', even printing T-shirts with Freddie Starr dressed as Rommel.

The stories just kept coming now. It fed itself when you had so many good people and such a big network. He couldn't remember the last time he'd actually followed up a lead himself or interviewed anyone. And as far as actually investigating or writing was concerned, he just didn't do it, and his name never appeared on a story. He missed it. Whenever he was asked for his occupation, he still wrote 'investigative journalist', but he should have prefaced it with 'former'.

*

They were in the small meeting room that connected to Sam's office. There were only six familiar faces now and Justine. Old habits die hard, and though he trusted his team, he told people on a 'need to know' basis. Every paper had a 'secret room', but it was self-defeating; everybody knew where it was, and when it was being used it meant a belter was on the cards.

Sam sat down at the head of the table. 'I guess some of you have been working with Justine there, she's on Donald's legal team.'

She smiled easily and looked around the table.

He had his laptop open and looked at CMS, the content management system. It showed him all 72 pages, neatly laid out. He could click on each page to blow it up, and just he and Frank had password access to change anything. He also had an A3 print-out that he would scribble pencil notes on.

Sam turned to Johnnie Brydon, his right hand man for the last ten years. He was an ex-policeman. Sam liked unconventional backgrounds.

'Right, what we got?'

Johnnie still looked like a policeman. 'Page one. Burke.'

It looked good now, properly laid out. YOU BURKE worked. They'd touched the picture well, though it didn't need much.

Next to it they had some girl from Corrie recreating the famous tennis poster, lifting her skirt to show her bottom. Johnnie said, 'That links to the Hot Bods section – you know Abby, Becks, Dan Osborne.'

'Who's he?' asked Sam.

'TOWIE.'

Sam wished he could be ignorant of this low water mark.

Then Johnnie led them through the whole paper. The usual depressing stuff – Danny Dyer, Rihanna or RiRi when over a single column, Lineker on Ipanema, a banker doing ketamine and meth, Kiefer Sutherland after another night out. 24 BEERS wasn't bad. A regular Harry theme seemed to be developing. Prince on the front, Redknapp on the back and Styles somewhere in-between.

He scanned the entire paper. 'Nothing on the hacking verdicts?'

'Old news.'

'It was Tuesday for God's sake.'

Johnnie said, 'Our readers don't care, it's *Guardian* stuff.'

Sam knew Johnnie was right. For him and his like, it had been a fascinating insight into the relationship between politicians, the police and the press, but in the end all that his readers wanted to know was if Simon Cowell really can change a nappy.

They carried on, commenting as they went, making minor changes to their own stuff, and adding more comments to be passed on. They got to CORRIE STAR IN VAJAZZLE SELFIE SHOCKER, and he didn't know whether to laugh or cry.

It was all vaguely depressing – a paper held together by football, reality shows, B-listers and listings. And all written in some ghastly new language he'd helped invent. Heartache, terror, shock, quiz, betrayal, romance, fury, spin, anguish, blasts, menaces, meltdowns, wannabes, beasts, brawls, perverts, psycho-killers, twerkers and tweeters, pitbulls and paedos, untold stories, top brass and – as if anybody thought it was – the truth.

They were up to page forty and on to book club and special offers. 'Johnnie, you take it from here, I've got stuff to do. Good job, everybody.'

*

Sam got back to his office in time to see Brazil kick off against Chile. While Terry was great as a sounding board, the most important man was the one closest to the story, the one on the ground. The man he had been twenty years ago. So he rang Damir Tanasijevic, the no-bullshit Serbian still out in Odessa. Sam had never figured out how Damir had survived the nineties in old Yugoslavia. The story was that he'd played soccer in the USA and used his dual nationality and languages to move around, keeping countless foreign photographers and hacks out of trouble, saving lives.

Damir answered. Sam knew what he would say.

'Privyet Plumski.'

'Privyet Damir. Anything happening?'

'Still working on a statement from the driver.'

He spoke perfect English, but his American accent and jargon couldn't win the battle against his Yugoslav origins.

'What's the issue?'

'Usual, money.'

'Just pay, rather have two. Housekeeper OK?'

'My guy's babysitting her in a hotel.'

'Any sign of the girls?'

'She said they were going on vacation somewhere. They won't go back to Kiev yet, I guess. We're looking.'

'Where would they go?'

'Not far, we're six hundred kilometres from Kiev and the same with Crimea. It's like Miami here, boiling, why leave?'

'OK, you're saying I shouldn't be worried?'

'No, boss. Chill.'

*

Saturdays were always the best day. At seven he went down and sat with Frank to watch extra time, and they went through the whole paper again.

People came and went asking advice and checking. It was pretty much open house on Saturday nights. What Sam loved about Frank was that even though he struggled to write a shopping list, he was a great editor. He listened, he led. He was an extrovert, people followed him, often purely out of curiosity.

Above all he knew what the reader wanted, and he didn't need an army of researchers or focus groups to know. He was the last of a dying breed. Frank liked the obvious comparison with Kelvin Mackenzie, but as he always said, 'Kelvin buggered off to the telly and topless darts; I'm still here.'

They'd kept the Burke story very tight, but word was out on the floor now and everybody knew. That's what put Sam on edge. It just needed one loose word. Any idiot could put tits on the front page, but how many people could put it in the context of a real belter of a story, particularly one which didn't involve a footballer or a soap star? The *Sunday Times* or *Observer* would have run this story.

Frank was looking at the CMS when he said, 'Fuck.'

'What?'

'I haven't got a leader on Burke.'

Sam knew they needed a serious 250-word piece, the paper's own editorial position.

'Get JR or Kerry to do it.'

'They're busy, come on, you want to go for the record?'

Sam laughed. 'Christ, when did I last try?'

Frank fished in his drawer and found a sheet. 'Right, the Speed Leader Leaderboard.' He scanned down it. 'You last had a go in October 2008, Jonathan Ross and Russell Brand and the prank call. You did it in three minutes, fifty-one seconds. It was brilliant.'

'What's the record now?'

'3:36. Henry Dean on Maggie when she popped her socks.'

'I don't write any more, you know that.'

Frank made clucking noises and flapped his arms. 'Chicken.'

Sam went over to Frank's desk. 'Move your arse.'

Frank got up. Sam locked his fingers and stretched out his arms, like a concert pianist about to start. 'Rules again?'

Frank read from the sheet. '250 words, plus or minus ten, no typos, no grammatical errors. Oh, and I have to agree it can be published.'

Sam pulled his chair in. He got a blank page up, set up word count, and just stared at it. He remembered at the height of his powers doing it in one sentence on Jeremy Thorpe. It was scary. Shit, he just needed the first line or word.

'Hold on. Give me a minute.'

Frank looked at his watch. 'Sod that. Three. Two. One. Go.'

He finished and stood up. Frank sat down and read it. 'No errors I can see. 242 words. I feel like Jeremy Clarkson. Sam Plummer, you did it in... three... '

'Get in.'

'Forty-one.'

'Bugger. But is it any good?' He realised he was desperate to know, and that what Frank thought was far more important than his lap time.

'OK, you tell me, I'll read it to you.'

Sam sat down and closed his eyes as Frank read it out loud.

'This newspaper stands for everything that is great about British journalism. We have always fought to maintain the highest standards, never flinching, never stepping down into the gutter. We have played by the rules. We have risen above the tawdry catalogue of shame. The appointment of Andy Coulson to a key role inside Number 10 was a colossal error of judgement by this government. The ensuing hacking trial needlessly exposed us all to the grubby world of the dark arts, to the seedy underbelly of Fleet Street. Nothing could have more clearly illustrated the sordid relationship between sections of our media, the police and the government. Now that very same government has done it again. Lord Nigel Burke was their misguided choice to oversee media reforms that would have taken away our freedom and put even more power in the hands of the very people we are here to bring to account. We have today done this country, and the fourth estate, a great service. We have exposed him, literally, as a shameless serial adulterer. More importantly, we have exposed him as a hypocrite, as a liar and as a cheat. Doing so is most definitely and undeniably in the public interest. His position is now untenable. This paper says good riddance. On the very day last week that Mr Coulson was found guilty, a well-known tabloid trumpeted that it was "a great day for red-tops". It wasn't. Today is.'

Sam wasn't sure. 'What do you think?'

'Honestly? It's a crying shame you stopped doing it. It's perfect.'

Frank cut and pasted it into page twenty-three. 'Right, next. You got the memo about meeting the Milky Bar Kid?'

'Do I really have to come in on a bloody Monday?'

'Jay wants to flex his muscles again. Show who's boss. It'll be the usual stuff, we just have to suck it up. I know it's not fast enough for you, but we can be out of here in five years, home free, and the paper will still be going then, probably. We're laughing.'

He checked his phone. There was an email from Justine, quoting extracts from the research his team had produced on the girls. He got the Burke story up and inserted the key facts. Irina was doing hotel management and, more impressively, Tatiana was at the Taras Shevchenko National University reading astrophysics. Was it important the world knew they weren't good-time girls? Justine thought so, but not really, and who the hell ever got to the last paragraph anyway?

# CHAPTER 3

## SATURDAY

Sam left his office at ten. He went down the stairs to go out via Frank's, who was still at it. 'I just talked to Harry, given me a good line about Roy Hodgson, going to use it in our Brazil post-mortem.' He said it as if it was going to be a government report of huge importance. He still had all the old football contacts and couldn't resist getting involved.

Sam said, 'For one minute I thought we might be Harry-free tomorrow.'

Way across the office he saw Justine heading out with her briefcase. More to himself he said, 'Should I stay or should I go?'

'What did you say?'

It took him a second to decide. 'I'm going to run, call you in a minute.'

He cut across the newsroom, calling Gary as he went, timing his run perfectly to meet her at the lifts.

'Good first week?' he asked, pushing the button.

'Not bad. Something else came up on the showbiz page.'

'Can I give you a lift? I mean car, not elevator,' he offered, stopping to face her.

The one coming down had about ten people in it.

He said, 'We'll take the next one.'

'No, come on, we'll squeeze in.'

He let her go first. They were very close, face-to-face. Sam was a shade over six feet, but their eyes were at the same level. She smiled but didn't say anything. He found it slightly unnerving.

When they got out she said, 'A lift to where?'

They crossed the lobby and he followed her out past security, through the revolving doors into the warm but still damp night.

'If you want to go to anywhere, my guy will take you. If you'd like to have something to eat, we'll take you there, which I'd like.'

'I should get back,' she said as they walked across the forecourt past a large, modern sculpture which Sam hated and had christened the blob.

'Fine, but you won't sleep, nobody ever does. It always takes a couple of hours and drinks to come down and stop thinking about it. Here's Gary.'

They were now at the kerb as Gary pulled up and got out to let Justine in the back. He put his hand out, 'Hi, I'm Gary.'

'Justine.'

She looked at him. She knew guys like Gary. They either wore tight clothes to show off their muscles and looked daft, or tried to hide them and looked cool. He looked cool, his long-sleeve black shirt hanging loose outside his jeans.

Sam said, 'You get in the front, I need to make a call.'

Doing background on the story, she'd Googled Gary and found nothing. Asking around, she found out who he was, but nobody knew any more than that he'd been in the army.

They set off west on Commercial Road. There was no jewellery or tattoos she could see, but he had what looked like a proper dive watch on his wrist. He made easy but smart small talk with her as he nosed the Range Rover right on to Tower Hill and headed west along the Embankment, asking about Burke and the story, which he seemed to know everything about.

Even though she knew, she said, 'Are you the Gary Lake that took the photos? They're great.'

'Thanks. Actually technically pretty easy – great line of sight, good light, no time pressure.'

'But still in the Ukraine.'

'In Ukraine. You don't say *the* Ukraine. It's like saying in the Wales.'

'Sorry.'

'Don't apologise. But yes, that was the challenge.'

From the way he talked, she sensed there was more to him.

'Are you just a photographer?'

He smiled.

'I drive too. Are you just a lawyer?'

Gary pulled up in West Street outside St Martin's Theatre. He looked up at the red neon sign. *The Mousetrap* was in its 63rd year. He really ought to go, he still didn't know who'd done it.

He kept the motor running.

Sam got out and leaned back in. 'You coming? Up to you.'

She thought about it then slid over. 'OK.'

*

They crossed the road and he held the door to the Ivy open for her. Its theatrical credentials had been established when the likes of Marlene Dietrich and Larry Olivier hung out there. It felt like a country house dining room, defined by the leaded harlequin windows and its art, but the originals were now gone, replaced by framed posters. Sam just liked it. It felt like home.

Marcus, the maître d', steered Justine to Sam's corner table. She'd detoured via the bathroom. She liked the way he stood for her and sat opposite her with his back to the room. It was laid for four, so they could have sat side-by-side and both had the view.

'This your table?'

'On Saturdays, late.'

'I've never been here.'

'I started coming when they relaunched it in the nineties. Richard Caring owns it now, not quite the same, but I like their club upstairs next door.'

'So, how are you feeling now about the story? Anticlimactic?'

'No, that's tomorrow. Right now I still own it. If I stood up and told everyone here, they'd be shocked. Burke will have friends in here.'

'But ten minutes after it's online it's not yours.'

'No matter what, it's still my story. They all know that.'

'And you go back to the next story.'

'People who say a week is a long time in politics should try running a Sunday paper. The crack is still breaking it and then how we ride the story, but it's frustrating when we have to wait seven days, watching the websites, the dailies and TV have a field day. You see that table of guys over my shoulder? They mostly work on tabloids. Members of what we call the Dirty Dozen. They'll have fun with this.'

'All from papers you hate?'

'It doesn't really work like that. There are some individuals I don't like, but I've got friends on all of them.'

'And that lot?'

'Hired and fired most of them, but we're OK.'

'Come on, so who should I know?'

He didn't need to turn round. 'See the bald guy in the pink shirt, with glasses?'

'Yes, he looks very dodgy.'

Sam laughed. 'That's Phil Nagle, from the *Sunday Times*, one of my best mates, managed to escape the tabs and write real stories. One of the nicest, straightest guys in the business. Look, it's easy to polarise it. It's a lovely idea that that lot and all those that were in the dock at the Old Bailey are bad, and that the others and I are truth-seeking evangelists. But we're not.'

'But you don't break the law.'

'One of my golden rules. The trouble is, once you start there's no going back.'

'But Burke's not a criminal.' She was getting animated. 'He might have an open marriage; he just shagged two girls. So what?'

'Should have told us then.'

She said, 'I'm sorry, that's lame.'

They broke off to order. As she looked at the menu he said, 'I always have the shepherd's pie.'

'I'll try that. Is someone joining us?'

He wondered if she was after safety in numbers.

'An old friend of mine and maybe Frank. You're right, it's not Profumo; there's no national security issues, but he's a soft target and a hypocrite.'

Justine saw a woman come in and sensed the moment she started to work her way across the room that this was the friend. She moved the way a runway model did, unfazed by whatever some daft designer asked her to wear. She might be a lot closer to Sam than her in age, but heads turned and she knew it. She looked familiar, maybe from the pages of *Hello*, but she couldn't place her. She stopped briefly at two tables, waved at the Dozen, then arrived. Sam stood to kiss her on both cheeks. A waiter appeared and she ordered a martini in Italian. Before he could introduce them, the woman said, 'I'm just going to chat to the Gandinis for a minute, will you order for me?'

'Your girlfriend?'

Sam laughed. 'That's Caroline Lomax. The boss's wife.'

'Oh, God, I didn't recognise her. She's very beautiful.'

'Bit of a chameleon. And she was.'

'No, she still is.'

'I meant she was my girlfriend, briefly, but a long, long time ago.'

'In a galaxy far, far away?'

'Something like that.'

She looked past him again. 'Is that the famous Roly Relton?'

Again he didn't turn round but said, 'The guy who looks like Jabba the Hutt? Big sweaty bloke, gold rings, with his napkin tucked in his shirt?'

'Yes. You don't like him?'

'I don't agree with the way he does business.'

'He does look fairly charmless.'

'He's a pig. We call him Roly Poly.'

She watched another of the Dozen get up and make his way over. He couldn't have been less like Relton, straight off the pages of *Tatler*'s little black book, his single-breasted, two button, navy suit cut only the way handmade suits ever were. He put his manicured hand on Sam's shoulder, who looked up at him, not answering, then turned and introduced himself to Justine. 'How do you do, Julian Mortlock,' he said, offering her his hand.

'Justine Walker,' she said, taking it. He kissed the back of her hand.

'Charmed. May I?' and he sat down before Sam could say no.

He focused on Sam. 'So Drainman, word on the street is that you've got a monster.'

Sam felt a knot in his stomach but tried not to show it.

'Really, whose word? Which street?'

'Just heard.' He turned to Justine, 'Are you working for Sam?'

'Not directly, I'm in the legal department.'

'Excellent.' He turned back to Sam. 'Anyway, just thought I'd ask if we're OK?'

'You and me? Why not? You don't work for me any more.'

'Water under the bridge as far as I'm concerned now.'

Sam said, 'Ancient history as far as I'm concerned.'

Mortlock stood up. 'No hard feelings?' He put out his hand.

'You know we still will never buy from you?'

'Understood.'

Sam shook his hand. 'Then none. And don't kiss it.'

'Very nice to meet you, Maxine.'

'Justine.'

Sam sensed anger in her voice. Did she have his talent to spot a fraud straight away? He liked that.

'Please forgive me, Justine.'

As he walked away she said, 'He couldn't know, could he?'

'No. Fishing. Old trick. I sensed you didn't like him.'

'Bit creepy, forgot my name. Not my type.'

'The look's a legacy of his working on the royals – handmade everything, school tie, you have to always look the part.'

She drank her wine. 'Drainman's quite funny.'

'Oh trust me, I've had every Plummer joke going. Every variant you can think of about plumbing new depths, Sam the Plumber, sinks, dumps, bends. Crossing the line with me was the plumb-line, I quite liked that. And think about it, plumbers are always in porn movies –a scantily clad cougar opens her front door to reveal every woman's ultimate fantasy: a bare-chested plumber in his work boots and a tool belt, saying "I'm here to unblock your drains' or 'I hear you have a ball-cock problem". Am I right?'

'Well, I can assure you it's not mine.'

She took another a sip of her wine. 'In mine he's a carpenter.'

She really was quite funny and ticking an awful lot of boxes, but she was still half his age. He was trying to read her. She'd let her hair down since their meeting. Her suit didn't look like a uniform any more. Did simply undoing just one more shirt button make that much difference, he wondered? Then he realised she wasn't wearing the bra she had been in the office earlier. When and where had that gone? Was she toying with him?

She said, 'Anyway, what was that all about?'

'Is Julian still there?'

She looked past him. 'No, I think he went out.'

'He and I haven't said more than hello since we parted company over ten years ago.'

'Did you fire him?'

'Technically he resigned, but everybody knows.'

'Why?'

'Frank hired Julian to work on the royals. He's part of that Cotswold set. He could do naturally what us grammar school boys never can. He was mine and Terry's protégé.'

'Terry?'

'Terry Thomas, editor before Frank.'

'What happened?'

'Talented boy. Julian was probably going to play cricket or rugby for England, but he did his shoulder on the Cresta

Run. His Dad's old money, got him a job at the *Telegraph*. Made a good fist of the "City Diary", but got caught up in insider dealing.'

Caroline came back and sat down. 'Hi, I'm Caroline.'

'Justine.'

Sam said, 'You seem busy.'

'I'm on this committee, running a big charity fashion show, in two weeks. Actually I'm really enjoying doing it, getting my teeth into something. I need to be busy.'

'That I know.'

'I'm recruiting. Fancy it?'

Sam laughed. 'Me, on the catwalk? Don't be ridiculous.' He turned to Justine. 'You should do it.'

'Stand up in front of people? I don't think so.'

The waiter arrived and topped up their wine glasses.

Justine said, 'You were saying?'

'I was explaining Julian, I'd told her about the *Telegraph*.'

Caroline said, 'Didn't Piers then hire him at *The Sun*? Then he came to the *Mail* and we worked together on Dempster. He was really good. Very charming – everybody gets seduced.'

'Did you?' said Justine.

'Sure, but not literally.'

Sam continued, 'Then Terry hired him, as Royal Editor, late nineties, then we reshuffled a year or so later when Terry took early retirement, and I made him my number two.'

'Your successor?' said Justine.

'That was the plan. He was fine for the first few years, then he got very ambitious and competitive. I was getting suspicious and then he broke the record for consecutive splashes, five.'

Caroline said, 'Nobody does that.'

'And then his next story was the last straw.'

Their food arrived, and Sam paused with the story. He looked at the two of them and thought it was like a time warp. He rewound to the office, Justine gliding across the office, reminding him of something. It was Caroline, when he met her in Paris, a 19-year-old dancer at the Crazy Horse, strutting near naked across the stage. If you could be that confident in front of five hundred tourists, anything in your clothes was easy. But it wasn't just that. It was the speed of thought, the eye contact, something in the way they held themselves. Two peas in a pod. For a second, Sam was back in 1982, just 22 and three years into his time at the paper. He remembered how isolated and frustrated he felt: Frank was all sorted on sport.

*One day, Frank said, 'Then do what I did, blag it.'*

*Two days later he was in a meeting. The paper's new colour supplement editor, Nicola, wanted a feature on sex spots in Paris.*

*He piped up, lying. 'I know Alain Bernardin.'*

*'Who the hell's he?' said Nicola.*

*'Owns the Crazy Horse, and my flatmate's sister's a dancer at the Moulin Rouge.'*

*'You speak frog?'*

*It was too late now. 'Of course.'*

*He prayed nobody asked him anything in French.*

*'Well, you'd better bloody come back with something good.'*

*How could he know that he would, just one weekend shaping his whole life. Journalistically, sartorially, and last but not least, sexually.*

'Paging Mr Sam Plummer,' said Caroline, raising her voice.

'Sorry, my mind wandered off then.'

'We could see that,' said Justine.

He felt quite like talking about something else but she carried on. 'So what was the story?'

Caroline said, 'He broke one of Sam's golden rules.'

'I was certain he was using somebody to hack phones. That's when it had all started, about 2001.'

'So why didn't he get prosecuted?'

'If I couldn't prove it, who else would? I could never figure his source. Frank and I let him go in 2003 I think. Then he did get arrested a couple of years later, but the case collapsed.'

'Why?'

'He got his stuff from a private investigator who was supposed to be on an exclusive with one of the bad guys, but he was greedy, so they were extra careful never to leave a trail.'

Caroline said, 'He's very clever. And that guy died anyway. Case closed.'

Sam said, 'But hacking was just a term for remotely accessing voice mails and caller ID spoofing. He was getting stuff that had to be coming from the police, and I mean serious stuff.'

'And nobody ever found out who or how. A mystery.'

'With us he really was the original rogue reporter.'

'And now he hates the fact that Frank and Sam won't buy anything off him.'

'What does he do now?'

'When he was sacked he got nearly quarter of a million because they cocked up the process, then another eighty grand to stop him publishing his book about it all. He used the money to set up on his own. Sort of upmarket Max Clifford.'

Caroline spotted someone else she had to talk to so slid off.

'So, what was the last straw?'

'You should be a barrister.'

'Sorry. It's interesting.'

'Complicated. Royal thing. I don't like to talk about it.'

She got the message. 'No further questions, your honour. So was Burke a typical story?'

'God, are we off again?'

'Sorry.'

'No, it's OK. Well I know you've read the file, yes. Text book really. Local tip off, seen with a young woman, but that's boring.'

'Why?'

'There's about ten guys sitting behind me, they all know I'm married... '

'Are you?'

'You sound surprised.'

'I thought you were single.'

'Why would you think that?'

She blushed and sounded like she was back-pedalling. 'In the office, you have a, you know, reputation.'

'Oh do I?' He was enjoying this. 'I am technically married, but we've been separated for years. But that's not the way our business works. If somebody wanted to expose me, I'd be a married father of two. They can see me sitting having dinner with you and Caroline. They could have a pap outside in five minutes, and when I just say goodnight to you or her on the pavement, they've got a story.'

'Except you're not Jeremy Clarkson.'

'Exactly, I'm anonymous. That's the way I like it and the way it's going to stay.'

She looked embarrassed so he thought it was a good time to ask. He pointed at her left hand. 'So what does your fiancé do?'

She regained her composure. 'Did. He was killed in Iraq.'

'So you wear that for sentimental reasons.'

She slid the ring off. 'No, for practical reasons, to stop all your guys at the paper hitting on me.'

'Does it work?'

She looked him in the eye and smiled. 'Clearly not.'

'I'm not... '

'I know. Only teasing. So, Burke.'

He loved the way she flirted harmlessly and regained control of the conversation. So in less than a minute she now knew he wasn't really married, and he knew she wasn't really engaged. But he also knew this didn't change anything. She was too young. And he was too old.

'Standard practice, kept tabs on him. When we knew he was spending nights at the first girl's place we stepped it up. When it moved from Kiev to the villa in Odessa, I sent Gary.'

'Gary's a snapper?'

'He is. Gary was in the army, he's very good at creeping up on people.'

'And shooting them.'

'Sort of. He's a wildlife photographer.'

'You are kidding me?'

'Well he does do it, and he has the credentials. It's actually cover to get the equipment in. But he did take a course, he's very thorough. He was in Ecuador doing Madonna adopting more kids or something and he got a photo of a very rare parakeet, I think – he became quite a cult figure, made the cover of *Ornithologist Monthly*. In fact that's what he always shows customs. You'd be amazed at the number of twitchers he finds.'

'Soldier, twitcher, pap, chauffeur. That's a great CV.'

'Think about it, military are the best guys – always the first into battle, they get you all the intelligence. You can't fight without communications. They're young, tough, operate on very little sleep, hold their drink, they take orders, real team ethos, can handle equipment in the field, will go anywhere – and in a tight corner they don't panic. Much more use than some spotty kid from Exeter with a degree in Media Studies.'

'Or a girl with a law degree.'

'Sorry.'

'But you think there's more.'

Was she was as smart as she seemed? 'Do you?'

'Maybe they're setting Burke up to blackmail him.'

'Possible, but it's bloody complicated just for that. And who would they be?'

'Maybe the girls are employed by some local so-called businessman, and our hero is getting sexual favours in return for something he's fixed back here – contacts, lobbying.'

'Top of the class. And that's what we need to find out.'

'And that would be huge. But you have no leads at all.'

'Correct. But we decided to run the story because we've got the juicy bit, sex always outsells intrigue. He knows we have it, and it's dead if it leaks or he breaks it.'

'Why would he do that?'

'Pre-emptive confession, on his terms. That's the problem – once this breaks, it's a feeding frenzy. Freelancers will do anything to try and rep Burke or the girls, sell their so-called side of the story.'

'Does that annoy you?'

'God no, I'd do exactly the same.'

'So where are the girls?'

'Damir has a head start, it'll take time to get people to Ukraine. You can't exactly ring John Simpson or Mark Austin in Crimea and say stop what you're doing, I've lost the Cheeky Girls – we really need to get them. Tell us what he was like in the sack, and get a photo shoot out of it.'

'Are you serious?'

'Sure, why not? You've seen them. Hardly shy and retiring. Good money, could be their ticket out. We could syndicate them for top dollar.'

*

Caroline came back, and Sam excused himself to make a call.

'So what do you do, Justine?'

She liked the way Caroline stopped scanning the room and put her phone down, giving her all her attention. 'Has to be on mute in here.'

'I'm a lawyer, on secondment. I just met Sam today, on a story.'

'I know the story.'

'Oh, of course.'

'It's a massive issue for all the owners. Burke is one of the prime movers on press regulation, and he's got more bad plans.'

Justine looked at Caroline, finding her ageless beauty and style almost intimidating.

'We need a free press, but they have to be accountable. You have to do that without the government interfering. Burke favours the heavy hand. That's why that lot over there are going to be very happy when Sam nails him.'

'What sort of plans?'

'OK, stop me if you've heard it. Leveson concluded that newspapers had, quote, wreaked havoc with the lives of innocent people. So we got a Royal Charter – which the government forced through, even though most papers tried to block it.'

'Why?'

'Papers think they should be self-regulating, to preserve freedom of the press. They don't think they should be controlled by the very people they want to bring to account.'

'Which is what this is all about, the blurred lines.'

'Exactly. So it's a bit of a fudge. The Press Recognition Panel, set up under the Charter, will decide if the self-regulation complies. So, a thing called IPSO.'

'What's that?'

'Independent Press Standards Organisation. It's being set up to enforce the Editor's Code – but not all papers will sign up.'

'Sounds very complicated.'

'And Burke's still in the thick of it. The whole thing doesn't now come into force until after the election next year, anyway.'

'So exposing their man Burke as a hypocrite is worth a lot?'

'No, it's priceless.'

'So why doesn't Sam put his name on the story?'

'Sam hates publicity. Ironic, isn't it?'

*

Sam came back and after some small talk, Justine excused herself. Sam walked her outside. Across the road the driver eased himself out of a black Escalade.

'That's Joseph, he'll take you, I need Gary here. Joseph was in the army with Gary, but as you can see he ate all the pies.'

'Where's he from?'

'Not sure, he's Joseph Kelly. Irish Jamaican? Ask him.'

'Well, thank you for dinner… and the day. It was fun.'

'My pleasure.'

'Will you be in tomorrow?'

'No. Have to be in on Monday. Finance meeting. The boy wonder wants us to cut costs.'

'Jay Lomax?'

'Like father unlike son. The only apple that defied Newton's Law and fell a long way from the tree.'

'So you don't rate him? He seemed OK to me.'

Sam was surprised they'd met. 'When did you meet him?'

'In the lift once. So, any plans for tomorrow?'

He didn't know why but he said, 'I'm spending tomorrow with my wife and daughter.'

She made no move to kiss him goodbye. She just got into the car and waved goodbye as Joseph eased out into the traffic. He checked his messages walking back, glad to find nothing urgent or interesting. Caroline was coming out and said, 'I've done the bill.'

'Thanks, shall we go up?'

'Wouldn't miss it for the world.'

They walked the twenty yards to the Ivy Club entrance and went upstairs.

It was in much the same style, but dominated by a long bar and dark brown leather armchairs and sofas. As they settled at the bar, Caroline said, 'What a beautiful girl.'

'Justine?'

'No, the coat-check girl. Yes, Justine.'

'Sorry. Think so?'

'Oh, come on.'

'Half my age.'

'No comment.'

He knew Justine was another fun episode closed and consigned to the file marked 'short pointless flirtations.' Unlike Caroline all those years ago.

*She'd been in charge since the day they met. At the Crazy Horse, they said he could interview 'the English one' the next morning. No, Monsieur Bernardin still never gave interviews. They gave him a ticket for the early show that night. He loved it, stunned by their impossible bodies and erotic routines. He went back to his hotel pathetically excited about meeting one of them in the flesh. He was still in every sense an innocent abroad.*

*The next morning the humourless PR lady took him into a windowless meeting room. 'No photos. No tape. Ten minutes.' It felt like a prison visit. A girl joined them. No make-up, no expression, no interest. A blank page. She was in a grey track suit. He gave it his best shot, but the ball just didn't come back over the net. He should have realised it would be a let-down. God, he was going home empty-handed. After five minutes she asked the PR if she could get her some water. As the door shut she leant forward, looking him in the eye for the first time. 'Sam, when she comes back you'll ask me one more question and say that's it. I'll meet you at Le Cou de la Girafe at one for lunch tomorrow, it's in Rue Paul Baudry. Can you remember that?' He nodded, scribbling. 'And for fuck's sake don't wear that suit, try and look cool. By the way, I'm Caroline.'*

'She moves like a dancer.'

'Really?'

'Takes one to know one. So what did you make of the results?'

'The trial?'

'No, the World Cup. Yes, the trial.'

The barman came over. 'Hi Jorg, usual please. Caroline?'

'Same please.'

'Predictable. Coulson and the others had to go down. Rebekah and Charlie, I'm not surprised.'

'Did you know when Murdoch was at the low point three summers ago, humbling himself in front of the select committee, News Corp was worth $35 billion. Now?'

'I don't know, double?'

'No. Nearly $90 billion. Go figure. What doesn't kill you… '

'So when they say hacking cost him $600 million… '

'Small change.'

'So you're a big picture person too now?'

'It's how they all think, Sam.'

'So where's Carson tonight?'

'At some boring men-only dinner with Chinese industrialists. Carson could talk about fibre optics all night.'

'Fascinating.'

'That's why we all love you, Sam – you're never boring, and you're always interesting.'

Sam laughed. 'Don't patronise me.'

'All the usual suspects in tonight,' she said, as they looked at the Dirty Dozen's table, almost full now.

She'd scared the living daylights out of him when they first met in Paris all those years ago, so far out of his depth he thought he was drowning. He still couldn't look at her without thinking that letting her go had been the biggest mistake of his life. Well, mistakes really, having done it twice.

Gary arrived carrying a courier-marked package. 'Hot off the press.'

She watched him look inside the envelope. 'Why do you bother? When's it on line?'

He looked at his watch. 'Exactly ten minutes, but this is a tradition. We all like it.' He turned to Gary. 'What about Justine?'

'Joseph said she listened to her messages and asked him to drop her at Boujis.'

'She have to wait?'

'No, straight in.' Sam wondered who she knew or was meeting that she could jump the queue. 'We got anybody inside tonight?'

Gary took a sheet from his jacket pocket. 'Let me see. Yes, Annabel or Alison.'

Caroline said, 'Bloody hell, do you boys ever stop? Leave the poor girl alone.'

'Sorry.'

'You don't think you're milking this, do you, boss?'

'You know me, I like a bit of a showdown. Don't get many days like this anymore.'

Gary took four copies from the envelope and walked over to the Dozen with them over his arm as if he was handing out *Evening Standard*s at the tube. They were just A3 printouts of the 1-4-5. He got there and said 'read all about it' as he passed them over, then gave a couple to others they knew in the room.

He knew exactly what they'd all be thinking – the good news that Burke was toast, the bad that Sam had done it again. Only his mate Phil Nagle looked across and gave him the thumbs up. Before the rest even acknowledged him, they were taking photos of the front page, calling and tweeting. He knew what would happen next. They would send a dozen guys and a TV crew to Burke's houses in Thurloe Square and Newbury. His phones would be ringing off their hooks.

He saw Mortlock take a copy off to a corner. He wondered who he would be calling, more annoyed and jealous than the rest put together. He knew he'd already be looking for an angle, to somehow get his nose in the trough.

Looking at it again, Caroline said, 'You know you couldn't art direct this better, almost surreal. Superfit.'

'You're not the first to say that.'

'I mean fit like athletes, not models or porn stars.'

She gathered her stuff. 'Carson wants me to meet him at Annabel's. I'll talk to you in the week.'

*

Sam bantered briefly with the Dozen and then met Gary outside. As they drove off he thought about it. Thirty years meant fifteen hundred editions, and he and Frank were closing in on five hundred front pages, of which maybe thirty were of any real significance.

Phil Nagle rang. 'You haven't got the girls, have you?' It was typical Phil. No bullshit.

'Between us. Nope. And Burke's gone to ground.'

'Worth us staking out his houses?'

'Gary says not.'

'Anybody running him?'

'Lawyers, I think. He's using Sherbrooks.'

'Can we talk in the week? It's already come down from above we all have to go big on this.'

'The regulatory side?'

'Sure, it's in all our interests to get rid of him. He's an arrogant arsehole. Stay in touch.'

Gary had pulled over in Grosvenor Square to read a message.

'Text from Damir. Girls left on a private jet to Linate.'

'Fuck, Ukraine bloke's I guess?'

Gary was typing. 'I'm asking the guy I know in ATC at Ringwood. What do you think?'

'I'm thinking what if that shit Mortlock finds out the real story? Some sort of blackmail or political corruption, something linked to Putin or Crimea.'

'Christ, that would be huge.'

'And all we did was catch him shagging.'

# CHAPTER 4

## SUNDAY 29th June – DAY 2

***The Sun on Sunday*: WATCH OUT PAEDO ABOUT**

***Sunday Express*: NURSES TO THE RESCUE**

Sam knew who or at least what he was the moment he opened the front door, standing across the street in his Belstaff biker jacket and jeans. The young guy starting firing as soon as he closed the door and turned towards the street. His first instinct was to duck, and hide his face, but he realised there was no point.

He held his stomach in, which in his case meant very slightly, put on his sunglasses, and walked right over and up to him.

'Got what you wanted?'

'Yes, thanks, Mr Plummer,' he said with no hint of apology, letting his long lens camera hang loose and pulling out a small digital in case anything developed at close quarters.

'Who you with?'

'Can't say.'

There was no point pursuing it. But it was very odd.

'Are you following me all today?'

'No, just here, that's all he wants.'

They all lied.

'OK. Well, I'm going in there for breakfast,' he said, pointing at the cafe on the corner. 'Why don't you have a coffee, too? I'll buy.'

The kid seemed OK with this and followed him into the Java cafe. Sam told him to sit down and went to the bar.

'Morning Ahmet.'

'Usual, Sam?'

'Two please. Enjoying the football?'

'No. Turkey didn't qualify.'

'Ah, sorry.' He unlocked his iPhone, and took a photo of the guy before going over with the coffees and said, 'There you go, kahve, Turkish coffee, best in the world, put hairs on your chest.'

'Thanks.'

As he put the coffee down for him, Sam picked up his bike keys and tossed them to Ahmet. 'He'll give you them back in thirty minutes, if you're a good boy. And you can pay for the coffees. Don't mix it, he's from Istanbul.'

'Very clever. Nice one.'

'What's your name?'

'David Bailey.' The kid seemed relaxed; he seemed to have what he'd been paid for.

As he nosed the Boxster out of the car park under his flat, he rang Frank on his hands free. 'Where are you?'

'Where do you bloody think? I'm in bed.'

'Sorry. I just got papped.'

'Really? Where?'

'Outside my flat.'

'Who were you with?'

'I was on my own. Check outside.'

He waited while Frank checked. 'Nobody I can see.'

Sam said, 'Well, it's very weird.'

'Any idea who?'

'Some cocky kid, Gary'll find out.'

*

Fifteen minutes later Sam was on Cromwell Road heading west. He flicked round the presets. Burke was getting huge airplay and making every bulletin. Near the Hogarth roundabout he pulled over and put the roof down while he emailed the photo to Gary. He was pretty certain nobody was following.

At the Woodstock roundabout he filled up and bought all the papers and a flat white from Costa next door. He took the biggest free table outside and started. One pile for rubbish – inserts, TV listings, most magazines, one for later – sport, arts, business, and one for now – the news. Depressingly, particularly for the Brazilian rain foresters, the first pile was the biggest. Everybody else was struggling – EU, the NHS, bloody Suárez.

At the next table he saw two guys, one looking at his story. They looked like they'd been up all night working on the M40, in their hi-viz jackets, yellow helmets on the table.

'Who is this Burke bloke?'

'Search me.'

'You seen these two birds?' He showed his mate the paper.

'Fuck.' He took the paper. 'See this, £10 off at Aldi.'

'Bloody hell, I'll get another copy. Another tea?'

He stood up and tossed the paper on the table as he left.

The guy was on to the sport now. Sam couldn't resist. 'Excuse me.'

He looked up. 'What?'

'Mind if I ask you what you thought of that story, on the front page?'

He looked suspicious. 'Why?'

'Well, I wrote it.'

He lightened up and turned to the story. 'You John Brydon?'

'No. I don't like my name in the papers, he works for me. I'm Sam.'

'Lloyd.'

'So what do you think, Lloyd?'

'About what?'

'Well, if you were telling a mate about it what would you say?'

'Oh. Um. Bloke off the telly shags two Russian birds.'

'Nothing more?'

He thought about it and looked quickly at the paper. 'Married bloke off the telly shags two hot Russian babes?'

'No wider implications?'

'His wife's pissed off?'

It was depressing. 'That's fair, I think she will be. Tell me, why did you pick it up and not the *Sunday Mirror* or the *People*?'

Lloyd looked at him as if he was an idiot and held up the front page. 'Ten quid off your next shop at Aldi.'

'Oh, I see.'

'I tell you what I would like to know though. Can I use two of these Aldi vouchers on one shop?'

'I've no idea.'

'Maybe if my wife and I have two trollies, we use one on each.'

Sam pulled his stuff together and got up. 'Lloyd, I think that must be worth a try. Thanks.'

So there he had it. Circulation would be up maybe thirty thousand and it would have nothing to do with his crack investigative team delivering the scoop of the year. It was some promotions guy that he'd never met, working out of the Slough office, making a deal with a cut-price German supermarket. And what was worse, it took up one third of the front page, his front page, and he had no idea how it worked.

As he walked away Lloyd called after him. 'Oi, mate.'

Sam turned round. 'Yes?'

'You going to have more pictures of the two birds?'

'We certainly will.'

On his way to the car he put the biggest pile in the bin outside, just as twenty million others would be doing soon enough.

Gary rang him as he was leaving. 'The plane was a Netjets, but we don't know who booked it or flew. Went to Paris not Milan.'

Sam was more interested in the photographer.

'Oh, it's Luke McIntyre, a new young guy, freelance.'

'He said it was what "*he*" wanted.'

'I don't understand,' said Gary.

'If it was you, wouldn't you say what "they" or "we" wanted, if you were working for me?'

'Perhaps. You sound worried about it?'

'It just doesn't make any sense.'

# CHAPTER 5

## SUNDAY

Past Oxford it was only another five miles to the house. He turned right in Charlbury, then left off the lane through the automatic gates, and halfway up the tree-lined drive he met Clare coming the other way in her white Range Rover, with Katie in the passenger seat beside her. They stopped side by side.

He looked up at her, wondering why she had to do the full Zara Philips just to ride out. The jacket, the tie, the make-up, even some sort of hairnet. All to ride a horse he'd paid twenty grand for that she couldn't jump over a garden bench.

'Hi girls.'

His wife pushed her Gucci sunglasses up on to her head. 'We're going riding, running late. We'll be back by eleven.'

Katie blew him a kiss. 'Sorry Dad, see you in a minute.' She'd made no effort at all. She looked great.

'Why aren't you all dolled up?'

She shrugged and pulled a funny face.

'The house is open,' said Clare, putting the car into gear and pushing her sunglasses down.

'Have fun, be careful,' he said, but they were off down the drive, tearing up the verge.

The house was a classic Cotswold pile. He went inside to drop his bag and get the dog. He'd put his foot down, Labrador or nothing. He went into the flat above the garage block where he kept some clothes and kit, and he went for a run with Geronimo at his heels, along the tracks that you could pick up at the end of the garden, past the paddock and stables. Gerry trotted alongside on the Evenlode towpath until they got to the village. He drank from the tap outside the church, cupping some in his hands for the dog. They ran back and then he swam a few laps. Getting out he saw his reflection full length in the pool house window. He'd never been with a woman who didn't hate the way he could stuff his face and never put on a pound.

They'd loved the place because nothing overlooked it; the nearest house was over a mile away. The irony wasn't lost on him, how much he valued his privacy. It was also why the kid Luke papping him was still niggling. He hadn't shagged anybody famous or married or both for months. And while he was still technically married, everybody knew that he and Clare had lived apart for years. So what was that about?

He used the outdoor shower and lay by the pool to get some sun. He didn't really want to, but he got his phone out of his bag and turned it on. Justine had texted him: 'Thx 4 dnr C U 2mrow.' He typed in 'U R wlcm' but thought it a bit naff and settled for 'Pleasure. Yes.'

He loved the quiet but he'd come back to spend time with Katie, who he never saw enough of. Had Clare taken her out just to annoy him?

The caller ID on one of his missed calls said 'Fergus #10.' He wasn't sure he approved of people moving from Fleet Street to politics.

He called him and said, 'You there?'

'Downing Street? No, I'm at home.'

'Amazed you didn't ring last night.'

'I know you think it's quiet, but it's not here.'

'All calm now after Coulson?'

'We should never have employed him, I blame Osborne. You would have been perfect.'

'You are joking. Too many kiss-and-tells.'

Fergus laughed. 'Maybe, but you are Mr Clean. Now, Burke.'

'Pleased?'

'Officially, obviously no, really embarrassing for us. Privately yes, I'm with you, he's an idiot.'

'Anything else?'

'Ukraine, very sensitive.'

'I don't think there's any political angle.'

'And who owns the villa?'

'Can't remember, nobody interesting.'

'OK, would you just keep us in the loop? We've got a delegation coming over soon, the whole Crimean thing is on a knife edge.'

Sam said, 'I hear you've been promoted.'

'Sort of, I think they've all forgotten I was once a journalist. But I'm still a humble Special Adviser.'

'You mean like Alastair Campbell, no real influence.'

He laughed. 'Yeah, something like that.'

*

When they got back, Clare went into the pool house and came out in a one piece, twirling her goggles. She looked fitter and slightly thinner than usual. Sam guessed she was getting laid.

She said, 'Big story today.'

'Joint effort with Frank.'

'A good day at the office then. Just another family destroyed.'

Before he could answer she dived in, swam a length underwater, and then effortlessly crawled another five. Sam knew he couldn't win so he never picked a fight.

She hung on to the side of the pool, her goggles up on her forehead, resting her chin on her crossed arms. 'Still try and do a hundred every day.'

He looked at her and thought it showed… and thought about the heating bills for the other pool indoors. And the personal trainer. Maybe it was him?

He thought back to when they first met on Concorde in 1991.

He'd got a tip from the guy they paid at Heathrow that Princess Di was on the next day's eleven o'clock to New York, so he bought a seat for the flight out and got 1C so he'd be across the aisle from her. But Di didn't show, so instead he chatted up Clare in the galley. She spent all four nights of the stopover with him at the Algonquin, hardly leaving the room.

Working minimum rests for BA, Clare was never home for more than four days, so even though they lived together, they didn't. She was funny, sexy and tall which were top three on his list, and then pregnant, which was right near the bottom. So they got married and she stopped flying. Sam was thirty-two and it seemed the right time, if nothing else. Katie was born and Felix followed a year later, but they soon realised it wasn't going to work. Never divorced, though. He reckoned it was cheaper, so he just paid the bills.

Looking back he wished he'd tried harder and not jumped into bed with other women the moment the going got tough. Maybe if he'd married Caroline it would have gone the same way? Now, twenty-two years on, he was resigned to his fate.

'Before you ask, I am seeing someone.'

'I wasn't going to.'

'You're not interested, are you?'

'He'll be younger, with no money, it won't last.'

'Sod off.' She said it without any malice or edge.

'So I'm right then?'

'You don't know it won't last.'

He laughed. 'I rest my case.'

'You?'

'No. Too set in my ways now.' He wouldn't tell her even if he was.

'Still shagging Caroline?'

'You need to change the record. She's married. To my boss.'

'Never stopped you before.'

That was how he made it work. Clare threw a punch, Sam would move away and change the subject. 'Heard from Felix?'

'Usual, one word texts.'

'Working their way up the coast still, aren't they?'

'He said Montevideo was fun. Tango lessons.'

'Well, that's what gap years are about. They went to a match in Porta Alegre. France game, I think.'

'Where's that?'

'On the coast, in the south. Frank got the tickets through ITV. They'll be in Rio soon, original plan was to watch England.'

Clare jumped out and picked up a towel. 'Katie's planning to cook you something special, so don't rush off. I'm going out. Might see you later,' she said, and she turned away.

'What the fuck is that?'

'What?'

'On your shoulder.'

'A butterfly. Grow up.'

Actually, he thought the tattoo looked quite good.

*

It was another world, quiet, green and clean. In the distance he could see a glider spiraling upwards in a thermal. He loved Sundays – there was the afterglow of a great story, and it was seven days from the next deadline.

Gerry slept in the shade. They set up lunch outside under the pergola. She'd always cooked. He could remember her tossing pancakes when she was eight or nine. Now she was preparing vichyssoise and an endive salad while he managed the barbecue and opened the Pinot Blanc. No matter how much crap Clare gave him, it was always worth it to see his kids.

'Your mother told me all about her new boyfriend.'

'You know it's the gardener?'

He didn't. 'Yes, Tarzan.'

'His name's Harvey. It won't last, she walks all over him.'

'And he lives with his parents,' he guessed.

'Oh, she told you.'

'Sort of.'

Sam liked to know the headlines, he didn't need to hear the details. He wasn't writing a story about it. 'How's Manchester?'

He turned the chicken on the barbecue.

'It's fine. I'm almost certain to get a 2:1. Depends on my dissertation.'

'You don't sound too enthused.'

'I need a good degree, and you know how hard it is getting a job these days. A first would make a difference.'

'How's the office?'

'It's OK, week to go.'

'It's not my fault the *Huffington Post* thing fell through. They know who you are?'

'Of course not, I'm Katie Mullins. You told me to.'

He knew using Clare's maiden name made sense, but it almost felt like she was disowning him.

'What's the deadline?'

'Couple of weeks, I can always get a couple more days.'

'If you change your view.'

'Well, that's not going to happen.'

'You got my comments, let's go through it after lunch.'

'Really, I'm fine, Dad.'

They got the food on the table and sat down. Sam poured her some water. He took a document from his bag and said, 'Right, your dissertation.'

'Dad, look I know you're really proud of me doing media studies.'

'And why shouldn't I be?'

'Because I'm interested in how we communicate now, not newspapers.'

'You can't think of it like that. I'm a journalist.'

'No, you're not.'

He picked up his front page. 'This is a great piece of journalism.'

'Maybe. But you didn't write it. You didn't go to Ukraine. You've never met Burke. You direct traffic.'

'What?'

'That's what you and the Fat Controller do.'

'Who the hell's the Fat Controller?'

'Frank, you must know that.'

'No I didn't. And who am I?'

'Somebody called you Jeff Tracy. Does that make sense?'

'He's the dad in *Thunderbirds*, never leaves Tracy Island, while his sons go off and save the world.'

He wondered if Clare had coached her to wind him up, or if it was genetic.

'Look, Dad, I have to write this, not you.'

'I'm not writing, I'm editing. When I put a headline on the front page, it's to make a lorry driver pick our paper up, rather than the *Sun on Sunday*. You'll be marked by some professor, on his second bottle of claret with *Downton* on the box. You have to grab his attention.'

'And you think THREE IN A BED will?'

'THE UNHOLY TRINITY is very good, but trust me, salacious outsells religious every time.'

'As the bishop said to the actress.'

Sam laughed. 'Very good. If you can combine both, it's paydirt.'

'And you changed my opening.'

She could see his red scribbles all over the first page. He put it face down on the table.

'Listen, the line about Rebekah Brooks lending Cameron a retired police horse being a great metaphor for the blurred lines between government, police and the press is brilliant. I just put it up front.'

'You really mean that?'

'I do. The last year, Leveson and the hacking trial, is all about that relationship. It's completely broken down.'

'But it's cheating if I talk to you.'

He admired her strict principles. He'd felt the same, but over time purity gave way to their more pragmatic application.

'Hang on, you read Peter Jukes and follow him on Twitter, what's the difference? It's just that you're actually talking to me.'

'Maybe.'

'But I like the fact you don't want to.'

'What?'

'Cheat. I'm encouraging, that's what I do. And you took our internship, and my advice comes with it, it's a package deal.'

She came round and hugged him. 'Sorry, Daddy. I do appreciate you and Frank having me, and I know you had a great story today.' She sat down again.

'I know there's a "but" coming.'

'But look at the way you tell it. Naked girls. Silly headlines. Not one word on the implications on media reform, the politics.'

'You might as well keep going.'

'That should be your story, your name, your words, in a serious newspaper or website. That's a comic.'

'You know it pays the bills. I'm not proud of it. No, that's not true. I'm proud of the story, but not, I don't know, the bigger picture.'

He liked her blind faith in him. That's how your kids could make you feel.

'Even if I could, what would we live on? I know it's hard for you to believe, but I do actually make more than most of what you call serious journalists.'

'Doesn't seem fair.'

'Five more years and I'm done. You and Felix will be working, and your mother will have married Alan Titchmarsh.'

'That's defeatist.'

'That's realistic,' he said, knowing she was right.

'But look on the bright side: Felix hero worships you. He thinks what you do is brilliant. He just wants to be you.'

'Well, he should try communicating then.'

'They post stuff on Facebook.'

'I'd love to see it, will you show me?'

'Sure.'

As they cleared up, he said, 'What are you on this week?'

She rolled her eyes. 'Bloody showbiz.'

'Let me speak to the Fat Controller.'

'Dad, please don't get involved.'

The alarm on his phone went. 'Come on, your godfather's on telly, let's go and watch. He loves this stuff.'

# CHAPTER 6

**MONDAY 30th June – DAY 3**

***Daily Star*: GIANT RATS INVADE BIG BRO HOUSE**

***Daily Mail*: HOW CHARLES INFLUENCED KEY POLICIES**

He found Frank in the newsroom chatting to a couple of guys who worked on the website. They seemed to be the only other ones in. 'You seen all the coverage?'

'The guys are showing me now. Looks good.'

'Just good?'

'Let's go in my office.'

Frank slammed the door behind them. 'The bastards did me this morning.'

'Who?'

'Louise opened the front door to pick up the papers, it freaked her out.'

'Same guy?'

'Yes. I rang Gary and he told me to take a picture from upstairs. Luke somebody, on a motor bike.'

'Shit. Very weird, I don't get it.'

Frank kicked the sofa. 'I told the little shit that if he uses a picture of my wife or family I'll kill him.'

'Ah, the measured approach.'

'Fuck him.'

'Frank, we've been doing it for ever. You're not Russell Crowe, calm down.'

'I wouldn't mind if I knew why.'

Sam laughed and said, 'It's probably a wind-up. Relax,' while thinking it was actually more than weird.

As they walked to the lift, Sam said, 'What exactly is this meeting with Jay about?'

'Our new fearless leader wants to have yet another budget meeting, about your department mostly. It's all numbers and new media. He keeps talking about page impressions and monetization.'

'He has to be happy after yesterday.'

Frank said, 'You know he wants to recruit a Chief Content Officer, what the fuck is that?'

Sam said, 'You were good on Sky. Look, it's the future, tablets not tabloids, charging people for content online.'

'All bollocks.'

Sam had never got to the bottom of the story that Jay had spent six figures refurbishing his monochrome office. He certainly couldn't see it. Big black and white framed photographs, uber modern furniture. Caroline had once said, 'E. L. James designed it.'

'Who?'

'*Fifty Shades of Grey.*'

Since then Jay's office was known as the E. L. James Suite.

*

'Thanks for coming, guys,' said Jay, who blended in, in black jeans and white shirt, looking like he'd come from the gym. He moved from his desk to the meeting table, offering water, but not tea or coffee. Two young consultants in grey suits that Frank vaguely recognised were there.

'Look, to come straight to the point...'

Frank held up the previous day's paper, interrupting him. 'What did you think?'

'Good. Thirty thousand up, I know,' said Jay, distracted.

'You know why?' said Sam.

'Because it's a good story, obviously. Can we move on?'

Sam turned to the two young consultants and said to one, 'What's your name?'

'Humphrey, sir.'

'Well, Humphrey, what do you think?'

He didn't look sure about speaking. 'Well, in my view, based on past data, and what I've seen overnight, I'd say maybe seventy per cent thanks to Aldi.'

'What?' said Jay. 'What are you talking about?'

Sam winked at Humphrey. Jay handed each of them a bound document. 'These are the current projections for this year and your forecast for next year, for your empire, Sam.'

'Department. It's a department.'

Sam was already bored and wondered where this was going. 'I've already read this. I'm on budget.'

Jay was turning pages. 'Page twenty-seven, all the disbursements that we just can't fully account for. Over twenty so-called freelancers and about a dozen more that are paid through offshore accounts. We don't even know their names.'

'Well we do, because I do. I'm afraid that's the deal – they wouldn't work for us if I told you their names. They're not all lowlife snitches. Remember who Deep Throat was.'

Jay clearly didn't. 'It's like the fucking CIA. Coverts, cash disbursements, private jets, surveillance, girls, technology, it just goes on.'

Sam shrugged his shoulders. 'It's simple. If you want to cut costs just tell me what the budget is, and I'll do it.'

'Would you?' Jay was clearly surprised.

'Of course, you're the boss.'

Jay sat back, trying to remember what they taught you at Harvard. 'Circulation is down three per cent,' he countered.

Sam said 'Ad revenue was down, it is everywhere, but on line was up 14 per cent, CPM's are strong, and we did 22 per cent up on syndication, of which over 90 per cent of that was my stuff. I made my numbers.'

Jay looked at the goons. Humphrey nodded.

'How do you know all this?' said Jay.

'Well, I can read. And I can add up. And I used to be able to write. Oh, and I've got share options, so the bottom line interests me. Have you seen the share price this morning?'

Jay shook his head.

'It's up 4 per cent this morning, off Burke. The whole sector's up.'

Sam had him on the ropes but now was not the time to put him away. 'Frank?'

Frank played it straight. 'Jay, it's your call, we'll cut if you want.'

Jay changed tack. 'And some of these expenses, we just don't get receipts or know what they're for. There's no audit trail.'

Sam knew he was in the home straight now. 'I've got to tell you that getting receipts from informers, doormen, drivers, pimps and drug dealers is not easy, and hookers just won't do it, allegedly. My team are the best, that's why they're here. This stuff doesn't come from Reuters or following Twitter. It's why Burke is on the front page, not Suárez. It's expensive, but you get what you pay for – a bit like your Ferrari California.'

Sam regretted the cheap shot and caught Humphrey trying not to laugh.

*

They were on the back stairs heading down. In his best Canadian accent, Frank said, 'I run the business, you run the paper.'

'Come on, he didn't ask for it. Not his fault he's born with the silver spoon in his mouth.'

'How do you know all those numbers?'

'It's his only language – if you can beat him at that, he has nowhere to go.'

'But we're hard on him every time. I'm not sure humiliating him in front of those guys is the best thing. I've taken the poster down.'

Sam said, 'I noticed. It was a bit much.'

Last Christmas, Johnnie had organised a large framed *Untouchables* film poster. Frank was photo-shopped in as Sean Connery in waistcoat with shotgun, and Sam as Kevin Costner in his trilby. Jay clearly hated the implication.

Sam looked at his phone as they walked and said, 'Ah, bingo. Burke's lawyers. Want to meet at twelve.'

# CHAPTER 7

## MONDAY

The best news was that it gave Sam a reason to call Justine and invite her, saying, 'It'll be a hoot, they must want to deal.'

She said she'd meet them at the offices in Fetter Lane. He wondered what she'd be wearing. When he got there with Frank she was already there, in a simple suit, looking like she'd come from the office. She poured coffee for Frank who was struggling to get the cellophane off the biscuit selection. 'Why do they do this, always at lawyers?' There were neat little rows of pencils and yellow pads, with pseudo modern art by the yard. Sam was impressed and surprised that Burke could afford Sherbrooks.

They waited. He was grateful she made no reference to dinner.

'Do we need to rehearse anything?'

'Let's just hear what they've got to say.' Sam could feel another of Frank's master classes coming on. 'They'll try and injunct us, stop us repeating it, publishing and syndicating more pictures. All bluff, they always end up making it worse.'

Sam said, 'This is damage limitation, they'll want to cut a deal. We'll be in control.' He was getting irritated. They were now ten minutes late. 'Let's give it five then we'll walk out.'

When they did come in, it all seemed choreographed, a touch melodramatic. The man who was clearly in charge introduced himself as Rupert Baxter-Ellis, ramrod straight and almost military. Wasn't eight people overkill?

Baxter-Ellis got straight into it with minimal formalities. 'Thank you for coming. Firstly, some housekeeping. We will supply you with draft minutes of this meeting. Secondly, you are aware that your group company secretary has signed an NDA?' He paused as Justine passed Frank a copy, who nodded.

'Which is binding on you and any group companies and freelance suppliers. Such material as we disclose is confidential until made public or you are required to disclose it by law. Furthermore, as you know, a meeting is taking place simultaneously in New York, since you will be aware that your sister publications ran much the same item there yesterday, and the substance of that meeting will be, or rather is, the same. So far so good?'

Frank said it was excellent. Justine was between them and Sam wrote 'blah blah' on his pad, pushing it towards her.

'I should add that we are acting for the entire family in this matter. Moving on. One, we are submitting a formal complaint to the Press Complaints Commission on the basis of breach of their Code of Conduct on two counts: firstly that it shows no respect for their private life and that the pictures were obtained by persistent pursuit.'

Sam couldn't read him. Was the pause for dramatic effect?

'However, you will be aware of the limited restraining powers of the PCC so, two, while one of my clients accepts that to some degree his life is of public interest, it was distressing to know photographs had been taken secretly over several days. They are suing you under the Human Rights Act for breach of their right to respect for their private life.'

Sam wrote a question mark now. Justine put her mouth close to his ear and whispered that yes, they could. She smelt good.

'And we shall be seeking an injunction preventing further publication of any related articles or photographs or video, repetition of the allegations, or any syndication or commercial exploitation thereof. And we will require all reference to our client to be removed from your website and other social media feeds.'

Frank tried to look at his watch without it being obvious. Twelve thirty, he could still be on time for lunch.

'Lastly... ' This longer pause, not for effect, made Sam nervous. Baxter-Ellis closed the file and stopped reading from his notes, making proper eye contact. 'Lastly, our clients will be bringing libel and privacy actions, commencing proceedings immediately, for defamation. You will receive the full basis of our claim in due course, but suffice to say that the main thrust of our argument will be that Miss Tatiana Svetlanova and Miss Irina Bezrukova are Lord Burke's daughters.'

There followed one of those long silences – Baxter-Ellis folding his arms and all of his cohorts staring them down, tasting something that had probably kept them up all night in anticipation, a magic moment in their little legal lives that they were going to savour. A story they could one day tell their mates a hundred times. 'You should have seen the look on their....'

Sam's mind filled with images of Burke at the villa, the girls, the affidavits, the first sightings in Kiev. It didn't make any sense.

Frank looked at Sam and they both realised they could think of nothing to say.

Justine saved them. 'Do you have any evidence in support of this?'

Baxter-Ellis pressed on. 'I do, Miss Walker.' One of the juniors slid a sheet across the desk. 'I am authorised to provide you with an affidavit from a Dr Timothy Whittet, of Harley Street, who carried out the blood and DNA tests on the young ladies. Positive tests. I am also authorised to provide you with notarised copies of their birth certificates, dated twenty-third of July 1992.' Yet another junior slid them across.

'What, both?' said Justine, studying them.

'Twins are usually born on the same day, in my experience.' No, he couldn't resist it, the merest smile.

Sam had been on the other end of this conversation a thousand times. He knew the trick was to stay calm, and not do what he wanted to, which was throw something against the wall. Like one of the spotty Herberts. What he needed was information. 'If they're twins, how come they have different names?'

'I believe one took their mother's maiden name, one their father's – or stepfather, technically. You should be aware that there is another dimension to this, though I'm afraid I'm not authorised to share it with you at this stage.'

Baxter-Ellis stood up. 'Gentlemen, Miss Walker, I suggest you and your lawyers meet with my team at say 3pm here to deal with details.' They knew the meeting was over.

Sam's mouth was dry. One minute he'd been teaching Jay basic newspaper economics, now he was in the headmaster's study getting six of the best. There was no dignified way to get out of there, just grab the papers and go. He let Justine and Frank out first, shoving Frank who seemed in shock.

Baxter-Ellis stood at the door as they filed out. Sam stopped as he got to him and said, 'Who have they sold it to?' He knew he shouldn't have as soon as he said it.

'I've no idea what you're talking about. There's a press conference tomorrow afternoon, I believe. I'm sure you'll be invited. Regarding damages, the word that comes to mind is substantive. Good day, Mr Plummer.' Smug had turned to nasty.

Rupert Baxter-Ellis shut the door behind them. Sam could hear them laughing as he walked away. He'd never met a Rupert he liked.

# CHAPTER 8

## MONDAY

Sam caught up with them on the pavement. Frank was on the phone. 'Really sorry, I've got to cancel.' He hung up. 'Jesus Christ.'

Sam looked back at Sherbrooks' office, and there at a first floor window was Burke, the trace of a smile on his face, using the universal sign language and mouthing 'wankers'. And the frustrating thing was, Sam couldn't argue with it.

Frank said, 'Fuck. Fuck.'

'Don't panic, Frank. Not yet. Just call Jay, he's the boss, and if they're doing the same in New York it's better he hears it from you first. I'd let him tell his dad.'

Sam ushered them across the road, dodging the traffic as he called. 'Mary, I need to speak to Donald. Yes, in Toronto, unless he's still fishing. OK, well, call me back. Let's go in here.'

They'd crossed Fetter Lane and were outside All Bar One. Justine took a call and hung back. Inside it was starting to fill up with lunchtime drinkers. Sky Sports News was on the screens, going back and forth between Wimbledon and Brazil.

Frank said, 'Well, this a fine mess.'

'I'm sorry.'

'We're going to be a laughing stock.'

'Are you thinking what I'm thinking?'

'That this is connected to the lad on our doorsteps?'

'Exactly.'

'So what does it mean?'

Sam said, 'Absolutely no fucking idea.'

Justine came in and sat down. Sam realised he'd probably blown it with her. One minute the guru and mentor, now the village idiot.

'I don't understand, why didn't he just deny it?' asked Justine.

'You start,' said Frank.

'We've had the pictures for nearly two weeks. He's known we were on to him for nearly ten days. Nobody else has a sniff. He stonewalled us all last week. The real story – which is clearly true – is worth what?'

'Ten, if anything,' said Frank.

'And why? Because it's a fluffy good news story, he'd only really sell it to a daily. And, the killer, what's the best picture? Him with two pretty students? Mother, who knows? Two illegitimate daughters is hardly a big deal. Pretty boring.'

'So he sits it out,' said Frank.

'And you are talking about a guy who is seriously media savvy and has an ego the size of a house. So he sues us for...?'

'Six figures?' said Frank. 'And he'll sue everybody else who followed us and wasn't careful.'

'Which is a lot of people. They do tend to trust us, me. Doesn't help us in the industry.'

'So everybody thinks he's a lad. Then he produces the girls to great fanfare, and he sells that story for a lot more – with our great pictures. Tax free wonga, as Kelvin called it,' said Frank.

'I have to admit, it's clever. Great piece of opportunism. His profile goes through the roof.'

Justine said, 'I'm sorry, the Government's adviser on media would play that game?'

Frank said, 'He can do his job best from the moral high ground. When this comes out, he's going to be on top of Everest.'

'Looking down on us at base camp,' said Sam.

Justine said, 'But I don't understand. You have the statements from the housekeeper and the driver.'

Frank snorted. Sam said, 'Worthless. Couple of opportunists, told and paid to say what we wanted to hear.'

'But you must be able to get them in court.'

'Even if we found them they'd just say it was sour grapes – and that they did it for the five grand we paid them both, told us what we wanted to hear.'

'But you've got them in a hotel, haven't you?'

Sam said, 'Let's see,' and rang Damir and told him the headlines. 'Go and see and ring me back.' He hung up. 'They'll be long gone. You should call Jay now.'

'Oh, God. I hate having to apologise to him for anything.'

Sam said, 'He's going to have his pound of flesh with this one.'

'So what happens now?'

Frank said, 'Well, I imagine you call your boss Donald and explain how your first assignment is probably going to result in our biggest ever settlement. Might even end up with the law being changed. You'll both be famous.'

'Or fired. I'm on secondment. They can easily get rid of me.'

'Frank's not being serious. You'll be fine,' said Sam.

For the first time she didn't look confident. Maybe that's why he lied to her. Jay would want as many scapegoats as possible, and Donald would look after himself.

After Frank left, she said, 'Do you really believe all that?'

'It wasn't some sleazy PR, it was the Queen's solicitors. They don't make that sort of stuff up.'

'Has this happened to you before?'

'Sure, been sued hundreds of times, made mistakes, but we usually settle or win. But it's usually round the edges, not something as black and white as this. Given his high profile and his background, the broadsheets and everyone else are going to have a field day. And it's really bad timing with the government.'

'Who's got the story?'

'*Daily Mail* I'm guessing, right up their street. It'll break tomorrow, definitely. Front page for two days, then probably

Thursday and Friday inside, easy enough to make it last four days. The Sundays will be fully primed by then.'

'Who's in charge?'

'Somebody will be running it for him, he can't manage this himself. What they often do is a split exclusive. Oddly the *Daily Mail* tend not to share with the *Mail on Sunday*, but the *Mail on Sunday* often share with the *Sunday Mirror*, or in the old days the *News of the World*. Then they'll do a TV exclusive, plus syndication.'

'And how much will it cost us?'

'Depends if they settle or we go to court. You're the expert.'

'Hardly. My CV looks really impressive now, doesn't it? Played one, lost one. As you so delicately pointed out.'

Sam said, 'Sorry. I'll ring Donald and Charlie for you. It was our fault, not yours.'

'Thank you. I mean it.'

She seemed to visibly relax, taking out a tissue and blowing her nose. He actually felt guilty that he'd put her through it, and he wondered what would happen to her.

'I have to go.' She stood up. 'Shall we meet later?'

He tried to sound relaxed about the offer, looking up at her. 'Probably makes sense.'

As Sam watched her walk away down the street, turning heads, he said to himself, 'Speak of the devil.' Across the street Burke had appeared with a guy he didn't recognise but looked like somebody from rent-a-heavy. He could see an earpiece coiled up into his ear as he checked both directions. He steered Burke across the pavement. They got into the back of a Mercedes with blacked out windows and sped away.

*

He called Gary to tell him all the bad news and ask him to back up all the photos and video on to a disc.

Gary said, 'You heard about Rolf Harris?'

'I'm guessing guilty.'

'Twelve counts.'

'Might keep us off a couple of front pages this week.'

Frank called to say Carson now wanted to meet today. 'He'd just landed. He called me, he hadn't heard.'

'Jay's a chicken. How did he take it?'

'Actually very calmly. I thought he'd go ballistic.'

'Probably in shock. Jay doesn't know what to do anyway.'

*

The private lift opened straight into Lomax's suite of offices. His PA Stephanie told them to go right in. There was no desk, it was more like a country drawing room. It couldn't have been less like his idiot son's E. L. James Suite.

Lomax waved them in. CNN was on the TV, muted. He was on the phone chatting in French, his feet on the coffee table. There were books and papers all over the tables, the biggest pile with an ice hockey puck as a paperweight. But it was his flattened nose, broad shoulders and the scar tissue above his eyes that made it easy to see that he really had played semi-pro hockey.

He finished the call. 'Sorry guys, have to go to Shanghai tonight now. Well, this is different. So what do we do?'

Sam spoke up. 'I suggest we wait until tomorrow. The injunction will stick. Then see. Cause you any problems?'

'Well, our mutual friend in New York who said he's sending me the case of Petrus is going to want it back.'

Sam knew he probably had ten far bigger things to worry about. But if he meant Murdoch was sending the Petrus that was quite funny.

'Who else do you think he might go after?'

Frank had a list with him. 'Couple of the Sundays panicked to get something out late, they look vulnerable. Today, your papers and a couple of others, they were more careful. Your TV stations ran it with some video.'

Sam said, 'The only thing that went viral is the clip of the two girls oiling each other.'

Carson said, 'He's no big deal outside the UK, just being a Lord makes it fun, I guess. You know what the issue is? This just strengthens him and therefore Cameron; they'll batter us on needing to be regulated. How's Jay coping?'

'Crapping himself about telling you,' said Sam.

'OK, well, don't tell him I know. I'll make him sweat a bit. Jay's mother is driving me mad. Good lesson.'

Sam realised his first wife was one of the ten far bigger things.

'Can you guys cut him some slack? He's not a bad kid, he needs to learn. You were young once.'

Carson Lomax had the relaxed, resigned air of a man who'd seen it all before, helped by thick skin and deep pockets. Frank was right – it was all a matter of perspective.

'So, was Burke single when they were conceived?'

Sam said, 'Yes, born July '92, so conceived late '91. We checked – Burke's engagement announcement was in *The Times* in February '93. I've no idea where they were conceived, could be anywhere. But at that time he was a single BBC reporter – news, Panorama, all over the place.'

'And the mother?'

'Nothing so far. Guessing she must be Ukrainian.'

'We're a bit isolated, won't have many friends on this one,' said Frank.

'Well, it's not hacking, is it? I'm not closing the paper.'

Though he didn't really know the business, Sam quite liked Carson. He could see why Caroline found him attractive. A man's man and a lady's man, at the same time.

'Well, let's see what tomorrow brings.'

Stephanie opened the door. 'Tokyo and Seoul are on the line.'

*

Sam decided to walk and reached Soho. Terry answered the phone on the third ring.

'Hello old boy, looked good.'

'Fuck up.'

'Really? Gone pear-shaped?'

'Banana-shaped.'

'Scale of one to ten?'

'Eleven.'

Sam crossed the road and cut through Newman Passage.

'Pray tell?'

'We're gagged, but they're his twin daughters.'

'Ah. That's different. Want me to come in?'

'Maybe, but you around?'

'Until Thursday, golf weekend. Le Touquet.'

Gary met him outside Soho House. It was the original one on Greek Street, tucked away behind an anonymous pale green door, opposite a minicab company, yards from Shaftesbury Avenue if you turned right and the sexual ambiguity of Old Compton Street if you turned left.

Buzzed in, they twisted their way up the stairs to the top floor. Sam had made Gary a member. It was full of media types, more TV and movies than the press. In its bizarre, inverted snobbery, they made you take your tie off. He put his phone on vibrate. They sat down and ordered two club sandwiches.

Justine texted. 'In office. Still meeting?'

Shit. He couldn't believe he'd forgotten her suggestion to meet later, so he texted straight back, 'Buy u dinner?' She agreed to meet him at eight in Colbert on Sloane Square.

Gary drank his regular Coke. He just fitted in wherever he was. He wouldn't look out of place if he walked over to the bar and hung with the advertising creatives or if he went out in the street and bantered with the minicab drivers opposite. He wasn't pumped from weights, but you just knew he wasn't a guy to cross, though Sam had never seen him lose his cool.

'When you were out there did anything strike you as odd?'

Gary fired up his laptop and moved to sit beside him. 'I've been looking at them for the last hour. At the time no, I'd have said something. But if they were posing, why do it for five days when they knew I had it after two?'

'But did it look like the girls were in on it?'

'You mean the posing for the cameras? Don't know. So you're asking whether Burke came up with this plan after we told him or while we were there?'

'Yes. And why did Burke go to Kiev?'

'Something to do with their mother or the guy who owns the villa?'

'Could be. Damir's trying to find out. Let's look at the pictures.'

Gary got them up and they scrolled through the endless shots.

Sam said, 'You see, yesterday they're foreplay, today they're horseplay. So which is it?'

He had to admit they were brilliant. For all the world they looked like some flabby oligarch with a couple of thousand dollar hookers, and then you looked again and it was a member of the House of Lords playing happy families.

Gary scrolled to the 'sex' shot in the bedroom.

Sam said, 'We didn't use that. You can't really see anything.'

'It's a four poster, with a mosquito net I think, that's the problem. That was early evening too and the light was crap.'

'But they're definitely having sex?'

'I don't think she's training to be a jockey, but she's doing all the work.'

Sam wanted to say, 'You get to a certain age,' but it was no time for jokes.

'Is it definitely Burke? Maybe it's a bodyguard.'

'They were both outside. And the woman's not the housekeeper, she's about eighteen stone.'

'So, how do you see it panning out this week, Sam?'

'Well, if I had it, then I'd go with the big revelation tomorrow, and I'd put Burke and his wife in to bat at the press conference later in the day – moral indignation, outrage etc etc. Wednesday I'd run the mother's story, must be one, plus maybe wheel out the twins. Thursday or Friday I'd really put the boot into us, probably me and Frank. Then live TV exclusive, Sky or ITN. Then recycle it all at the weekend, dual exclusives, with new pictures. They might own them by then, suspect we'll have to hand them over.'

'You think that with young Luke on your doorsteps means they're going to have a go at you two?' said Gary.

'Well, if it was me, I would. I'd go heavily on the hypocrite. I'm still technically married and I'm up there as "muckraker in chief". Probably try for a kiss and tell.'

'Plenty to choose from.'

'That's not really very helpful.'

'Sorry, but would they really do that to a fellow journalist?'

'It's very unusual, mostly because the public don't care much or know who we are.'

'Well, they do now.'

Sam was still looking at the photos. 'Stop there, who's that?'

He pointed at a wide shot of the villa, two men getting out of a car to the right and beyond the villa.

'The bigger guy is security – stayed in that outbuilding. The other one, don't know. Saw him a few times. Never outside though.'

'Can you zoom in?'

He was a slight figure in a trilby, carrying a briefcase. He said, 'Do you think that's the guy running the process now? Bit risky knowing we're watching – but explains the shades and hat, and why he never came out.'

'Maybe he's the one shagging the girl?'

'Not that I ever saw.'

Sam looked at the shot, and said, 'Well, somebody's getting fucked here, and it's not just us.'

*

They bounced around the story but got nowhere. Gary offered to drive him to his dinner. In the car Frank called. They called him back on Bluetooth and put him on the car speakers.

'I've got the story' said Frank.

'Just give us the worst.'

'The girls' mother was a journalist, Ukrainian, a dissident really, that he met and had an affair with in 1991 while working for the Beeb. Katia Svetlanova. She got pregnant and wanted to have it. She had twins and he said he'd support them, which he did, even when she was imprisoned for six months.'

'Tell me it gets better.'

'I'm afraid not. She then married a local businessman, Artem Bezrukov. He looked after the girls. But they split up about ten years later. Seems a bit dodgy, lost a lot of money, but still well connected. Two years ago she got cancer, serious. Burke and his wife went out there – Sarah had known all along, met her, promised to look after them and to get the girls out of the country, convinced they would be exploited.'

'Oh, God. That it?'

'I've updated Damir. For the moment, yes, but there must be more. I don't know.'

'Is she dead?'

'Assume so, yes.'

'So that answers the question about the other dimension. The mother's a martyr. And Burke's a saint. We're screwed.'

*

They pulled up in Sloane Gardens and parked so they could see Sloane Square tube and the entrance to the restaurant.

'Maybe I'm just getting lazy. Should have seen it.'

'These things happen,' said Gary.

'Not to me they don't. And we've got nothing to come back with. We're gagged and they're all going to have a field day at our expense. Well, this is cock-up, not conspiracy. Burke just took advantage – all the lights turned green and he put his foot down and went for it. I told you he's smart, he knows our game.'

'Well, that's true,' said Gary.

'Our best defence is that it was a genuine mistake. As far as libel or privacy's concerned, what real harm's been done? He comes out a hero – he stuck by her and the girls.'

They sat in silence for a while. Sam knew at times like these you had to focus on hard facts, nothing else could be assumed. 'All we know for certain is that those two girls are his daughters.'

'And he refused to deny the allegation.'

'But he now looks likes the perfect regulator. He beat us at our own game.'

Justine came out of the tube in front of them and Gary tooted. 'She's a nice girl, and smart.'

'True. She is. Think she's slightly worried about breaking the world record for the world's shortest legal career.'

He got out, telling Gary not to wait, and met her on the pavement, where she kissed him on both cheeks as Gary pulled away.

*

They gave him the table he liked in the corner by the window. It was curved and worked best if you sat side by side on the red leather banquette. It really did feel like an old French bistro, with its checkerboard tiled floor and massive art nouveau posters.

It was the first time he'd seen her not dressed for work, in a simple summer dress and flats, her hair loose. She was really easy company, funny, attractive. She was genuinely interested in him, and he knew she too was in a hole.

After they'd ordered she asked him how it was going and he said, 'Can I suggest that we have a break from that?' He turned his phone off. 'There, tell me about you.'

'What do you want to know?'

'OK. Tell me about your parents.'

'My dad Percy works for BP in Melbourne, he's remarried. Don't really see him. My mother Helen lives in the South of France.'

'And where did you grow up?'

'In Bristol, then went to Cheltenham Ladies College.'

'Ah, hockey sticks and big green knickers.'

'Not always.'

He noticed she wasn't wearing the engagement ring. After a few more questions he said, 'Have you got a boyfriend?'

She laughed and said, 'You're very forward.'

'Enquiring mind. It's my job.'

'I don't believe in sex outside marriage.'

He was surprised. 'Really?'

'Not me, you. You're married. I don't date married men.'

'I told you. I'm not really married.'

'They all say that.'

'Clare and I haven't shared a bed or a house for years.'

'They all say that too.'

Sam laughed.

'Work's exposed me to a lot of married men.'

Every time she lobbed out an ambiguous line, he wondered if she was flirting. Even if it was stupid, and he made a fool of himself, he wanted to find out.

'And yours?'

'What?'

'Parents.'

'They're both long dead.' Maybe when, or if, he got to know her better, he would tell her. 'My mother was a nymphomaniac who drank herself to death, but not until after she had driven my father to hang himself.' It was easy to guess it explained a lot about his relationship with women.

'So you and Caroline, was that before or after your marriage broke down?'

This he never told anybody. It was too important, and nobody would believe him anyway.

*He found Le Cou de la Girafe just off the Champs-Élysées. He was early and Caroline walked in fashionably late. 'You look vaguely cool. Was the suit on sale or return from Burtons?'*

*'I binned it.'*

*'I bet you've still got your M and S Y-fronts on though.'*

*He went bright red. She was very cool and he was way out of his depth, even though she was probably nineteen. Her hair was dark and cut short and spiky – they all performed in identical wigs – there was no make-up, though her cheek bones stood out, and she had big perfect teeth.*

*She ordered in French, 'You can interview me now. Three questions.'*

*'Which one were you last night?'*

*'Very predictable. Night off. We're on a rota. I'm on tonight. Two more.'*

*'How did you get here?'*

*'Subway.'*

*'That can't count.'*

*'Usual, studying here, spotted, auditioned, good money.'*

*He'd read the press pack so he now knew the breasts he was trying desperately not to stare at, straining bra-less against her tight white T-shirt, were the required 34B. She started to ask him questions, seeming genuinely interested in what he did.*

*'I'm one of the Guards in bearskins in the opening routine. See if you can spot me after that.'*

*He took the ticket she offered. 'Come.'*

*'I'll try. What were you studying?'*

*'One. Am studying. Journalism – surely you worked that out?'*

'Way before. She was working in Paris, dancing. I was doing a feature on Paris nightspots. What about you, after Exeter?'

'Four years in private practice, boring, then the job in the Group, based in Bath, which was great fun.' He added it up – it made her about 26 or 27. Would that be wrong? Maybe not, movie stars did it all the time. Look at Bruce Willis.

She seemed perfectly happy just chatting. They had a second

bottle, and half of him thought what the hell he would do if something did happen and he couldn't manage it or fell asleep. He ordered a double macchiato, and gave up on a plan.

It was a warm night. Outside she said, 'No Gary?'

'My flat's a walk from here.' He looked across Sloane Square. 'Can I get you a cab?'

'Is it close?'

'What?'

'Your flat, stupid.'

They walked down the King's Road, diverting through Duke of York Square where he showed her the Taschen bookshop. In the window was the huge limited edition Helmut Newton book. As they went past the Pheasantry, she linked arms with him, and at the flat she made it easy for him to kiss her as they got into the lift. He felt like he'd had two Viagra, not two bottles of Viognier. Her hands were undoing his belt as he fumbled with the front door key. They got as far as the rug in the hall, him pushing up her dress. He was amazed he lasted as long as he did.

'God, if I'd known you weren't wearing knickers I'd have never got through dinner.'

During the night he woke up. It was still warm, the windows wide open. He looked at her, naked and unmarked, no tan line, no tattoos, no wrinkles, not even studs in her ears. Nothing. She rolled on to her back, and he remembered when a Brazilian was vaguely shocking. Now it was nothing.

When he came back from the bathroom she was propped up on the pillows. 'Come here, big boy.' This time they took their time. He somehow managed to hold on and come with her, hoping in that moment that he might see her again.

In the morning he was surprised that she was right over on his side of the bed asleep, latched on to him. The sun was up and when she shifted he went to the bathroom. With the cabinet mirror angled, he could see the scratches on his back. He wondered where the hell this was going, but he felt good about her, and she made him feel good about himself. Too often he'd subscribed to the definition of eternity as the time between when a man comes and a woman goes. He'd shoved girls out at all hours into minicabs with excuses about early starts. But he wanted her to stay. Yes, he wanted more great sex, but he just wanted her around. When had he last felt like that? She came in wearing just his unbuttoned shirt, standing behind him. 'Ooh, sorry about your back.'

'It'll heal.'

'You're in good shape.'

'If you say "for your age" I won't be happy.'

She kissed one of the weals on his shoulder and reached round. 'Let me wash your back in the shower.'

Stone-cold sober in the unforgiving bathroom light, her body looked as ludicrous as it had last night. If he knew one thing for certain, it was that the day could and would only get worse.

# CHAPTER 9

## TUESDAY 1st July – DAY 4

***The Sun*: ROLF AND SAVILE STALKED BROADMOOR TOGETHER**
***Daily Star*: VEGAS SHOCKER: ROONEY ROBBED ON HOLIDAY**

Sam didn't really want to face the day. He turned on the TV and his phone. Texts and emails poured in. He left it on silent and ignored the calls.

Burke was the big story on the BBC *Breakfast* sofa. One of the presenters held up the *Mail* front page, with Sam the focus of the story. They read the story together on line and looked at some others. They had the shot that Luke had grabbed downstairs.

'Why are they writing about me? Frank's the editor, Johnnie's name is on the story. Carson's the owner, and Jay.'

'But everybody knows it's you.'

'In the industry, yes, it's like somebody's stoking the fire.'

'Like who?'

'No idea.'

He looked at it. LIAR LIAR above the story didn't help. Referring to him as 'a dodgy Plummer' was lame. But it still hurt.

It also now appeared that Burke had been struggling to get visas for the girls and to get them out before the story broke. They had made it by just hours, they claimed, which made him look even worse. It also explained Burke's silence and all the time he'd spent in Kiev, presumably at the British consulate.

Justine sat opposite him having breakfast, back in his shirt. She looked good in it. He read an email on his phone. 'You remember the guy at the Ivy?'

'The smooth one?'

'Yes. Julian Mortlock. Rumour is he's working for Burke. No surprise, he had to hire somebody. His lawyers probably suggested it.'

'What was the last straw?'

She seemed to remember everything he said and could just pick up wherever he left off. 'When you fired him.'

He turned down the TV. If he couldn't tell her, who could he tell? 'He was on the Royals. Whether he got it hacking or not I don't know, he might have reverse engineered it.'

'What's that?'

'With voicemail hacks, you use the information to go off and get a genuine lead, to cover your tracks. But the hack tells you where to look. A senior guy in the Royal Household's son, 17 or 18, was going out with a 15-year-old girl. Good kids, good families. They're at some party at Windsor Castle, and they have a quickie upstairs.'

'So UNDERAGE SEX IN QUEEN'S BEDROOM.'

'That's the headline. I really couldn't see it doing anybody any good. They were all nice people. I refused to run it.'

She was starting to think Sam was a contradiction. He was supposed to run a ruthless tabloid machine.

'So you're a softie really.'

'Don't tell anybody.'

'Well, you weren't last night.'

She went to the sink with her plate, then jumped back. 'There's two photographers opposite.'

'Shit. They see you?'

'Don't think so.'

'Stay away from the windows.'

He went out and up one floor to sneak a look from the landing. He recognised Luke again but not the other. Had they followed them home? He went back down.

'Wait thirty minutes and make sure they've gone.'

He fetched a baseball cap, sweatshirt, tracksuit bottoms and some trainers. 'Put these on.'

He explained how to lock up and leave through the basement and up the car park ramp. 'Sam, I can't be seen involved in this.'

He was surprised how nervous she sounded.

'I know this won't sound right, but it's not about you, it's about me. I won't let any harm come to you. You have to trust me.'

'OK.'

He dressed, then got an Uber that was two minutes away. He kissed her goodbye, then went out, where they took some shots.

'Hi Luke, good to see you again.'

'Hi Sam.' To his back he added, 'I made you famous.'

Sam went back and right up to him. 'Just understand this Luke McIntyre, you little turd. You're freelance. If you step out of line I will sue you personally. I will make your life hell. You will never work again. Understand?'

The kid looked petrified. 'Sorry, Sam.'

'Excuse me?'

'Mr Plummer.'

The other older guy was still taking shots. 'And what's your name?'

'Fuck off.'

He wanted to rip the camera off him and smash it against the wall, but he turned away.

He got the Uber driver to slowly lap the block. He called her. 'It's OK, they left. I'll call you later. You going in?'

'Should I?'

'No. I'll tell Frank. The lawyers have got it now.'

She said, 'I really enjoyed last night.'

'Me too.'

He realised that was probably the understatement of the decade.

*

For twenty years he had walked into the newsroom like the lion king entering his den. It was his territory and he was the alpha male. He didn't need a job title or big office to show he was the main man. Today it went quiet and people avoided eye contact as he made his way to Frank's office.

Mary sat outside. 'Morning, Sam.'

'What happened, somebody die?'

'Jay's upstairs with outside lawyers.'

Frank shut the door, which was always a bad sign. Through the glass the staff could see the debate unfolding – Frank sat at his desk, Sam circling, with all the TVs off.

'You're being unreasonable. Look what's happening.'

'Like what?'

'We had three outside the house this morning. Louise told them to bugger off. Half of Fleet Street on your tail, like the PCC using us as a scapegoat, like every other paper making you the point of the story. What's that about?'

'So what happened to collective responsibility?'

'It's your picture all over the *Mail*, not mine, in their so-called exclusive. I'm next, obviously.'

Sam slumped onto the sofa. 'Not so fucking untouchable now.'

'Well, we invented the rules, we should know how to win.'

'I hope you're right.'

Frank came and sat down opposite him, leaning forward. He tossed the *Mail* on the coffee table. Sam had only seen it on line. On the front page it said INNOCENT VICTIM above a picture of Burke.

Frank said, 'Look, now it's my turn to be Captain Sensible. Young Jay wants to flex his muscles, he's got the authority. We need to sort out Burke, and we've got to let this blow over. You being here doesn't help. I don't see why telling everyone you need some time off is a big deal.'

'There's a team upstairs who found Martin Bormann. How long do you think it would take them to figure it out?'

'No, they didn't. This is about lawyers now. But like the others we're not in court. Listen, you're not being suspended.'

'Oh, thanks.'

'But it's easier if you're not around, can you not see that? They think we're out of touch, and maybe they're right.'

'It looks like I'm running away.'

'The tables are turned. You may not have noticed it, but when we nail people, that's what they tend to do. Except we call it going into hiding.'

'You know Mortlock's running Burke.'

'I heard, and that's another reason to go. Once he's on your case.'

Sam held a cushion to his chest and leaned back into the sofa, looking deflated. 'Frank, maybe it's my time of life, but I just don't know what to do.'

'Oh fuck, don't go all Mariella Frostrup on me.'

'I am not going through menopause.'

'Well, we know that, because that involves reduction in testosterone levels, and you're still doing it for Britain.'

'It's not funny.'

'No, it's boring, it's your bloody mid-life crisis that we've been discussing for the last ten years.'

Mary came in and said, 'It's starting.' She picked up the TV remote and sat down next to Sam. Frank opened the balcony doors, lit a cigarette and poured them coffee.

*

A cutaway during the preamble showed the room at the Savoy packed with journalists, photographers and TV crews. He saw Gary and Mortlock and plenty more he recognised. He picked up the remote and pressed record. He'd need to watch it all again. He paused the next wide shot.

Mary said, 'Isn't that Katie next to Terry?'

On one side of Burke sat his supportive wife, Lady Sarah, and on the other was Baxter-Ellis, the lawyer. Behind them, a *Daily Mail* branded backdrop.

And of course the press conference was like masterpiece theatre, the man was a pro. While Neil Hamilton looked about as comfortable as Jeremy Paxman doing *Jackanory*, Burke had spent years looking down the lens, live, sincere, on network television, and this was a cow he was going to milk.

He 'read' a prepared statement which he might have referred to once, for effect, and got in every message. Privacy, stress, children, family values, human rights, invasion of privacy, responsibility, death, marriage, freedom of the press, moral outrage. And of course he managed to work in a reference to Sam as a 'despicable bottom feeder'. Apart from his position on the euro, it had something for everyone.

And all the time Lady Sarah sat there limp and vulnerable, red and doe-eyed, standing by her man, champion of the people.

Baxter-Ellis invited questions, and our hero was just as good at these, explaining that the girls' mother was still in Ukraine undergoing treatment for cancer and that they were providing support. 'Her tragic illness was the catalyst for me going to Ukraine to rescue the girls, a delicate operation that was so nearly sabotaged by the reckless intervention of one newspaper.'

Yes, he would sue. No, the girls were not available today. Yes, his wife had known right from the outset. Yes, his 'good friend' the Prime Minister had expressed his personal support. No, he did not wish to comment on the extent of the litigation. Yes, he would of course continue to support his twin daughters. And intercepting a question directed at her, no, his wife would not be making any comment today.

*

They watched the immediate analysis on Sky News, then Frank muted it. 'Well, that couldn't have gone much worse.'

'Word perfect. Bloody Mortlock. Even I'm starting to believe him,' said Sam.

'They're his daughters, for God's sake. There's a DNA test. Give it a rest.'

'Sorry. And the mother's not dead.'

'Not sure if that's good or bad. She's not a martyr now, but it's another story. More pain and suffering.'

'You can't always be the smartest guy in the room. Always a first time.'

'Like being suspended?'

'You're not suspended… though we could be.'

'Are you serious?'

'Try reading your contract.' Frank was getting exasperated. 'You're not running away, but you are being a hypocrite and a wimp. Week in, week out, we, you, tear people to pieces in print. You never bat an eyelid. Now you get a teaspoonful of your own medicine, you can't handle it.'

Sam went over to the window, hands stuffed in his jeans, looking across to St Paul's. It had never occurred to him that he wouldn't leave on his own terms. He'd always imagined a big dinner, awards, a book deal, nice pieces in every paper.

'Maybe you're right. Frank, do you ever stop and wonder why we do this, shovelling shit?'

'I only do philosophy in the pub, after seven, on Fridays.'

'I need to do something. I can't bloody go on holiday, mid-story.'

'Sam, the reason we win, the reason we always win, is that when we get on to somebody they get emotional, they panic. We stay calm. We think. Now you're behaving just like them.'

Sam knew he was right.

'You're the story now. You have to go.'

'Where?'

Frank thought about it. 'Go and stay in my place.'

Sam knew that Frank had always been good on property, always on the move, trading up, borrowing against his options. Frank had bought a villa in Spain in the late nineties, which Louise and their five kids loved.

'Are you sure?'

'I don't rent it out, it's empty.'

'And do what?'

'I don't know. Do some stuff on the Spanish economy, or Gareth Bale, or King Carlos abdicating.'

'You are joking?'

'Gibraltar then, you can see it from the roof. The dodgy fag imports, they say everybody should be on four packs a day. Got a better idea?'

'I'm an investigative journalist. I investigate. Remember?'

'Vaguely. Actually, tell you what then. Chalky White.'

Sam laughed and went back to the sofa. Frank might as well have asked him to be their opera critic. The old PLUMMING NEW DEPTHS tagline swam into view.

'Jesus, Frank. Me, work on the Bermuda Triangle of journalism? Nothing original or interesting has been written about John White in maybe ten years. I haven't spoken to him for at least fifteen. Has anybody seen him? Do we care?'

'We got a lead from Terry. It's the government's last chance to extradite him. Time limit or kids or something.'

'Bollocks. An annual event,' said Sam.

'Seriously. Terry said a really good old source. I'm not going to beg Sam, don't do it for me. Have you got a better idea?'

'World Cup?'

'You can't gatecrash your son's gap year. And you don't really like football.'

'Yes I do.'

'Who did Germany beat yesterday?'

'OK, you made your point.'

'Ignore White then, make up your own reason. I don't give a shit. Do what you always do on holiday. Take a bird.'

'Oh, yes, that's just what we all need. Married man with bird at your villa. I'll buy some Vilebrequins and take two.'

Frank said, 'You see, you're happier already.'

Sam got up. 'I'll go in the morning.'

*

From his office he called Justine and asked her for lunch and a favour, which he said he'd explain. He went back to his department, pleased to see Terry come back from the Savoy ten minutes later. 'Thought you might like some moral support.'

Sam envied him; he'd gone on his own terms, head high. But he'd packed it in too young. He was still a genius.

If nothing else Sam had to try to make this look real. If in doubt do nothing. Buy some time. He rang Katie and told her to come up.

Sam looked around at the office. 'If this is my last day here ever it'll be yours too. You thought of that?'

'Chin up. Worse things happen at sea.'

'Terry, I don't want to go out this way, shuffling out through a side door with my stuff in a cardboard box. How was it?'

'I'm afraid your worst nightmare. What's your plan?'

'Few days off, going to Frank's place in Spain.'

'Excellent idea. You should do something, work.'

'I thought Chalky White. Coming up for possible extradition.'

'Excellent again. But I know that. It was me who told Frank.'

'Oh yes, he said that. I just need an excuse.'

'The tip was genuine, might be something.'

Katie arrived, closely followed by Johnnie, who Sam introduced. 'This is Katie, my eldest. Katie, this is Johnnie, my number two.'

Johnnie said, 'Really?'

'I'm on work experience. Dad thinks I'll get more out of it if I use Mum's name.'

'I'm OK with that,' said Johnnie.

'Don't tell anybody, but can you keep an eye on her? Just you and Frank know.' Sam turned to Katie 'Did I see you at the Burke conference? To see your dad get a kicking.'

'That's not fair at all. I wanted to go. I went to find out what's going on, to see if I could help.'

'I'm sorry, that was out of order. Terry and I were talking about Chalky White.'

'The poor man's Ronnie Biggs,' said Johnnie.

Sam looked at his watch. He had a couple of hours before he met Justine, and he always loved listening to Terry talk about the old days. 'Off you go Obi Wan, no rush.'

'Yes and no, he was.' Sam started reading emails, half listening. 'The real issue was timing. Biggs was in '63. The right wing establishment were really struggling to come to terms with the new outlook, the Beatles, sexual freedom. Profumo was a disaster, and MacMillan and co. took a really hard line on law and order. John White, inevitably "Chalky", was the late eighties, Thatcher Government, liberal attitudes, much more enlightened.'

'Tell us about Biggs first, Katie will enjoy it.'

'Biggs was small time, hopeless. He got caught house-breaking because his tools were wrapped in his newspaper which had his address on the top. He'd gone straight, got married, and had the chance to buy his council house for £500 which he didn't have. Ironically he won that much on a double the day before the job but he was committed.'

'Why did they use him?' asked Katie.

'The train robbers? Wrong place, wrong time. He just knew Bruce Reynolds who put the job together.'

'But didn't he whack the guard or something?'

'I'm afraid we all know you shouldn't believe everything you read in the papers. Everyone thinks so, but there were no guns at

Cheddington. Biggs never even got out of the car. But he did get his share of the two and a half million.'

Sam took over. 'Then the central theme emerged. Is a sentence punishment, discouragement to others? The judge...'

'Judge Edmund. Hardliner,' said Terry.

'Said the famous bit about the game not being worth the candle.'

'The alluring candle.'

'What did that mean?' asked Katie.

'It meant you couldn't get five years, do three, and retire on the proceeds. Thirty years for unarmed robbery was way over the top. And no parole either. Where Biggs and White were similar is that they both really struggled to do time. Biggs just couldn't take it – young family and money on the outside, they said they could get him out, and in '64 he went up a rope ladder and over the wall with three others.'

'And went to Brazil,' said Johnnie.

'Well, no,' said Terry, who was now on a roll. 'Melbourne. He then went to Brazil. The rest we all know.'

'And White?'

Sam moved to sit next to Katie.

Terry said, 'Well, unlike Sam I never met him. Birmingham chap. He was known as a Peterman, a safe breaker, usually worked alone. Never armed, out of hours, you know, bookies, shops, factories. Always in trouble, did some short spells inside. But he got caught again, asked for dozens to be taken into consideration, got six years, did four, out in his late twenties. Couple of years later got caught doing a big country pile.'

'And escaped,' said Johnnie.

'In June '86 it says here,' said Katie, looking at her laptop.

Sam said, 'Well, he was sprung while he was being transferred. Overpowered the policeman driving, but no harm done. He was looking at ten years. Disappeared for a couple of months, then turned up in Spain. No wife or kids, no money stashed.'

Katie had some pictures up. 'Here you go.' Sam scrolled

through them, remembering the time fondly. The dodgy haircuts, everybody dressed like Crocket and Tubbs.

Katie said, 'Looks a bit of a playboy.'

'He was. Terry sent me down there. I was still quite junior. But at that time he wasn't a massive story. Boring crime, small time, no gang, no victims. I'd just started for you, and you said it was a good one to cut my teeth on. Just not sexy, was he?'

'Not to start with. No national outcry. There was always a suggestion that there was a technical problem with the evidence, that if they'd got him back it might not have stuck, so the government might have wasted brownie points with the Spanish. Sleeping dogs. Just another one having cocktails with Barbara Windsor.'

'It was about two years in, he'd gone completely native,' said Sam. 'Big party animal, gold chains, night clubs, suntanned girlfriends, B-list actresses, guys like Ronnie Knight. Knight was the main man, armed robber, and he really flaunted it and taunted the police. And everybody called White "El Blanco".'

Katie said, 'These photos are hysterical. He looks like Elvis in Vegas.'

'Not a very original name, I know. He played to it – white suits, white cars. Ronnie had a club called R Knights in Marbella and an Indian restaurant. Chalky had a night club with Ronnie in Puerto Banus called White Knights and a bar called Blanco's which redefined naff. White leather sofas, white everything, the bar was covered with whale foreskin. They said Barry White was coming to the opening party. Cilla Black came, I think.'

Sam knew this was all academic and a waste of time, but he was enjoying seeing Katie engaged, enjoying Terry talking.

'Did you actually meet him, Dad?' asked Katie.

'Oh yes, twice down there, and we spoke sometimes after that on the phone. Funnily enough I quite liked him. Yes, he was flash, but there was something about him, bit of a disconnect with his image. I met his Mum, too, back here. He was very easy to deal with, quick mind. It came out that he'd also done some big houses, and in one he'd stolen some jewellery. The press started comparing him to Raffles.'

'As in Sherlock Holmes?' asked Katie.

'Very good, but not quite,' said Terry. 'Raffles was created by Arthur Conan Doyle's brother-in-law. A deliberate inversion of Sherlock Holmes, a gentleman thief, if you like. Anyway, jewel thief is a better story than breaking into factories in Bromsgrove.'

'I always thought he was a contradiction,' said Sam. 'Everybody here bracketed him with the hardcore expat villains, but he never struck me as like them. I found out he did local charity work down there. He was very good-looking, charming. He created this image that didn't really reflect the crime. We lapped it up.'

'On the so-called Costa del Crime,' said Johnnie. 'We'd go down to try and nick them but it was so hard. The Spanish made it impossible, they were all in their pockets. We wanted Chalky back for the PR value but you just couldn't get near him.'

'Well, it was like that for years, but about five years ago they launched Operation Captura – the Serious Crime lot – offering anonymity for tip offs,' said Sam. 'They've got about forty so far. It's all easier with these European arrest warrants.'

'Why didn't the Spanish just extradite them?' asked Katie.

'Because of the ongoing spat about Gibraltar. Always made it tricky to get anything done diplomatically,' Terry explained. 'Some went to Mallorca, more to Cyprus, but that's not looking so clever now. The Spanish were mostly interested in the ones that carried on, human trafficking, prostitution rings, bringing in marijuana and cocaine from Morocco. The ones just spending money and playing golf were generally harmless.'

'But then there was the Bolwell incident,' said Terry.

'What was that?' asked Katie.

'Pete Bolwell, crime correspondent, legend. He was known as Bolly, as in Bollinger, always lived it large. He'd been all over the Chalky story for years, filed good stuff, rumours he was getting close to something big. You knew him Sam, didn't you?'

'I visited him in hospital. He was beaten really badly one night, outside Málaga. Ruptured his spleen, lost a lot of blood, left in a coma. He was in intensive care for about a month, then his paper paid for an air ambulance to fly him home.'

'A sign to warn people off?' asked Katie.

'I was shocked. I'd met Chalky just a few months before, he didn't strike me as that sort of guy.'

'They often don't,' added Terry.

'Paul told me he couldn't be absolutely certain, but there was nobody else it could be, it had to be Chalky's guys.'

Johnnie looked puzzled. 'I never heard about that.'

'We all knew, but he didn't want us to write it. His wife Emma is a real ball-breaker, she'd have grounded him. And he didn't want to spook his kids, so it was written up as a mugging. But we all knew. I think it's why he gave it up.'

'What does he do now?' asked Katie.

'He's P.J. Flint, the crime writer. Made a fortune.'

'Are you sure it's safe, Dad?'

'He'll be fine,' said Terry.

She wasn't convinced. 'You're not the one going.'

Terry wanted to move on. 'Anyway, the rumour is they might get Chalky back, last chance.'

Katie seemed energised. 'Really, shall I get the files out?'

'That would be great,' said Sam, realising it would be a good way to stay in touch with her.

Johnnie said, 'I'll show you later, but I need to get stuff done.'

Terry left, too, leaving him alone with Katie.

'It's really appalling how they're all treating you.'

'I just made a mistake, it'll blow over. If you want to leave I'll get in you in somewhere.'

'I'm staying. Can I work on Chalky White?'

He wanted to say there wouldn't be any work, but she looked enthused. 'Terry got you interested?'

'He's amazing, isn't he?'

'He certainly is.'

'In the pub last night somebody said you'll get a Shafta for this. What's that?'

Sam laughed, glad to get the chance to lighten the mood. 'Well, they don't exist anymore. Like our Baftas, it celebrated the best stories we all made up. A guy I worked with called Geoff Baker kicked it off in the eighties with PRINCESS MARGARET TO APPEAR IN CROSSROADS.'

'What's Crossroads?'

'Very early soap, set in a motel made of cardboard outside Birmingham.'

'Sounds rubbish.'

'It was. Since then there have been loads, like JACKO'S CHIMP TO TESTIFY. Frank got done for WEREWOLF SEIZED IN SOUTHEND. If it was still going I would have voted for ARGIES TRAIN KILLER SEAL TO EAT PRINCE HARRY.'

'That's just stupid.'

'I got the Michael Fish prediction award once for saying Bill Nighy was going to be the next Dr Who.'

'Stop it Dad, it's not funny.'

'Actually it was then, but I think that's why we stopped. It was basically publicising our cock-ups. You may have noticed we're trying to behave now.'

'Did you make this one up?'

'No, it looks like a simple cock-up. The Shafta motto was "It was true at the time". I thought it was.'

After she'd gone he worked his way through his emails and sorted his diary. He got Gary to come up.

'Can you take it all down? I don't want to be seen doing it.'

Gary made three trips, using the back stairs. At the door Sam looked back for a few seconds and wondered if he'd be back and who might next sit in his chair. He turned off the light, and walked away.

*

The Phene was a pub in Chelsea he hadn't been to for years, where George Best drank himself to death. Now it was all bleached pine and red leather. He quite liked it. Justine texted to say she was late, so he took a corner table and ordered a glass of Pinot Bianco, but not in a pint glass as George always did. He took the *Mail* out of his bag. There was an extended piece about him on page seven: PUBLIC ENEMY seemed a bit strong. He'd always got on fine with those guys. Maybe they'd decided Burke was now in for the long run so they'd back him. The sound was down on the wall-mounted TV but Sky News were showing the press conference, and then they cut up an old head shot of him. He looked round to see if anybody was looking at him.

He wondered if he was being followed now. Maybe one of the bar staff was a spotter for a paper, ringing somebody to get a photographer over. He went outside and checked. When he came back he moved to a quiet corner booth away from the line of sight of the bar's CCTV.

By the time Justine arrived he knew what he had to do.

She saw the *Mail*. 'Thanks for keeping me out of it.'

'No problem, not hard. Nobody knows about us.' He looked around and said, 'Look, I think this is going to get worse. You OK?'

'Bit stressed.'

'I'm going away.'

She looked genuinely disappointed. 'Where?'

'Spain.' He hadn't planned it but he said, 'Come with me.'

'I can't. My deal. I have to meet Donald on Thursday, when he's back.'

'So what are your plans until then?'

'I'm off this, they're not giving me anything else, so not much point going in until I see Donald. I can wait but I don't want being fired on my CV, probably better to go quietly.'

'You'll be fine.'

'Easy for you to say.'

'You will, girl of your talents.'

She stiffened. 'Meaning what, exactly?'

'You're qualified, attractive. Girls like you are always OK.' That didn't come out as he planned.

'So that's it, is it? I'm twenty-six and at the start of my career, so not as much at stake with you fifty-seven and at the end of yours. Girls like me?'

'I didn't...'

'So I just turn up in a short skirt and stick my tits out and I'll be fine?'

And she was gone, in tears.

He followed her into the street and grabbed her arm, then let go, realising the shot would be just what they wanted.

'I'm sorry, that was all wrong. And for God's sake, don't start crying.'

'Let go of me.'

'And I'm fifty-four anyway.'

She laughed and wiped the back of her hand across her cheek.

He looked round. 'I don't want to sound paranoid but we shouldn't be seen together in public.'

She looked at him, thinking, then said, 'My place is close.'

*

She gave him the address and he sent her on ahead. He waited ten minutes then walked there. He hadn't forgotten how it worked. As he walked down the street he checked the cars, walked a hundred yards past her front door, then looped back.

She buzzed him up. When he got there the door was on the latch. He shut the door behind him and turned round. 'Jesus.'

'What do you think?'

She was in what he guessed was the bedroom doorway. He wasn't sure he'd seen anything like it. Well, not since the Max Mosley story.

'Does it come with a whip?'

She laughed and did a twirl. He couldn't figure out what

actually held it together, and marvelled how every main area of interest was exposed and framed.

'If they remake *Catwoman* as a porn movie, that's the outfit.'

'Now now, no pussy jokes.'

*

Propped against the pillows he looked at her, sitting at the end of the bed, naked, the bizarre outfit back in the tack room, he guessed. She was reading his employment contract. They'd just picked up where they left off last time, but going to the next level, moving round the flat, having fun. It made him feel good, but where could it go? He was getting on a plane.

'I have to advise you, Mr Plummer, that I am still technically an employee of Canadian Media Holdings Inc, and I am not allowed to act for you, under Law Society rules. I could be disbarred.'

'I do love it when you talk dirty. So, could they fire me?'

'Well, pretty standard, they could make you redundant, give you twelve months' notice, but you've got one of those amazing pensions which nobody does any more. You get two thirds of your exit salary, index linked, in perpetuity.'

'So that's secure?'

'Well, I need to read the whole thing but unless you did something very naughty I would think so. Let's find termination.'

He looked at her, transfixed.

'Right. Here we go. Well, you obviously work exclusively for the paper.'

'Well, I do some moonlighting, the odd film review, done some stuff for *Private Eye*.'

'OK, I wouldn't bother about that. They can terminate you immediately for, one, bankruptcy.'

'No.'

'Becoming a patient as defined by the Mental Health Act 1983.'

'No.'

'Convicted, criminal offence?'

'No, not yet. You are 18, aren't you?'

'Very funny. Found guilty of any dishonesty relating to the company?'

'Pass.'

She looked at him over the top of her glasses. 'Next, we'll come back to that. Serious or gross misconduct. Can include harassment or discrimination, blah blah blah. Yes, no??'

'Pass.'

'Properly carry out duties, and then a general one all about insider dealing, confidentiality, duty of care.'

She put down the contract and crawled up the bed towards him, pulling the sheet down towards her. 'Mr Plummer, you had two passes.' She sat astride him, looking down. 'Dishonesty?'

'Look, I've been there thirty odd years, but I stuck to my rules. Most of what we do involves subterfuge, cash, informants, policemen, stings. It's all grey, it's not dodgy.'

'They could never prove that, it would need to be something properly dishonest. How bad have you been?' She reached behind her and squeezed his balls. 'Can I remind you, Mr Plummer, you are under oath.'

'Ow. OK. Well, I did once rent a villa on Mustique for a stake out. Put this Dutch journalist in there. She had to try and get close to Mick Jagger. Amazing place, took it for a month. But a mate of his turned up with a yacht and they buggered off to watch the cricket. Then I sort of got involved with the girl and I needed a break, so we just had a holiday. Big parties, boats, charged the lot. Even the dope.'

She slid back down the bed. 'But Mr Plummer, I put it to you that that's not really very naughty.'

'Objection, your honour. Counsel has my dick in her mouth.'

She paused and looked up. 'Overruled.'

He had no idea where he was finding the energy. She was back lying face down at the end of the bed.

'I still haven't heard your famous golden rules.'

'There's three. Don't break the law you know.'

'Seems marginal.'

'This is not law-breaking, it's just what happens, creative accounting. Two, don't confuse fact with opinion.'

'Get that.'

'And remember who you write for and work for.'

'That's four. And apart from that, anything goes?'

'No, I have other ones. If ever I write a book, I'll expand it to the Ten Commandments.'

'Like?'

'Play the ball, not the man.'

'So Moses, what does that mean?'

'Like now with me, or Michael Gove with education, it's much easier to target the man than the issue. It's not actually about me, it's about the way the press behave. Same with Coulson.'

She went to the kitchen and came back with some cranberry juice. He felt guilty for so wanting to take a photo. Just for the record. He'd really have liked one of her in the bondage outfit.

'This is a cool place, is this the top floor?'

'Yep. Friend of mine bought it, but she's with a law firm in Hong Kong for two years, she's never lived here.'

'Very minimalist.'

'Architect owned it. Everything works but it's not very homely.'

She picked up the contract. 'Leaving aside your rules, if they did start digging, what would be the worst?'

He looked at her and thought she could ask him to jump out the window and he probably would.

'OK, I'll tell you my favourite. Ten years ago, we did a sting on a racehorse trainer, Jasper Slipper. Basically he, a vet and a bloodstock agent, were scamming owners, buying duff horses. I posed as an owner called Harry Zain, set up a bank account, and bought two horses, Bouncing Ed and a donkey called Booboo Bob, a three-year-old. Great bloodline, he was by Galileo, but Bob wasn't sound – one race at Newbury, broke down. I'd gone a bit soft on Bob so rather than turn him into burgers for Tesco, Frank and I said we'd pay his fees until they sold him. We got all three of them, Slipper went down. Anyway, a year or so later, out of the blue, I got a cheque, maybe £500, for stud fees. He'd been put out, and I'd forgotten we'd bought him. So I banked it – Terry, Frank and I had a big lunch and laughed about it. Next thing, one of his offspring finished second in the 1,000 Guineas, and the cheques got bigger and more frequent. We stuck them in the offshore account. Then the bloodline went ballistic, we won two Group Ones with Bonzo Dog, and the cheques just got bigger. We still own one leg of the Bonz, he's at stud now.'

'And has Bonzo followed in Bob's footsteps?'

'Not exactly. I spoke to them last week; they said he is without doubt the most enthusiastic one there, but he just keeps firing blanks. He's so good natured I think we'll stable him at home. Clare can ride him.'

'Sounds alright.'

'Bob was the star. Died last year, seventy in man years, going right to the end. My inspiration, really. Still the only horse to have put seven kids through private school. Mine and Frank's.'

'Nobody got hurt. You provided for your family, that's not a bad choice. You said yourself this is a cut-throat business.'

She tossed the contract on the floor and moved back next to him, her hand sliding down his stomach. The doorbell rang.

Her hand kept going. 'Who is that?'

'Shit, it's the taxi. I have to go.'

'Today? Ignore it.'

'You're not making this easy.'

She threw back the sheet and looked down. 'Hello vicar. Right, off you go. But it's official, you're not a journalist, you're a very naughty boy.'

Sadly he knew the first bit was definitely true.

# CHAPTER 10

## WEDNESDAY 2nd July – DAY 5

***Daily Telegraph*: NEW LAW TO TACKLE REVENGE PORN**

***Evening Standard*: MAN DIES IN PUNCH 4 PUNCH INTERNET CRAZE**

Marbella was bad enough even without school holidays, and rather than advertise his trip he'd booked the first flight to Seville, preferring three hours on the open road to the delights of the traffic system and Málaga airport, which was always patrolled by low-life stringers waiting for footballers and soap stars.

This way he could arrive at Frank's place in the hills above El Madroñal without going near the coast roads.

But his Iberia flight had been delayed. He could have finished what Justine had started. He'd had a few drinks to pass the time and some more on the flight, so he checked into the airport Radisson. There was no rush now.

It might have been hot in London, but this was something else. The air conditioning in the Hertz rental couldn't keep up, so he just opened all the windows and thought about the swim and cold beer he'd have when he got there.

He couldn't stop thinking about what had happened. It was

odd in the modern digital age that he had not one picture of her on his phone. He'd been with her twice and they'd had sex six times. Great sex. After the first mind-bogglingly quick quickie, each time had been longer and more intense. He felt like he had jump-leads attached to his 23-year-old self.

His mobile rang. The caller ID said Stefano. He ignored it. He didn't want to talk to any journalists, even mates. Within five minutes curiosity got the better of him – Stefano was one of the good guys. Living in Rome, half English, working in a restaurant, he got close to Gazza in the mid-nineties when he played for Lazio. Frank paid him for stories, and when Gazza went to Glasgow, Stef followed. In the end he actually turned out to be a good writer, writing as Steve Angel.

He pulled over. 'Hi Stefano, what's happening at the *Mirror* then?'

'Good, Sam. You sound like you're abroad.'

Sam laughed. 'Nice try, Stef.'

'Sorry. Really quiet week I'm afraid, so we've got a lot to fill, and it's a great story. I'm afraid they think I'm best qualified to do you.'

'Well you are, I taught you everything you know. Go on then.'

'Since you're still married, we're doing the women. The headline's PLUMMER'S MATES.'

'Original. OK. Off you go.'

'Sharon Stone.'

'No. Stood next to her once, at some party.'

'But it was a great story. Liz Hurley?'

'Don't be daft.' None of these had ever been written about, they were just urban myths – the odd one true – that helped establish his reputation.

'Look, I don't mind if you write it, it's just if the women do – to make it simple, why don't I just give you some?' So he gave Stefano the names of a couple who he knew wouldn't mind, and would be glad of the publicity. One was an ex-model who'd been on TV in the jungle, the other was an actress who was lucky now to get panto. 'Just call them and check, will you?'

'OK. Not mentioning Caroline.'

'That would be unwise. How's the family?'

'Good. That French actress, Isabelle somebody?'

Sam laughed. 'Stef, it was you started that one, you idiot. No.'

*

The housekeeper couldn't meet him until later so he drove across country. About halfway he stopped in a small town called Montellano and found a cafe with Wi-Fi.

On BBC iPlayer some lawyer gave a pretty good analysis of where they stood legally. Sam spent his life walking the fine Human Rights line between invasion of privacy and public interest. She then explained what had happened with Max Mosley, the Princes – and of course, Kate sunbathing topless, which had changed the entire media landscape.

So many texts and emails poured in it was getting ridiculous, but one caught his eye – to call George Hodgson. That was odd. He was old school, one of Terry's generation.

'Hey Hodgy, how is sunny Nottingham?'

'Hi Sam, quiet, but as you know that's why I left.'

'Heart OK now?'

'Yes, little battery keeps me ticking over.'

'Still retired, I hope.'

'Basically. Look, it's probably nothing, but I was having dinner in Sat Bains last night.'

'Sounds glamorous.'

'Actually it's got a Michelin star. Julian was in there.'

'Really. Where is it?'

'Near here. Just thought it strange, with all that's going on.'

'You're not kidding. Who was he with?'

'Well that's the thing. A woman. As I walked past I said hello, and you know what Julian's like on manners, but he didn't introduce me and even more weird was that she tried to hide her face.'

'Some married woman he's shagging?'

'Oh no, I've seen Julian's birds; she was older, not like his mother, but maybe fifty, well dressed.'

'Find out who she was?'

'No. I saw him ask for the bill, so I got my daughter to go to the loo, and she got a shot on her phone. I'll email it to you.'

'What do you think?'

'Nobody here knows her, restaurant guys didn't either. I'd say odds are she's somebody's mistress, or her husband's playing away.'

'Agree. Look, thanks, stay in touch.'

Sam loved it on so many levels. His mates were standing by him, and there was Hodgy, who should have his feet up, but the merest sniff of a story and he just slotted back into the old ways. The photo came through from Hodgy. He didn't recognise her, but it was a poor shot, out of focus, her profile partly obscured.

*

The housekeeper let him in, then set off back down the hill on her moped, trailing smoke. The villa wasn't the conventional white box. Frank's wife Louise was the one with taste. It was almost bohemian, set in a huge olive grove, the walls a burnt orange so it looked more Mexican or Moroccan. Frank had bought the adjacent plots with his neighbours so nobody could build and spoil the view of the sea, maybe a thousand feet below and ten miles away. Sam tossed the keys on the hall table and fetched his luggage from the car.

His clothes were damp, and he threw them in the laundry basket. He swam and washed his hair under the outdoor shower. He fetched a cold Estrella and tried to log on but he realised he didn't know the Wi-Fi code. He went inside and put his iPhone on charge, then tried and failed to get the TV working.

He was just wondering when he should ring Justine when she called. He was glad to hear from her. 'What's happening?'

'Donald's too busy to meet, I got an email.'

'Good deal?'

'It's fair.'

'Well, I'm not going to say you'll be fine. I'm really sorry. When?'

'Three months' money, go now, full confidentiality provisions. They'll give me a reference. Could be worse.'

'You sound OK.'

'Well, I'm not really. I've let a lot of people down.'

'Well, my offer stands.'

'To come down?'

'Yes.' He so wanted her to say yes. 'It's lovely here.'

'Really?'

'Sure, I've got so much credit at my travel agent from unused business tickets over the years, and a zillion air miles.'

She didn't answer. He filled the silence, realising he was pressing. Was he already really wishfully thinking he and Justine were a couple? 'But don't if you don't want to, up to you.'

There was a pause. She said, 'Look, let me get my deal signed, should be tomorrow. Can you email me the travel agent details? I need to sort some stuff, but I'd like to come. Hold on.'

He waited for a few moments.

She came back and said, 'I have to go. Call you later.'

*

Back outside by the pool he realised just how quiet it was. After two more beers he felt quite mellow. All he could hear were the cicadas buzzing.

Then he checked his missed calls and added them to his list. Top was Caroline.

'I'm in Spain.'

'I know, Frank told me everything.'

'Where are you?'

'I'm in London, Carson's travelling. I'm working on the fashion show, enjoying it.'

'What's up?'

'Decision time.'

'You should take the deal. Swallow your pride.'

'It's not just the deal.'

'God, I can read you like a book. You're sleeping with that Justine and she's fried your brain.'

'I don't want to talk about my love life.'

She laughed. 'Christ, you're the one who always says you only have a sex life.'

God, she was right. 'You know what's really scary?'

'Tell me.'

'She reminds me of you.'

'Not sure how I feel about that. So you going to fuck up again?'

'Caroline, she's 26 years old. Do I need that?'

'Sounds like you do.'

'I made the mistake with you because I was too young, now I'm going to make it because I'm too old.'

'Sam, we both made the mistake, not you. I let you go, too.'

*He went back to the Crazy Horse that night. With her short, dark hair tucked under the platinum, fringed wig she looked just like all the others and he couldn't pick her out. He badly wanted to put a body to the face. While the magician was on, a Mountie found him at the bar and asked him to follow him. They went down and out through the basement kitchen into an alleyway. Two security guys stood there, and a row of maybe ten black Renaults. She was leaning against the first one, chatting to the driver.*

*'Doing anything?'*

*'How come you've finished?'*

*'That's your second question. I hope the last one's good, rubbish so far. This is Jérôme.'*

*'Hi Jérôme.'*

*He opened the door and they got into the back. Her hair was wet. She was wearing a short, very short, black leather skirt. More like a wide belt. Her legs were so long she had to sit sideways behind Jérôme, facing him. 'I'm not in the finale. You only need eight for it, and there's eleven of us each night. Did you see me?'*

*'Polly Underground?'*

*'No, that's Helga. I was one of the leopards, in the cage.'*

*'Ah, "spot me", that was the clue.'*

*'Shit, you do listen. Girls like that.' She put her hand in his lap and kissed him on the mouth. 'That's very flattering.'*

*'Been like it since eleven this morning.'*

*She laughed. 'My stage name is "Nooka Karamel". They offered me that or "Zula Zazou". Couldn't really be up there as Caroline Logan, could I?'*

*At her place they got into the lift, and they kissed all the way up to the top floor. There was no one home and they did it on the hall floor. Her skirt hiked up round her waist, his trousers round his ankles. It was over in seconds.*

*'Blimey, you're keen,' she said, laughing.*

*'In truth,' he said, propped on his elbows, 'I nearly came in the lift.'*

*He pushed himself up. He said, 'I have to say, the Saloon's new media relations policy is a real improvement,' when all he really wanted to say was sorry or thank you. She stretched out a leg and kicked the door shut.*

*

Katie was working late in the office. She wasn't sure why but she was drawn to researching Chalky White. She refused to believe it was journalistic instinct, more that it was wanting to help and motivate Sam, worried that he was about to throw in the towel. She was starting to appreciate that his reputation was worth protecting, whatever she thought about the profession. Her phone rang.

'Is that Kate Plummer?'

'Katie. Who's this?'

'It's Harry Thompson, from Heathrow. I'm trying to reach your father. I've just got some information for him.'

She was already developing a cynical default setting.

'Oh. Look, I'm really sorry, you'll appreciate I'm very wary about talking to strangers.'

Harry laughed. 'You are a chip off the old block. Hold on.'

She heard him tapping away.

'Christmas before last, he took you and Felix to Cape Town, you got upgraded to business, coming back to First. Put you in 1A.'

'Ah, you're that Harry. Thank you, by the way.'

'Pleasure. Look, I keep an eye out here for him. Given what's going on I don't want to call anybody else.'

'How did you get my number?'

'You and Felix are in the BA database. You've got silver cards.'

'So what's the story?'

'I tip him off if any of the main guys go anywhere. I'm sorry I've only just come back on, but there's a guy called Matt Cooney, he flew to Sao Paulo yesterday on TAM, would have got there at five this morning.'

'Maybe he's working on the World Cup?'

'Trust me, he won't be.'

'Harry, can I ask you, do you ever think about the ethics of this?'

'What?'

'Ringing my dad, or anybody else, with this information?'

'I'm protecting your kid brother here.'

'I know, thanks.'

He sounded confused. 'Are you saying you don't want me to call you again?'

The more she got sucked into this world, the more she realised it was more about guidelines than rules, that maybe sometimes the end did justify the means. Anyway, this was family. 'No Harry, sorry. Please do call me.'

She tried to ring Sam but his phone seemed to be dead. She Googled Matt Cooney who looked pretty young and clearly didn't work on sport. She tried and failed to call Felix, so warned him by text, Whatsapp and email, with links to photos, and gave him all the instructions she could think of, signing off with 'FFS avoid COONEY at all costs.'

She went on his Facebook, wondering if Felix had stuck with Lampard8 as his password, given even she knew he was leaving Chelsea. She could see that they'd watched Argentina beat Switzerland the day before, and at the weekend they were heading up the Brazil coast via the islands off Angra dos Reis. But it was too late. There was a clear trail that showed where they'd all been and where they were going. It looked like TripAdvisor. It was all harmless stuff – bare bottoms on the Bolivian salt flats.

Johnnie Brydon came past. 'What are you still doing here?'

'I'm researching that Chalky White.'

'What do you think?'

'Great story. But I'm puzzled.'

'About what?' He perched on the edge of the desk.

She wasn't sure how to articulate it. 'He was part of all these really nasty villains, yet he doesn't quite fit the mould, does he?'

'A contradiction?'

'Maybe. Do you know a journalist called Matt Cooney?'

'Yes, why?'

'He seems to be taking an interest in our family.'

'Well, be careful, he's the new kid on the block. Works for Roly Relton mostly. Nasty piece of work.'

# CHAPTER 11

**THURSDAY 3rd July – DAY 6**

***The Sun*: RAPE SUSPECT PASSES X-FACTOR AUDITION**

***The Scotsman*: MURRAY OUT OF WIMBLEDON**

***Daily Mirror*: JIHADIST THREAT TO UK: BE AFRAID**

He'd slept in the guest room, with the double doors that led out on to the balcony above the pool open. Overnight his phone seemed to have died. It was charged but he had no signal or messages. He went to the house phone and saw it had a sticker saying 'No outgoing calls' in English and Spanish.

He rebooted his phone, took it on his run, but nothing. He came back and swam. It was odd having nothing to read, watch or check. He went out to the road to see if anybody was watching the house, then found Frank's binoculars and scanned the hillside. He didn't feel paranoid, he just thought he should.

He was getting used to the quiet life when the house phone rang. He thought about ignoring it but knew who it would be.

'Hi, Frank.'

'Hi, Dad, it's me.'

He realised he wanted to hear her voice more than anybody's.

'Hey baby. How did you get this number?'

'Your mobile seems out of service, and your email has an out of office message, but I've only just been able to get hold of Frank.'

'I think they've barred it, nice eh? In case we get cut off, can you ask him what the Wi-Fi code is and whether I can unblock this phone? He must do it to stop the staff ringing their relatives.'

'Sure.'

'And tell Gary about my phone, maybe he can check. And ask Frank where the TV instructions are, I can't get Sky to work – I'm feeling sort of cut off from the outside world.'

'That must be awful.'

'Actually it's OK. Use my Gmail account.'

'Have you seen the *Mirror*?'

'No, but it'll be Steve Angel's PLUMMER'S MATES piece. He called me – ex-girlfriends.'

'You knew?'

'Sure, he's a friend. It's what I would do, portray me as a family man cheating on his wife.'

'I don't mind about you, but it demeans the women.'

'You're not reading it properly. It doesn't. Virtually all of them at the time, or now, wanted the publicity. I never wanted it. I kept that stuff out of the papers. You at work already?'

'Of course. I'm reading up about the Costa del Crime.'

She sounded genuinely engaged and he didn't want to dampen her enthusiasm. 'The bottom line is I'll have to do the deal. I won't be able to pursue it. And it is an old story.'

'That's not what Terry says. He's been helping me. Maybe he knows more than you.'

Sam laughed. 'I'm not taking on you and Terry. And he does.'

'Anyway, that's not why I called you.' She told him about the call from Harry and Matt Cooney going to São Paulo.

'Shit. God, I hate that Roland Relton. Cooney's his new protégé.'

She explained how she'd cleaned up all Felix's social media and all the instructions she'd sent him. 'Did I do the right thing?'

'You did. Does your mother know?'

'God no.'

'Well, don't tell her.'

'Dad, can I ask you a question? Isn't Harry at Heathrow giving you flight information illegal?'

He suddenly felt defensive. 'What's your point?'

'You always say your first golden rule is you don't break the law. I'm not making a point, I'm just asking a question.'

'OK, well, let me ask you, did you act on it?'

'Yes. But two wrongs don't make a right.'

'It's what I call a grey area. Matt Cooney's bad news. Just try and reach Felix.'

'Of course I will.'

'You know there's only one problem with your plan.'

'Which is?'

'When did your little brother ever do what you told him?'

*

Six thousand miles away it was 3am in São Paulo. The boys had a great table in Bagatelle, which seemed to be the hottest place in town. And maybe the most expensive, which in São Paulo was saying something. On the table was a magnum of Grey Goose vodka in an ice bucket. After midnight it morphed seamlessly from a restaurant into a night club. The lights went down, the DJ wound it up, girls danced on the tables. The place was jumping, rammed with uber cool young Paulistanos.

Felix and Oliver were wedged between two hookers, both in impossibly tight, short dresses. Simon was well gone, and Matt Cooney was now Aidan Rogers, an expat luxury watch dealer from Miami, there as a guest of Hublot for the World Cup, on expenses. Oliver leaned in to one of the girls, speaking Portuguese. Whatever he said, she laughed.

*

Around 8.30am Sam drove down to Benahavis to do a food shop and buy the English papers they printed locally – *Telegraph, Mail, Times* – and he sat outside a cafe in the square sipping a cortado and skimming them. It was developing as he knew it would. Burke the hero and victim, SAINT NIGEL. Sam the villain, THE FAKE SNAKE. Every media outlet wanted to get rid of Burke, but they had to run with it.

He logged on to the Wi-Fi and Googled himself. A bunch of stories came up. *The Mirror* piece was OK – they'd been kind to Clare but still managed to work some good names in there; they'd even managed to find the one picture of him with Naomi Campbell, chatting at some awards dinner. He couldn't believe they'd used PLUMMING NEW DEPTHS. No real harm was done, but while that was tittle-tattle, the broadsheets were savaging him and Frank.

Katie had emailed him the villa's Wi-Fi code and said Frank's property manager had sorted the phone and that Felix would call him.

He Skyped Clare.

'Why are you Skyping me? You know what I look like.'

He did, and he wondered why she had so much make-up on and her hair done. Did she want to be papped? Was she going to use the BMW and drive round with the roof down?

'My phone's died. Have you seen the *Mirror*?'

'Of course I have, my mother rang me. She's mortified.'

From her tone he realised it wasn't make-up. It was war paint. And she was on the warpath.

'Any paps following you?'

'No, of course not. Is there anybody you haven't screwed?'

'Look, they want to get me, it's open season, all I want to do is keep you lot out of it.'

'I think Katie should leave the paper.'

'Well, you tell her. They won't find out, she's not using my name.'

'What about Felix?'

'He's in Brazil, they won't go after him.'

Over the years he'd found lying to her very easy. Mostly because it made life easier. She didn't need to know Felix was possibly in trouble.

'It doesn't change the fact that all the tabloids are telling the world that you're a serial shagger and a hypocrite.'

'Hypocrite's a bit harsh.'

'This is no laughing matter.'

'I'm sorry.'

'And I've had Louise on, she's told me about the deal you and Frank have been offered. I assume you're going to take it, too?'

'I'm deliberating, but Frank should.'

'Well, stop. You've got a son and daughter to support. You've got security, you can't just throw it away because you made one mistake.'

Sam knew that getting her to support him on a matter of principle had no chance, so he lied. 'It's the kid, Jay Lomax, he's overreacting. It'll all blow over.'

'Bollocks.' Now she was angry. 'Please don't use the family as some poker chip. Don't screw up now. Take the deal.'

'Don't worry. Maybe you should go away for a few days.'

'I can look after myself, Sam.'

He thought that was a bit rich but let it go.

*

After lunch Sam went upstairs and showered and then went out to the balcony. Standing there he could look south, along the coast a few miles down below him towards Gibraltar, and then on to the horizon and what he assumed was the hazy outline of Morocco.

Then he looked around again. This time not to see what he could see, but to see who could see him, from where. His eyes scanned the trees, then he looked up. He wondered if they had drones, then if that was the most paranoid, if not stupid, thought he'd ever had. And who was 'they' anyway?

The phone rang in the bedroom and he went back in.

'Hi Dad.'

'Felix, thank God, how are you?'

'I'm great. Katie told me everything. Bastards.'

'So did you get all the messages, avoid that Cooney?'

'Yes and no.'

Sam could tell from his voice something had happened. He took the cordless out on to the balcony.

'He found us.'

'Of course he did, that's what we do.'

'We went with it.'

Sam sensed this could be the last thing he needed.

'You do know Oli's Mum is Brazilian, don't you?'

'I didn't.'

'He grew up in São Paulo. His elder brother sorted two girls to come with us, we went to this amazing place. Cooney said he was a watch dealer. Oli and I didn't really drink, just pretended to. We got Simon to go toe-to-toe with him, because he does tend to go OTT, but he can handle it. We kept topping up Cooney who got smashed. He doesn't know it but he picked up the tab for about three tables, and I clocked his pin. We put a sleeping pill in his last drink.'

'Jesus, Felix.'

'Back at the Sheraton, Oli bunged the concierge and told him it was Cooney's stag weekend. So we cleaned out his room. He'd used the same pin for the hotel safe.'

'Everybody does.'

'You told me that one.'

Sam was feeling nervous about this. 'Did I?'

'I mean everything. Clothes, computer, phone, passport, the lot. We drained his credit cards at the hotel ATM. When they maxed out, we put in the wrong pin until the machine ate them. Afterwards we gave all his stuff to the concierge and told him to blank him for 24 hours.'

As they talked, Sam watched a car winding up from the coast, the late afternoon sun catching it in the hairpin bends.

'I've got a terrible feeling I know where this is going.'

'I don't think so, Dad.'

The car emerged on the long drive that twisted up through the olive trees, trailing a dust cloud.

'Shit. Somebody's coming, look, I need to know everything.'

'I'm sorry if I did the wrong thing.'

'Felix, if your mother ever finds out, the official line is I'm furious. Let's see how it plays out. Just whatever you do, keep your phone on. I'll pay. I need to know the rest. Get Katie to call me on the house phone now. Got to go.'

He got down as the silver Mercedes S600 crunched across the gravel and pulled up. The windows were blacked out and he wondered who knew he was here. For one second he thought which direction he would run if he had to.

A man got out of the back. Sam relaxed. They all joked in the office that Donald Whelan had no heart. He certainly had no sense of humour. Sam knew him no better than all those years ago, but they had kept each other out of trouble. It was a relationship based on respect, not friendship.

Sam said, 'Hey Donald, this is a pleasant surprise,' as they shook hands. 'You haven't made a house call in twenty years. Come and have a cold beer, you look like you need one.'

'Just a quick one, can't stay long. I've only made this trip because I want you to hear this from me face-to-face. I owe you that.' As they walked he gave Sam the day's papers and a brown A4 envelope. 'You always tell us in the office that the first rule of holes is if you're in one, stop digging.'

'So how deep is this hole?'

'This would be a sinkhole. You know, where the earth opens up and you just keep going.'

'I know. And this?' said Sam holding up the envelope.

'Your lifeline. Go now, quietly, keep all your rights. Full benefits. One year's money and gardening leave.'

'So one story goes tits up, and five days on all this happens?'

'Who gives a toss about the story, any story?'

'Me?'

'I know you do, Sam, but you know it's more than that. That's a get out of jail free card. Frankly it's more generous than they need to be. As the Group's senior lawyer, I advise you to get your own to look at it. And as your friend my advice is just sign it. I'll email a copy.'

'I'm guessing there'll be a deadline.'

'True. The offer stands until close of play Monday, it's all in there. Don't talk to anyone at the paper, all through me.'

'And if I don't?'

'I hate to say this, but the Milky Bar Kid will fire you for all that other crap, which I know you know they know. In this deal, that's all history, no comebacks. If some of that stuff comes out it'll look really bad. You'll get nothing, and you'll be unemployable.'

'They've blocked my phone.'

'Sorry, that's HR being overenthusiastic. I'll sort that.'

Donald was starting to sweat. Sam wondered how he thought a pinstripe suit could possibly be a sensible choice. 'Sorry. Where's that beer? Lovely place, can we sit outside?'

'Sure, I'll meet you on the terrace.'

While he was in the kitchen, Katie called on the house phone. 'Listen, I have to be quick. Felix went off-piste. Drop everything. I need you to get him on a conference call with you, Gary and Terry, not on an office phone, and not with Frank. Just go through the whole thing. Whatever Terry says, both of you do it.' He hung up and went out with an ice bucket and four Estrellas.

They sat in the shade of the fig tree. Donald had loosened his tie. 'I've called about your phone, they said ten minutes. The deal's good. Trust me, just take it.'

Sam opened two beers.

'And what about my reputation?'

Donald mopped his face with his handkerchief. 'Grow up. You're not Woodward or Bernstein.'

*

He'd found a spot with good cover on high ground about a half a mile to the west so the sun would be behind him as the day unfolded. It gave him a good view of the pool, and if the curtains stayed open, the master bedroom. The irony of the view didn't escape him, with Sam and Donald sharing beers by the pool.

Through the telescopic lens he had the driver in the crosshairs, leaning against the car. He recognised the guy but couldn't place him. He watched him grind out his cigarette underfoot, then go to the boot and take out a small rucksack. He looked round and then went into the villa through the front door.

He put the scope down, rested the Canon EOS with its 70/200 telephoto lens on his jacket, and rolled up on a rock to get a stable platform. He got glimpses of the driver moving through the villa, on both floors, and took some shots, switching to video when he was in the master bedroom. The guy knew what he was doing, in and out in maybe fifteen minutes.

High above he saw a Bonelli's Eagle, its distinctive white underside rising and circling in a thermal, and took some shots of it.

*

Sam said, 'By any standards it was a proper exposé. It ticked just about every box – sex, politics, intrigue. Best photos in years.'

'You've got to have some perspective. They weren't aerial photographs of nuclear installations, they were girls with their tits out. Please.'

'So for the first time ever we're not going to try and defend our actions at all?'

'We screwed up, for God's sake.'

He could see Donald running out of patience.

'Still a good story.'

'If you like historical fiction. It's my problem now, not yours. The only thing that matters is how much I get us out for.'

Donald was right. Each year they agreed their 'legal' budget, which was their combined reasonable projection of what it would cost to fight and settle libel and damages after they made mistakes. Now he was the mistake, and the price attached to it was in the envelope.

'So, come on Don, conspiracy or cock-up?'

'Cock-up. Yours, ours. The boot's on the other foot, and you can't take it, because that boot is up your arse. You're confused; you keep telling people it's a cock-up to see how it sounds.'

Sam knew he was right.

'A conspiracy is a massively complex, planned piece of misdirection. Like the theory that the Chinese murdered Kennedy and tried to frame the KGB for it so America would declare war on Russia.'

Sam hated arguing with Donald.

'This was opportunism, pure and simple. He did it for two things. Money and ego. We all hate him, we're all after him. He's the untouchable now.'

Donald stood up. 'Anyway, I need to go, we have to fly back through Nice and collect Carson. They lent me the jet.'

'Of course they did.'

He walked Donald back to the car. 'Call me if you want any advice. There's nothing tricky in there.'

'I'm sure.'

'Thanks for the beers.' The driver shut the door, and as he walked round Donald lowered his window and said, 'Sam, this is a no-brainer: Don't. Fuck. It. Up.'

*

He sat by the pool and read the letter. It did look fair, generous even. It made sense but he needed a lawyer to look at it.

About an hour later he heard his phone inside come to life,

filling up with emails and texts. Then it rang, showing a Spanish number.

Gary said, 'Go outside now.'

He stepped out on to the terrace. 'I am.'

'Don't use the house phone or talk in the house. No email.'

'Bit James Bond isn't it? How long for?'

Gary was already gone but Sam knew by his tone he meant it.

*

Back in London, Terry and Katie walked across Lower Thames Street, into the office, and up to the reception desk.

'Katie Plummer to see Roland Relton.'

'Do you have an appointment?'

'Just tell him I'm here.'

In the lift up Terry said, 'Are you alright?'

'Not sure, aren't we rushing into this?'

'No time like the present, we have the advantage. Don't want them forewarned. It'll be fine – trust me. He'll just assume we're here to trade and protect Felix.'

'Well, I'm a twenty-year-old intern. I'm only here to put Britain's most notorious editor in his place, get the paper off our backs, protect my brother's reputation, and maybe save my Dad's job. So no pressure.'

Terry laughed. 'That's my girl. You'll be fine.'

The newsroom was buzzing; maybe a daily just felt different. It looked exciting and intimidating. A PA showed them in. Relton was in his office with about ten people at his long polished meeting table. He remained sitting there with his feet up and said, 'Well, look what the cat's brought in.'

Katie and Terry sat down at the empty end of the conference table.

'Fire away Tel, we need a laugh. We've been looking for you, Miss Plummer.'

'And my little brother.'

'Well, we've found him. We've got a great spread on their South American naughties. Bit of Argie bargie.'

The table all laughed. Katie said 'That's very funny, Mr Relton.'

She wanted to reach for a glass of water but her hands were shaking. Terry poured her one, his hand rock steady.

'Team, this is Terry Thomas, likes to think of himself as a Fleet Street legend. Couldn't cut it, gave up. Bit of a clown.'

'If you say so, old boy. Not so keen on the old H2O. Any chance of a cup of tea?'

Relton turned serious and put his feet down. 'Fuck off, Terry. Get on with it. We love a grovel. You've got two minutes.'

She found Relton very intimidating, but felt safe with Terry there. She said to the guy on a laptop, 'Is that the one connected to the big screen?'

'Yes, sweetheart, it is.'

She went and sat next to him and gave him a memory stick.

Terry said, 'We'll talk you through it, just a few shots.'

Relton said, 'Shall we close the curtains?' The table laughed again.

She said, 'Do you mind if I drive?'

Terry was impressed; she was milking it. The first couple of shots were from the restaurant. Just a fun boys' night out.

'Right, this is the guys, you all know them, in Bagatelle last night, and there's your man.'

The shot showed Matt Cooney with them, aka Aidan Rogers.

Relton acted innocent. 'Who's he?'

She kept it going. 'Aidan Rogers, a watch dealer.'

She put up the next three shots. Cooney's passport, business cards and office security pass.

Relton said nothing, sitting back.

'By the way, have you heard from him?'

Relton folded his arms.

Terry looked around. 'Katie, I think we'll take that as a no.'

'Next, in his hotel room, bit pissed.'

Terry thought he looked more than drunk. 'And next, Exhibit A.'

She paused for effect before she tapped the key.

'Fucking hell,' said Relton.

They all stared at the shot. Matt Cooney was on his back, stark naked, propped on a pillow, a rictus grin on his face. One naked girl was astride him, the other was up the other end, steering a nipple towards his mouth. Katie did think the boys had styled it well – the vodka bottle, the discarded underwear. It wasn't exactly Tracey Emin's bed, but not far off.

Terry stood up, looking at his watch. 'Time's up, what a shame. Come on, Katie.'

Relton jumped up. 'Hang on. Hang on. Sit down, Terry.'

Terry stood his ground. 'Next.'

Katie scrolled through the shots. 'In case any of you don't know, Mr Cooney is married, with two small children.'

'If I was running it, maybe THREE IN A BED? Too obvious?' said Terry.

They all just looked at him.

'Next. This is Felix's mate Simon with the girls.'

'I do think you have to admire the photojournalism and how young Simon entered into the spirit of the enterprise,' said Terry.

'And when Terry says young Simon, can anybody tell me how old he is?' said Katie, hitting her stride now.

They all looked at each other.

'No? Well, he's seventeen. Anybody know what a minor is in Brazil?'

Again nothing.

'And Oli's middle name is Marcelo because?'

'Katie, maybe we're going too fast. Explain it to them.'

'He's half Brazilian, has a passport and his mother's a criminal lawyer.'

Relton said, 'Shit.'

Nobody spoke as Terry circled until he was directly behind

Relton. 'Yes, 18. Coercing a minor? Up you get fat boy, down the other end please.'

Relton slowly got to his feet, went to the far end and sat down.

Terry looked at the Felix mock-ups in front of him, then swept them on to the floor.

Relton folded his arms 'Yep. Come on then.'

'Britain's finest outfoxed by two kids and, what was it, a clown?'

'How much?'

'Twenty-five thousand. Guineas.'

'That's impossible, don't be stupid.'

'Each. And a full family ceasefire. Take it or leave it.'

Relton just looked at Terry who stared him down.

'Deal,' said Relton.

*

As she closed the door behind them, the shakes returned. Terry watched her and held her arm. 'Relax, you'll be fine. Come on.'

'Shouldn't we have told them we're not actually in the business of wrecking marriages?'

'In what way?'

'Well, Cooney was unconscious before they got to the room. Nothing at all happened, with him or the boys or girls.'

'Oh, God no, get the money in the bank first, then make him sweat.'

She loved Terry. As they headed out across the office she said, 'So is Dad still fair game?'

'Well he has to be, that's the trade.'

'Seems harsh.'

'They won't go big now, they wanted an exclusive angle. How do you feel?'

'I'm thinking it was an unbelievable high. That was surreal. Did I just do something where the end justifies the means?'

'Not at all, self defence. If somebody comes at you with

a cricket bat, you're allowed to take it off them and give them a spanking.'

'Do unto others?'

'Exactly.'

'All fair in love and war?'

'Think that's enough clichés. You defended yourself – that's the game we play.'

'I do now have one problem, though.'

'Which is?'

'I might have to rewrite my thesis.'

*

Frank had sent Sam the TV instructions, and while he tried to get on to Sky, he wondered what Terry had in mind for Relton. He was sure he heard a noise, but the maid wasn't coming. He picked up the poker from next to the fire. Gary appeared in the doorway, with his finger to his lips.

Sam mouthed, 'What the fuck?'

Gary beckoned him to follow outside.

'Fuck, you scared me. I did think when you said "go outside" how you knew I was inside.'

'Can't be too careful.'

'You're paranoid.'

They sat in the shade and Gary pulled his laptop from his bag.

'How long you been here?'

'Got the last flight to Madrid last night, drove down. Slept in the woods, it was lovely.'

'Why did you do that?'

'Look at these.'

Gary started scrolling through shots.

'That's those guys parked up watching the house. And this looks like a drive-by.'

'Shit. I knew I was being watched, just felt it.'

'Of course you did. This is much more interesting.'

Gary started the sequence of Donald arriving. 'Your friend Donald. And Donald's friend.'

Sam watched in amazement as Donald's so-called driver moved from room to room. Gary switched to video. 'He's a pro.'

Fucking Donald. 'I'm shocked.'

'No, you don't know that Donald knew.'

'True. Can you get rid of the bugs?'

Gary said, 'You must be joking. We leave them in place. The longer they don't think we're on to them, the better.'

'Why didn't you tell me you were here?'

'If people see me, it scares them off. I need to stay invisible too. The house is being watched; I wanted to watch them.'

'Who is it?'

'That lad Luke and another guy. Didn't recognise him.' He decided not to worry Sam by telling him the other drive-by looked like pros, maybe Americans.

Gary gave him a mobile. 'Use this pay as you go for anything sensitive. I've put your contacts in it. Terry and Katie have it, oh and Frank. I'm going to give you a full digital makeover.'

'Thanks. Fancy a beer?'

'Sure. By the way I've been terminated, and they took the cars back.'

'Sorry to hear that.'

'No surprise. Terry hasn't even got that. They just told him not to come to the office again. We're off the entry system too.'

'Forty years for Terry, nice way to finish.'

'Terry sounds to me like he's just getting started.'

*

As Sam went back into the house for the beers, Frank called on the house phone.

'Blimey. Nobody had this number twenty-four hours ago, now it's like the Samaritans. I'll call you straight back.'

Sam called him outside from his new mobile and told him about the bugs.

'That's unbelievable. Listen, I've just been in with Jay. He offered for me to work until the end of the year. They made it clear it was take it or leave it.'

'On what basis?'

'Restructuring. Said they had stuff on you, and since I was responsible for your actions, I could get the same treatment.'

'What stuff?'

'Jesus, they could dredge up anything, couldn't they? Think about it. Can you account for every penny, every deal? There's something going on. Jay's out of his depth here.'

'Well, Donald made me the same offer basically. But you should take it, it's a good deal.'

'Maybe, and I'm to tell you to down tools. I need your badge and gun. There's a statement going out later that you're suspended pending an internal investigation. Sorry, Sam.'

'And Chalky White?'

'Fuck Chalky White.'

*

He rang Terry. 'Been trying to reach you. You spoke to Felix?'

'Of course.'

'So what are you going to do?' said Sam.

'Do, old boy? It's done.'

'Bloody hell, how?'

'I think Katie should tell you.'

She took him through it. When she told him about the photos he said, 'Prostitutes, I assume?'

'No, they were students Oli's brother knew. They do some glamour modelling on the side. There was no sex. They gave them each a grand, they were thrilled.'

She put Terry back on.

'Twenty-five each for the kids. Clare and the kids off limits.'

'Bloody hell. Great job'

He went back inside, where Gary was opening the beers.'

'Couldn't wait for the beer. There's no bug in here, I've got it. Just keep the door shut.'

Gary opened up Sam's laptop. 'This is still OK, but obviously be careful with company email. I've set you up with a new Gmail account. All your contacts are there. If anybody emails you on your work account, they get an Out of Office message. But I can access them all and I'll forward them your new details. All the key people like family have your new number and email. I backed up all this, too, so everything's on there – files, calendar, emails, photos. It's logged in to the Wi-Fi. I've set you up for all the news sites behind the paywall. You're back in business.'

'How did you get the TV working?'

'Well, I turned it on, not difficult.'

'What about leaving the bugs?'

'He'd expect one or two failures, so I've left the ones in the bedrooms, the one next door, and the one in the land line. Just act naturally, but nothing confidential in those rooms.'

'You're a genius.'

'Hardly, simple stuff.'

'Did you look at that photo Hodgy sent ?'

Gary got it up on his phone and they looked at the mystery woman's profile, out of focus.

'Can you enhance that?'

'You've been watching too much HBO. We can't do much with it.'

'Well, it's not critical, just odd timing.'

Gary got up and started to pack his stuff away.

'Better if I sleep outside and keep an eye on you.'

'Gary, you didn't have to do all this.'

Gary stopped and looked him in the eye. 'Sam, for a lot of reasons, I did.'

*

He'd unplugged the landline in the bedroom and muted his new mobile so he could get some sleep. In the middle of the night he came back from the bathroom and checked his messages. A text from Frank read MIRROR. He went down and logged on. The shots were from across the street, from a floor higher, maybe on the roof. The two guys outside his flat on the Tuesday morning were understandable – they'd doorstepped him before, and anybody could have seen them in Colbert or walking down the King's Road and rung it in. But how the hell did they get the shots through the windows the night before?

While he was clearly visible in, thank God, his pink boxers, her face wasn't in any shot. But her body was, in the tiniest white g-string. He knew why – she wasn't the story, but they'd have worked out who she was. She was the follow-up, and they'd try to buy her 'story'. His bedroom was at the back so they couldn't have any of that or the bathroom. Could they have got the first one, on the floor? Or the CCTV on the stairs?

There was no way he could sleep now. He'd been so stupid. Carson was unhappy; Jay Lomax would think it was just more ammunition. Clare was going to kill him, and Katie would be appalled. And worst, Justine. He thought of her, in her flat, fast asleep. She was going to wake up, hear the news, and panic. It might kill her exit deal. She'd probably, quite reasonably, never want to see him again, but it was too early to call her. He texted: 'Read *Mirror*, don't panic, call me at this number xx.'

# CHAPTER 12

**FRIDAY 4th July – DAY 7**

***The Independent*: TORIES UNDER FIRE FOR LINKS TO PRO RUSSIAN LOBBYISTS**

***The Sun*: 'MAGA-LEWD': GIRL PERFORMS 24 SEX ACTS FOR £4 COCKTAIL**

***Daily Mail*: HOLIDAY CHAOS LOOMS IN AIR TERROR ALERT**

He killed time watching it spread across social media and onto other websites. He could see why they called them 'virals'. It was unstoppable. When he'd had enough, he went for a long run and came back to Gary making breakfast.

'I locked up.'

Gary laughed. 'Of course you did.'

'You seen it?'

'Of course. Doesn't look good.'

'I can't get hold of her.'

'It's probably freaked her out and she's gone into hiding.'

'They must know who she is.'

'True.'

'Can you send Joseph round to her flat? She might need help.' Sam gave him her address.

Gary said, 'Only a thought, but maybe cover off Katie?'

'Good idea. She's the one I'm worried about.'

'Hi Dad, I'm just arriving at the office. I've seen it.'

'And?'

'Is it that girl from the office?'

'Yes, sorry.'

'Dad, stop apologising.'

'Just not used to being on the receiving end. You don't mind?'

'I know what you do, Dad, I've just never seen the pictures.'

He was surprised how relaxed she seemed.

'Mum told me they've offered you a great deal.'

'She wants me to take it. And she wants you to quit.'

'I think you should do what you think is right. And I'm not going anywhere.'

'That means a lot.'

'I have to go, late for the editorial meeting.'

Sam got an email from Justine: 'I'm fine, no paps, no contact from *Mirror*/anybody, phone off. Deal done. Need break. Seems no harm done to me, sorry bad for you. Talk later? Justine xx. PS Nice pics. My bum looked good didn't it! Xx.'

He admired that she was probably putting on a brave face to make him feel better.

Donald rang him. 'Sam, I've seen the *Mirror*.'

'I'm sorry about that.'

'Well, it doesn't help, but forget it. Just to let you know nothing's changed, just sign your deal, I'll sort it all out.'

'Thanks.'

'I saw you got a lawyer. Good man. By Monday.'

He felt a lot better with Justine and Katie onside and his deal on the table.

Gary said, 'Katie and Terry keep copying us in on emails about Chalky White, what's that all about?'

'He's got her interested, he thinks there's a story there. No harm.'

'Where does he live now?'

'In the countryside, it's in one of Terry's emails.'

'What's happening on Burke?'

'Everyone's saying Mortlock's got them all hidden away. Loads lined up for Sunday, including TV.'

Sam could just tell that Mortlock was making all the right moves. He hated it.

'I wonder where?'

*

One hour behind and about twelve hundred miles due north, Lady Sarah Burke was nursing a cup of Earl Grey in the kitchen of a house she didn't know the address of. She knew it was Surrey because they had driven down the A3 and turned off at Cobham. It had a large, walled garden and the drive was guarded by electronic gates. Nobody had line of sight to the house or garden. Each time she looked out, there were two guys on patrol.

Every minute was torture. The house arrest, the make-up, the canned interviews, the posed happy family shots. All the talk about money. And Julian Mortlock, who kept saying it would all be done with by Monday, and she'd be home. She had a terrible feeling it wouldn't be, and neither would she.

She tossed a paper on the table. 'So, was she at the villa while you were cavorting?' She put an emphasis on the last word and refused, as always, to call the twins' mother by her name.

Burke sighed. 'Katia. You know her name. I told you, she's in Kiev, recuperating.'

'Did you have to enter into it with such gusto?' Again the last word stressed.

'I understand, but they are my daughters. They're finally getting out; you always agreed it was the right thing to do.'

'I suppose so.'

'Sarah, let's be clear, the reason we now have financial problems is because your delusional half-wit brother Piers destroyed the family business, of which you own, or owned, half.'

'You always bring that up, don't you?'

'Oh, so you want to downsize, do you? I'm just trying to do what's right for everybody. It's not easy.'

She lit a cigarette and changed the subject. 'And where are the cheeky girls?'

Burke wished they hadn't used that line in the paper. It was going to stick.

'I think they're doing some photos.'

'What sort of photos?'

'I don't know, background, stuff to reflect their student life.'

*

Sarah didn't know it, but the house was less than a mile away and much more modern, with a bigger pool. Tatiana was adjusting the focal length on the Takahashi TSA-102S APO Refractor Telescope that stood on a tripod on the terrace.

She said to the photographer Morgan in her almost perfect English, 'This is a fantastic piece of equipment. 816mm focal length at f8 and gives you up to a 3.06 field at 16X. Amazing light transmission and excellent contrast – all the surfaces are fully anti-reflection, multi-coated and the tube interior is knife-edge baffled. Weighs just five kilos. Very, very cool.'

Morgan tried to look interested. 'Can you tilt your head back just a bit, love?'

Tatiana was bent over slightly, looking in the viewfinder, but she did and it took the shadow off her face. She was wearing a mortar board and high heels. That was it.

The girls weren't convinced it was the best idea, but Mortlock said they could keep and split the fifteen thousand they were getting for the teaser in the *Mirror,* the spread in *FHM,* and worldwide syndication. Burke had been over the day before to do some boring 'proud father' shots that would look fine in *Hello* or the *Times*. They seemed relaxed about the nude stuff when Mortlock said it doubled the price, and they all agreed not to burden Burke with the fact they were going that far.

Irina was in the kitchen, just an apron for her to go with the heels, making the traditional dish of Kapusniak soup. She was doing the video version for the website, with the apron barely covering anything, looking in the camera saying, 'And for this you need salo, which is pork fat, and sauerkraut.' With her stronger accent she even made pork fat sound sexy. She served it with sour cream and Korovai, a bread she made.

She made enough to feed the entire crew, including the buffed male model called Finnian they drafted in to wear the Vilebrequins. They could not understand why half the crew called him Finn, and the other half said Mickey.

Irina ended her piece by popping a bottle of Obolon beer on the work surface and saying, 'Nasdrovia,' then taking a proper slug. Finn asked her, 'How do you girls eat this stuff and stay so fit?'

Irina took the apron off, and put on shorts and a T-shirt. 'When we were young, gymnastics, like everybody. Then we got too tall. Tatiana plays volleyball now, indoor winter, beach in the summer. I spend most of my time in the pool.'

He then asked the obvious question: 'Why are you doing this?'

Irina said, 'Why not? This will be fun, we'll make some money, then we will go back to further education, maybe here.'

'We want a life that can be independent of Ukraine.'

The photographer knew they were novices but had to admit they were naturals. Finally, he took one very conservative shot of Tatiana wearing glasses and a white lab coat, next to the telescope. 'I can tell for a fact that this is the first and last shot I shall ever take for the *New Scientist*.'

'Really?' said his assistant.

'Yes, really. I was told to.'

She was so pleased she undid the buttons and flashed the stockings and suspenders underneath.

He fired off some more. 'That might just be the money shot.'

# CHAPTER 13

## FRIDAY

Damir was in a café outside the Bontiak Hotel on Irininskya Street. Across the road was the office of VFS Global. He flicked through the Ekxpres while he smoked and drank his espresso, watching VFS's front door. He'd worked with Sam for nearly ten years, his only newspaper client. He'd failed to make it as a player with Red Star, played briefly in Belgium, then ended up in the late seventies in Tampa in the early days of American soccer, playing for the Rowdies where his lack of pace didn't seem to matter.

He hung out with Rodney Marsh and guys from all over the world. With his bandit looks he got work as a TV extra, and games in New York meant nights out with Pelé, Chinaglia and the boys. He married a local girl, got a passport, got divorced. Tito died in 1980 and he went back to Yugoslavia – the borders opened and he became a fixer, getting foreign movie companies to make films there on good tax deals, acting as an agent for the exodus of footballers. Now he chose what he did, working for Sam, fixing deals for footballers, clubs and the odd movie star.

His mobile rang. 'Hey Plumski. Glad you called, Johnnie rang me, told me to go home and that we're dropping Burke.'

'So you back in Belgrade?'

'Hell no, I'm still in Kiev.'

'You think the mother's there?'

'I'm working on it. Katia sounds like a party girl. Activist's a bit strong. Her ex-husband's the guy.'

'How come?'

'The ex, Artem Bezrukov, is a well-connected local guy, but his great mate is Nikolay Pavlovich, he owns the villa – mega rich. Nicky's extremely close to Oleksandr Vilkul who's Deputy Prime Minister, responsible for industrial development. I have to call you back.'

A man was coming out of VFS, they made eye contact, and Damir set off down the street. At the corner he stopped and, as agreed, let the man walk past and waited. He made sure they weren't being followed, then trailed him until they reached Starbucks.

They shook hands. 'I'm Damir.'

'Viktor.'

As Damir got up to get the coffees, he tossed his paper on the table and said, 'Great article on page 8.'

Viktor opened the paper and took the envelope.

When he came back, he said, 'Thanks for coming. So explain how this works here.'

'My father saw you play, said you were good.'

'Too slow.'

He laughed. 'He did say that too. In a lot of places, the UK Border Agency is run by commercial third parties; that's what VFS does here. We don't make the decisions, we just run the process.'

'So the embassy gets involved?'

'Well, we need biometric information – they have to come in person, give us their fingerprints and we take their photograph. Most applications are pretty standard, but they do check. It's been a lot tougher just recently.'

'Of course. So what do you know about the two girls?'

'I was here when they came in, I processed all of them.'

'What do you mean all?'

'The girls and their mother.'

This was news to Damir. If she got the visa, why didn't she get on the plane with the girls?

'What sort of visa?'

'They all wanted General Visit ones, for up to six months max. We get 80% of those through in ten days, but it can take three months.'

'When did they come in?'

'Only about two weeks ago, so they were cutting it fine anyway.'

'So what happened?'

'Well, of course the mother had been in prison, very briefly, as a dissident, so she has a criminal record. The girls are twins but have different surnames. And of course the girls' father, sorry stepfather, is well-known. So we knew the Embassy would get involved. We have to put the status of the application online, and they told us to say it was pending, as opposed to in process. So it was on hold. They all seemed pretty agitated.'

'Then what?'

'Two days later my boss came to see me and said it was all approved but upgraded to LTV, Long Term Visit.'

'How did the mother look? Sick, thin?'

'Looked like the girls' mother. Normal.'

'I know it's a big ask, but could I see the applications?'

Viktor stood up and offered his hand. 'Good to meet you. By the way, you were right, great article on page 8.'

Damir opened the paper slightly and saw the A4 envelope. He was most interested in the mother's. He went into the men's room to look at them and saw that Viktor had given him their forms and photos. Even with her hair back, looking straight at the camera, unsmiling, the mother was still a very good-looking woman. She wasn't emaciated, she just had great cheekbones.

Walking down the street he called Sam and said, 'Trust me, the girls got their looks from their mother.'

'What's the story?'

'She got a visa too. They were all fast-tracked and upgraded. But she wasn't on the jet.'

'Why on earth would she do that?'
'Get the visa? No idea. Treatment somewhere, Switzerland?'
'Maybe. What are you going to do next?'
'You always say that. Wait and see,' said Damir.
He hailed a cab and said, 'British Embassy.'

# CHAPTER 14

## FRIDAY

Gary and Sam set off on the seventy odd miles to Jerez airport to collect Terry, with Gary driving his rental Audi.

'Why didn't you tell me he was coming?'

'We thought you might put your foot down. We both think it'll do you good.'

'Well, it's not going to achieve anything. Oh, God, I hope he doesn't want me to play golf.'

After about ten minutes Gary said, 'We're being followed.'

'Can I look round?'

'Sure, they're way back. It's McIntyre and the other guy. They put a tracker on the car.'

Gary turned off the main road, and after a few miles the tarmac ended. 'Always rent a four wheel drive. Old trick.'

Sam admired Gary's skills on the loose surface, all the time looking at his phone, the Q5 trailing a dust cloud. He pulled up on the brow of a hill and got out. 'Come on.'

They looked back down the hill. As the dust cleared, they saw the BMW, buried up to its axles, the two guys hands on hips.

'Did you plan this?'

'I recced it yesterday.'

Gary retrieved the tracker. 'Come on.' They drove back down and pulled alongside.

Gary got out. 'Hey Luke. And who are you?'

'Fuck off.'

'I think this is yours.' He lobbed him the tracker.

'Don't think a BMW ever won Paris Dakar. Not a car, anyway.' He leaned into their car and took their two Evian bottles, emptying them in the dirt. 'Twelve miles, nearest town. Five to the road.'

The guy said, 'Barry Harrison.'

'I'm guessing you're new to this, Bazzer?'

Sam remembered where he'd seen him. 'Oh, you were the guy with Burke, at the lawyers.'

Harrison's mobile rang. In a moment Gary grabbed his right arm and spun him round, pushing him against the car. He reached in his pocket and took out the phone. He tossed it to Sam who looked at the caller ID. Julian Mortlock. Gary could see what he was thinking and shook his head. Sam ended the call.

Gary took some pictures of the two guys next to the buried car. Then he took Luke's phone. 'You can get them from the villa later.'

Barry said, 'I'm going to get you for assault, theft, phone hacking, stealing data. And you, Plummer, I thought you were Mr Clean. Dirt on your hands now, eh?'

'Barry, this isn't Jeremy Kyle. Shut up and listen.'

Sam loved the way Gary could just say it slightly differently and it made him do it.

Gary gave Sam the floor. 'I have no problem with you guys working for Mortlock. I know it's not personal for you two. I've been there. Do your job. But this meeting never happened.'

Barry relaxed slightly.

'Of course, if Mortlock's broken the law, and this ends up with the police, then you're both in it with him.'

Gary went to the car and came back with a tow-rope and two Cokes from the cooler box. 'As I said, twelve miles.'

As they towed them out, Sam said, 'I haven't been in the field for years, I'd forgotten how much fun it is.'

'What's the line in your movie?'

'Which one?'

'*The Untouchables*. They take one, you take one, or something.'

Sam said, 'If they put one of our guys in the hospital, we put one of theirs in the morgue.'

'I like that idea. Want me to scan their phones?'

'No. The flip side of that is I'm not stooping to Mortlock's level. We do it my way or not at all.'

Gary went back and unhooked the rope. 'Don't follow us. And you won't find the tracker on your car, I did it properly. And here are your phones. Your lucky day.'

# CHAPTER 15

## FRIDAY

While they waited at Jerez airport, Sam rang Francis Kenyon, the employment lawyer he'd emailed the draft compromise agreement to and connected with Donald.

'What do you think?'

'It's very straightforward. They've sent me your employment contract and other stuff, we can easily do it by end of Monday.'

'Do me a favour, Francis. Just do a mark-up, but be really pedantic, and go back on Monday morning with more questions.'

'I should take some tax advice too.'

'OK do that, sounds better. Then send them the mark-up but make it subject to my comments.'

'You want to buy some time?'

'Just so you understand, Francis, they're putting me under a lot of pressure to sign this, on all fronts. It's my only leverage.'

'We could get it done today if you really want to.'

Sam knew there was some logic in this, but he knew that once he signed, it would close a chapter in his life.

'I appreciate the thought, but I'm going to wait.'

Sam knew he was letting his heart rule his head. Maybe it was the deadline mentality, going right down to the wire. And what was going to happen over a weekend stuck in Spain? Maybe it was just knowing his world, where anything could.

*

They watched Terry come through with a porter carrying his leather suitcase and golf clubs, escorted by a lady from BA.

Sam said, 'It's Alan bloody Whicker.'

'I'm loving his blazer. And the Panama.'

Terry reached them, doffed the hat, and said, 'Morning campers. This is Charlotte.'

'How did you ever manage to work undercover?' said Sam.

'Master of disguise when needed. They called me the Scarlet Pimpernel of Fleet Street.'

'They did not.'

'True. Anyway, hello boys, always look the part, I say. Lunch?'

As they walked to the car, Terry said, 'I've had a look in the old Michelin and there's a marvelous little bodega about ten miles from here, on the way. I've got the address. Andiamo.'

'That's Italian,' said Sam, tipping the porter.

They found the place in Alcala easily. It was full of locals, and they took a quiet corner table. They ordered, and Sam got Terry to take him through the confrontation with Relton. When he was done he said, 'But that's not what we're here to talk about. Full review. From the beginning, we're all free agents now, we've got all day. Want to hear it all my lovelies, and I mean all.'

So Terry and Sam shared the wine, and they took him through it, Gary focusing on Ukraine, and Sam on the events of the last few days. He skipped over Justine, but Terry insisted, 'No, want to hear that bit too.' So Sam went into all the details – the first date, the liaison, the small talk, the second time, in her flat, her getting fired – with Terry endlessly probing.

'This feels like an interrogation. You're not George Smiley.'

'Well, you say that,' said Terry.

'But my relationship with Justine is none of your business, it's irrelevant.'

'Let me be the judge. You will have my opinion shortly, which will be based on all the facts.'

When Sam really had finished, Terry untucked his napkin and paused to take a drink. '2007, very good year for Ribeiro.'

'Well?'

'Based on everything I've heard, and already know, there is only one conclusion. I'm afraid, Sam, that it's staring you full in the face.'

'What is?'

'You of all people. I'm amazed.'

'For God's sake, what?'

Terry put his hand on Sam's arm. 'You're not going to like what I'm going to say.'

'I'm a grown-up.'

'Honeytrap.'

They just sat there all looking at each other, then Sam finally laughed and said, 'No, Terry, not possible, not with what happened, the way it did.'

Sam's mind was racing back through everything. 'No way.'

'Dear boy, textbook. Can't say we invented it, oldest trick in the book, of course, but it's a classic.'

'Not Justine, it wasn't like that. Not possible.'

'They all say that.'

'Gary? Back me up.'

Gary leaned back in his chair, trying to put it together. 'Hang on, I wasn't in the bedroom. Bloody hell, Sam, maybe.'

Sam felt sick.

'Alright, you asked for it, dear boy, here we go. Had you ever met her before?'

'No.'

'Do you know anything about her?'

'Not really.'

'But you have tried to find out?'

'Yes.'

'And you can't.'

'Not really.'

'Show me a photo on your phone.'

'Aren't any.'

'Who seduced who?'

He said, 'Fifty, fifty,' but he knew that wasn't true.

'Sex in the rooms with street view?'

'Yes, you saw the *Mirror*.'

'So why at your place the first time?' said Terry.

'Shit, the photographers outside the flat, so I would leave her alone in the flat.'

Gary said, 'So you had to leave her in there while you drew their fire.'

God, she'd seemed so vulnerable, so scared. All he'd wanted to do was protect her. Was that really all a set-up?

'Textbook. And why her place the second time?'

Sam knew exactly where this was going. 'Oh, God.'

'Exactly. Lights, camera, action.'

'Surveillance.'

'You got it. Did she get you to reveal, shall we say, corporate indiscretions?'

'Oh fuck.'

'Your moonlighting?'

'Shit.'

'Language. Just tell me you didn't tell her about Bob the wonder horse.'

Sam didn't reply.

'You are a twit. I rest my case.'

For too many reasons he wanted Terry to be wrong, but he had to assume the worst. He knew that what he'd told her could finish him, give Jay all he needed. The stories were like a buffet, help yourself – freelancing, dodgy dealing, airline tickets, the horse. They all just needed the slightest spin and he was screwed. And how long was she in the flat – could she have copied the keys?

But he said, 'You guys are paranoid. You might be wrong.'

Terry picked up the *Mirror*.

'We can't see her face and she's not named. Whoever's running her wants to keep his or her powder dry. You don't burn assets like that.'

'We always protected them, you taught me that.'

'I know, funny how you don't see it when it's right under your nose.'

Sam needed to regain control. 'OK, if you're right, we know how it works. She's in on it, paid off, and they have all the ammunition. It's a big Sunday splash. I'm toast.'

'Burnt toast.'

'I can sort this out. I'm going to ring Justine.'

'Wake up, old boy, there is no Justine.'

'Sorry Sam, but I think he's right,' said Gary.

'Of course I am. Did I teach you nothing? Think about it. Right now she doesn't know you're on to her. So we now have the high ground. And remember, somebody's put her up to this. She's being paid.'

'Who by?' said Gary, tapping away on his keyboard.

'By whom. Well chaps, as we all know, only two groups of people run these sorts of ops. The intelligence services and us. So who's your money on?'

'Relton?' said Sam.

'He was after Felix,' said Terry. 'He wouldn't do it. You know perfectly well who it is.'

'One horse race,' said Gary. 'Julian Mortlock.'

Gary connected to the Wi-Fi and moved round so they could all see his laptop.

'Look at this. I've got access to the CCTV at your flat.'

'You're kidding,' said Sam.

'How many times do I have to tell you that I watch your back, and it's what I do. Easy. What date was she there?'

'Arrived Monday, left Tuesday.'

Gary typed in the date. 'Time?'

'Got there about eleven.'

'Here we go.' In black and white stop-frame, Sam watched himself and Justine go through the front door, then on the four-way split screen, going into the lift and kissing.

'Lovely move Sammy, chapeau,' said Terry.

'Do we have to see this?'

More from the overhead shot in the lift, then coming out of the lift, Sam watched himself push her up against the wall, his hands on her hips, moving down. He looked at it, shocked that it could all be an act.

'Bravo. The master at work.'

'Terry, fuck off.'

'Note she's just carrying a small handbag, gents,' said Gary.

Gary scrolled through to the next morning and saw Sam leave at 08.43. Justine appeared at 10.16 with a Waitrose shopping bag.

Sam said, 'All my notebooks are there. Old diaries, contacts. Files. Everything.'

'I've got Joseph on his way round to check and do the locks, then he'll try her place. I'll get the car.'

When Gary was gone, Terry looked at Sam, deep in thought. He had always felt paternal about Sam. He wanted to put his arm round him. 'You're smitten, aren't you?'

'Well, I was.'

'Worse than Caroline?'

He wanted to say yes but lied. 'I don't know. No.'

'I'm so sorry. We've been in worse scrapes than this.'

Sam thought about it but couldn't think when. Now he really was going to be a laughing stock. He put his head in his hands.

'Terry, you know me as well as anybody. I never made a decision in my life. I did what my parents told me until I joined the paper, which was luck. I married Clare because I had to. I've never divorced or changed jobs, and I cocked it up with Caroline because I was indecisive. Twice.'

'I'd say that was a fair assessment.'

'And here I am, finally facing the first fork in the road. Quit or fight? And I have no idea what to do. What would you do?'

'Well, I did quit.'

'On your terms.'

'Listen, you'll make the right choice, I'll help you.'

'Thanks.'

'Let me summarise. One: the girl.'

'Not Justine any more then?

'She's not a Justine. One – the girl is a separate issue. Irrespective of Burke they – assume that prick Mortlock – have used her to get stuff on you so they can pressure you and Frank. He just got to her to get the dirt on you. Two – as we stand there is not one shred of evidence that Burke planned this. A scam would be fraud, so you'd have to prove it is planned – in advance – not just opportunism. In my professional opinion, that's impossible, certainly in any sensible timeframe. Three – you have a great deal on the table, which means we can forget one and two.'

'You might be able to. I can't.'

'Sam, one of your golden rules is play the ball, not the man.'

'And I'm playing Mortlock and Burke.'

'Exactly. And you're getting emotional. And you're loved up.'

A word popped into Sam's head. He leaned back and a smile spread across his face. 'So I am right. Conspiracy.'

'Half right. The girl clearly, but not Burke.'

'It's a start,' said Sam.

'I agree. Here's the conspiracy theory. Mortlock is very, very clever. He's been waiting for somebody to arrive at the paper who he could turn and then get stuff on you from the inside. She'll have money problems, whatever. Come on. We invented this.'

'But she didn't just turn up, she was hired as legal cover, seconded. That could only be Jay or Donald. She's a lawyer.'

'You sure?'

'Look, you can fake an orgasm, you can't pretend to be a lawyer for five weeks.' They both laughed.

'Oh sorry, a woman with a body and brains, not exactly a first for you.'

'Not now, Terry, please.'

'But it's a good point, Mortlock just has her as a mole. He finds out from her that we've got Burke on the hook, so he gets to Burke, tips him off, and tells him how he can make himself a real hero, and some pin money, with no risk. Capisce?'

'That's Italian, too, but yes, I do.'

'It's win-win for Mortlock and Burke.'

'But how did Mortlock find her?'

'Maybe somebody in your offices tipped him off. He's good at cultivating people. It still looks like cock-up, not conspiracy. You've had a great career. You can trouser all the money from your options and pension. Keep your lifestyle. You take the money.'

'Really?'

'Dear boy, you're normally the rational one. Ignore who did it. The full story, with pictures, will be in this Sunday. She'll be history, but it's going to be a graphic, blow-by-blow account, as it were. Plus the notebooks, the stories. You should sign.'

Gary pulled up outside and came back in.

'It's a rotten bet, Sam, don't make it,' said Terry. 'I've worked with you for thirty years – you might have been the best I've seen.'

'What do you mean, have been?'

'They got lucky finding a cross between Perry Mason and Christine Keeler – she's a fine piece of work. Great asset if you've got a smart lawyer who'll do the old horizontal rain dance. A veritable modern day Mata Hari.'

'She fried your brain,' said Gary.

Terry stood up and they all walked outside. Over the years, giving Sam sound advice that he knew he would ignore had served them both well.

Sam said, 'Staggering what can happen in seven days.'

'The next seven might be the same.'

'I doubt that. So what shall I do, oh wise one?'

'Think you just have to ride out Sunday. You don't need to sign until Monday night. Let's keep our options open until the last minute. Knowledge is power. And time we can always buy.'

'Fair enough.'

Sam sat in the front next to Gary. He turned round and said, 'You seem back on top form, Terry.'

'Had the old MOT last week, looked like I might fail.'

'Engine?'

'I'll spare you the gory details, but more exhaust-related. Got the all clear. Firing on all cylinders.'

'Thanks for Katie, she seems to be fired up, too.'

'She loved taking on Relton, and I've got her interested in Chalky White as a piece of modern media history.'

'Her cynicism seems to have mellowed.'

Terry handed him a file. 'She wanted me to give you her notes.'

'You read this?'

'Of course.'

Sam handed it back. 'Tell you what, why don't you go and find him? You'd love it.'

Terry refused to take it. 'No, I'm going back to the airport. We need to find the aforementioned Miss Mata Hari. You guys need to be here.'

Sam flicked through the file. 'She's done a good job.'

'Good teacher.'

He could see it was a serious piece of research. It was fully indexed. She'd got old Spanish articles translated. She had transcripts of her calls. He went back to the one-page summary at the front. Half of it was dedicated to the evolution of his profile and the central contradictions, of the playboy hard man image. Where was the actual evidence of his criminal activity on the Costa del Crime? She asked why he still kept a vulgar pile in Marbella but never used it, living instead in a farmhouse near Córdoba, allegedly. On the contacts page there was just a grid reference, but only the Marbella address. No numbers, no email. The 'El Blanco' man in the white suit party photos seemed to pop up twice a year. That was it.

Sam remembered the last time he met him – 1988. He liked him. He wouldn't take cash for the piece, but Sam delivered something for him to his mum in Walsall and gave her the cash anyway. He didn't want to sound as interested as he now was.

'OK. The Chalky tip we got, where did it come from?'

Terry said, 'Through me, very old contact.'

'Who is he?'

'Was. Government. But then they only offer life membership.'

'MI6?'

'Sort of. They never call it that. SIS is OK but the Firm is better.'

Sam closed the file. 'If I have time, it'll be for Katie.'

'Understood, old chap.'

They both knew what he really meant. MI6 mandarins tended to provide better leads than nightclub sleb spotters, and unlike the police they never wanted paying.

*

They dropped Terry at the airport. In the car on the way back to the villa, Sam looked at the file again. The summary and index was classic Terry. Then he said, 'Fuck,' and banged the dashboard.

'What?'

'I told Justine who Katie is. She saw her photo in my flat and recognised her from the office. I told her she was using her mother's maiden name. Mortlock will use it against me and Frank.'

'Well, there's nothing you can do, she's gone.'

They drove in silence. Maybe she'd dated Mortlock; maybe she still was. The thought of her fucking him made him feel nauseous. He now realised there was every chance it was a reality. Mortlock's reputation as a swordsman was based on him having 'the best column in Fleet Street'. Stories abounded about girls, forewarned but intrigued, who simply couldn't handle it. He remembered being irrationally angry when he first heard. It was bad enough he had a younger rival in the newsroom, he didn't want one in the bedroom.

'I'm thinking how she did it.'

'Did what?'

'Filmed me. Us.'

'At your place? Loads of ways. Laptop, phone. You can get one in just about anything in the house – smoke alarm, plug – but she had to bring it with her. That small bag could do it –

glasses, watch, book, lipstick. Stills and video. You'd be amazed at the quality.'

'Oh great, that's really reassuring.'

'HD, colour, sound.'

'Yes, I got it.'

'But from what you said, there was no time at your place when you got there – on the floor, impressive – in the bedroom she could set up, in the bathroom no.'

'Not very encouraging.'

'But the second time, at her place, could be a full multi-camera studio set-up.'

'Gary, that really doesn't help.'

'I think we'd all like to see it at the IMAX, and apart from Kermode, in 3D.'

'It's actually not funny.'

'Don't ask if you don't want honest answers. Lots of ways to get it out there.'

'As Colin Farrell learned.'

'If you measure up to him, I'd be impressed.'

They drove on, Sam reading the file, marking it up as he went. His phone beeped. 'Bloody hell, text from you know who.'

'You mean we don't know who.'

'Exactly. "Really sorry can't come. Bit complicated. J."'

'Still using J. Jezebel maybe? Kisses on the end?'

'Two.'

Gary said, 'I know it's hard, but you really mustn't. We have to keep it going. Don't call.'

'Why not? I can pretend everything's normal.'

'Sam, listen to me. You can't. Don't. As you like to say, if in doubt, do nowt.'

There was so much he wanted to ask her. As the countryside sped by, he read the text over and over, looking for some clue. It took him five full minutes to compose a reply. 'No problemo. XX Sam.'

'Did she make you wear a condom?'

'No.'

'Blimey. Beyond the call of duty.'

Sam thought about all they'd done. It was fine being an urban myth, but he just wasn't ready to join the celebrity section on PornHub. 'Really Gary, you have no idea.'

'Guess we all will on Sunday.'

# CHAPTER 16

## FRIDAY

Carson Lomax had always had Gulfstreams, working his way up to a G5, but the Global Express was something else. It had a range of over 6,000 miles so it could do the East Coast to London or Nice in one hop. It was faster at 0.8 Mach but he most liked that it was built by Bombardier in his home town of Toronto. The 14 seats were rarely filled. It had D1-LMX on the tail. They were wheels-up from TAG Aviation Farnborough at 1630, climbed to 28,000 feet in just ten minutes and levelled off.

Carson finished a call and took a Labatt Blue and pretzels from Rachael, the stewardess that he liked to stay with the plane. She dated one of his two Swiss pilots, Dieter, who based themselves and the plane in Geneva, mostly for tax reasons.

Jay sat next to Mortlock, opposite Carson, and had already given his father a heads-up on appointing him as Editor, knowing he had no chance without his approval. Carson knew Mortlock was on a roll with headline grabbing stories.

'Julian's been very useful. He's advising Burke right now.'

'So where are we with that?'

'Donald is working on the details, globally, not going to be as bad as we thought.'

'Why?'

'May I?' said Mortlock. Carson noticed how he was controlling the narrative, as if he'd worked out a storyline.

'We've done the *Mail* deal. We're getting all the others done; we need some of your photos.'

'And Burke needs the money,' said Carson.

Mortlock laughed. 'That would be an understatement.'

'So you're working for Burke, his family, the *Mail* and us. No conflict of interest, then?'

Mortlock looked him in the eye 'No. Right now I'm working for myself. If I was employed by you, it would be different.'

Carson Lomax looked at the two of them. Mortlock had balls but he wasn't fooling him, he clearly knew every trick in the book. Poor young Jay didn't even know which book. What was the risk of finding out if Jay could cut it? Could these two really make a better team than Frank and Sam?

'And what about the Untouchables?' said Carson.

Jay said, 'All under control. They'll take the deals, they have to. They're the ones stopping progress. We can really cut the headcount, invest in new media, rebrand, relaunch.' Carson could hear his son drifting off into management speak.

'Still hurts the bottom line,' said Carson.

'Not really, exceptional items. Like everybody, we had a bigger litigation contingency this year, but we've hardly used any.'

'You mean they haven't made any mistakes for a while.'

Jay knew this was true, but let it pass.

They talked some more about the paper before Carson changed the subject.

'So how are the wedding plans?'

'Angelina and her mom have it under control.'

'And Angie's fine about moving over?'

'Absolutely.'

He wasn't convinced about Jay marrying the only daughter of Nick DeLorenzo, New York new money, at their family estate on Long Island.

'You sorted the prenup?'

'Nearly.'

'Get it done. What are you boys doing tonight?'

Julian said, 'I'm introducing him to some fun spots.'

'Low key tonight, Dad.'

'Just remember, what happens in Vegas.'

*

Sam and Gary were on the sofa drinking beer, watching Germany beat France. Mary rang from Frank's office. 'How's it going, Sam?'

'I wouldn't exactly say swimmingly. Couple of snags.'

'Thought you might be interested in this. Carson and Jay are on their way to Paris.'

'Right,' said Sam, not seeing that it was very interesting.

'There was a late addition to the manifest.'

Now he was interested. He could guess but said, 'Go on.'

'Julian Mortlock. Only Carson's going on to Sardinia. They're staying at the Crillon, using Elite Limousines.'

'You're an angel.'

'Good luck.'

Sam called Jérôme, his guy in Paris since Caroline's Crazy Horse days, who still used the Arsenal season tickets.

'I have a really big favour, a job tonight.'

'Under control.'

Sam laughed. 'I haven't told you what it is yet.'

'Jay Lomax and Julian Mortlock. On their way now in an Elite to the Crillon. Then they're going out.'

Sam laughed. 'You know where?'

'Sam, you do ask stupid questions. Full cover?'

'Please.'

'This one's *à la maison.*'

*When he woke up next to Caroline in Paris all those years ago, it was Jérôme he met in the kitchen making breakfast. Six Crazy Horse girls from around the world shared the flat. They all seemed remarkably normal, clothed.*

*He told them about the feature and they promised to help. Caroline took him out, helped him buy some cool clothes. She talked about school, her parents, life in Kent, what she missed. When she found out he had to go back the next day, she told him to stay through the weekend. He called Frank and persuaded him to tell the office some whopper, which they bought. He told Frank what was really happening, but he didn't believe him. 'Sam, it's me, Frank. Get a grip. You are not staying in an apartment with six strippers and shagging one called Nooka. You've lost your passport, haven't you?'*

*The next morning, Jérôme drove them all to Bernardin's huge country estate near Orsay, an hour outside Paris. 'No cameras, Sam.'*

*He met Bernardin, played a set of tennis with him, and let him win. Walking across the lawns back towards the house, he'd said, 'Caroline says you are a good guy.'*

*'Thank you.'*

*'Well, she's a special one. How is your story going?'*

*So Sam told him, including the overwhelming feelings of unreality and inadequacy. They reached the pool. Caroline walked him round and introduced him to the girls, who all sunbathed nude. 'Tan lines, strictly verboten.'*

*Jérôme took a few photos, putting Sam in some.*

*At the end of the day, Alain took him on one side. 'It was good to meet you, Sam. If I can help you, you let me know.'*

*'Well, today was fantastic, thank you. That was obviously all off the record.'*

*'Who said?'*

*'Your people said.'*

*'They say lots of things for me. You do what you think is right. For you and for Caroline.'*

# CHAPTER 17

## FRIDAY

Mortlock and Jay were in the stretch limo heading in. Jay chatted to the driver in French then said, 'Where are we going?'

'Friend of mine, Michel, runs a model agency here. We're meeting him and some of his girls for drinks and dinner at Costes, then a club, maybe the Buddha-Bar.'

'We just need to road test it all for the stag.'

'Might go somewhere else for that later.'

'Well, you passed the audition,' said Jay.

'Once you got me on the plane and you stuck to the script, it could only go one way. Just get those two bozos to sign, let me take care of the rest.'

'Under control. Donald went down and hand-delivered the deal to give him some encouraging words. Frank's there, poised to sign.'

'Good.'

Jay said, 'Do you think they've worked out Justine?'

'No chance.'

'She's amazing.'

'I think she might be one of the best I've used. She trained well.'

'Don't forget I found her,' said Jay. His gullibility never ceased to amaze Mortlock. He tried and failed to think of anybody he'd ever met who was so easy to manage.

*

Carson skimmed Jay's boring and predictable report as he flew on to Sardinia. It was full of the 'management speak' bullshit he hated. People were being transitioned and backfilled, never fired. They were drilling down even though they weren't in the oil business or dentists. Problems were issues. One of his managers in California had actually once said, 'Let's cross the sidewalk and see what the view looks like from over there.' Nobody just told you anything, they gave you a 'heads-up'. Everything was leveraged via a paradigm shift. Carson always went straight to the cash flow – Jay and his little army of consultants couldn't bullshit that.

They touched down at Costa Smerelda Airport in Olbia. Customs met him at the bottom of the steps, and he walked the fifty metres to their helicopter. He told the pilot to skip the scenic route so they flew due north for ten minutes. The *Hic Salta* was repositioned at Porto Cervo, off Cale de Volpe. As they came in to land, Lomax could see at least another twenty superyachts. He joined Caroline on the rear deck for dinner.

He kissed her on the cheek. 'So your mate got 18 months.'

She said, 'Andy Coulson is not my mate, you know that.'

He sat down. 'And for a minute I thought we had Burke.'

She said, 'How's Jay doing?'

'You want to know about Sam.'

Caroline said, 'He's a proud man.'

'Well, very soon he's going to be a rich man.'

'Sort of.'

'He made a mistake.'

'What happened to collective responsibility? Your son's the CEO.'

'Jay didn't know what was going on. Nobody's getting hurt here.'

'Newspapers normally put up a fight. You just rolled over.'

'Look,' said Carson, 'he and Frank have been running that place the same way for years. New blood.'

'So this is purely an exercise to see if your son can cut it?'

'Kills two birds with one stone. I'm a deal man, not a paperboy.'

'So it's not personal?'

'Sam didn't make us the profits, he kept us out of jail and in business. We owe him for that. If he takes the deal, he's set.'

'And if he doesn't?'

'You can take a horse to water.'

They ate in silence for a moment. She hated the thought that one day she might have to take sides.

'So what exactly is your point, Caroline?'

She paused and took a deep breath. 'I'm sorry. Just don't underestimate Sam.'

Lomax laughed. 'I can look after myself.'

# CHAPTER 18

## SATURDAY 5th July – DAY 8

***The Guardian*: COULSON JAILED FOR 18 MONTHS**

***Daily Express*: JAILED ROLF'S FINAL SHAME**

Gary was up early and long gone before Sam surfaced.

The previous evening they'd driven to Benahavis and had dinner in a quiet restaurant just outside town that Frank had recommended, steering away from the tourists. Their shadows Barry Harrison and Luke McIntyre were nowhere to be seen, but they didn't like being in the house with the bugs.

Sam had said, 'I should call Justine if I'm acting normal, shouldn't I?'

'No. Joseph tried, the phone's dead, and emails are bouncing. And he can't figure who rented that flat. It's over.'

Sam took stock – it was time to play 'find the lady'. They had to get to Justine somehow, and Terry was on his own there. And now that Katia had a visa, Damir had the whole of Europe to cover in pursuit of the elusive mother. They'd agreed that Gary should catch the first flight home and that Sam would sit it out, with his priority to get his employment lawyer to work on his deal.

After breakfast he rang Katie. 'You at the office?'

'Heading in.'

He'd toyed with telling her about the honeytrap, about what she would see the next morning. He rationalised he shouldn't, but in reality he knew he was scared to.

'Have you looked at my Chalky White file?'

He could tell she wanted him to say yes. 'Terry gave it to me. I glanced at it.'

'Oh.'

'I'm kidding. I read it. Three times.'

'Wow.'

'It's really good. Question. Not as your Dad, as an editor. Explain the trend thing.'

'Well, over the years the local coverage became more supportive – family, charity work. The UK coverage was regular, always coinciding with some celebrity in town, but it became less frequent. And there was less about associating with hard criminals, more all that Raffles stuff.'

'Interesting.'

'I've got an Excel spreadsheet showing the timeline.'

'Blimey. Send it to me. And what's your conclusion?'

'Terry might be right, maybe they are about to get him back. Looks like he's been trying to improve his image, cultivate goodwill – with the Spanish to support him and with us, in case he ends up back here.'

'Makes sense.'

They talked some more and she said, 'Are you going to try and find him?'

'I can't lie to you, I don't know.'

Just the pause was enough to show she was disappointed.

'I'll try.'

'Dad, my instincts tell me there's something wrong.'

He laughed. 'It took me forty years to develop my journalistic intuition, and it's still getting me into trouble.'

'Well, female intuition then, we're born with that.'

*

As he sat on the terrace, his new safe mobile rang. He really wasn't in the mood. 'Hey Clare.'

'Don't hey Clare me, what the hell is going on?'

'I'm OK, thanks for asking.'

'You signed?'

'I have until Monday.'

'Look Sam, I know how this works, tomorrow can only be bad. You and that tart are going to be all over the papers.'

'That's true. But I can't stop it.'

'Have you any idea how embarrassing that is going to be for me?'

'Not as much as for me.'

'Hardly, she looks like a porn star. Can't you sign today?'

'No. I have to go.' He hung up.

He knew Barry and Luke's BMW was parked down the hill in the shade, safe in the knowledge that with Gary gone they could keep up with Frank's Fiat Panda. He hated being spied on.

*

He found a small rucksack in one of the kid's rooms and put a change of clothes in it, along with his laptop and chargers and his wash bag. He and Frank had many shared interests, and one was sitting in the garage downstairs.

He'd pulled off the dust sheet the previous night to check the battery and fuel levels, and he just looked at it. The MV Agusta F4CC. He remembered a review he'd read for it. Something like: 'If power is the ultimate aphrodisiac, then this is the planet's most sexually charged motorcycle.' They'd built just 100, and they had the only one in the UK, which cost a staggering £75,000 in 1998. They did an outrageous and marginally dodgy contra deal and Frank paid trade price. They'd had trials bikes. He'd been on the back of Randy Mamola's Honda at Brands Hatch where he nearly frightened him to death. He'd entered one amateur race and fallen off, calling it a day when he saw Katie's little face when he got back to the pits.

Frank had shipped it down on Spanish plates. He had two helmets in the garage, his full-face Shoei in West Ham colours and an open-face matt black Arai for mates, which Sam took. Frank's leathers were too loose so he just took a black Calvin Green golf jacket off a hook and some Alpinestar gloves. He noticed Gary's nice touch, covering the plates with duct tape. The roar of the engine filled the garage as he eased it off the stand.

The garage door ground up and he eased out, zapping it shut. Then he gunned it down the hill past the BMW, u-turned it and came back, pulling alongside. Barry looked up at him, still clearly pissed off.

'Nice car boys, the Panda won't start. Try and keep up.'

'Wow,' said Luke – and he took a photo.

Sam pulled away steadily and they followed. As they crested the hill and the road straightened, he couldn't resist it and turned to give them the trademark V sign that Barry Sheene liked to give Kenny Roberts every time he passed him. His heart was hammering and the adrenaline was flowing even before he opened the throttle and wheelied it, then dropped the front wheel. And with that, he made the jump to light speed and was gone.

When he slowed, he laughed at the moment. Was it a great metaphor? Giving two fingers to the industry – though he had just done that, literally – and riding off into the sunset. No, he'd literally done that as well.

'Shit,' said Barry.

'Can you believe that?' said Luke.

'I know, what a prick.'

Luke was animated. 'No, that was an MV Agusta, the F4CC.'

'Oh, get a life.'

'With the titanium frame.'

'Do I look like I give a toss?' said Barry, doing a dodgy three-point turn.

'You said he's a has-been. He just wheelied a one hundred grand superbike, like he's Casey fucking Stoner.'

'Oh shut up.'

'He gave you a Barry Sheene.'

'A what?'

'He's a dude. And he shagged Sharon Stone.'

'No he did not. Jesus.'

'It was in the papers.'

'Exactly. Enough,' said Barry as they drove back the way they came.

*

He'd set off north towards Ronda. They didn't have an exact address for White, just the grid reference which Gary had worked out was about 10 kilometres east of Cordoba, so about 300 kilometres away. Gary had found the spot on Google maps and printed it out for him.

After about 20 kilometres, Sam pulled over and took the tape off the number plates. He drank some water and checked his phone and that nobody was following him, which would have been impressive. Despite Katie's work, he knew White was probably a wild goose chase, but he admired how Terry had enthused her, and it reminded him why he was so wonderful to work for. He also felt mildly stimulated that for the first time in years he was on the ground, in pursuit of a story, albeit one that had died a horrible death years ago. And that, for the first time in about a week, he wasn't being watched, and he really was alone.

He had all weekend to kill, so he'd worked out a scenic route, stopping at the Fuente de Piedra lagoon, where he swam and sunbathed, watching the pink flamingos. He'd stopped in Campillos to get petrol and then bought a sandwich in a café, always paying cash. At one point he cruised along with some Germans, mostly on big Honda Gullwings. Then he shook hands with the lead guy, waved goodbye, and rode away. When he stopped, any who saw the bike would come over, just to look at and admire it. This was the country of Dani Pedrosa, Jorge Lorenzo and now Marc Márquez, who looked about fifteen.

He texted Frank to call on his new mobile, from another line.

Frank called him straight back.

'Broadsword to Danny Boy.'

'Very funny, Frank.'

'Aren't you getting a bit paranoid about all this?'

'You'll never guess what I'm doing. Out and about, with your Italian love child.'

Frank laughed. 'Just don't drop it. Where are you?'

'Just out touring, got nothing to do.'

'Liar. Looking forward to tomorrow?'

'Well, it'll be all about the pictures.'

'Terry told me the full story. Can't believe you fell for it.'

'Neither can I. Talk to you later.'

He saw he had a missed call. 'Hi Hodgy.'

'That woman up here with Mortlock.'

'Gary tried with the picture, couldn't do anything. Thank your daughter, though.'

'No, I've got news. A waiter came back from his hols and remembered her from another place. Langar Hall.'

Sam said, 'OK, I'll try and send somebody.'

'No, I'm on my way.'

'Hodgy, you don't need to do this.'

'Actually I do. Let me tell you Sam, if you quit you'll find out why. Walking away is not as easy as you think.'

As he ended the call, the phone rang again.

'Bad news 007, you've failed the test.'

'What test?'

Gary was laughing. 'How to disappear.'

'I've done exactly what you told me, to the letter.'

'You're all over the Twittersphere.'

'I have not tweeted.'

'That Luke might not be as stupid as he looks. He took a

picture of you on the bike, tweeted it and tagged it Agusta and F4CC and a few others like *Motor Cycle News*. The official Agusta Twitter feed picked it up and retweeted it.'

'So what?'

'Well, everybody else who photographed it on your travels did the same – like those Germans. So with geo tags I can see your route and timeline all the way to that last Repsol garage. Pretty obvious you're heading towards Córdoba.'

'Sorry, Q.'

'Just don't let it get photographed any more. When you get there, you might want to hire a car.'

Sam felt stupid. Yet another mistake.

'You want the good news?'

'Please.'

'I've been round to your flat, which was clean, fitted new locks and wiped Justine off the CCTV.'

'Thanks.'

'But there's bad news. Joseph went round to her place. It's not her place. Been on a short lease. It was empty, nothing. And I mean nothing.'

'Who rented it?'

'Trying to find out, but short sublet for cash probably.'

'What are you doing?'

'I'm on my way to Odessa, some loose ends.'

If only Gary could as easily wipe Justine from his memory. It was getting too much like a Saturday in the office, plus flamingos. He wanted to get back to the freedom of the road.

*

By five he thought he'd found the right place, but it was a crossroads in the middle of nowhere. He rode about five kilometres in each direction but never saw an entrance or any buildings. Looking around he couldn't see any high ground where he could get a view. What had he been expecting, a neon sign saying 'Welcome to Rancho Blanco'? He realised he didn't know what he would do if he'd found it, and worse, he had no plan B. 'You idiot,' he said out loud.

As he sat in the shade of a tree studying his map, he heard a car approaching from the south and then saw it appear, trailing a dust cloud. The police car pulled up and an officer got out. He didn't look like a helpful traffic cop.

'Are you broken down?'

Sam stood up, 'No, I'm fine, thanks.'

'Nice bike.'

'How did you know I was English?'

Another guy in plain clothes went over to look at the bike.

Sam said, 'Who's your friend?'

'You look English. Are you lost?'

'I know where I am. I'm trying to find an Englishman who lives near here, Mr John White. Some call him Chalky or El Blanco.'

Sam kept looking round at the guy examining the bike. The officer took off his sunglasses. 'Are you insured?'

'I am but I don't have the papers with me.'

'Licence?'

As Sam got it from his rucksack, the guy started taking photos of the bike on his phone.

'Hey, please don't do that.'

The guy ignored him.

'Please don't post it.' He knew he was wasting his breath.

The officer took his licence and they both got back in the car.

Sam watched them, the officer on the phone. After maybe five minutes, he came back and handed Sam the licence. 'I've not heard of your Señor White. Are you staying near here?'

Sam knew there was no point lying. 'The Mezquita.'

'Very good hotel. Try La Juderia for dinner, it's a short walk.'

'I will. Thanks, officer.'

'Captain. Have a nice day.'

As they drove away, Terry rang. 'How's it going, lad?'

Sam didn't want to admit he wasn't doing very well and said, 'I'm at the crossroads.'

'Ah, the eternal challenge that man has faced down the centuries. The Devil leaving you there, the Faustian pact.'

'No Socrates, I'm at the crossroads, in the road. Where you sent me?'

'Oh, I see.'

'And I can't see any entrance, nothing.'

'Oh dear. Well my advice, knock it on the head. You did your best, Katie will appreciate you tried.'

Terry was back saying the opposite of what he meant.

'You're probably right. I'll head back in the morning.'

Sam headed into Córdoba. He filled the bike on the outskirts of town, in case he had to get away early, then checked in, leaving the bike in the hotel's garage. Gary had booked and paid in advance, using a name he had made up. When he went out, he folded a small square of paper, wedged it in the door frame, about six inches off the ground, and hung the Do Not Disturb sign. An old trick. He drew a blank with the concierge and barman on White. Maybe it was reality he was out of touch with. He didn't have one single lead; he couldn't really count the restaurant recommendation. But, and it was a big but, when the local police take an interest, it usually means you are on to something.

The hotel was three star but felt like two, right in the centre next to the Cathedral-Mosque. He walked along its north side and found La Juderia in five minutes, tucked down a back street. Clearly a local place, not for tourists. The waiter, who spoke no English but looked just like Manuel from *Fawlty Towers*, found him a big corner table.

Manuel shuffled back with a draught Dorada and then a small plate of Iberico ham, offering no menu or wine list. Sam thought nothing of it and started reading the *Wall Street Journal* he'd picked up in the hotel reception.

Manuel appeared again, naming the dishes as he put them down: 'Pimientos de padrón, queso con anchoas, mejillones rellenos y croquetas.' He took the beer glass and was soon back with a glass of white wine: 'Castillo de San Diego Palomino Fina Vino de la Tierra de Cadiz.' Sam wondered how long this could go on for.

For some time, it appeared. He could only assume it was the policeman's way of staying in control. As a journalist he knew that anything was better than being ignored. He had to go with it. As Sam read, Manuel shuttled backwards and forwards. A glass of red came: 'Ariyanas Tinto de Ensamblaje.'

Manuel finally brought him a small coffee. Sam said, 'La cuenta, por favor,' probably the only phrase apart from asking for a beer he could do in six languages.

'You ordered nothing. señor, so no cuenta for you.'

So nothing was happening, and it stopped being funny. He wondered who was watching him, knowing he had to retrace his steps to the hotel. He'd come here to get away from being watched. He took a detour which meant a longer walk back, sticking to the main road past the Cathedral-Mosque, walking along the river.

He was glad when Caroline called. It gave him a chance to stop and look round without seeming unnatural. He took her through the honeytrap.

'You don't sound surprised.'

She said, 'It's what you used to get me to do.'

'You didn't sleep with them, you just got them on the hook.'

'If you say so.'

He ignored that.

'So you braced for tomorrow?'

'It's going to be ugly,' said Sam.

'And to think I was part of a select group who know what you're like in the sack.'

'Did you talk to Carson about it all?'

'Sam, he's a fair man, just don't cross him. There's a dark side. Keep your head down, sign your deal. Where are you?'

'At the villa.'

He didn't like lying but he was making mistakes, and telling anybody what they didn't need to know was page one stuff.

The Do Not Disturb sign was there, but the small piece of paper wedged in the doorframe was on the floor. He put his ear to the door and listened, but heard nothing. He double locked the door behind him, drew the curtains, and put the TV on loud. He had no idea how to search for listening devices and couldn't believe they'd install a camera. He emptied his rucksack on the bed. He couldn't see any sign it had been searched, but he had so little stuff. Not bringing Katie's file had at least been a smart move. Being watched was one thing, but this was another level. Somebody was invading his space and knew how to do it. Had he walked into some trap? Was Mortlock behind this? He just wished Gary was around. It always felt safer.

He wrote up his notes, the first he'd made on the road in maybe fifteen years.

Finally he wrote a short email to Katie. 'Hi Baby, For Your Eyes Only. In Córdoba in pursuit of Britain's Most Wanted. I'm very out of touch but loving it. Bit of a dead end so far but Guardia taking interest – good sign. Don't want to let you down. Love, Daddy. PS Need sleep so phone off. Going to be ugly overnight online re me and Justine. Been a bit stupid. Need to explain. Speak to me first. Xx'

# CHAPTER 19

**SUNDAY 6th July – DAY 9**

***The Sun on Sunday*: TERROR TWINS: SISTERS 16 FLEE TO FIGHT IN SYRIA**

***The Independent*: LEON BRITTAN QUESTIONED BY POLICE OVER SEX ATTACKS**

He woke early, showered, and settled down to look at it. He logged on and said out loud, 'Here we go.'

*The Sun on Sunday* front page splash filled the screen. He'd been thinking they'd been pretty quiet all week. He just looked at it with his mouth open, not sure if he should laugh or cry. There was a touch of genius about the photo they'd used.

And there was the headline: TIT FOR TAT. The story read, TOY BOY REVENGE. Disgraced hack's wife says anything you can do.' Clare was by the pool and Harvey the gardener was standing next to her, with his ridiculously buffed physique. There were two more pages inside. They couldn't resist YOU BERK over a short piece on Sam being duped – paying the man who mowed his lawn to shag his wife. It was all photos – the open top BMW, the Range Rover, the horses, shopping with Harvey, and one of them snogging at Daylesford.

His immediate thought was that Harvey had sold his story,

but the shots of him looked like they'd come off Facebook and an old modelling card, and he wasn't quoted. But Clare was. There were lines that could only come from her. 'Harvey is like a sex machine' and 'Sam lost interest in sex'. The truth was 'disgraced hack' hurt far more.

He surfed the web but there was nothing new on him. A few had picked up on Clare. The cheeky twins were there in the *Mirror*, great photos. It didn't make any sense. He and Justine just had to break today, why would anybody hold it back? Bloody hell, maybe after all that, Terry was wrong about the honeytrap?

What he did know was that he had to get into damage limitation mode, so he turned on his phone and let it download endless messages while he cleaned his teeth. He went back to the balcony and called Clare, but before he could speak, she just screamed and ranted. She'd done about a minute and burst into tears before he said, 'Clare, shut up.'

While he was furious, he knew it wouldn't help to show it. He heard her blow her nose.

'Calm down. You spoke to somebody. All the stuff about the house, us, the sex with Harvey Wallbanger. Who was it?'

'I don't know. Nobody.'

'OK. If it was me and I wanted to get you to talk about me and Harvey in the sack, I'd send a woman.'

'But I haven't met anybody new this week.'

'It won't be this week. And I'd send somebody in the same boat. Someone sexy.'

'Oh, God.'

'What?'

'This Greek woman, Theadora. I met her riding. She's married to some shipping guy, a real cougar.'

'And she told you all about her sex life, too.'

'Yes, in great detail. All about this Argentinian polo player.'

'A lie. When did you meet her? It's important.'

'Two months ago? No, Easter. Party at the polo club.'

'Got a picture?'

'Don't think so. Thea stayed twice, said she was having a really tough time with her husband.'

'OK, this is what you're going to do. Email Gary with everything you know about her. Name, mobile, email, car. Try to get a photo from the party or the club. Don't speak to her or anybody you don't know. How many paps at the gate now?'

'About four, I shut it. Can't you stop them?'

'Not unless you're Harry Styles, no. Lock up and go out the back. Take Gerry with you. Find somebody who'll look after him and lend you a car. Go to your mother's.'

'You are joking.'

'Just do it, you might be surprised. Where's Mellors?'

'He was a gamekeeper, not a gardener.'

'Whatever. Harvey.'

'Sailing in Cornwall. Some race with his mates.'

'For what it's worth I'd say he's not in on it.'

'Thanks. That was supposed to be you on the front page again, Sam, with that girl.'

That was true. It was odd – while he didn't exactly have the moral high ground, he was definitely in better shape.

'Look, I've done everything to keep you and the kids out of it. I was always OK to draw their fire.'

'And I never said you'd lost interest in sex, just with me.'

Sam laughed. 'I know how it works.'

She was calm now. 'I'm so sorry. What does it all mean?'

'I need to think. Just that somebody wants to hurt me, and has wanted to for some time. Plenty of people with grudges in our business. You slept with anybody famous recently?'

'Very funny. That's your department.'

He sensed her mellowing.

'By the way, you looked good in the pictures.'

'I did, didn't I?'

'I know what you looked for first. Cellulite.'

'God, you still read me like a book. There wasn't any.'

'Air brushed out.'

She was laughing now. 'Bastard.'

'I'm joking. And the kids are fine.'

'Thanks Sam, I really appreciate all that. Talk soon.'

*

He went back to Sunday's websites. *The Mail* and *Mirror* both led with Burke. Mortlock had done a good job carving it up. They each had Gary's pictures, but the *Mirror* went heavily with all the naughty stuff done with the twins. The shot with the telescope had HEAVENLY BODIES as the predictable tagline.

What most interested Sam was that the mother Katia was nowhere to be seen, but she was still referred to as 'having treatment'.

Elsewhere, Sam and Frank were still getting a kicking, with Carson now getting dragged into it. There were reams of criticism from rent-a-quote politicians, media commentators and regulators. Another kiss-and-tell was harmless enough – great sexy pictures of Sam's then girlfriend in her heyday, more in the jungle covered in ants, eating something's genitalia, a middling sexual reference for Sam, and some nonsense about a jealous husband.

Frank's TOWIE front page was a shocker. As Sam skimmed it, Frank called. Sam went back out on to the balcony.

'Can I speak with the disgraced hack please?'

'Fuck off, Frank.'

'You jammy sod, you could slide off sandpaper. How's Clare?'

'Chastened.'

'When did they do her?'

'Some Greek bird, goes back to Easter.'

'Blimey, so way before Burke. Anything new on him?'

'Not that I heard. Gary's gone back to Odessa, don't know why. The mother still puzzles me. Didn't fly. Nobody can find her. She's the best part of the story, why Burke did it.'

'Look, daft thought. You naked on the front page is bad, but it rocks the boat. What if all they want is for us to sign and bugger off?'

'So somebody held it back?'

'Yes, as leverage. Clare's a warning shot.'

'No shit, Sherlock.'

'What do you think?'

'Come on. So the honeytrap is linked to getting us out? I don't see that. And anyway, Sherlock Holmes on speed couldn't crack it by five tomorrow.'

'I did say it was a daft thought.'

The hotel phone rang inside. 'Hold on one second.'

'Mr Plummer?'

'Yes.' He swore under his breath and muttered, 'Don't tell them your name, Pike.'

'Sorry?'

How many more stupid mistakes could he make? After all that trouble to register and pay under a false name.

'Could you come down please? There's somebody here to see you.'

Back on the balcony he said, 'Frank, I have to go. I think my career as Jason Bourne is over.'

*

In reception was the same police officer.

'Mr Plummer, Captain Mendez.'

'Hello again, Captain.'

'I'm afraid bad news, a break-in here last night. A car and your lovely motorcycle stolen.'

If he was lying, he was very good at it.

'And?'

'I will join you shortly. We have to ask some questions.'

He needed a proper coffee so he crossed the road to the café and sat outside with a cortado and an ensaïmada. He failed to reach Gary, so he texted him: 'Tracker still on bike? Stolen. Trace?'

Mendez came over and sat down. 'I have your details from yesterday. Here is my card. I have spoken to the hotel and they will repay your room cost. They are very sorry. If we do not find it, I will give you a reference for your claim.'

'OK, thanks. Which car?'

'Excuse me?'

'Which car was stolen?'

'Oh I see. I think it was a Seat, a white one.'

This time he knew he was lying.

'You said you are staying near Malaga.'

'Did I?'

'There is a train in thirty minutes. It would be my pleasure to drive you there, if that is OK?'

Sam said, 'Sure.'

He went back to get his bag. He was going to ask the receptionist the same car question, but Mendez was there. He drove him to the station, helped him buy a ticket and walked him to the train. They shook hands. 'Goodbye, Mr Plummer.'

Sam got on the train and moved forward through the carriages. Gary texted back: 'Yes. Coords to follow.' It was still five minutes until the train left. He got to the front carriage and looked out of the window, but he couldn't see Mendez. He changed out of his jeans into shorts and a T-shirt and left the helmet on the seat. 'Sorry, Frank.'

Checking it was clear again, he jumped down and went into the waiting room on the platform.

Gary called. 'What's going on?'

'I think I've been run out of town.'

'Well, the bike's not far from those crossroads. I'll text the coordinates, just put it into Maps on your phone, that'll get you right there. By car it says 18 clicks.'

'Thanks. You still in Odessa?'

'Going tomorrow, now.'

A train pulled in on the other platform. He slipped in with the crowd, then out into the street. A taxi was too risky, so he started walking. At a garage at the edge of town he bought some water, a local map, a baseball cap and some sun cream, and he worked out where he was trying to get to. He avoided the main roads, and once he reached the countryside walked on trails wherever he could, using the GPS on his phone and the map. Despite all his cock-ups, he was on it. Whatever it was.

He trudged along, the sun high in the sky. He stopped by a stream, where he took off his T-shirt and laid it out on a rock in the sun to dry. He splashed water on his face and refilled his bottle. Sitting against the trunk of a tree, the only sign of life he could see was a goat silhouetted on a ridge about half a mile away. If Mendez came back, would he turn nasty? Like the cop trying and failing to run Rambo out of town?

He wondered what would happen if he went cold turkey. There was no doubt he was a news junkie, but what if he cancelled the newspapers, literally and metaphorically? Just signed off and ignored it all? He'd be remembered as the Don Bradman of journalism. The Don needed just 12 in his last innings for a test average of a hundred, but failed and was left stranded on 99.99. Sam would be remembered for his last cock-up, but if he didn't read about it, so what? And nobody ever called the Don disgraced.

He'd miss Frank, but he was off too now. And Terry, but he was gone already. The golden years had been the three of them working together.

He rang Hodgy who said, 'Not quite what I was expecting on the front pages.'

'Nor me. I thought your old mates were going to get stuck in. Any joy?'

'Yes and no. They don't know who she is, but she ate there a couple of times with Doug Slateford. He's a mega-rich software guy, sixtyish, serial tech investor.'

'Married?'

'Grown up kids, divorced. Very low profile. They said they always had a laptop open on the table.'

'They sharing a room?'

'They weren't sure. He stays there.'

'Is his office nearby?'

'Not exactly. San Francisco. Expat Brit, moved there about thirty years ago with Honeywell, then started his own business.'

'Thanks again Hodgy, stay in touch.'

*

After another hour or so, he thought he was in the exact spot, but he was on a road with an unmarked track leading off it. There was no Agusta.

He called Gary who said, 'You're right on top of it.'

'OK, thanks.'

He looked around. A few yards up the track was a battered mailbox on the ground. Inside was the tracker, wired to a couple of AA batteries. What was this? Some Japanese game show?

He put it in his rucksack, thinking at least Gary would know where he was. The unmade road wound on for what felt like miles. He went over cattle grids and through three gates, closing each behind him, before he finally crested a hill. Spread out in front of him was a vast estate.

He'd been walking for nearly three hours. He couldn't see any buildings, but a rough wooden sign pointed to 'Casa' so he carried on. He crossed a river, still winding through endless olive groves and vineyards, before coming to what he assumed was a bodega, a huge sprawl of stables, barns and outbuildings. Beyond that, he could see a large, old two-storey house.

A couple of farm workers saw him but paid little notice. Another appeared and pointed to the larger house. He could see a figure in the distance on the terrace.

He was about two hundred yards away when the man went back inside, then reappeared. He wasn't anybody he recognized.

He looked like one of the farmhands, in a loose check shirt and faded jeans. His face was in the shade of shabby cowboy hat. He had something hanging loose in his left hand. He stopped about fifty yards away, wondering if this was how Gary Cooper felt in *High Noon*.

'There's a man who looks like he could do with a cold beer,' said the man.

'You are not fucking kidding.'

It wasn't like summiting Everest, but Sam felt ridiculously proud. He wanted to ring Katie.

'Welcome to Casa Montilla.'

Chalky White had two beers in his hand. 'Long time no see. Twenty-two years.' They shook hands.

A maid appeared and took his rucksack. Chalky led him to the shade and they sat down. He opened the two Estrellas. Chalky handed one over and Sam noticed his rough hands, like a farmer's.

'You look surprised, Sam.'

'Well, I guess I was expecting the man from del Monte, not Clint Eastwood.'

'Don't believe what you read in the papers. You made good time.'

'What was all that about? The Challenge Anneka bollocks.'

'The restaurant? Wanted to be sure you were alone and you had an appetite. For the chase.'

'And today?'

'To see if you could still cut it. You don't get out much, I hear.'

'I'm a bit rusty.'

'And I haven't survived this long by advertising. There's a lot at stake here.'

'Like what?'

Sam could see some information coming at last.

'Your reputation, what else?'

'Oh, I see.'

'Short trip from the Tabloid King to disgraced hack.'

Sam looked at him. He hadn't changed much in twenty odd years. Still fit, good-looking, and just as effortlessly charming. But he thought about Katie's note. The cultivated profile. All those villains he mixed with. Bolwell battered, in his hospital bed. Had he just never seen the real Chalky?

Sam finished his beer in no time, so Chalky said, 'Come on, you need to freshen up first.'

The main house was laid out around three sides of the courtyard, dominated by an ornate fountain. They walked out through an arch and across the lawns to another house, in the same style, with white stucco walls and faded red roof tiles.

'This is the guest house, treat it as your own.' They walked through it and out of the back, where it had its own small walled garden with a pool. Everywhere Sam looked, it was understated and stylish, as far as possible from what he had imagined.

'Have a swim, get changed. There are some clothes if you need them, then I'll show you round.'

Whatever Sam thought, it was too late. He had to go with it.

They started at the garage block, close to the house, just beyond the floodlit clay tennis court. It looked more like a Dutch barn, with big sliding doors. The working vehicles were outside: two Toyota 4×4s, an old Ford flatbed, and a quad bike.

Sam was surprised to see two young guys had the Agusta on a stand. They looked at him suspiciously.

'These are my sons, Alex and Ignacio, but we all call him Nacho.'

Sam offered his hand.

'Boys, he is an old friend, to be trusted.'

They all shook hands. The elder one, Nacho, smiled and said, 'These old ones are easy to hot wire, sorry.'

'Who rode it back?'

Alex said, 'I did.'

'He races.' Chalky said it with real pride.

'You look about twelve. Listen, I've got a problem.' He explained the Twitter issue.

Chalky turned to Alex. 'You still testing at Jerez tomorrow?'

'Yep, going to drive down this afternoon.'

'Change of plan,' said Chalky. 'Take the Agusta.'

Alex's face lit up. 'Fantastic.'

Sam said, 'I left the helmet on the train.'

'We'll find something similar. You got the keys?'

'Sure. Let people photograph it, but try and keep out of shot.'

Chalky said, 'But bring it back in the truck. Put a sheet on it.'

'OK Papa, got it.'

As they were leaving, White said, 'Notice anything?'

Sam looked at Chalky's cars. 'They're all boring, and none of them are white.'

'Very good. I borrow the Bentley for photos. Ghastly thing.'

They walked across to the stables. White walked along, patting and stroking the horses. 'You know what these are?'

'Horses?'

'Very good. They're picador horses, we breed them. Bullfighting is still big here. The tercio de varas is the first part of the bullfight, when the two riders have lances. They have to weaken the bull so he drops his head. It's when you find out if the bull has courage, wants to charge, to fight.'

'Do they have padding?'

'Sure, it's called a peto, but a hundred years ago, no. The picador was the main attraction, so the horses were in much more danger. These ones in here are all retired.'

He opened a stall and showed him the scars on the grey's sides. 'And of course they're blindfolded. So they can't see the bull, but sure as hell they can hear it and smell it. This is Marta.'

'A mare?'

'Why not, some of the best. Retired when she was ten, which is pretty good going. She was a star in her own right. And women have a higher pain threshold, you must know that.'

'As my wife never failed to remind me.'

Chalky laughed. 'You ride?'

'Sort of,' he said, though he couldn't remember the last time.

Sam watched him. The easy way he was with the boys, the farmhands, even the horses. If he wasn't real, it was one hell of an act. They went along to the tack room, White issuing instructions in Spanish as he went. Inside was a long rack of leather riding boots.

White gave him a well-worn pair. 'Try those on for size, tuck your jeans in. They zip up the back. And you'll need a hat, pick one off the rack. Leave your phone.'

'Is this the bit where you drop me down the disused mine shaft?'

Chalky stopped and said, 'Who told you about that?'

Sam laughed. 'Read it somewhere.'

They went back outside where two stable lads were sorting out the two horses.

'You ride Marta.'

*

They headed out on a track that wound through the olive groves. The horses seemed to know the way and White just rested his hands on the pommel, the reins loose in one hand. With his other he took a soft pack of Ducados from his shirt pocket.

'How come nobody gets to you?'

'I employ a lot of locals. They're private people.'

'You employ Captain Mendez?'

'We have an understanding. To be honest, a few journos got close, we just make it difficult. Let's just say a few had bad experiences, and that's why I tend to be visible on the coast. I drip feed my appearances down there.'

Sam wondered what 'bad experiences' meant exactly.

'You know I never talk to anybody about this, and I mean anybody?'

'I'm guessing there's a reason.'

'Well, there are only two reasons I'd speak to you. One, you remember?'

'Sure, the second time I came out, the last time, did a story.'

'I meant the girl.'

'We got photos of you with that young Spanish girl, student wasn't she? Good ones, on your boat, topless.'

'Exactly. She was from a very good Catholic family, could have caused me a lot of problems, her more. We made a deal.'

'I got that Bond girl, Jessica somebody, to pose some shots with you.'

'Exactly. I haven't forgotten it. And?'

'You wouldn't take the five grand we offered, and I took that package home for your mum. Rita?'

'Yes. Which you delivered, unopened, and gave her the money anyway. And despite the fact she jabbered away to you about God knows what, you never mentioned or used it.'

'I liked her. What's number two?'

White laughed. 'You're more in the shit than me.'

'How much do you know?' asked Sam, who realised Marta needed no input from him at all.

'Well, I can read. But there must be more to it since you're down here sitting on your arse.'

'No. I'm looking for you.'

'Don't make me laugh. You haven't left your office in years.'

'They want to fire me over the Burke story,'

'But that's just one of those things, happens all the time.'

'OK then. My old editor got my daughter interested in you and the Costa del Crime. I came for her.'

'Really?'

'That came out wrong. It was the catalyst. I didn't walk across Spain for her.'

'Good. Who was the old editor?'

'Henry Thomas, Terry to everybody. You meet him?'

'No.'

As they rode, White prompted him and he told him the whole story, about Burke and his own problems.

'So the logical thing is to sign your deal tomorrow and ride off in to the sunset. I'll lend you Marta. And the hat.'

'Your turn,' said Sam, flapping at the flies. 'So come on, what happened to you?'

'From when?'

'Well I know the story up until you got here, we all do.'

'If you say so.'

'As I recall, you were all Flash Harry, then you went all Howard Hughes.'

'The penny dropped. I realised I was spending all my time with some pretty unsavoury characters. These were proper gangsters – GBH, drug dealers, the Time Bandits.'

'Who were they?'

'Those timeshare scammers who nicked people's life savings. I'd never touched anybody, and I only stole from offices, factories. I'm not saying I was Robin Hood, but I was low key.'

'You did jewellery from houses, didn't you?'

'Just once, but the media liked that side of it. That whole Raffles crap.'

'But you still ran.'

'True, but you'll have to take my word for it, I was trying to go straight. Job at Currys, studying electrical engineering at night school, business studies on Open University. I was fixing TVs and installing car radios to make ends meet.'

'Doesn't explain how you own a farm the size of Kent.'

'It's not that big. I got bored with all that nightclub bollocks very early on. I had a mate here who was a bit of a techie, so we started a business installing security systems.'

'Ironic.'

'I know, but it worked. We gave 10% to a local guy, ex-policeman. He kept people off our backs and sent us lots of work. My partner went back to England after a couple of years. I expanded into mobile phones, telecoms, then when Sky launched in '91, it just took off. We started doing home entertainment, computer systems, and then boats, shops, offices. We tied in with the developers and opened in Alicante, Mallorca and Girona. And I did property, on my own account.'

'But you still had Blanco's?'

'I needed something that people could write about – the bar was perfect. But I was a silent partner. I'd go in once in a while, dress up, do photos, then go back to ground. I kept the glitzy villa in Marbella, but I moved up this way. I hired a local PR company, and one in England, to manage what got out. We had a very well thought out plan. The whole idea was for people to get bored of me, but I fed you lot enough to keep you happy.'

'Well, it worked.' And Sam realised Katie had been right.

'And it worked with the locals. I've employed a lot of people; I do my charity work. They know what I'm really like.'

'A double life.'

'Something like that.'

Sam wondered if anybody really could lead a double life.

They'd been riding along a river and came to a spot where it widened out into a small lagoon. Under a tree were a couple of benches and a cooler box. They let the horses drink and then Chalky loosened the girths and tied them up in the shade.

'The ones we don't chuck down the mineshaft, we drown here.'

Sam thought it was a good line, but this was the guy who was responsible for his mate Pete Bolwell being nearly kicked to death because he got too close. Sam remembered his face, black and blue, the network of stitches, the missing teeth.

White popped two cold beers from the box.

'The business was great cash flow, and I put mine in property and a bunch of tech stocks. We had an American client from Palo Alto who came over for the polo at Sotogrande. He put me into good long-term stuff like Intel and Apple. Then we sold the company in 2006, so I focussed on property, but I could see that was a bubble and the Spanish economy's been under water for ages, so I got rid of all the bricks and mortar. Swiss guy looks after my investments now; I'm mostly in funds.'

'And this?'

'My wife's from Córdoba, so we always wanted to be round here. We bought this with the sale proceeds about seven years ago.'

Chalky had his boots up on the cooler box, and he lit up another Ducados.

Sam looked round and said, 'And you're going to tell me you miss Birmingham?'

'I do sometimes. My mum died last year and my dad's far too ill to travel now. Miss Villa. Mates. A pint of Banks's. All the stuff you take for granted. Freedom of choice really, I guess. Look, nobody's going to remember me as a good son, or husband, father, businessman. I'm always going to be linked to the two Ronnies, Biggs and Knight, and all those thugs down here.'

They rode on, coming to the vineyards and, beyond that, the winery itself, where White showed him the presses and the bottling plant. 'I'll get a couple of cases dropped at Frank's place, and the UK distributor will send you some.'

After another hour they got back to the house. While it was discreet, he'd noticed razor wire every time they were near a boundary and CCTV on all the buildings. A stable lad took the horses, and White took Sam to the guest house. His clothes had been laundered and laid out and his phone was on charge. There were two new plain white T-shirts and pairs of boxers, still in their El Corte Ingles bags. Sky News was on the plasma screen. He thought if he'd actually had to write something, FARMER WHITE IS A NICE BLOKE wasn't much of a headline. He had a full house – missed calls, texts, emails. But in that moment he realised he didn't need to look at any of it, left it, and turned off the TV. What couldn't wait? Then he realised what couldn't and went back. He texted Katie: 'Gotcha. With your man. Tell nobody. Not even Terry. xx'

*

The table was laid up under the wisteria-covered pergola. It looked like it could seat maybe twenty people, but just three places were laid at one end. He sat down and waited.

Chalky appeared. 'Sam, this is my wife, Sofia.'

Sam shook her hand and knew exactly who she was. You didn't forget women that beautiful or elegant, however old they were.

With just the slightest trace of an accent she said, 'Hello Sam, you remember?'

'Through a telephoto lens, yes.' He would have made the joke about her not wearing much then, but he sensed she was staying cool, not smiling at all.

'On the boat, Sofia is the reason I saw the light. We've just celebrated twenty-five years.'

'Congratulations. Weren't you a medical student?'

'I was, and went on and qualified as what you call a GP. I still do some locum work, but this place keeps us really busy.'

They sat and chatted. Chalky said, 'Every single thing on this table is from the farm. Even water from the well. The tomatoes, the lamb, the bread.'

'And the wine.'

'Of course, I thought about calling the white "El Blanco", but it's a bit obvious and would only attract more attention.'

'It's very good. Dry, fruity, bit like a soave.'

'Exactly. Same grape. 4,000 cases a year of this.'

A woman who Sofia introduced as Maria shuttled back and forth bringing food and clearing plates. It was magical. The dead calm, the light. All they could hear was the river, and occasionally the horses, far off.

At the end of the meal, Sofia said she had to do some work, and they stood up to let her go. He watched her leave. Sam knew his own marriage was a charade, but Chalky's looked very real.

Chalky shut the door to the house. They sat on the cane sofas at the other end of the terrace, with a bottle of unmarked red and two glasses in front of them. Chalky offered him a cigar and cutter. Sam got it going.

Chalky said, 'So not much of a story then, sorry.'

'Well, it is, but we haven't got a business section.'

'Nor farming, I hear.'

'Big Mac and a bottle of Blue Nun for our readers.'

Chalky leaned forward and Sam sensed the change of mood. 'Now, can we agree this is all off the record, until I say otherwise?'

He'd never broken that rule in his life. Was this a story? He could only say one thing. 'Yes. Off the record.'

Chalky put out his hand. Sam shook on it.

'Right, well, what I'm going to tell you now is more than that. It's a secret. You can't tell anybody – not Frank, your daughter, lawyers, nobody.'

'OK.'

'And you can't discuss it with my family. Say it.'

'Whatever you tell me, I will not disclose to anybody, including but not limited to your family.'

Chalky lit a match and took a while to get his cigar going. 'The British Government are never going to get me home.'

'Are you sure about that?'

'Positive.'

'Because?'

Chalky drew on his cigar, then exhaled, stretching his arms along the sofa. Then he lowered his voice. 'Because they got me out.'

'I don't understand.'

'They sprung me. MI6. It was the Firm who brought me here.'

'You're fucking kidding.'

White drew on his cigar, leaned forward, and stared him down.

'Jesus, you're not.'

He just couldn't get his head round it. He kept thinking about what Katie had written: *It's like there's some sort of pattern or control. What's real?*

'I'm lost for words.'

'Good. Are you sitting comfortably? Let's begin.'

He had no tape recorder and no pad. He needed to stop drinking and concentrate.

Chalky started. 'Once upon a time, a small time criminal learned his lesson. He confessed his sins, did his time, which he hated, went straight, got a job, learned a trade, and swore to his parents that he would never, ever be a naughty boy again. He was building a good life. Then he met some very nice men who asked him to do them a big big favour. All he had to do was break into a big house and just photograph something, not even steal anything. For twenty-five thousand big ones. Cash. And he knew they were nice men because they could prove they were MI6.'

Sam decided he would mentally count off how many things were hard to believe. That wasn't one. Terry told him MI6 did that stuff all the time. 'What Peter Wright wrote about in *Spycatcher*.'

'Exactly. That was big money then. I knew I could use it to pay the deposit on a flat and start my business. Said it was a Russian's place, mate of Gorbachev. I signed the Official Secrets Act. They gave me half up front and guaranteed me immunity and protection.'

'Then what happened?'

'Well, the intelligence services' 11th commandment is "thou shalt not get caught". It was a black bag job.'

'What's that?'

'Break in, to get intelligence. They knew the layout and the safe model, which I knew I could easily crack. The house alarm was primitive. They gave me a miniature camera. I just had to photograph any documents.'

'But you got caught.'

'Yes, but I got the safe open, took the shots, closed it. Then I heard noises and headed back to the window but they had security and they got me. I'd done what the spooks told me, though. I'd already grabbed some stuff off the desk – cash, a watch, a silver box – so they thought I was just a burglar.'

'Did they rough you up or anything?'

'No, just made me empty my pockets. They called the police who took me to the local nick. I used my one call to the lawyer they'd given me. He turned up and said it might actually take a few days to get me out. I started to worry, I had nothing in writing. So I told him I'd been caught before I opened the safe.'

'For insurance?'

'Exactly. As I sat there in the holding cell, I just got more and more pissed off. So I thought I'd keep it.'

'But you emptied your pockets. How did you do it?'

'Easy, I'd bought one of those asthma inhalers and took the insides out – it was perfect to hide the little roll of film. My plan was if I got caught I'd put the film in that and dump the camera.'

'Because nobody would ever take the inhaler off you.'

'Correct. But I didn't have time in the house, so when I closed the safe I just stuffed the camera down my Y-fronts. When I got to the nick I said I was bursting, so they took me to the loo. I made the transfer and dropped the camera in the cistern.'

'How long did they take?'

'About a week. I was panicking. I assumed it would all happen behind the scenes, with a sergeant walking in any minute and saying, "Mr White, I'm afraid there's been a terrible mistake, you're free to go." But on my first transfer, they sprung me. I was the only prisoner in the van.'

'Didn't you overpower the guard?'

'No, that was all bollocks. Spin, as you call it. I never even saw him. They put me in the back of a car with a blanket over me. Straight to Fishguard. And outside town they gave me a change of clothes and a fake passport and put me in this fully laden Volvo estate with a woman and two kids. We drove on to the ferry. Never saw her again. It was going to Bilbao so I just waited, and with about an hour to go this Joe introduced himself, and we drove off in a Seat with Spanish plates. Went to a little house in the middle of nowhere, where they briefed me and he babysat me for two weeks. They took the passport off me and he taught me to play backgammon. I got quite good. Then another guy arrived and he brought me down here.'

'Did you see Joe again?'

Chalky laughed. 'A Joe is what they call agents. He said his name was Adam, and no, never.'

'So you just got passed on?'

'Exactly. When I arrived here my only possession was that inhaler. Proper story now?'

'Well, it is. But nobody is going to believe that. Can you prove any of it?'

'I'll come to that.'

He thought about using the old trick of going to the loo and scribbling notes. But he pressed on.

'What happened to the film?'

'Stored it in a dry place, then after about three months I borrowed a studio from an English guy who did lots of pap stuff, and I developed two sets.'

'Where are they?'

'One's with my lawyer in London, with instructions if I die. The other's in a safe deposit box in a Málaga bank.'

'Anything interesting?'

'Letters, bank statements, some foreign language stuff, one list of names. Meant nothing to me. But no photos, no plans for the invasion of Poland, no pictures of headless sex.'

'Shame. So what happened when you got here?'

'The Joe who brought me down here, Jonathan Wilkins, was my handler, bit younger than me, mid-twenties. A Second Secretary based in Madrid. Clearly picked him so we'd get on. Wilko had a good cover story. Rich dad, Leicester car dealer, babysitting their villa and yacht down here. He did odd jobs. First guy to do karaoke down here. To be honest he seemed to like the playboy life even more than me. I think it was his first proper overseas posting – spoke good Spanish, played tennis and golf, seriously fit bloke. He could charm the birds out of the trees, straight into bed, without passing Go.'

Sam was certain Wilkins or Wilko wasn't in the file. He needed Katie to check that.

'How long did he stay?'

'The plan was simple. The Firm were going to square it with the Russians and the police. The last thing the Russians needed was a trial in the UK. I'd give myself up after six months, come back to a trial where there'd be a problem with evidence or whatever, get a suspended sentence, pick up where I left off.'

'But?'

'Two things. They didn't really get stuck into organised crime until later, in the mid-nineties, but they wanted to infiltrate the exiles down here for intel and they weren't getting anywhere. I turned up like the prodigal. I'd spent my twenties in and out of places like Wandsworth and Belmarsh, with some guys who now lived here, and the ones who came on holiday. I was perfect.'

'So the Firm started using you.'

'Exactly. And secondly, frankly, I was bloody good at it.'

'And they wanted you to carry on.'

'Well, it was three things really. I also just loved it – you have no idea of the buzz. I had a great lifestyle, my parents came over, and I was building a legit business. Why go back?'

'Logical.'

'I'd been going straight back home for four years or so, but it was tough. Spain was giving me all I'd ever wanted and more.'

'Who was the business partner?'

'Wilko, my handler. He got moved on after about two or three years. But blimey did he know electronics and security, just mind-boggling. We went fifty-fifty. I put his share in a nominee company, but he was low key, the boys didn't know he was my partner, and I sent his annual dividend to the Cayman Islands.'

'Did he tell his bosses?'

'The case officers back home? Don't know, didn't ask. All I knew was I was having the time of my life, and they kept sending me more of what they called clients. The Firm was minding my back and funding my business; I was living it up, girls, parties. And Wilko was categorically my best mate, he didn't want to leave.'

'But he did?'

'Suddenly. It's very weird when somebody close to you just walks out. You've probably never had it.'

'Actually, I have.'

'Oh yes, sorry. Justine or whatever. Anyway, somebody else had turned up. Spook called Hardy Cobbold. Anything came up, it went through Cobbold, then after two years of him, others.'

'And you were never tempted to tell Wilko or Cobbold about the stuff from the safe?'

'They seemed to have just forgotten about it, moved on – they'd paid me the balance for the job. I thought it might piss them off. Sleeping dogs.'

'And you were now a proper asset.'

'Full on. A proper Joe.'

'But you kept sending the money?'

'To Wilko? Yes, and the proceeds of the sale. Must be just sitting there.'

'How much?'

'A few million.'

'And that was that?'

'I'd do odd jobs down on the coast mostly, I had the perfect cover. I'd signed the Official Secrets Act, and they were still subbing me, so I was virtually on the payroll. Can you imagine how valuable we were to them? We bugged and followed all sorts – Saudis, Russians, Americans, some Brits, even the Spanish – and they taught me loads of stuff. It was great fun at the start.'

'You'll be telling me next you kept a diary.'

'More a log. And photos.'

Sam knew, if verifiable, this could take it to another level.

'But coming up to ten years in I was getting bored. It's why I sold the business – they couldn't stop me, and it got rid of my cover story. It was great in the early days with Wilko, but Cobbold and the others weren't much fun.'

'So if this story about the government finally getting you back is bullshit, why am I here?'

'You're the ace journalist, you tell me.'

'I'm just a disgraced hack.'

'Come on.'

'All right. You think in the age of whistleblowers, Snowden and Assange, that this might come out anyway?'

'Even under freedom of information. That's one.'

Sam had worked it out. 'So week one is CHALKY WHITE SUPERSPY and then the world goes mad, and by the following Sunday it's CHALKY WHITE SUPERGRASS.'

'And every criminal and their kids are after me and my family. I'd be a dead man walking.'

'Not to mention the secret service of about half a dozen of our so-called allies.'

'Correct. How would you like your tea, Mr White? Milk, sugar, Polonium-210?'

'So you need to manage it.'

'Exactly. That's where you come in.'

'And you need the Firm on side too, and ideally that means Wilko. And you have no idea who Wilko is, or where he is, or if he's even alive.'

'Ah, you haven't lost it. That certainly was the case ... ' Chalky got up and went into the house. He came back and dropped a *Daily Telegraph* on Sam's lap. Sam looked at the circled article on page five: SPYMASTER HEADS TO NUMBER TEN. It was clearly based on a press release. The photo had no credit. A man was standing next to a uniformed general and a senior police officer. Next to them, in his dark suit and tie, he looked every inch the typical senior civil servant. Could that really be the playboy Wilko? The narrative was dull, a succession of foreign postings and admin roles. He noticed Spain was not on the list.

'He's about to take over as Chairman of the Joint Intelligence Committee. And of course he's not Jonathan or Jon Wilkins.'

'Sir Leonard Fox, age 53.'

'First time he's put his head above the parapet in over twenty-five years. I recognised the photo, first one I've seen since he was down here.'

'Big job, isn't it?'

'Massive. He's still a member of the Firm but he's seconded, and it's high profile. This is part of the Cabinet Office. It means he meets the PM on a regular basis. The committee's them and MI5, GCHQ, the CIA, everybody.'

'The words skeleton and cupboard come to mind.'

'Wilko, sorry Fox, is not a civil servant, he's a spy. And I don't mean a cryptographer. A proper one, like in the movies.'

'And you're the embarrassing cousin they don't want to talk about.'

'Got it in one. Very good.'

Chalky topped up Sam's glass.

'I'm OK.'

He laughed. 'You're worried you'll forget it all. I do like you, Sam. Have a drink, we'll do it all again. You can tape it.'

He took a sip, put down his glass and pressed on. 'How the hell did you keep all this a secret?'

'Well, they do it for a living. Very simple in my case, I didn't tell anybody. And I mean nobody. My lawyer, parents, Sofia, the children.'

'Sofia doesn't know?'

'She fell in love with me for what she thought I was. She accepted it. I didn't want to burden her.'

'So why now?'

Chalky pointed at Fox's face, staring out at them both from the newspaper. 'I've done exactly the same as him, served my country loyally for nearly thirty years. He's a knight of the realm, a public figure. I'm still a fugitive. I want Sofia, my children, to know the truth. My mum died not knowing; I don't want my dad to as well. I want to go home, on my terms.'

Sam had heard the slight tremble in his voice and said, 'Are they sympathetic?'

'A couple, but not really.'

'Is it hard to talk about?'

Chalky exhaled. 'Very weird. Today, with you, I feel like I've pulled the pin out of the hand grenade and I can't put it back in.'

*

Sam went back to his room, took out his laptop, and started writing. It took him just over an hour to get it down. Then he started writing up the earlier stuff when they'd been on the tour of the farm. Everything told him that Chalky was telling the truth. But he had also thought Burke was a fraud and that Justine loved him. If these things came in threes, he was in trouble. He needed to talk to Terry but knew he couldn't. He was about to call Katie but looked around the room. Would Chalky bug it? Surely not.

Still, he went outside. 'Can you talk?'

'Yes. You still with him?'

'At his farm. You can't tell anybody, not even Frank or Terry. I need you to start doing some proper deep background, get on the database, focus on the time from when he was arrested for about three years. How are you covering this at the office?'

'I told them it's for my thesis.'

'Good girl, stick with that. Look for known associates. Go through picture libraries, see who's with him a lot.'

'Anyone in particular?'

'Jonathan Wilkins. Always known as Wilko. Have to go, call waiting.'

'Love you.'

'Love you, too.'

Sam switched calls. Frank got straight to the point. 'Have you found White yet?'

It felt weird lying to Frank; they had no secrets. 'No, I think I'm losing my touch. Stop fishing. When I've got something to tell you, I will.'

A white lie was OK with Frank. Sam said, 'Went riding today, met Lord Lucan, on Shergar.'

'Can't sell that; too far-fetched. When you back?'

'Don't know, that lawyer Kenyon's on my deal. He sorting yours?'

'Yes. Maybe we have more time now, with the Clare thing. Shit only happens on Sundays. They seem keener to get yours done.'

'Who was that freelancer down here, had his own photo agency, did everybody's stuff?'

'Jez Clifton. El Snappa, we called him. Good but very tricky. I couldn't stand him.'

'That's the guy. Got any contact details?'

'He must be retired or dead now. I'll text you the last number I had for him.'

Sam said, 'I'll call you tomorrow. Promise.'

He knew he had to do two things: get Katie to validate Wilko and the early years, then get to him now.

*

Sam rang Gary. 'There's a guy called Sir Leonard Fox... '

'On loan from the Firm to chair JIC at Number 10.'

'One day I'll tell you something you don't know.'

'Unlikely. Go on.'

'Any way we could find him, get to him? This week?'

'Sure, we can find where he lives pretty easily. His movements we'll have to work on. I see you sorted the bike.'

'Where is it?'

'At some race meeting at Jerez now. There's a great shot of it in the pits with Pedrosa looking at it. That'll go viral.'

*

He went online and found the Clifton website. He'd never met him but he knew the type. He kept guys like him all over the world going. Guys who fed the tabs with what they wanted, from there to St Tropez, from LA to Cape Town. Red carpets. Boats. Slebs. Suntans. Tits. On the homepage was his shot in a *Mail* article on Marbella by Piers Morgan under the headline BUTLINS FOR BILLIONAIRES. The site was pretty basic, with no searchable archive. It had a number that went to a dual language message telling him to call during office hours, which it gave as Tuesday to Friday, ten to four, which hardly put it at the leading edge in the digital age.

At about eight, Chalky came by. 'Sorry, I forgot we're going to mass, then having a late dinner with some friends. I don't think we can risk taking you, and it'll all be Spanish anyway.'

'I'm fine, got plenty to do.'

'By the way, I meant to tell you the room's not bugged.'

'I didn't think it was.'

Chalky laughed. 'So why you making all your calls outside? See you tomorrow.'

Sam was impressed by how he'd caught him out. Was that tradecraft? Sam now knew he was up against an invisible, moving and anonymous enemy. Who had been after him for months? He had to know. He hated doing it, but a process of elimination looked the only way. He dialled the number.

'Roland Relton.'

'Roly, it's Sam Plummer. I need a favour.'

'Is this a wind-up?'

'No. I just want to know if it was you who put the woman on to Clare, back in March.'

There was a pause. 'What, you mean sold it on after your Katie and Terry bullied me into a ceasefire?'

'Yes. And you can forget the fifty grand.'

'Good story, but scout's honour, wasn't us. And I don't know who did, and I wasn't offered it.'

'OK, thanks.'

'By the way, your kids have got balls. And if Felix's are bigger than his sister's, he must be walking bow-legged.'

Sam laughed. 'I'll tell them.'

'And I made the deal with her, not you. We're transferring the money today.'

'Thanks.'

'You really need me to tell you whose fingerprints are all over it?'

'To be honest, no. Think I've got it now.'

# CHAPTER 20

**MONDAY 7th July – DAY 10**

***Daily Express*: 86 DEGREE HEATWAVE IS ON THE WAY**

***The Sun*: VIP PAEDOS. ABUSE OF POWER: TEBBIT TELLS OF MP COVER-UP**

***Daily Mail*: DJOKOVIC CROWNED CHAMPION**

Lady Sarah Burke sat at the kitchen table, drinking tea and drawing on her Silk Cut. Even though they were back at the family house in deepest Wiltshire, she was still not happy. Sarah knew now she shouldn't have married him. It was hard to tell who was more bored in the marriage. He'd lasted six months until he was unfaithful with a Delta stewardess called Megan he met on a flight to LA. She'd lasted a bit longer but was still annoyed that she'd done something so clichéd as bonking the milkman.

Burke sat opposite her, working his way through the papers, while Julian Mortlock paced around.

She said, 'Seriously, how much longer is this going to go on, Julian?'

Mortlock sat down. 'I'm so sorry, Sarah.'

'Of course you are.'

'Look, I know it's a bore. I've done a deal, if you're OK with it of course, for a general photocall at ten. So you've an hour to get ready, then an interview with ITN, not live, and then they'll all go. I've told them there's nothing else.'

'What about the ones up in the woods?'

'There's nobody up in the woods, I promise.'

Sarah lit another cigarette from the last, dropping the stub down the waste disposal. 'I'll go get ready. Downtrodden or upbeat?'

'Country housewife look, I think. Shame we haven't got the dogs or kids,' said Mortlock.

'It is, isn't it, Julian?'

After she left, Mortlock shut the door. He buttered a piece of cold toast. 'All fine. Everybody's happy with the numbers yesterday. More stuff with the twins this week – bit serious, bit fun. You're shortlisted for *Question Time*, and the *Telegraph* are doing a profile on Saturday. We need to spend Wednesday in town doing one-to-ones. I think we should push the stuff for the Americans, good money there. I'm trying for a flying visit this week to do a one-off on CNN with Piers Morgan.'

'And what about Katia?'

'Everybody's just accepted that she's in Kiev having treatment. Be pretty ghoulish to track her down. We've given them all some more photos and good quotes, so they're happy.'

'We close to settling with the paper?'

'Terms are agreed, just the lawyers doing their stuff.'

'And Plummer and the other guy?'

'Frank Chappell. Signing their deals this afternoon. The story about Sam's wife didn't help him.'

'Where did that come from?'

'No idea.'

Burke's naivety staggered Mortlock. This man was supposed to be shaping the Government's media policy. It was perfect that Burke was seen as media-savvy, and thought he was, but in reality he had no idea what really went on or how it worked.

The lack of respect was mutual. While one part of Burke was thrilled at the money and the way Mortlock had pulled it all together, the other still found that, despite the effortless charm and shared background, he represented all that he hated about tabloid journalism. In his brave new world, he would clip their wings.

*

When Sam wandered over to the house, nobody was around, so he took a coffee back and sat at the table on the terrace, reading his marked up termination agreement. He needed time to think today. He'd laughed at Terry's description of the crossroads as a Faustian pact. But the fact was he had to make a choice. Lomax the devil, his offer tangible and bankable. The other road, Chalky's story, that was – the more he thought about it – the best he'd ever had. And right now he was certain he was the only journalist in the world who had it. The deal was the bird in the hand; Chalky was still a flight of fancy. It was true, Burke was a mess and had ruined his life. People only remembered your last story, and Chalky would trump everything. But he couldn't have both. There simply wasn't time.

*

Sam got back from a run through the olive groves and saw Frank had texted a mobile number for Jez Clifton, which he rang. He got an answer on the third attempt.

'Clifton.'

'Jez, it's Sam Plummer. I need to see you.'

'Get in the queue tomorrow. Ring for an appointment.'

'Jez, I really need your help.'

'Clearly. Ring the office tomorrow. We're closed Mondays. Talk to Emilia.' He hung up.

He knew he had to keep his options open, so he rang his lawyer. 'Hi Francis, have you sent the mark-up to them yet?'

'Went this morning, Mr Plummer. Told them comments on the tax would be later. I thought I was on a go-slow?'

'Call me Sam. Change of plan. Do a sensible final mark-up. Tell them I'm flying back tomorrow afternoon and it remains subject to my comments. Tell them I'll do a call on any outstanding points, and that I want to sign at four on Wednesday, at your offices.'

'OK, I'll do that.'

'Be very friendly so they think it's all on track. And tell them it has to be Donald Whelan who comes and signs – that's non-negotiable. And it's the same for Frank. Just send me an email or text this number.'

He knew if it became a game, he'd have to play it with Donald. And he still hadn't figured out whose side he was on.

*

He lay on the bed just to check his emails and fell asleep, shocked to wake up four hours later. He had a swim and an outdoor cold shower to get him going. Outside, Chalky was back and by his Jeep on the phone. As Sam walked over, Chalky said, 'It's for you,' and handed him the phone.

Sam was puzzled but took it and said, 'Hello?'

'Sam, it's Jez Clifton, sorry about earlier.'

He looked at Chalky who just shrugged his shoulders.

'Six too early tomorrow?'

'I can do six,' said Sam, while Chalky nodded.

'You'll want to get away before Barry Harrison arrives. I'll get out what you need.'

The alarms bells were ringing. Clifton seemed by nature an unfriendly guy, and now he had joined Katie and Gary in knowing what he was doing.

'What time is he there?'

'Nine, then someone from the *Sun* at ten and some agency guy after that.'

'Appreciate it. See you tomorrow morning.'

Sam gave Chalky his phone. 'How does he know what I want?'

Chalky lit a Ducados. 'Because I told him.'

'Shit. Do you trust him?'

'Sure, why not?'

Sam didn't like him being almost blasé about it. 'He's seeing Barry Harrison, who works for Mortlock.'

'Really? Come on, let's go.'

They got in the Jeep and set off, driving on in silence for a while.

'I'm not happy, Chalky, this could blow it.'

'And ruin your exclusive?'

It was below the belt but a fair shot. Sam had known the story for 24 hours. Chalky had lived it for 24 years. It was his property.

'Sam, it's all about control.'

'You mean the Firm controlling you?'

'And who I control.'

The penny dropped. 'Oh, God, you own Jez Clifton.'

'Basically, yes. Think about it, every story from down here is picture-led. He controls supply. I was in surveillance, and so's he. Every story about me is about the pictures – girls, white suits, nightclubs, B-listers, bling, boats. So we worked together. Profitable for him, useful for me. Every newspaper used him because he got the best stuff. He didn't know it, but a lot of his stuff was for the Firm – he had perfect cover for sticking a camera in somebody's face. Anybody else turned up, they had a bad time.'

'You warned them off.'

'Let's just say it was a lot easier if you went through Jez.'

Chalky pulled over on the dirt track and turned off the ignition. 'Sam, we need to get something straight here.'

'What?'

'If you want to take your deal and forget this, that's fine. I value your advice anyway.'

'I appreciate that.'

'But you've got to stop this paranoia. I have given you the story. I trust you.'

'It's just... I don't know. I don't feel in control.'

'Well, you're not. It's my story. You're in control of your destiny, your deal. This is mine and I'd like you to come along.'

'Understood.'

The more he learned, the more he thought of Katie's notes, the media strategy. 'So who planned all that media side?'

'Not sure. They clearly knew it really well. I always knew which journos to trust, who to feed stuff to.'

'Interesting.'

'They came up with the whole plan. Me going to the coast occasionally and showing off, living it large, then disappearing again. I told Clifton what to drip feed, who to help.'

Sam was surprised but guessed it fitted. He remembered the odd conversation he'd had with Chalky back then, and how business-like he was. He needed to talk to Terry; he was the one who understood that world.

'I've got to ask you something.'

'Shoot.'

'You nearly killed my friend Pete Bolwell.'

Chalky laughed.

'I saw him, he was a mess. It's not funny.'

'I was fond of Bolly, he liked a party. But he fell in with some bad guys here – the worst. What do you have in common with him, apart from journalism and partying?'

'Well, he likes the women.'

'No. You both like married women. And when they're married to criminals and you shag them, it's a very bad career move. I found out, when I got there, they'd beaten the shit out of him and had him strung up by the ankles, naked. The guy, Colombian, I won't tell you who, was going to cut his cock and balls off, stuff them in his mouth, then let him bleed to death. It's what they do to rapists in their country.'

'Jesus. What did you do?'

'It doesn't matter, but we walked out. Well, actually, I carried him out.'

'You went alone?'

'You remember he went missing for a week? I kept him in a private hospital up here. I had to make sure I was the first one to speak to him when he came round. I made it clear that if he said who'd done it, he was dead, so blaming me was no bad thing. But he could never say I rescued him. It warned others off and I got more street cred down here.'

'We reported it as a mugging but all assumed you were to be avoided.'

'Clever, eh? I had to keep my public profile as "Raffles the gentleman thief" but make you lot and the local thugs think I was not to be messed with.'

'And Bolly's never breathed a word.'

'Would you? And he never will. Not after what he saw.'

He started the car. Sam knew that was the end of it.

*

At the vineyard, the table was set outside for dinner, under a sprawling elm tree. Sam was surprised to see maybe twenty people there, with Chalky's family and Sam at one end. A pig was on a spit, all the cava and wine in unlabelled bottles.

Chalky and the boys seemed pretty open, but Sofia clearly wasn't. Over dinner they talked mostly about Sam's plight, which Sofia and the boys seemed to find amusing, until he explained the honeytrap… which they found hysterical. It felt terrible making light of something that was hurting him, but he needed their trust and it seemed to bring them together.

After dinner he found himself alone with Sofia. She said, 'I'm not quite sure why you're here. He doesn't ever talk to journalists.'

'I think he's amused by me being in bigger trouble than him.'

'Well, you're not. You're deciding whether or not to accept a big pay-off. Chalky's facing being dragged back to spend ten years in a prison cell. It's what we all live with. Every minute of every day. So?'

He couldn't tell, but he felt he'd been invited.

'I didn't betray you twenty years ago.'

'You still got a story, it was just with another girl.'

'I didn't betray Chalky's trust then, and I wouldn't now.'

'Trust. You expect me to accept that from a working journalist?'

'But I'm not.'

'A journalist? Or working?'

'Fair enough. Well, I'm not working, but I'd like to think that I'll always be a journalist.'

He sensed her relax slightly. 'I'm sorry if I seem angry. It's impossible to know who to trust.'

'In my own way, I know what you mean.'

She seemed to move on. 'It's awful. Mainly because the man I know is a good man, good husband, good father. I believe he's an honest man. I married the man on the run, the boys were born into it. It's tougher for them.'

Sam realised how bizarre this was, that she had been with this man for over twenty-five years, yet he was the one that knew the truth. And that she was right.

'Sam, do you think they'll get him back this time?'

'I'm afraid I'm not a lawyer or a civil servant, so I can't tell you. All the Gibraltar tension with the boats probably helps him a little. But if it really is the British Government's last chance, maybe they'll push for it. It's good PR on law and order.'

'That's not very reassuring.'

'Sorry, the bottom line is I simply don't know.' At least that was the truth. Sort of.

# CHAPTER 21

**TUESDAY 8th July – DAY 11**

***Daily Telegraph*: YOU WON'T FLY IF YOUR PHONE'S FLAT**

***Independent*: SCOTTISH YES VOTE WOULD BE WORSE THAN BANKING CRISIS**

***The Sun*: PAGE 3 SAVED MY LIFE**

Gary had cleared immigration at Chisinau just after midnight. Customs ignored him. He'd been on Monday's last Air Moldova flight from Bucharest, having got there on Tarom Air from Heathrow. He knew he'd probably have to leave Odessa in a hurry, and crossing the border back into Moldova made the most sense if it all went wrong.

Damir had got a local guy to meet him at the airport. He gave him the keys to a battered old Toyota Land Cruiser and told him insurance was in the glove box and false Ukrainian plates were in with the spare wheel if he needed to run. The TomTom he always travelled with showed 175km, and 2 hours 23 minutes. The border at Kichurhian was at about halfway.

Arriving at crossings in the middle of the night usually worked best. Tired, bored, junior guards, and no queues. He crossed without needing any birdwatching diversions. He found a lorry park on the outskirts of Odessa and went to sleep.

*

The alarm woke Sam at four. Chalky had told him to pack everything and that the boys would get the bike back to Frank's when the coast was clear. He was showered and packed when Maria came with a coffee and some scrambled eggs.

Chalky was on the steps kissing Sofia goodbye. He had a battered canvas satchel over his shoulder and a big leather holdall. Where the hell was he going? Sofia was in her dressing gown and waved an unsmiling goodbye to Sam as they got into the pick-up. She looked like she'd had no sleep, and she'd definitely been crying.

Just before six they were on an industrial estate near Malaga airport, driving steadily through the long line of drab offices and units. It felt like the outskirts of Slough. Chalky pointed and said, 'That's one of mine, home entertainment – does all the Sky stuff and sound systems, villas, boats, hotels. Here we go.'

They came up on an unmarked, two-storey grey box.

'Doesn't believe in advertising then.'

An old, dark green XJ6 was parked outside.

'No need. That's Jez's. Can't see anybody else.' They cruised past and, at the end of the road, turned round and came back, but it was deserted. The way he handled the car and looked around reminded him of Gary. Did they learn this stuff somewhere? Chalky parked at the back, reversing into a bay.

Chalky said, 'Just so you know, some of Jez's stuff is what I wanted kept quiet. Some Wilko.'

They went to a door with a small sign saying Clifton Photo Agency, where Jez met them. They all shook hands and went up to his office. This was clearly a challenge in itself for big Jez, out of breath after one flight. He wasn't just fat, he was grey. Sam looked at the drinks cabinet and stacked duty free cartons of 200 Senior Service. 'How long you been here, Jez?'

'Not sure what you mean, but all night and thirty-one years.'

It certainly smelled like the first bit was true. Clifton really was as nondescript as his office and most picture editors he'd ever met. 'So, Sam. Still enjoying the ladies, I see.'

Chalky said, 'Shut up Jez, that's not funny.'

'I hear you've got stuff on me.'

'I have. And I've never sold it.'

'And he's not selling it now either. I told Jez we wanted everything that features the two guys that I worked with in those early days. Wilkins and then Cobbold,' said Chalky.

'Chalk and cheese, those two,' said Jez at the window, letting in some fresh air and half closing the blinds. 'Can't be too careful.' He had his laptop connected to the big screen.

Sam could tell there was no way Clifton knew anything about Chalky's double life or these guys.

'Wilkins first.'

'You have to remember he was camera shy,' said Chalky. 'His dad was rich, he had a big trust fund. Being seen with me and a load of villains was a very bad idea. And the last thing he needed was his dad knowing he'd gone into business with me. So we helped him stay out of sight.'

Jez laughed. 'Didn't stop you though.'

Sam said, 'So you took pictures, for insurance.'

'In my nature, and Jez's. Leopard, spots.'

Jez scrolled through. 'We got pictures, we just never used them, and I warned the other guys off. I could always get them something better than a spoilt rich kid.'

Wilkins was in every shot. Bars, boats, pools, parties, the beach. All linen, pastels and Ray-Bans.

Sam looked at them as any good editor would. 'Not bad, but they just make him somebody on the Costa having fun. Doesn't even prove you know him, just that you were in the same place.'

Jez got up and said to Chalky, 'Shall I?'

He nodded.

Jez went to the safe in the corner.

'One of ours, nobody can break into that.'

Jez opened it and came back with an A4 envelope. 'Maybe, but they live in a safe deposit box in town normally.'

Sam started flicking through the photos. He'd seen loads of it in his time, mostly unusable. A lot was clearly covert surveillance, some grainy, some black and white. Some famous. Some not. The most common theme was naked flesh. Sam went through them one by one, holding them up for explanation.

'We did a fair bit of coke then. You almost had to, to fit in.'

'That's me and him with a Moroccan guy called Lotfi, heroin and illegal immigrants.'

'That's coming out of the bank where he paid all the money in.'

'Bloody hell, what are these?' said Sam

'Before I met Sofia, thank God. Hidden camera at the Marbella Club. Just got out of hand.'

'Is that... ?'

'Yes, last contract. At Fulham, or QPR. The four girls were in from Norway, shooting some vodka commercial.'

'And this?'

It was a close-up of Wilkins at the airport in a dark suit. Jez said, 'We always had someone at the airport. Notice anything?'

Sam picked up the magnifier from the desk and studied it. 'Handmade suit. Rolex. BA flight. Copy of the *Times*. Nobody famous at check-in.'

Clifton smiled. 'Losing your touch, Sam?'

Sam tossed the photo on the desk. 'He's wearing a wedding ring.'

'I'm impressed. Only time I ever saw it. Next time I saw him, I looked – there was a very faint white mark, soon went in the sun.'

'And Hardy Cobbold?'

Jez gave him another envelope. As he looked through them he said, 'After the Lord Mayor's Show.'

'Sadly no party animal,' said Chalky.

Sam knew why straightaway. Cobbold was coming out of a bar with a man, arms linked. Sam held it up. 'Friend of Dorothy?'

'Explained everything, really. That's him with some waiter he picked up. Pretty harmless. We got loads of that stuff.'

'Don't think gay guy is much of a story.'

Sam wanted to add, 'Certainly not in the Firm,' but knew he couldn't. 'Can I keep these?'

'They're your copies, Sam. And the stuff on the screen. Jez'll email you the file. Just don't share it.'

Sam went back through them. 'Who's that guy, he's in a few – the one who looks like Super Mario?'

'Hector González, a pro at the Marbella tennis club – the only guy who Wilko couldn't beat. Known as?' prompted Chalky, with a grin.

'I'm going for Speedy,' said Sam.

'Correct, which was ironic considering I never saw him break a sweat. Jez, have you got that tennis shot?'

Jez put a shot up on the screen of a tennis four at the net. 'This was a pro-celeb tennis match.'

'That's Vitas Gerulaitis, been retired then for a couple of years.'

'Very good, lot of the pros then came down for the little tournament. Hard to believe I was the celeb, but Wilko had coached me. I was quite solid.'

'He wasn't called Speedy because of his tennis,' said Jez.

Chalky said, 'He was everybody's favourite dealer. Always had the best gear, best rates. Could get you whatever you wanted. He hung out with me and Wilko a lot.'

They heard a car outside. Jez went to the window and looked through the blinds. 'Harrison's early.'

Sam said, 'No surprise. What will you give him?'

'Give? Nothing. I'm selling to him. He'll want some stuff on you. I won't sell, don't worry.'

'Hang on, won't that look odd? Why not give him something?'

'Let's see what I've got.' He started searching.

'Here you go.'

Sam looked at the montage of shots of him with a leggy blonde.

Chalky said, 'Christ she's hot, you horny bastard. Who's she?'

'Tell him, Jez.'

'That's Sam's wife, Clare.'

Chalky laughed. 'She looks like Sharon Stone.'

Sam knew it was true. 'Tell Harrison it is. It's one of those stupid rumours that's knocking around anyway. Give him the ones that look like it could be.'

'Done.'

*

They thanked Jez, left through the back door, and drove off without seeing Harrison.

'Tell me about the guy Speedy.'

'I think Wilko used him to get to people, information. Find their weak spots.'

'Drugs and tennis, good mix.'

'Girls, too – he was always in demand, fantastic guy. He was at Columbia University I think, with Vitas, played Davis Cup for Mexico. He knew all that era, Muster, Wilander.'

'Be good in the story, fun pictures. You stayed in touch?'

'Not exactly. He's dead.'

'When?'

'He just disappeared, back then, into thin air. He'd been hanging around a lot with this Egyptian guy, nasty piece of work called Wally, Waleed Khalifa, who we all thought was controlling drugs coming in, mostly from Tripoli. Never saw him over here again, but Speedy just vanished. His car was found outside his place. Inside was his passport, money. He didn't pack or say anything to his girlfriend.'

'Did Wilko check?'

'He tried but no record of a flight, nobody had seen him. Everybody assumed Wally had him taken out and that he was probably fish food. Very sad, great guy. What are you thinking?'

He needed to feed this all to Katie, see if she could find something.

'Nothing. Where we going now?'

'Do you play golf?'

'Well, yes, but I haven't got time, really.'

'Of course you have. Relax.'

Up to now he'd gone with the flow, but this was getting ridiculous.

As they drove, Sam texted Katie to research Speedy González and Waleed Kalifa, giving her the headlines. Twenty minutes later they drove into Las Brisas Golf Club. Chalky waved at the security guard, drove up past the clubhouse to the far end of the practice ground and parked. Nacho was there, his helmet off, his trials bike on its stand. He came over and dropped the tailgate, taking out a plank. As they took out their bags, Nacho started the bike and rode it up on to the flatbed, then tied it down.

'Where are the golf clubs?'

Chalky looked at his watch. 'Here in a minute.'

Nacho embraced his father. If there was any emotion, they kept it hidden. He drove off, leaving them alone.

Sam stood there with his arms folded. 'Is this more *Challenge Anneka* bollocks?'

Chalky was looking past him. 'Actually, you're very warm. Look.'

Sam turned round and saw a light low in the sky, then heard the sound of the helicopter. It came in over the trees, touching down but staying running. Chalky got in the front, Sam the back. As they climbed Sam unhooked the headphones.

'Hear me, Sam?'

'Roger.'

'Can't fly out of Málaga, it's a zoo. All the golf courses have pads and landing rights, all the local rich boys do this.'

'Where are we going?'

'Granada, about an hour, plenty of time. Enjoy the view.'

*

Gary stopped at McDonald's for breakfast then made his way to the spot where he'd taken all the photos. He scanned the property with his scope.

It looked pretty bare and uninviting now with the sunbeds and parasols stored, all the shutters closed, under a grey morning sky. The tennis net had gone and the lawn badly needed a mow. There was one car, an old Ford pick-up, in the drive. They'd moved some of the large potted palms, so the view of the pool was partly obstructed. He recognised the one security guy, sitting smoking on the garden wall. After a while he saw the other one, coming out helping a cleaner with black rubbish bags for the bins.

He knew it was a long shot and risky. And Damir had said, 'Be careful, these guys don't take prisoners.' Just being taken prisoner would be a result. This was Ukraine. Whether he got out or not, it would be a diplomatic incident either way.

*

They set off east along the coast. Chalky pointed out the sights. The Marbella Club where they'd taken so many photos. The high-rise horrors of Torremolinos. Countless golf courses. Once they got past Málaga they cut north inland. Flying over open country, Sam wondered who or what they were going to see in Granada. Ten minutes out, he realised the answer was probably nobody. He heard the pilot talking to Air Traffic Control, and in the distance he could see commercial airliners lined out on their final approach.

Federico Garcia Airport had a single runway running east-west. They came straight in from the south and landed at the east end of the terminal on one of two white H marks painted in circles. About twenty small planes were parked up, mostly props and just one small jet. Its door was open, a pilot standing there in a short-sleeved, white shirt.

Sam and Chalky carried their bags the short distance to a small, single-storey office. Sam's curiosity was aroused but balanced by the growing irritation. Why couldn't Chalky just tell him and drop the *Magical Mystery Tour* stuff?

Chalky said, 'Just act normal. I'm Dennis Mortimer.'

'Of course you are. And who the fuck am I, Peter Shilton?'

'Act normal. No, forget that. Relax.'

In the office they were met by another pilot in uniform who introduced herself as Rebecca. They put their bags through the X-ray machine. A policeman glanced at their passports, compared them to a manifest, then waved them through, all the time smoking and holding an animated conversation on a landline. He didn't even look at them.

*

They walked out and across to the jet. Rebecca introduced Simon, the co-pilot. The Learjet 40 had six seats, four facing each other and two behind. Sam sat facing backwards, across from and opposite Chalky, who said, 'Only way to fly,' and put his feet up on the empty seat opposite.

'Dennis Mortimer? The Villa player?'

'In joke.' Chalky passed him the passport.

Sam flicked through it, looking at the various stamps. The oldest was for Morocco two years ago. 'You been to England on this?'

'Not until now.'

'What?'

'I'm going to England.'

'You really are mad.'

'Now or never.'

Sam realised that was probably true. He handed it back. 'Whose plane is this?'

'English friend of mine, lives in Marrakesh. Wouldn't risk a foreign plane. The helicopter's a mate's over here.'

'Where are we going exactly?'

'Well, we are not going anywhere. Too risky putting you on a manifest to the UK. Ironically you're the hot one.' Chalky fished in his satchel and produced an easyJet boarding pass. 'We're dropping you in Asturias.'

'Where's that?'

'Nice little airport, serves Oviedo on the north coast. You're on the 13.15 to Gatwick.'

'Oh, great.'

Sam looked at the easyJet boarding pass. So they'd been in his room, or got his passport details some other way. It wasn't worth making an issue about it now.

'I got you speedy boarding. And seat 1C.'

'That'll make all the difference.'

'I'm going into Oxford. Very low key there, I'm told. I'll meet you in London. I need to give you another mobile number. I know Fox is in the UK, and I know where he lives.'

'He'll turn you in, won't he?'

'Maybe. Maybe not.'

'Where are you staying?'

'I'll do B and Bs or pubs for cash.'

Sam thought about it. 'Best would be Terry's place. What about a car?'

'The airport fixed me a driver.'

'Don't do that, cancel it. I'll get Gary to sort one.'

Sam was always amazed how steeply and quickly they climbed; he reckoned landing to wheels up in Granada had been a twenty minute turnaround at most.

'One thing I don't understand, Sam, why not sign your deal, take the money, and let somebody else front this, pull the strings behind the scenes?'

'I can't. The deal's generous, but onerous. I sign now but see no money for three months. I have to tell them where I am, no contact with anybody, and the penalties are really heavy. This is one of those gardening leave deals where they actually want me to be in the garden. If I become what's called a bad leaver I lose all my share options, everything. That's millions.'

'But you want it all?'

'And a deal's a deal. I have to at least try.'

Chalky looked out along the wing. 'Well, let's hope this isn't the biggest mistake of my life, too. Ten years in Belmarsh is not on my bucket list. You're angry I didn't ask your advice.'

'This is reckless. No, it's lunacy.'

'You'd have tried to talk me out of it.'

'If they catch you, it's open season.'

'OK, here's the thing. I made it pretty clear to my London handlers that I wanted out. We went backwards and forwards, they seemed sympathetic, but it was taking forever.'

'How long has this been going on?'

'Two or three years. You'll appreciate that some think the Firm's a lifetime commitment. Then finally I had to meet a Joe in Madrid, late last year. I thought it was good news. But he was very junior, off-hand, just said they had a new Chief coming in, Sir Christopher Lines, and it was all on hold. I was really pissed off.'

'So what happened?'

'This was the weird bit. About a month later I got a call from a spook called Archie Hunter, who I'd never met.'

'How do you know he was for real?'

'Standard, short, coded exchange. Told me it was a one-to-one. Sounded old school, said he was sorry that there had been no action but Lines was taking a firm line on all this, and they'd review it in five years. It made no sense. But the next bit was interesting. What he said was, "So please just keep your head down, whatever you do don't rock the boat, or we might have to take action." And guess who Archie Hunter is.'

'No idea.'

'First Villa captain to lift the FA Cup, in 1884.'

'Coincidence?'

Chalky laughed and gave him a look.

Sam was starting to understand the way Chalky worked. 'So it was a message?'

'From somebody. His exact words: *Sorry for lack of action. Don't rock the boat or we'll have to take action*. Yes.'

'Aha.'

'That's why we're on the plane. We're rocking the boat.'

*

Terry got off the District line at Tower Hill and walked up Prescot Street to the Princess of Prussia, a Shepherd Neame pub, knowing he had exactly eight minutes in hand. He would normally court attention, twirling his brolly, in a bowler hat, with a red carnation, or even all three. But today he was in a navy linen jacket and panama, low key by his standards.

Not much had changed since Terry started drinking there when he joined the paper in '84. It was a classic, dark Victorian boozer, with leather-topped bar stools and engraved glass panels over the bar.

He shook hands with Tim behind the bar who said, 'Usual, Mr Thomas?'

'Two please, Tim.'

He watched him take two highball glasses from the fridge, fill them with ice, add two shots of Bombay Sapphire, then run a wedge of lime round the rim and add a twist of the rind.

As he did it, he said, 'Where did this come from?'

'In Calcutta we used to go to the Tollygunge Club. There was a barman called Benu, known as Benny, that's how he made them.'

'Never lemon?'

'Always lime. James Bond liked it with the juice of a whole one.'

Mary walked in, on cue. He kissed her on both cheeks. 'Are you all right being seen with me?'

'Oh sod them, who cares? More importantly, how are you?'

Terry had hired Mary in the late eighties, and she had worked her way up and across until she virtually ran HR, and then she got made Carson Lomax's PA since she knew everybody and everything. But he was never there, so when Frank's secretary left, she went back to the action.

'I'm relaxed. Sam's finding it a bit harder.'

'Can we go in the garden so I can have a fag?'

He steered her to a table at the far end that gave him a view of the small, walled beer garden and the door to the pub.

Terry took a folded A4 sheet from his inside pocket and said, 'Do you know who this is?'

It was a blow up of the guy from the villa who planted the bugs, leaning against the Mercedes.

'I think his name is Jean-Luc something, works on the boat. Maybe in the chalet, too, mostly security.'

'In Whistler?'

'No, the one in Courchevel. French or maybe French-Canadian. Military or police background. Can I keep this?'

'As long as you don't show anybody. Who would he be employed by?'

'Oh, the BVI Holding Company, they all are, and that's the company that owns the boats and jets.'

'Is Donald on the board of that?'

'Sure, he's on the board of everything.'

'And do Group employ Justine? Or did they?'

'Well no, and neither did anybody else.'

'How do you mean?'

'Jay said she was on secondment from another Group company.'

'But you checked.'

'Well, I have now. I've got access to the entire Group payroll. She's not on it, never has been.'

'So how does she get paid?'

'No idea. Rumour is she has history with Jay.'

'Do you have any contact details for her, number, address?'

'Nothing. When Frank told me what happened with Sam, I looked. Sorry.'

'We just can't find her, not even Gary.'

She reached in her bag and took out a memory stick. 'That's the photo for her security pass.'

'Thank you.'

'Least I could do. Is Sam going to take the deal?'

'He's looking at insurance.'

Mary held up the A4 sheet and raised her eyebrows.

'Exactly,' said Terry.

*

The jet was ten minutes out from Asturias. The pilot came back and said, 'I've spoken to the ground staff. You're technically in transit, so we'll drop you at the terminal. They'll take you straight to the gate. They know we cleared in Granada.'

'Thanks.'

Chalky said, 'I'm afraid we're early. You'll have a bit of a wait.'

'Fine. Joseph will be at Oxford. He'll drive you to Terry's. We'll use that as a base. Stay there. All things being equal Gary should be back. We'll sit down together and see where we are. If he and Terry both draw blanks, we're a bit stuffed.'

The jet came to a stop. They both got out, Chalky to stretch his legs. Was this him saying goodbye to Spain and everything it meant?

'Good luck, partner,' said Chalky.

Sam took his hand. 'Do you really think between us we can make this work?'

'Soon find out. I'll meet you there tonight. Or will you promise to visit me when I'm back inside?'

'Not funny.'

*

Sam connected to the airport Wi-Fi. He Googled the date that Pete Bolwell had disappeared, in August '89, then added 'Colombia.' Nothing. He changed it to the next day and added 'death.' Again a blank. Then he deleted 'Colombia,' did the whole month of August, and tried 'drugs-related.' And there it was, ten days later, one short paragraph in *Euro Weekly News*, the local English language newspaper. 'Three bodies have been found by police in a derelict barn in remote woodland west of Ojén. Police have not been able to identify the male victims, but believe it is another drugs-related incident in the recent spate of gangland turf war killings.' That was it, but it was tenuous at best. He was going to leave it, then he sent an email to his Venezuelan mate Cheche in Miami.

On the flight he put his phone on silent so he could keep doing emails and texts until the last minute. Clare was nagging him about whether the deal was signed and everybody else was just checking in and asking for news. The lawyer Francis confirmed that all was in hand for Donald to come over at four on Wednesday, so he sent Donald a friendly note. When they landed, the first text he read when he turned his phone on was from Joseph – 'The eagle has landed. With Dennis the Menace.'

The next was from Gary, asking him to call. Urgent.

'I'm fucked here.'

'Why?'

'Shift changed at two but four guys turned up. It's brightened up and they're having a bloody barbecue, swimming, and right now they're trying to put up the tennis net. If any girls come I'm guessing it'll be an all-nighter, and I'll have to abort.'

'I'm still confused why you actually need to get in?'

'Do you really think I'd be here if there wasn't at least some chance?'

This was a fair point. Gary knew what he was doing.

*

It was very strange arriving at Gatwick. It felt like a movie, though not exactly *Midnight Express*. He felt he was going to get stopped at any moment. He still hadn't got an ePassport so he had to queue. The immigration officer looked at his passport and then him. As she held it face down under the scanner, she said, 'Where have you come from, sir?'

'Asturias.'

She looked at him.

'It's in Spain.'

'I'm aware of that, sir. I'm an immigration officer.'

'Sorry.'

'Where did you start your journey?'

'Granada.'

'Interesting route.'

She handed him his passport but didn't let go. She smiled and said, 'If I were you, Mr Plummer, I think I might have stayed out there. Good luck.'

When he got through customs, there was one photographer there who must have had a line to easyJet or BA. He took a couple of shots as Sam walked over to take the Gatwick Express to Victoria. He couldn't see the guy when he got to the platform, but to be safe he did the old 'French Connection' last minute entry and repeated it when he got on the District line to Whitechapel. He then set off to walk the ten minutes to Chance Street. He did one last minute double-back, but it looked clear.

As he walked up the street, the lights flashed on a Ford Mondeo, and Sam could see it was Joseph, with Chalky next to him, a Yankees baseball cap pulled down over his eyes.

Sam got in the back. 'Hello boys, all good?'

'Painless,' said Chalky.

'Bit understated for you, isn't it?' said Sam to Joseph.

'Escalade gets too much attention.' The Mondeo made Joseph look even bigger than he was, his head touching the roof.

Chalky looked different to Sam. Hunched down in his seat, eyes darting around, he wasn't the same man as he was on home turf, master of all he surveyed. 'Are you OK?'

'I went to see my dad. We had time, Joseph took me. He's in a hospice in Banbury.'

So he had already changed the plan. 'How did you do that?'

'I called my aunt, said a very old friend of Dad's wanted to visit, and asked her to leave his name.'

'Did it work?'

'Fine, he's got his own room, I pay for it.'

'How is he?'

'Well he's just about with it, but he's dying.'

'Did you tell him?'

'I did. My mother died without knowing, I couldn't do it again.'

'What did he say?'

Chalky just looked out of the window.

*

Gary sat there watching the Odessa villa and knew all he could do was wait. The light was fading and he switched to the night scope. His phone vibrated and showed Frank was calling from his safe phone. Gary adjusted his headset.

'What's happening, Gary?'

'Nothing since you called me two hours ago.'

'What can you see?'

Gary wasn't going to burden Frank with knowledge or problems. The four guys were relaxing now, drinking beer.

'Birds.'

'Aha. More action?'

'Starlings, curlews, the odd sparrow hawk, vultures.'

Gary knew what Frank would say next, he always did.

'Well, call me when you see some tits.'

*

Chalky looked around. 'I didn't get to London much in my youth, but Shoreditch was a dump.'

'All changed now, uber cool, Shoreditch House is in the next street, silicone roundabout's here. Can we really trust this guy?'

'He's my lawyer.'

'How did you get the meeting?'

'I rang him, told him I had a mate, Mr Morley, who needed to see him urgently. He's been my lawyer for the last ten years, the old one retired.'

'And he's been a pain in my arse for longer.'

'You have to park that. You ever meet him?'

'No.'

As they approached, Sam could see a huge guy all in black at the door. His leather trench coat almost reached the floor. He was wearing black leather gloves and wrap-around shades. The wire from his earpiece went down inside his collar.

Sam thought he must have been melting. 'Christ, a lawyer with bouncers.'

As they arrived, Chalky said to the man, 'Tony Morley for Paul Goodman.' The giant turned his back and spoke into his sleeve.

'Tony Morley?' said Sam.

'Don't worry, he supports Orient.'

The door buzzed and the bouncer ushered them in. They stood in a small hallway, almost like an airlock, with a CCTV camera winking down at them. The next door swung open and they walked into a reception. It was all white and chrome, with a huge, two-storey chandelier. Dominating one wall was a gilt framed oil painting of Paul Goodman, trying to look like a country gent but doing about as well as Chris Eubank.

Sam said, 'Looks like the ballroom on the *Titanic*.'

A ludicrously pneumatic receptionist tottered round to meet them and squeaked, 'Mr Morley, I presume?'

Chalky put out his hand and said, 'My associate.'

Sam said, 'Mr Cowans, Gordon Cowans.'

'Please follow me.'

She wiggled across the shag pile in front of them and opened the double doors that led to her boss's office.

When they walked in, Paul Goodman had his back to them, sitting in a high-backed swivel chair. He turned and stood in one movement, clearly practised for effect. But after a perfect double take he stood there, frozen, lost for words. Sam could virtually see his face in Goodman's silver suit. His beige shoes could only be described as winklepickers. Outside his cream silk shirt and over his paisley tie hung a gold chain. There was a ring on every finger and a Franck Mueller hanging loosely on his wrist. Sam could see four mobiles on his desk.

'Hello, Paul,' said Chalky.

'Gordon fucking Bennett.'

He came round his desk and embraced Chalky. Then they stood at arms' length, still holding each other.

Goodman said, 'I just can't believe it. What? Why?'

He then turned to Sam and offered his hand. 'You must be Mr Cowans, good to meet you. I saw you play.'

Sam said, 'The pleasure's all mine.'

Goodman gave him a look. 'I'll stick with Sam.'

The office had faux Doric columns, two real looking Jack Vettrianos on the wall, and a white grand piano. A long shelf behind his desk was cluttered with framed photos – in black tie with Shirley Bassey, fishing with Barry Hearn, at a fight with Frank Bruno. His certificates were on the wall. The only thing Sam had seen like it was when he'd interviewed Bob Guccione in Palm Springs in the early nineties, but he also had a white tiger and a naked girl on roller skates who brought the cocktails.

'I have to ask you – which came first, Saul or Paul?' said Sam.

'Who the hell is Saul?' asked Chalky.

'*Breaking Bad*, it's a cult American TV show,' said Sam.

'Few years ago they did a profile of me on cable TV in the States, which I now regret, and the rumour is they based the sleazeball character on that. I did have "Better Call Paul" on my cards a long time ago.'

Chalky was clearly not in the mood for banter. He was behaving like a fugitive. 'Can we get on with it, guys?'

'Sure.'

'Is the upstairs thing I've heard about for real?'

'It certainly is, Mr White. Shall we go, gentlemen?'

Goodman pressed a button under his desk and a bookcase slid to one side to expose a lift door. It was as much as Sam could do not to burst out laughing. It was like a Bond villain. Could anybody really be impressed by all this nonsense? He couldn't wait to get upstairs – no doubt some sort of Austin Powers shag pad. Once inside it had one button and they went up to the top floor, Sam reckoned the tenth, and they stepped straight out into a penthouse apartment. 'Help yourselves guys, give me a minute.'

Goodman went off into what Sam assumed was a bedroom.

Sam looked round. 'What the fuck?' The room was in absurdly good taste and could have been on the cover of *Wallpaper*. He looked closely at one painting which looked like a real Edward Hopper.

Goodman appeared in faded jeans and a navy polo shirt, barefoot. All the jewellery was gone.

'It's an act, Sam. It's what my clients expect, and it puts the opposition on the back foot.' The cockney accent was still there, but all the edgy aggression was gone.

'Well, you had me fooled. And I mean for years.'

'To be honest I did used to be a bit like that.'

It was the oldest trick in the book. Let people see what they want to see. Sam did it himself all the time.

'Before you tell me anything, Sam, give me a fiver.'

Sam handed it over, puzzled.

'Now you're a client,' said Chalky. 'Client privilege. Take your time, meter's running. Only kidding.'

'Before we do, can I just ask if you work with Julian Mortlock?'

'No, Sam. Not if I don't have to. Don't like him.'

So they each took him through everything. It took half an hour, during which a charming girl appeared with tea and biscuits. The more questions Goodman asked, the more impressed Sam became. When they'd finished, Goodman said, 'Sam, we could probably take them to court for constructive dismissal.'

'But?'

'It would take months, maybe years with appeals. Your family would get dragged in, everything you've ever done would be exposed, and it would be very expensive.'

'They wouldn't want that either.'

'True, but young Lomax is a stubborn little shit, and it sets an example that they're not to be messed with. It wouldn't be a jury trial, and the chances of getting a judge who sides with the establishment are pretty good.'

'So?'

'It's a good deal. So you're here because you want to buy time and see if you can nail Burke, take Mortlock with him, and get to the bottom of what Justine was up to. I like the sound of her. And you, Chalky?'

'I'm sorry I didn't tell you. I just decided my only chance was to tell nobody, not even Sofia.'

'Understood. Does she know now?'

'No, she's going to kill me.'

'Perfectly reasonable. I reckon we'd get her off.'

'I know it sounds unbelievable, but it's true. It all happened, Paul.'

'Let me tell you, it has to be true. Not even the love child of John le Carré and Agatha Christie could possibly make that up.'

Goodman moved to the edge of his sofa, ready for action.

'OK, I'm in. What do you want me to do? Actually forget that, I know. First up you want me to scare the shit out of Donald Whelan.'

'Four tomorrow, buy us time,' said Sam.

'The pleasure will be all mine. Can you email me the draft contracts?'

Sam pulled a copy from his bag. 'Can you scan this? I'll get Frank's emailed.'

'Sure. But we can't meet at his office or here.'

'No, it's at the employment lawyer's place. If either or both of these play out, we're going to need a lot of legal work this week.'

'I hope you guys aren't thinking of leaning on Fox with the photos.'

'Only as last resort,' said Sam.

Goodman called down, and the bouncer got Joseph to drive into the basement. 'You should go out that way.'

'You still got my stuff?' asked Chalky.

'Everything you gave me is in a safe deposit box at the bank, I wouldn't want to keep that here. Where do you want it?'

'Terry's,' said Sam, and wrote down the address for him.

'If Gary gets back in time we're going to have a meeting there tomorrow, then go to see Donald from there. You up for that?'

'You bet.'

'Why not bring it with you?'

'OK.'

In the lift, Sam said, 'Maybe you could... ?'

'Dress down? More Lord Goodman than Saul Goodman? Of course.'

In the basement Sam looked at the matt pearl white Bentley, with red leather seats and the registration SUE 1. 'And for God's sake, don't come in that.'

*

Joseph drove Sam and Chalky all the way back across town, crawling through the rush hour traffic. He got Joseph to go back along the embankment; Chalky couldn't get enough of it. He'd seen it all on TV, but it felt different. Cleaner, cooler. Most of the ugly buildings had gone. Everybody was on bicycles.

'I guess most of this is new to you.'

'Well, the Tower of London was there. But not the Eye. And they were talking about developing Battersea Power Station when I left.'

'Well, it's happening now.'

'My God, it's changed.'

'So, you haven't seen this since the eighties?'

'Does Birmingham look like this now?'

'Er, not exactly.'

They were stuck in traffic outside a pub in Pimlico. Chalky looked at it. 'That's what I miss.' The Orange was on a corner, a

Georgian building on three floors. Drinkers sat outside on trestle tables under blue umbrellas.

'I wonder what they serve? You know, real beer.'

'Didn't you serve bitter in your bar in Spain?'

'Not the same.'

Sam looked round. 'Come on, Joseph, let's help the man.'

Joseph pulled up on a single yellow line and went into the pub. He came back and said to Chalky, 'Doom Bar, Pride or Speckled Hen?'

'I've no idea.'

Sam stepped in. 'Two pints of Doom Bar, straight glasses and don't let them fob you off with plastic ones.'

'Plastic glasses?'

'Health and Safety, all bollocks. After twenty years your first pint should be in a proper glass.'

Sam knew they ought to stay there, but drinking pints in a car would only attract more suspicion. When Joseph came back, they left him by it and walked over to a bench on the grass opposite the pub. 'Just act normal.'

A tramp came and perched on the end.

'Friend of yours?' said Chalky.

'Ex-editor of the *Sun*.'

Chalky took a long draught.

'Worth the wait?'

'Not bad. Nice drop.'

Chalky seemed more relaxed now, finding his feet.

'Excuse me, sir.'

Chalky turned round. The tramp was holding out a paper cup. 'Spare the price of a cup of tea?'

Sam saw what Chalky did, finding some coins with one hand and a note with the other. He dropped them into the cup together. 'Our secret, don't tell anybody.'

'Bless you, sir.'

Chalky turned back to listen to Sam's question. 'Would you have come back anyway, just to find Fox?'

'Hypothetical. Don't know,' replied Chalky. 'Your dad's your dad, isn't he? But I do need to bring it to a head.'

Joseph caught Sam's eye and tapped his watch.

Sam knew they were pushing it. 'Right. Come on.'

'What about a curry?'

'We always defer to Terry on matters Indian.' Sam was halfway through his Doom Bar and gave it to the tramp. Back in the car he called Terry. 'We fancy a curry Memsaab.'

'I beg your pardon?' said Terry.

'Oh sorry, an Indian supper mother.'

'That's more like it. Well I haven't got the time or fresh ingredients. Do you know the Star of India?'

'On the Brompton Road?'

'Yes. Ask for Ravi. How many?'

'Four including you.'

'Right-o. I'll ring them now.'

'Shall I pick up some Cobras?'

'I'm fairly sure I can do better than something brewed in Burton-on-Trent.'

They got to Terry's house in Drayton Gardens at seven. It was a beautiful, white Georgian terrace, over four floors, a stone's throw from The Boltons. He opened the door in a velvet smoking jacket and brocade slippers. 'Evening, gentlemen.'

'John White, meet Henry Thomas. Terry, Chalky.'

They shook hands.

'I'll be outside, keep an eye out,' said Joseph.

Terry led them inside. Chalky was no expert, but every painting and piece of furniture looked not just valuable, but important.

The ground floor was a big, open plan kitchen with a pale, York stone floor stretching the full length of the house. French doors opened to the terrace and garden.

Terry took the food. 'Right, give me that lot, the plates are warming. Game starts in an hour.'

The World Cup had passed Sam by. 'I've lost track, which game?'

'Brazil-Germany, semi-final. That's as good as it gets. I do hope they stuff the Germans.'

Chalky showered and they had dinner, Terry giving his usual discourse on Indian food. He produced imported chilled Kalyani Black Label beer, and then a red wine. 'Try this, Krsma Cabernet Sauvignon 2011. It's not bad, from Hampi in North Karnataka.'

Chalky said, 'Not bad at all, good follow through.'

Terry said, 'Steer clear of the whites, generally filth.'

'I'll send you some good whites.'

Sam wasn't surprised to see Terry and Chalky getting on, as if they'd known each other for years. He realised they all felt safe. He trusted Terry, Joseph was outside. It had been a long crazy day – he would write it up during the match.

They cleared up and settled down to watch the game on ITV. Clive Tyldesley and Lee Dixon started analysing the team line-ups and Sam fell asleep.

# CHAPTER 22

## TUESDAY

It would be dark soon so Gary packed up his stuff and went back to the car, picking his way carefully. It wasn't going well. He'd give it one last go and then cut his losses.

He changed into all black. Jeans, polo neck, and a woolly hat that rolled down into a balaclava. He put a dozen heavy duty zip lock ties in his back left pocket, some loosely threaded in the right. He cut two short lengths of black duct tape and stuck one to each thigh of his jeans. He put the roll in his small black rucksack with the night scope, his iPhone still on vibrate, and a torch.

Then he drove to the point he'd already chosen nearer the house so he could make the quickest exit. He waited and watched. After about an hour, an old Audi arrived. Two guys got out and had a laugh and smoke with the four party animals, who then left. Normal service resumed; two he could probably handle.

There was no time for a proper recce now. One was taller and lumbered around, looked older, maybe 110 kilos; he reminded him of Meatloaf. The other was younger, shorter, and fitter. Clearly the boss, he looked more of a handful. He went straight inside. Meatloaf went to the terrace and sat down.

Gary gave it five minutes, then hopped over the wall beyond the tennis court and worked his way up to the villa. The big guy was clearly just plain lazy, sitting on a chair bathed in light from the house. He couldn't see a gun.

Gary rolled down the balaclava for effect, walked up behind him, then stepped in front, put the scope against his temple, and gave him the universal sign to keep quiet. At that angle and with that level of fear, there was no chance Meatloaf would realise it wasn't a gun. He peeled one length of the duct tape off his jeans and stuck it over the guy's mouth. Then he took a looped zip lock and held it out. Meatloaf slipped his hands in while Gary pulled it tight and stepped back, motioning for him to kneel down. He put the scope in his backpack and zip-locked Meatloaf's ankles. Then he cut the hand ties and retied a new one behind his back, finally laying him on his side, where he couldn't move.

Gary circled the house, and through the blinds he could see the other guy on the Playstation, sitting on a sofa with his back to the wall. He had a Coke on the table next to his gun – an Uzi. Unless the guy shot him, it was extremely unlikely he'd get the better of him. But it was a risk.

The house phone rang and he saw the guy get up. Gary couldn't see if he'd left the room, but saw he'd left his gun. A lazy, basic mistake, but then, who was going to turn up? Gary went in via the kitchen, waited until he heard him hang up, then just ran headlong into the room. It took Gary two seconds to cover the ground and floor the guy with his shoulder, hitting him just below his ribs. He knew that he might be an athlete, but he wasn't a pro.

With Gary on him, he struggled to catch his breath and said in Ukrainian what Gary assumed was, 'Please don't hit me.'

'I guess you're asking me not to hurt you. You speak English?'

'A little.'

Ten minutes later, Gary sat on the arm of the sofa looking at the two men. He had them on two dining chairs, side by side, down to their socks and underpants. Meatloaf's grubby grey boxers, the pretty boy's black Calvin Kleins. Their outside hands were zip-locked to the chairs, the middle ones together, so they looked like they were holding hands. Humiliation was always best for information.

He took out his iPhone and said, 'Smile.' They didn't – well, Meatloaf couldn't.

'Fuck you,' said the young one.

'Does fatboy speak English?'

'No.'

Gary went upstairs and then round the house, doing what he had to do. He got back to the main room and said, 'I haven't stolen anything. I'm guessing you two would like to work again?'

The young guy said nothing.

'I'll take that as a yes. If you say anything to anybody about tonight, I'll post the photos on Facebook, Twitter and Instagram, and send them to every newspaper I can think of. Oh, and to Mr Pavlovich, you know, the guy who owns the villa and pays you. So, give me the name and number of somebody you really trust, and I'll call them later. They can come and get you.'

The guy gave him a name and number.

'Does Oksana speak English?'

'Not great, but yes.'

'And your name?'

'Ivan. And he is Vasiliy,' he said, gesturing to Meatloaf.

Gary scrolled through pictures on his iPhone until he found the one of the housekeeper. 'Where do I find her, Ivan?'

'If I help you, you keep her out of it, and I give you something.'

'Better be good.'

'That's her. Same person I told you to call. My mother Oksana, they use her.'

'OK, it's a deal, but I need your number, too.'

Ivan gave it to him. 'Top drawer of the desk, behind us. You the one took the photos?'

'Yes. I'll text you.'

He went to the desk and found an envelope. 'This blue one?'

Ivan nodded.

He didn't look inside, just put it in his rucksack. As with the other stuff he'd collected, he'd know its true value later.

Then he lifted his own sweater and unbuttoned his shirt,

and from his money belt he took out a clear, sealed, waterproof Aloksak bag stuffed with notes, the cash he always had as last resort if he had to buy his way out.

Ivan looked at him, fully engaged.

'Much easier to keep your mother out of it if I can find the girls' mother.'

'I think France, maybe.'

'Very interesting, but no use. I need a city, an address.'

'I can find it probably. I need money.'

Gary counted out some notes. 'One thousand euros. In the next 24 hours, latest.' He counted out two thousand more. 'I'll hide this within a kilometre of here. It's yours if you deliver.'

'Understand.'

Gary put the first instalment in Ivan's lap. 'Talk tomorrow.'

Gary unplugged the landline phones and put them in a bin bag with their mobiles, clothes and the one gun, which he dumped by the car. Down the road he buried the two thousand by a road sign, put a rock on top and took a flash photo. If Ivan didn't come through, Damir's guy could collect the cash one day. He was now ten minutes ahead of schedule, and two hours later he crossed the border near the coast at Palanca to avoid the border guards who might think his trip remarkably short. As soon as he was through, he had a pleasant, short chat with Ivan's mother, the housekeeper. The boys would be rescued early, and her English was good enough to understand where he'd put their stuff.

At the Airport Marriot, he met Damir's guy who dropped him at the terminal in time to get the Austrian Airlines flight at 5.35 via Vienna, which would get him to Heathrow at 9.30 if he made the connection.

*

Just as Gary had been hopping over the wall, Terry woke Sam, which he'd asked him to do at ten. He always fell asleep in front of the football. Terry and Chalky were at the kitchen table, laughing and working their way through some cheddar and one of Chalky's finest reds that he'd brought on the jet.

'Good sleep?' asked Terry.

'I did, thanks. Who won?'

'Germany, seven-one,' said Chalky.

Sam laughed. 'Come on, really.'

'They were five-nil up in thirty minutes.'

'You're not joking, are you?'

'Rabbits in headlights, could have been ten. Like life really, just when you think you've seen everything.'

'Blimey. Good chat?' said Sam.

'Terry's a mine of information.'

Terry said, 'I assume you can't go home. You OK with the sofa? Seems to work for you.'

'Fine, but I'm popping out. Can you give me a key?'

'Of course, old chap. So, what's the plan for tomorrow?'

'If Gary's on time, he'll be here mid-morning. I've told Katie to phone in sick, so she'll be here. Paul Goodman's coming. We'll just review everything. See what Gary's got, if anything.'

*

Sam went out in to the street and saw Joseph coming over.

'Slight change of plan.'

'Don't tell me, Wilkins isn't there.'

'You mean Sir Leonard Fox?'

'Sorry, yes, Fox.'

'I've got a guy down in Wimbledon. He and his wife Fiona had dinner. She left and took a mini-cab back up here to town. I found out he's hosting some sort of meeting near there tomorrow morning.'

'Good stuff.'

'So we should go earlier. Leave at eight thirty?'

'Will you tell Chalky?'

'Sure. Where you going?'

'A friend's, nearby. Seen anybody suspicious?'

'You're good.'

He'd have happily slept through but Caroline was having dinner round the corner and she'd suggested he join at the end. He walked down to the Brompton Road. He wondered if people would recognise him all the time now. Would he always look over his shoulder? He did then, but didn't see anybody.

She said she'd call, so he sat outside the tapas bar Tendido Cero and read a *Standard* that he picked up off the bar. He could see Caroline at a window table in the sister restaurant Cambio de Tercio opposite, talking to a guy he didn't recognise. It was stupid but he still didn't like the thought of her with other men.

*When he got back from Paris he wrote up the Crazy Horse piece which he faxed to both Caroline and Bernardin for approval, pretty certain Alain would change his mind. He'd told the guys at work what had happened, which they all took with a pinch of salt.*

*Frank had said, 'I know we occasionally make stuff up but it has to be based on some facts.'*

*Two days later a courier arrived. He'd enclosed a stack of negatives and prints – including the girls and him round the pool. Alain's note wished him luck, told him to always be a gentleman, and assigned him the copyright personally to the photos.*

*

*The paper syndicated his piece worldwide. His share was double his salary. They transferred him to features, putting him just four pages away from the front.*

*

*She starting dating some French heartthrob actor and they lost touch. She followed him to Hollywood where they married in a hurry and divorced even quicker. Sam got a ridiculous amount of pleasure nailing him later, cheating on his second wife. Alone at*

*25, she got an intern job at the* Enquirer. *As she said, 'Intelligent, funny, bilingual, former exotic dancer with GSOH wants to meet people. In LA? Come on, form a queue.' She met everybody. She kept her name, Caroline, but she pronounced it Carol-een. Dubois was a better calling card than Logan.*

*She wanted to come home so he gave her a job on the paper. They slept together once and it was a disaster. As he lay there, annoyed, she said, 'We'll always have Paris.' He laughed so hard, he knew in that moment that they would forever be friends.*

His phone rang and broke his train of thought. It was Gary.

'Breaking for the border.'

'Get anything?'

'Haven't had a chance to look yet, tight schedule. I'll start when I get to the airport. I made contact with the housekeeper. Think I may have already traded her in the transfer window.'

'Explain.'

'Her son was one of the guards. He's trying to get me the girls' mother. He says she's in France, but I need more than that. If not, I've read him wrong and it's cost me three thousand euros.'

*

Caroline walked out and Sam saw her insist the man take her driver. As they drove off she waved him over. 'Let's sit at the back.'

'Good idea. Who was he?'

'Friend of Carson's, launching some high-end glossy, wants me to do a monthly column.'

'Going to do it?'

'Think I can do better than that.'

'God, do I smell a comeback?'

'Watch this space.'

He brought her up to date, telling her everything – apart from the truth about Chalky.

'Justine's still got to you, hasn't she?'

'But I'm the last person who should fall for it.'

'You taught me, don't forget.'

'OK, but I never paid you to have sex with anybody.'

'That's true, and I never did. And you don't know that she was.'

'Explain.'

'You don't know how far she was paid to go.'

'I appreciate you're trying to make feel better. So she was paid to what, kiss me?'

'Maybe.'

She paid the bill. As they left she said, 'Where are you staying?'

'Terry's sofa. Can't go to my place, it's bound to be staked out.'

'Come back to mine, Carson's away.'

'You sure?'

'We've got eight bloody bedrooms.'

'How's the fashion show?'

'Going to be brilliant.'

They walked on. 'You seem to find this funny.'

'Sorry. But nobody died. You fell for a beautiful girl who fucked your brains out, and you loved every minute of it.'

He looked at her, knowing exactly what she was going to say next.

'And look what happened last time.'

*

It took them ten minutes to walk to the Lomax house in Onslow Square. The maid let them in and made them tea.

'Tell me where you are with your deal. You going to sign?'

There was no point lying to Caroline. 'I don't want to put you in a position where you have to lie to Carson.'

'Let me worry about that.'

'I can sign my deal tomorrow. Well, later today really. All done.'

'You can but you might not?'

'Why decide until the last minute? Anything could happen tomorrow.'

'Yes, like get a lot worse.'

'That can't possibly happen, everything is sorted. The deal is fine, security for life really, but I have to sit on my hands for a year, so I do have to be a good boy.'

'You can do that.'

'What does Carson say about it all?'

'He's letting Jay find his feet. I think he'd like to find a way for him to fail, then his mother will get off his back.'

'Jay's mother?'

'Yes, you know the paper has no real future long-term. He'll make some clever deal. I'm not sure he'll even be in the UK much longer. He says all the politicians are just wet, and he can't stand Miliband.'

'He say anything about me or Burke?'

'He has this strange view of life that everybody is expendable, including family. It's almost some Keyser Söze thing, there's nothing he can't walk away from.'

'That was Robert De Niro in *Heat*. Keyser Söze was happy to shoot his son.'

'Well, that's what he might be doing.'

# CHAPTER 23

**WEDNESDAY 9th July – DAY 12**

***Daily Express*: MIGRANTS DO TAKE OUR JOBS**

***Evening Standard*: STUDENT HID CASH FOR JIHAD IN HER KNICKERS**

***O Globo*: 7-1 HUMILHAÇÃO!**

When he got up there was a note outside his bedroom door. 'Dodgy tapas, I think. Bad night. Help yourself. Talk later. CX.'

The maid gave him breakfast. BBC *Breakfast* was on but nothing much was happening. He flicked through the papers, football everywhere. Bloody Germans.

*

He closed her front door behind him and turned to face the street. In that single moment he knew he was completely fucked. Caroline had been right: it could get worse. Leaning against a car opposite was Julian Mortlock, his legs crossed, a smile on his face. He started clapping, very slowly. Behind him on the pavement, Luke was taking shots.

Mortlock stopped and said, 'Good night?'

Sam walked slowly down the steps. For a second he thought about running.

Mortlock held the car door open for him. 'Shall we?'

Barry Harrison was at the wheel. He said, 'No babysitter with you today then?'

Sam ignored him and got in the back. He started to text Caroline.

'I wouldn't bother her, the coast's clear. We got what we need.'

'Us going in last night, and me coming out.'

'I don't need a fire, I just need smoke. Who said that?'

This was clearly Mortlock's strategy – play him at his own game. Quote his lines back at him.

'I have to make one call,' said Sam

'Sure.' Mortlock seemed relaxed. He should be, he had all the cards.

Sam got out and called Joseph. 'I'm with Mortlock. Pick me up in about twenty minutes at the bottom of Callow Street. Bring my bag. Just keep the man from del Monte hidden.'

'You got it.'

Sam got back in. He needed time to think. Maybe the office had just slowed him down. It wouldn't be the end for him; he'd sign today before it broke, but it could wreck Caroline's marriage. Would Carson believe her? It wouldn't look good.

'How long you been following me?'

'A while. It's Caroline we've been on. I knew you'd pop up. You can't leave it alone, can you?'

'Carson is not going to be happy.'

'This is like Tony and Wendy, who cares if anything happened? You're just a bonus, with Burke.'

'This off the record?'

'Sure, for now. Yes.'

'I've got no defence. Burke's a cock-up.'

'As is Caroline,' said Mortlock.

'Nothing happened. And that's on the record.'

'Doesn't matter. I've got you with other women.'

'So you've got me screwing around. So what?' Sam knew this was lame.

'You're married.'

'Technically, but everybody knows I have girlfriends.'

'True. But she's the wife of one of the world's rich and powerful. And your boss, for the moment.'

'Are you listening to me? I am not sleeping with her.'

'I told you, I don't care.'

'What do you have?'

Mortlock took out a notebook and flicked through. 'Well, on the last point, with you, the Hotel Beau-Rivage in Geneva, over at Blakes, few times. The Bristol in Paris.'

'They weren't liaisons, we just met. If I stayed, I had my own room.'

'If you say so. Then her with others.'

Sam didn't believe him. 'How long you been on this? Is this some sort of Linklater film project?'

They were into the game now. 'I know about Justine, too, the hot bird from the Ivy.'

This was it, he thought. Was Mortlock going to admit the honeytrap?

'She's an adult, and she's single. Hardly a story.'

'She works for the paper. Her dad's a vicar.'

That was news. 'I didn't know that. You can prove it?'

'That her dad's a vicar?'

He hated that Mortlock was playing with him. 'No. That she slept with me. Her face wasn't in the pictures. Nobody's named her.'

'Nobody's going to put it all out there on day one. Drip feed, you always said.'

So he wasn't saying he knew, just somebody did. He was clever. Sam knew that flattery and submission was the only way to go. 'You've done a good job.'

'Thanks. And of course I've got access to the corporate fraud stuff that's on offer.'

So Justine really had done a number on him. Very clever the way he said 'on offer', to put himself one step away from Justine.

'So, more PLUMMER'S MATES again this weekend?'

'Think I can do better than that, but Caroline is the main story. The corporate stuff is a can of worms – we all got creative on our expenses. Love the horse story, I remember it. THE STUD isn't a bad headline.'

'And you gathered all this information legally?'

'Certainly did.'

Sam wanted to say, 'That's a first, then,' but didn't. 'Seriously, you ran Burke well. How did you get him?'

'Old pals act.'

'Logical.'

'When you were on to him, he called me, panicking. I just told him to focus on getting the twins out, keep his mouth shut and say no comment. You chose to run it. More fool you.'

'Fair enough. What's next?'

'Twins are easy, *FHM*, *Strictly*, *Big Brother*. Tatiana really does want to be an astrophysicist, though. Think I've persuaded her to have a gap year, make a load of money first.'

'The mother?'

'Not good, got her in a clinic in Austria, more treatment. Fifty-fifty, they say. Either way a good story – martyr or miracle.'

Sam knew at least part of this was a lie. Mortlock certainly wouldn't be stupid enough to tell him where she was.

Mortlock said, 'Burke's arrogant. Marriage a sham, bad investments. Needs the money – trying to push him in the US. He's bloody good on camera.'

This was like the old days. Sam was keeping the conversation going, trying to buy thinking time. And on top of that remember every word, every nuance.

'Look, Julian, I know you've done nothing I wouldn't have done, so no hard feelings. The only thing that's pissing me off is young Lomax. I'm fair game, but not Frank and the others that will go down with his management reviews.'

'Sam, it's all bad, and it's going to break this Sunday, so why don't you sign your deal and we'll all be winners? I'll bury the finance stuff.'

'Did you do Clare?'

'God no.' Sam so wanted to hit the liar now.

'And you keep Frank out of it too.'

'No, it was both of you, and bloody Terry – he's gone already.'

Mortlock stopped smirking and lowered his voice. 'Sam, I've waited eleven years for this. You set out to destroy me, and you nearly did.' Sam wanted to say that he'd done that without his help but didn't. 'You think you're so fucking perfect, up there in your ivory tower. Well, now you and Frank are going to find out what it's like with the world looking down on you.' He leaned back.

Sam knew there was no point coming back with anything. He offered his hand. 'You win. It's a deal.'

Julian cracked his smile again and took it. 'Good move, Drainman. Gotcha.'

They shook hands on the pavement for the last shot. Mortlock had all the cards. All he had to do was lay them down, full house, and scoop the pot. As Sam walked down the street he turned everything over in his mind, against the backdrop that Mortlock had played him perfectly. He'd used every kind of move that Sam used to be legendary for. It was genius.

*

Sam made sure he wasn't being followed and climbed into the back of Joseph's car. Chalky said, 'About time. I've been under this effing blanket.'

He told them what had happened as they drove, ending with, 'Let's go fox hunting.'

# CHAPTER 24

## WEDNESDAY

Joseph went round the back past the All England Club where the workers were derigging.

'My guy says there's just one bodyguard with him today. That's his house, the one with the black gates. Look at the CCTV cameras.'

'Look like military installations,' said Sam.

'They are.'

Joseph parked at the end of the road, with a view of the Common. He looked at his watch and said, 'Wait. He's due over there in forty minutes.' He pointed across the common to Cannizaro House. 'It's the only way he can get there, and he seems to like walking.'

After about ten minutes Joseph said, 'Don't look round, bandits at six o'clock. Looks like just him, and the dog, on this side.'

Fox strolled past with a Springer spaniel. He looked for all the world like an accountant, just without the suit jacket – but Sam could see he was still fit. When he was well past, Sam and Chalky got out and followed him, at about ten yards.

Fox stopped, and slowly turned round. 'Guys, why don't you put a flashing light on the roof and take out ads in the press?'

'Wilko, you are a prick.'

Sam wasn't sure which way it was going to go, but Fox came back, started to laugh, and they went into a bear hug.

'Dennis Mortimer, as I live and breathe.'

'You knew?' said Chalky. He looked genuinely shocked.

'Jesus, we run national security, we try and keep an eye on people, especially you two blundering round Western Europe. I'm surprised you're not in burkas. I cancelled a trip so I could be here. We reckoned Wimbledon would be easier than you trying to break into Legoland.'

Fox broke away to shake Sam's hand. 'Hello, Sam. Look, let me and Chalky have five minutes on the Common. Park up outside the house, we'll come back and chat.'

'OK,' said Sam, 'be gentle with him.'

Sam listened to them laughing as Fox took Chalky's arm and they set off to the common. Fox was immediately impressive. He hadn't lost his looks or his charm. He wondered what he'd really done in the last twenty years. Given his talents, there was simply no way it could have been as dull as his Wikipedia entry. Assistant Undersecretary jobs. GCSE in Geneva. Singapore. Brussels. Luxembourg. Ottawa.

Sam got in the car with Joseph who said, 'Fucking legend that bloke.'

'In Wikipedia he's only been in places where they lock you up for dropping litter.'

Joseph got out. 'I'd better keep an eye on them.'

At the road Fox said, 'Chalky, sit.' The dog did.

'You are kidding me?'

'Called the last one Blanco. I liked the idea of still having you around.'

They crossed the road.

'How is Sofia?'

'Stressed. She thinks I may not come back.'

'Christ. You never told her?'

'No, decided not to.'

'That was bold. And how's your dad?'

'Not good. You know, don't you?'

'You went to see him? Of course. We knew the flight. GCHQ

did that. We just made contact with Joseph while he was waiting to pick you up at Oxford, told him to tell us your plan and we'd give you a clear run. It's what we do, you know that.'

'Why would Joseph do that?'

'Let's say old pals act.'

'Well, thanks. My biggest regret is I couldn't do it for Mum.'

'She knew.'

'What?'

'When she was dying, I went to see her.'

Chalky stopped and turned to face him. 'How?'

'You had her in that private hospital. Getting access was easy.'

'Did she understand?'

'I'm pretty certain. Rita was lovely. I knew it would be important to you.'

'Oh my God, thank you.' Chalky hugged Fox, then moved on, rubbing away a tear. Fox gave him a few seconds and then caught up.

'I'm sorry the Firm's been dicking you around, difference of opinion internally.'

'You've been involved?'

'Aware, not my section,' Fox took an A4 scan of Chalky's passport from his pocket. 'Not bad at all. Beard's good.'

'I grow it just for trips. Never been in the press.'

'We first picked it up two years ago when you went to Casablanca. Let's do a lap of the pond, then go back.'

Joseph stood watching them. A jogger came by and stopped to stretch using a wooden bench. Joseph looked at him and said, 'You with Fox?'

Unfazed, the guy said, 'Yep. You with Mr White?'

'Yes. Joseph.'

'We know. Crispin.' The guy jogged off. He was the fourth that he'd spotted, not counting the tail across town. He hadn't mentioned it; he didn't want to spook Chalky. The Firm were taking this very seriously.

Chalky said, 'There were times I wondered if you were still alive.'

'I was one of the very low-profile ones. You've signed the Act so I can tell you. I was a Joe for a long time. A proper spook.'

'I assumed that.'

'Then about two years ago our friends told me I'd be groomed for a more public role.'

'No more Wilkins?'

'I was only Wilkins with you. Then it was others. But now it's just Fox. I'm coming out.'

'And I want to come home.'

'I figured that out.'

Chalky said, 'Actually it's not that… it's coming out, too. For thirty years you've been a hero. You've got a knighthood. Now your reward is public life and a great, high-profile role at Number Ten. I did my bit, too. I did the jobs, I kept my mouth shut, but my kids use Sofia's name, none of us can come here, and sometimes they have to deny me. And no matter how much they love me, they think I'm a small-time villain. Is that fair?'

'Hang on, we set you up. You're a millionaire – you took the money.'

'It's not always about money.'

'And life's not always fair. But you're right. I paid a price, too.'

'Really?'

'My first wife and my second marriage.'

'I'm sorry. Why did you stop using me?'

'When you sold up and moved to Córdoba, we already had two people inside the business. We had another Joe outside, so we were covered. We only needed you for odd stuff.'

'I've had virtually no contact for about five years.'

'We like sleepers.'

They sat on a bench overlooking the pond. 'The only contact recently was about my negotiation to come back. I thought we were getting there, then when Chris Lines made C, he apparently pulled the plug.'

'Hardliner, I'm afraid, not my favourite.'

'Then one of your guys called Archie Hunter called me and said whatever I did, not to rock the boat.'

'Never heard of him.'

'So I took it as a message to rock the boat.'

'Really?' said Fox.

'Why else would they get somebody from Vauxhall Cross to tell me that?'

Fox stood up. 'Good question. I've absolutely no idea.'

As they got near the house Chalky stopped and said, 'Wilko, sorry Len, did you ever think I might have worried about you?'

'They thought we were getting too close, which was fair. They don't like us to.'

'When I saw you in the *Telegraph*, it was still a shock.'

As they walked on Fox said, 'Let's see if we can do something about it. Not easy. But at least the boat's rocking.'

They picked up Sam at the car, went into the garden and sat at a table on the terrace. It was a big detached Wimbledon pile, with manicured lawns and landscaped flower beds. A man who looked like he did about two hours of free weights every day before breakfast came out with a pot of tea. Incongruously he had on a Bake Off apron and a Walther P99 on his hip.

'So Sam, where are you up to?' asked Fox, as he poured the tea.

Sam sensed Fox rarely asked questions he didn't already know the answer to.

'Personally I'm half out of the door. Burke's a bad story but they've offered me a good deal.'

'And where are you with Chalky?'

'I know the full story. But that's all it is. A story.'

'So tell me, if you were to publish, what would you need?'

'Without any proof it would play as Chalky had lost his marbles, the ramblings of a deluded bitter man, and nobody would run it. "I was abducted by aliens" territory. But there's lots of ways to get it out there, you know that – online, abroad, just Twitter would do. You guys wouldn't like it and somebody might talk. There's enough disgruntled ex-spies about.'

'That is possible.'

Fox wanted to take his time, but Chalky had been waiting years for this conversation and was already irritated.

'The whole point is that you confirm it so I can come back to the UK a free man, no arrest warrant. And with all the WikiLeaks, Snowden, NSA, whistleblowers stuff, there must be a chance it will leak at some point,' said Sam.

Fox sipped his tea and said, 'Again possible.'

'And we've got the new twenty-year rule.'

'Maybe. I do hate the term whistleblower. Makes it sounds like it's in the public interest. It's not – it's plain treachery.'

Sam wasn't sure Chalky was playing it well, pushing too hard, showing his hand. Fox looked like he was withdrawing. Chalky had never even rehearsed this conversation, while Fox had clearly played the part a hundred times. And he wasn't going to be hurried. 'Maybe. So what would it take?'

'Ideally you say you ran Chalky, on the record.'

'Me? Never going to happen. The Firm doesn't do that.'

'We've got the pictures, other stuff.'

'I'll pretend I didn't hear that. Seriously, you don't want to play that game. Jez Clifton's archive? And yes, I was married, but she died in a car crash before I met you. Next.'

Chalky looked genuinely concerned. 'I never knew that.'

'She was driving, over the limit. And she was pregnant.'

Sam and Chalky didn't know what to say.

Fox leaned forward. 'If this comes out in the wrong way, there might be repercussions, for both of us.'

'Doesn't need to be you personally, we need somebody in the Government to confirm.'

'Very, very difficult. I need more.'

Sam and Chalky looked at each other. Sam nodded.

Fox picked up on it. 'What's going on?'

'I'll give you more. I did get in the safe. And I took pictures.'

For the first time, Fox became animated, nearly spilling his tea.

'You are fucking joking.'

'No, I am fucking not. I was so pissed off with you guys. I had nothing in writing. I kept it as insurance.'

Fox laughed. 'You sneaky bastard. Great move. Anything good?'

'Couldn't say. There is one list of English-looking names.'

Fox looked at Sam. 'Do you need it for the story?'

'Ideally, but not critical. Could stick to the line he didn't get into the safe. Hold that back, at least until we know what it means. I just need the Firm confirming you hired him and got him out. I don't need to expose the work in Spain.'

'OK.'

'OK I understand or OK I'll get it for you?'

'Former. Next?'

'What about Cobbold?'

'You can't have him, he's dead. And he's not Cobbold.'

'I'm sorry to hear that,' said Chalky. 'Natural causes?'

'Depends on your point of view. AIDS-related. You got pictures of him?'

'We have,' said Sam, who wanted to get back to the story. 'It was twenty-five years ago. The safe stuff can't be relevant.'

Fox got up, walked round the table and lit a cigarette. 'You never know with intelligence. Why do you think we had the old twenty-year rule? It's information. So, where are the pictures?'

'My lawyer, here, another copy in a bank in Málaga. Do you want to see it?'

'If you show me, I have to report back. No incriminating photos?'

'No photos at all, just documents,' said Chalky.

'That's good. You hang on to it, might be good for you. And don't say you told me. Look, I'm in transition so I don't have much authority now. I can't make the call. Chalky, I want to help.'

Sam simply didn't believe people like Fox were ever powerless.

Chalky said, 'So what do we do?'

'I can't guarantee your safety, but I'll do what I can. Stay out of sight. How long you here?'

Chalky said, 'Same way back, Thursday afternoon. Problem is, every Brit that I met down there will think I grassed on them. I'm going to need help on that.'

'You're not kidding.' Fox gave them both a card. 'These are secure private numbers and email. Send me your contacts.'

Fox gave Sam a handwritten note. 'When this is over you'll need a break. This is a great hotel in the south of France, lot of people go there to recuperate. Really suggest you try it, sooner rather than later.'

Sam put it in his pocket, puzzled. 'Thanks.'

Fox stood up. 'To be clear, if I help, it's for Chalky.'

'Understood.'

'When do you want to write this?'

'This Sunday ideally.'

Fox laughed. 'That's ridiculous. Have you seen how fast we move? Talk soon.'

*

Back in the car Sam said to Chalky, 'Do you think he'll help?'

'As much as those guys ever do.'

'He bent over backwards to see us, and you haven't been arrested. Yet. They're letting you roam free, but the police might not. I wouldn't run on the pitch at Villa Park just yet.'

Chalky said, 'You notice the one thing he didn't mention?'

'The money in the Caymans – in his name.'

'Exactly. We've still got that.'

He thought it funny that they were now engaged directly with the Firm, the only other organisation he knew that operated as dirtily or cleverly as the tabloid press. Sam said, 'That Fox is a piece of work. Wouldn't trust him as far as I could throw him.'

Chalky looked out of the window and said, 'You, maybe. I'd trust him with my life. Well, I did. And I will now.'

*

Sam had got Joseph to drop him at Wimbledon station. He couldn't put off telling Frank any longer. He was waiting for him upstairs at the back in Costa when he got into town.

Sam got a flat white and sat down. 'So, Chalky.'

'Finally. So what's the story?'

'You're not going to believe me.'

'Try me.'

'Chalky's a spy. MI6 recruited him, he did the job for them.'

'Bloody hell. I knew it was something big. Terry told me not to take no for an answer.'

'Why didn't you tell me?'

Frank shrugged his shoulders. 'He asked me not to.'

'But we don't have secrets, Frank.'

'Hang on. You didn't tell me you'd found Chalky.'

Sam looked at Frank, and wondered if this was some sort of turning point in their relationship. Then he said, 'Actually what I wanted to say is I've thought about it long and hard. We should take the money – and run.'

'Hang on, rewind. Something's happened.'

'Mortlock doorstepped me – I stayed at Caroline's last night.'

'Are you fucking mad?'

'Nothing happened, it just looks bad.'

'Bad? Looks bad? It looks catastrophic. Let me think who could be worse – the Queen? Are you still shagging her?'

'Give me some credit. No. Mortlock's been on her tail for ages. If Jay or Carson get wind of this they won't sign our deals in a million years, we'll be dead meat. And a nightmare for Caroline.'

'But we're on the verge of two incredible stories.'

'I know, but Chalky's going far too slowly, I keep hitting brick walls. And MI6 will never confirm. It's like pulling teeth.'

'He told you off the record, didn't he?'

'Yes. Look, it's the same with Burke, we just haven't got any evidence. The truth will come out one day anyway. They don't need either of us – Chalky's a man on a mission, and Mortlock will slip up eventually, he's not as clever as he thinks he is. So let him play at being editor for a bit. It won't be our problem any more.

Frank leaned back, looking resigned. 'You know, you're probably right. We're going round in circles.'

Sam finished his coffee. 'It's so frustrating.'

They sat there for a while just looking at each other. Then Frank said, 'No. Come on Sam, we can't go out like this. Why don't we just see what today brings? Have your meeting and I'll see you at the lawyers. I thought you had a cunning plan.'

Sam stood up. 'OK partner, one last shot. Then that's it. You know in the office you're the Fat Controller?'

'Really?'

'And I'm Jeff Tracy.'

'*Thunderbirds* Jeff Tracy?'

'Exactly.'

'Not bad, and you are the puppet, we can see the strings.'

'And bloody Mortlock's pulling them.'

# CHAPTER 25

## WEDNESDAY

Terry opened the front door to Sam. He said hello to Gary, who was unloading Pret a Manger bags on to plates and putting water on the table. He waved at Paul Goodman, who was on his mobile and dressed in his casual attire – no bling in sight.

Terry said, 'Come on, she's upstairs.'

They went up, Sam wondering if he meant Caroline or Katie, and who he was keener to see. He knew when he saw Katie, studying the books on Terry's shelves.

She was putting one back. 'Amazing collection.'

'Thank you, a lifetime's work.'

The drawing room ran the length of the house and felt like it hadn't changed since the thirties. They looked at the books lining two walls, mostly on Terry's passion, military history, and a lot reflecting his early life on the Indian subcontinent. With his years on foreign desks and knowledge of the intelligence services, Sam wanted to discuss Chalky, but that would have to wait a little longer.

Sam heard footsteps coming down from the bedroom above and saw Katie put her hand over her mouth. 'Oh my God.'

'You must be Katie, I've heard so much about you.' Chalky put out his hand.

'Gosh, you're real.'

Chalky laughed. 'Well, that's true. I hear you've been doing a great job on me.'

She blushed. 'With some help from these two.'

'Let's go down, they look like they need to chat.'

As they walked away, Katie turned and pulled a face at Sam, who just smiled and shrugged.

'Great girl you've got there, Sam.'

'Thanks, Terry, I appreciate what you've done for her.'

'So, how's it looking, old boy?'

'Not good.' They sat down in two armchairs, facing each other. Sam took him through the whole day.

Terry said, 'Let me summarise. I will try and stick to the facts. He has you spending the night with Caroline and evidence over the years of you with her and maybe of her with others.'

'Correct.'

'But no extramarital *in flagrante delicto*.'

'If you mean was she putting it about while married to Carson, no.'

'And he's got your friend, the fragrant Justine, with young Jay?'

'Yes. And Jay's bought it – literally. God knows why.'

'He's got you being financially creative, shall we say?'

'Yes.'

'He's got Burke in his pocket, and you can't prove anything.'

'Yes.'

'He's lined himself up to take Frank's job.'

'Yes.'

'And he's put you out on the street, the disgraced former hack.'

Sam rolled his eyes. 'Thanks. Yes.'

'Your turn, you know how it works. Play it back.'

Sam was ready. 'Is he really going to sell me and Caroline to a paper?'

'Not in a hurry. Would any owner really want to expose Carson and make him look stupid?'

'And Mortlock wants to work for Carson, so if he did he'd have to use a middleman, but too risky.'

'Expenses fraud? Worst can of worms you could open on Fleet Street. We make the MPs look like beginners.'

'Speak for yourself. But yes, glass houses and stones.'

'He did the Clare sting to put pressure on me.'

'Correct, he knows you can handle it. Your weak spot is family. He probably fed Felix to Roly Relton, too.'

'So, it's all just pressure on us to sign and bugger off.'

'Exactly.'

'OK, Obi-Wan, if Justine's Mata Hari, how come he hasn't played his best card?'

'Yes, I have to say that is rather baffling.'

Terry got up and walked around. 'So by now Mortlock's flush, on a retainer with Jay as his fixer cum minder, managing Burke and the twins, been paid for Caroline who he's got on toast, has Justine working as a prize asset, and last but not least got you and Frank strapped into the ejector seats.'

'So Jay's all over us to save the pennies and Mortlock's using the company like an ATM.'

'You have to admit, it's a brilliant wheeze.'

'And on top of it all he gets back in to run the paper after Frank and I have been fired into space.'

'You think so?'

'It's the ultimate revenge.'

'That's the trouble with apprentices, old boy: they have this nasty habit of turning into sorcerers.'

*

Downstairs Sam looked at the table and said, 'No, Terry, you sit at the end. You're the editor, always have been for me.'

'You sure, old boy?'

'I don't think I can be objective, I'm too involved.'

Terry stood up. 'Order, order. Welcome everybody, particularly Chalky, since I know you made a big effort to get here.'

Sam looked round at everybody laughing, including Caroline now – all the people there who mattered to him and had stuck by him, except Frank.

'And I can honestly say I have no idea at all why you're here. I can also safely say, Chalky, that if you're a story, it will be the first time we've had the target in the room.'

They were all thinking the same. A household name that they all only knew from the pages of newspapers was sat there, drinking a cup of tea.

'First item on the agenda – find the lady. Gary.'

Gary put Justine's security pass photo up on the big screen. Sam could feel them all looking at him. 'Still all we have is her name, Justine Walker. She's not on the Lomax payroll, in any company. Nothing on Facebook, Google or LinkedIn. Can't find her on any lawyer lists or databases. We need her real name.'

Paul Goodman said, 'Wonder if she's normally blonde. Gary, can you tweak her ID photo?'

'Photoshop is the word. Sure, and we'll lose the glasses. But I'm afraid that's it on her.'

Terry moved on. 'Next item, the chap from Frank's villa.'

The next shot was the driver who planted the bugs at the villa.

'That's Jean-Luc Lavelle,' said Terry. 'Employed by the Group. French-Canadian, ex-naval police. Mostly works on the boat that sails out of Monaco. Been with the company for about four years. Close to Jay – done some yacht races with him.'

Sam said, 'So we know who he is but not who told him to do it.'

'It can't be Carson,' said Caroline, almost defensively.

They all looked at Sam. 'Take your pick. Donald, Jay, Mortlock?'

'This isn't going that well, team. Gary?'

'To cut a long story short, I got into the villa in Odessa and recovered my stuff.'

'Is that legal?' asked Goodman.

'In Ukraine, yes,' said Gary.

Goodman laughed, but Sam stepped in. 'This is important. Is everything you've done out there legal?'

'Damir says it's a grey area. He checked with the local lawyer, and he says we can argue it is.'

'I'm not convinced.'

'Well, invading Crimea was illegal,' said Caroline, 'but I didn't hear about anybody getting arrested for that either.'

'OK, so when you say stuff, what exactly are we talking about?'

Sam knew Gary so well. It was coming, in his own time. 'I'll show you. Remember this, one of my original ones?'

In the shot he put up on the screen, there were two security guys in the villa's drive and a man going in with a briefcase.

'Ah, our famous mystery man,' said Sam.

'Sorry, what do you mean?' said Goodman.

Gary zoomed in. 'We just couldn't ever figure him out.'

'The guys are in shorts and it looks about forty degrees, but he's wearing a hat and what looks like a white raincoat,' said Katie.

'Very good,' said Gary. 'And I never worked out who he was. Not security – and he never came outside, except to leave.'

'Probably there for business,' said Sam. 'Looks like a slimy lawyer. No offence, Paul.'

'None taken.'

Gary said, 'OK, we switch to video, inside. I've edited it.'

'Bloody hell,' said Sam. 'How did you...?'

'Don't ask,' said Gary.

The black and white wide angle showed him coming in, walking across the living room and tossing the raincoat on the sofa. Underneath he had on a pale suit. Then he went up the stairs and out of shot. Cut to a camera on the landing which had him going into a bedroom.

Gary said, 'And hey presto, five minutes later.'

A tall girl came out, long hair down, barefoot, in a kaftan. Gary froze it, blurred.

'Another girl,' said Sam. 'So he was getting laid after all. Mystery solved.'

'Hang on a minute,' said Terry. 'Hardly solved. Who is she?'

Gary put up three grainy black and white headshots that looked like photo booth passport photos. 'Damir's visa application shots.'

'Oh my God, they're not twins, they're bloody triplets,' said Chalky.

Sam got up and went over to the screen, laughing. 'You need to go to Specsavers. From the left Tatiana, Irina, and this is Katia. She's not a girl, she's the mother.'

'Bloody hell,' said Terry. 'Right, boys and girls, that again doesn't prove anything, except that she was there and that she doesn't look to me like she's at death's door. But what do we learn, anybody?'

Katie put her hand up.

'Darling girl, you don't need to put your hand up.'

'The disguise means they knew somebody was watching.'

'Very good. But I'm afraid that the fact that our friend Lord Burke is still bonking the twins' mother is hardly Pulitzer Prize stuff. So he's human.'

Sam could see Gary wanted to move on. 'That's not our only proof. I leaned on the security guards. Actually one, Ivan, was quite helpful. We reached a deal and he gave me these.'

A sheet came up on the screen.

'My flight details. And Damir's. They knew when we were there. Next.' It was a sheet of writing, in what they all assumed was Ukrainian.

'Damir translated it for me – briefing notes for the housekeeper. Exactly what she had to say and not say, looks like a crib sheet. But no date, don't know who wrote it, so not sure on value. And finally, Exhibit A.'

Sam knew all too well that Gary would save the best until last. A black and white shot came up of the villa, taken from the same spot as Gary had used. It was covered with scribbles – mostly crosses and arrows.

'I don't understand. Is that one of yours?' said Sam.

'No, look at this.'

He put the shot up next to his now infamous front page pool shot of Burke cavorting with the twins.

'This is like that kids thing, spot the differences,' said Katie.

'Exactly,' said Gary. 'So that big bush, with the cross on it, is gone.'

'And the bins, and the washing line.'

'And where it says "upgrade", the white plastic loungers have gone and they've got nice wooden ones and matching towels. Caroline, you said it looked art-directed. It was.'

'I don't see what this proves,' said Terry.

Gary went back to just the black and white, rotated it ninety degrees and zoomed in on the top corner. 'See that?'

Sam was still standing by the screen and read it out loud. 'ACL and a UK fax number.'

Gary got up the website for JMA, Julian Mortlock Associates. 'Let's go to Contact Us. Read the fax number.'

'Brilliant,' said Sam.

'And you'll see JMA is the trading name of Alborz Consulting Limited.'

'ACL. And it's his handwriting, too.'

'The date's the thing,' said Terry.

'Three weeks ago. It's stone cold proof,' said Gary.

Sam banged the table. 'Love it. Even Frank said they were perfect, like Helmut Newton. He was right. Mortlock art-directed it. The whole thing was a set-up.'

'And the sex shots?' said Terry.

Gary put the shot up. 'You see, through the net curtain it's very hazy – they were new, too. That's Burke with the mother. She's the same shape, long dark hair. It's impossible to tell.'

Katie said, 'You had to think he was shagging the twins, not her. And she's supposed to be having chemotherapy in Kiev.'

'Not playing hide the sausage with Lord Nigel Burke,' said Terry. 'But he's right back in the frame as a love rat.'

Sam went over to Gary and kissed him on the forehead. 'You're a genius. I love you.'

'Oh, God, he's going to cry,' said Katie.

'No. But I just knew it. I knew he was a fraud.'

Terry said, 'Word of caution, old fruit. Fraud equals crime, but call me old-fashioned, I believe it still requires a trial.'

'I'd say a year to prepare, another year in court,' said Goodman. 'Behind closed doors, millions on lawyers. Every other paper would love it. Everybody here giving evidence.'

Sam thought about it. 'Terry, that's why you're in the chair. You're right. We need a quicker, better way.'

'Sit down. Sam, let me think. OK, let's do this properly, still plenty on the agenda, we're not there yet and we've got no time to spare. We need to close down every angle. We need to find Justine, she's the missing link. I think the only way to do it is you walk us through it again, Sam, sorry. Step by step.'

'In front of Katie and Caroline?'

'In your own time, old boy.'

So Sam went back to the beginning and went over it. He got to the bit about taking her back to his flat.

'I've got that CCTV stuff saved on here.'

'Gary, we really do not need to see that.'

'We really should,' said Caroline smiling.

Terry saved him. 'I think not. But the devil's in the detail.'

'What was she wearing? Anything?' asked Caroline.

'Not really. Well, the G-string at my place, you saw it in the papers.'

'Oh, come on, Sam. Set-ups are always better if you get kinky shots, naked's boring. What was she wearing the second time, at her place?'

'Jesus. Sort of sexy underwear.'

'Victoria's Secret?' said Chalky.

'Not exactly.'

'Janet Reger?' said Terry. When they all laughed he said, 'What's funny?'

'It was definitely not Janet Reger. It looked like it came from a tack room.'

'Ah, right,' said Katie. 'Chains?'

'Horses don't wear chains, no. Lot of crisscrossing, tassels. Actually she said she got it from a shop in Covent Garden.'

'You still online?' Katie asked Gary. He got the browser up and slid the laptop to her. She typed away. 'How about this? Coco de Mer. Let's see if we get lucky and go straight to Bondage. 'The Erotic Emporium, may all your fantasies come true."'

'Yes please,' said Gary as a picture came up.

'How about this – the William Wilde Basque and Strap Suspender Belt?'. A snip at £365.'

'Boys will be boys,' said Caroline. 'I wore something like that at the Crazy.'

Sam folded his arms. 'It wasn't latex.'

Katie moved on, reading out loud, 'The Godiva Balcony Bra and Spanking Knicker. With optional Ilya wing leather wrist cuffs'

Sam wondered how on earth Katie knew about this stuff.

'Do people really wear this at home?' asked Terry.

'It had straps, and some red in it.'

She kept searching. 'Like this? The Bordelle Bondage Angela Dress with Brazilian Webbed Thong.'

Chalky's mouth was open. 'Bloody hell, it's another world.'

'More on view. Really, just straps. And I said it was basically red.'

It comes in red, Daddy.'

'You're all enjoying this, aren't you?'

He looked around at them all nodding.

As she clicked around, Sam said, 'Stop.' He stood up, and went to the plasma screen. 'There, top left.'

Katie got it up full screen. 'The Persephone Playsuit – inspired by the Queen of the Underworld's fabled majesty, beauty and strength.'

'Does that include the nipple things?' said Chalky.

'That's it.'

Goodman read from the screen and said, 'What are "multiple bondage inspired styling options"?'

'I guess that means you can wear it backwards,' said Gary.

'OK, so that's what she wore, but she could have bought it anywhere,' said Terry.

Katie scrolled down. 'No, they've just got just one shop, Covent Garden. There or mail order.'

'Good girl Katie, great job,' said Terry.

Sam sat down and looked at Katie, who was having a giggling fit. He put his hands up. 'Shush everybody. Look, you all need to know this. Mortlock doorstepped me this morning at Caroline's.'

'Nothing happened, and nothing has for years.'

'He's been having us both followed on and off. And Clare.'

Katie said, 'So he didn't sell you and Justine last weekend because he had Mum, put more pressure on us that way.'

'Correct,' said Terry. 'He's planning to sell your dad and Justine this weekend.'

'With photos of Justine in her bondage merkin,' said Caroline.

'Exactly. But he didn't taunt me with those. Bit odd.'

'So maybe he hasn't got them yet,' said Goodman.

Sam hadn't thought of that.

Goodman carried on. 'If I was her, and she's any sort of lawyer, she'll only hand it over when she gets her money.'

Sam hadn't thought of that either.

*

Before Sam could suggest it, Terry said, 'Let's all take a break, reconvene in fifteen minutes for round two: Chalky.' Goodman and Chalky went off in to a huddle. Sam still didn't know if Chalky was ready to talk about it.

Gary said to Sam, 'Just got an email from my Ukrainian pal.' He read it from his phone. '"Sorry Gary best we give you she flies Nice (France). Yesterday. Try find more. My mother say thank you. Ivan." Not much help, could be anywhere, including Italy.'

'Maybe not,' said Sam. He went to his jacket, fished out the note Fox had given him and gave it to Gary. 'Look this up.'

Sam looked at it on Gary's laptop. 'Very cool. We'd better check she is actually there.'

Gary started dialling. 'Well, in France you always have to show your passport at reception.'

He spoke into his phone, 'Mrs Katia Svetlanova, please. I can spell it.'

'Please hold while I connect you.'

He was put through and let it ring once before hanging up. 'She's there.'

'Bloody hell, finally a lead. Get back to Damir. Tell him to drop everything and get there as quick as he can.'

*

Terry tapped on his glass with a teaspoon to restore order. 'Now then, this falls under any other business really since I have no idea what's coming. Chalky, the floor is yours.'

As Chalky told his story, Sam watched their reactions. Katie looked shocked; Terry caught his eye.

When he finished, Katie said, 'That all makes sense.'

'Explain,' said Terry.

'Nobody ever really understood how you escaped or how you got to Spain. And when you got there you seemed to always be one step ahead of the police.'

'That's right, I was.'

'Jesus Christ,' said Terry. 'So Burgess of the Yard and the boys in blue trying to get you back was a charade?'

'No, that was for real, the spooks couldn't risk telling the police. They'd sell it to you lot.'

'Harsh but fair,' said Sam.

'So I was in a tug-of-war between the Firm, the police, and the Spanish authorities. Couldn't tell them... they're the worst.'

They carried on. Sam enjoyed watching Katie take the lead, asking many of the questions he'd asked a few days before. He gave Gary a memory stick. On screen they introduced everybody to Sir Leonard Fox, formerly known as the playboy spy Wilko.

Katie was off again. ‘So, someone managed your image with the press – them?’

‘Yes, planned in great detail, very clever. Drip fed the right messages at the right time, controlled the photos.’

‘Any idea who?’ said Terry.

‘No.’

‘Dad asked me to do some research around the time Wilko was there. You asked me to check out the guy Speedy González, the drug dealer. Gary, can you?’

He put up a shot of a smooth-looking swarthy guy in a sharp suit at some party with a blonde on each arm.

‘My God, Waleed Khalifa. Egyptian. Known as Wally, nasty piece of work,’ said Chalky. ‘Speedy could sort you a line, but Wally brought it in by the boatload.’

‘Remind me,’ said Sam, ‘how does this all fit in?’

‘Johnnie put me in touch with your man in Cairo.’

‘Idris,’ said Sam.

‘Yes. He went off and we checked. Muslim burials are very regimented, but he was apparently buried at sea. Idris traced his death certificate. 26th of October 1989.’

‘Jesus, that’s about when Speedy vanished,’ said Chalky. ‘I always assumed Wally killed him.’

‘Day after,’ said Katie.

‘So they killed them both,’ said Chalky.

‘They?’ asked Sam.

‘No idea, gang warfare. CIA. Us?’

There was a pause while they all seemed to be thinking what to ask next, then Terry broke the silence. ‘So Fox liked a good time, but “the spy who shagged birds” or “man did coke in the eighties” is not much of a story. Where’s the proof?’

‘We’re counting on Fox to verify.’

‘No chance. Tell me you’re not thinking of blackmailing him with those Jez Clifton photos?’

'Last resort, but no. I made him my business partner. Even after he left I sent the dividends to the Caymans. And when I sold it, I sent his share of the sale. A big number.'

'All the signs are Fox is sympathetic.' said Sam.

'Sympathy's no good. We need him on the record.'

'Speak of the devil, a text. He asks are we on Skype or G+ whatever that is, Gary you want to connect us?' Sam gave him his phone.

*

Gary tapped away, and as Fox came up on the laptop, he turned it to face Sam. Fox looked like he was in his kitchen at home. He said, 'Who's in the room with you, Sam?', clearly agitated.

Caroline caught Sam's eye and shook her head, mouthing 'no'.

'Terry Thomas, Chalky, Paul Goodman our lawyer.'

'Goodman? Jesus.'

'And Gary, who... '

'I know who Gary is. Get him in front of the screen.'

Gary moved the laptop back so he and Sam were both in shot.

'What the fuck are you clowns doing?'

'What do you mean?'

'Gary's gone to Ukraine, a country we are working very hard to improve our relations with, where you might just have noticed it's all going off. You broke in, put a gun to a man's head... '

'I didn't put a gun... '

'Shut up. We need our friends there. You've broken into the house of a key political figure, bugged it, beaten up two guys who work for him, and stolen his property. Do you know who owns that house?'

Sam said, 'We did originally think it was Artem Bezrukov, the girls' stepfather.'

'And now you know he doesn't. For the benefit of those in the room, the owner is his mate, and ours, Nikolay Pavlovich. Ludicrously well-connected, the guy who originally saved the mother, got her out of jail.'

'Friend of Burke's too?'

'I don't give a flying fuck about Burke. He's your problem. Burke is of no use to us or the country, he just wants to make money and get his leg over. On Friday, the Prime Minister of Ukraine's arriving in London, with a so-called trade delegation, and you've been trashing his mate's villa.'

Gary wasn't going to let that go. 'Len, that's not right.'

'Whatever. In Ukraine they've all seen the photos now. It looks like he's been running a brothel. And you've got to give up that bird shit bird-watching cover story. We all had you on the radar when you crossed the border and they're connecting you with us, not the paper.'

Sam was confused by this. 'Why?'

'Oh come on, Sam – Gary was behind enemy lines in Iran for months. He's not actually best known for hanging around outside nightclubs.'

'I did not have a gun. He just thought I did.'

'You tied up his guys in their underpants.'

'Actually it was textbook covert ops stuff,' said Gary.

'We didn't break any local laws,' said Sam, hopefully.

'We'll have to agree to differ on that. And if you use anything from the villa, we'll disown you. All bets are off.'

'And me?' said Chalky.

Fox went quiet. Chalky's intervention seemed to stop the rant in its tracks. He finally said, much more quietly, 'Ukraine's my problem more than yours. Unfortunately, yours is worse.'

Sam didn't see how it could be any worse. 'What do you mean?'

'The *Evening Standard* contacted the police. They've been offered a photo that seems to show you and Chalky having a pint in Pimlico yesterday. Is that remotely possible?'

'I didn't think it was a risk,' said Chalky.

'Christ. So you play the game for twenty years and get caught out having a pint? Did I teach you nothing? Might staying out of sight not be vaguely sensible? Did you have a car?'

'Joseph was driving, in my car,' said Gary.

'Well it looks like a criminal offence. The paper told the police, and the trade will probably be a positive ID from the photos and CCTV footage, which they'll find from somewhere and share with them. Then they'll just go in the number plate database and trace your journey. Is the car where you are now?'

'Yes, Joseph's outside.'

'Get him to move it now. Change one digit with tape, unless you've got spare plates. Ideally underground without being traced. To be clear, under the 1961 Criminal Justice Act, the harbouring of a fugitive is an offence.'

'And they'll go for perverting the course of justice and assisting an offender,' said Goodman. 'Statutory offences, jail term.'

'Thanks, Paul,' said Sam, 'that's really helpful.'

'I'm your lawyer.'

'It'll take them a while to figure out it's you in the photo and to get somebody to confirm it's Chalky. Look.'

Fox held up his mobile to the camera to show them. Chalky was full face, Sam's head turned away.

'It was taken from a bus, some woman on her phone.'

'What do we do?' asked Sam.

'Is your mate's jet here now?'

'No, coming back late tomorrow.'

'You and Chalky get on a plane tonight, tomorrow's too late.'

'Scheduled?' said Chalky.

'Well, we can't fly you, but I think I can cover you. The Mortimer passport is still clean – take the first BA flight you can to Seville or anywhere in Spain except Córdoba or Málaga. Sam, you need to go too. The police will want to interview you, and when they can't find you, they'll issue an arrest warrant. Then you won't be able to fly, you'll come up at passport check.'

Sam was shocked. 'Can you delay that?'

'Don't ask questions like that. I just need you guys off the estate – unless you hear from me, assume that you're good to go. The other guys can hold the fort. Terry and Goodman are probably fine, Joseph and Gary should be careful.'

Chalky said, 'Are we still on?' He sounded worried.

Fox sounded on a short fuse. 'I need to sort out the Ukrainian shit fight here first. Christ, I'm supposed to be giving up this life.'

'I've so missed working with you, Wilko,' said Chalky. 'The laughs, the banter, the light touch.'

Fox said, 'Ditto,' and hung up.

'Dare I say it, but if that's him being sympathetic I'd hate to see him when he's got the hump,' said Caroline. 'I wonder if Fox is going solo on this?'

'Very difficult, they just don't work like that,' said Terry. 'And he himself said he's virtually out of the Firm. JIC Chair is a connected but different job, new bosses, different protocols. I don't see he could risk it. Now, in case any of you missed it, Fox said if we use the stuff from the villa he'll disown Chalky. Anybody?'

Caroline said, 'Sadly, what it means is you can't have both stories.'

'Ah, back at those infernal crossroads, Sam,' said Terry.

Sam knew Caroline was right. He looked around and knew he had to make the call. 'It's no contest. Chalky is the scoop of the decade.'

Gary had his laptop open. 'Last Seville flight at seven-ten. BA.'

'I won't make that. You go, Chalky.'

'No no. If you can get out of the meeting by five-thirty, I will. Give your luggage to Joseph, he'll take Chalky. I'll book you on.'

'Is that risky? Maybe buy a ticket there?'

'Let's trust Fox that we'll know if we have to abort. If you don't get out, I'll take you to a safe house.'

'We've got at least half an hour,' said Terry. 'Can we get back to the matter at hand? Shall we look at what was in the safe? That would be logical, MI6 must have thought it was awfully important.'

Gary had loaded the disc Goodman had given him. 'Here we go.'

A letter came up on the plasma. It was over two pages, packed with text and numbers, heavily annotated.

'That's Russian text,' said Gary. He zoomed in on the

letterhead. 'I'd say that was some Russian state department, we can find out.' He moved the zoom about. 'It's addressed to Anatoliy Kubashov at Stoke Court, is that the place, Chalky?'

'That I broke into? Yes, big pile near Ascot.'

Sam looked at his laptop. 'According to Wiki, Kubashov, son of a diplomat, school in America, import-export. Aviation, armaments. Picture of him with Gorbachev.'

'Kids?'

Sam scrolled down. 'A daughter. Married. Anastasia, there's a link to her. Here we go. Anna Slack, dual citizen, married to some American, she works at the UN in New York.'

'Keep going,' said Terry.

'I'll get the letter translated.'

'Don't waste your time. I got this Russian hooker to translate it years ago, it's harmless.'

Gary pressed on with the other documents. 'These certificates are Russian, look like bearer bonds. The bank statements are from a Swiss bank in Zurich, but no narrative, just numbers. And finally this.'

It was a list of names, British-looking. One had the suffix G.

'I'll Google them,' said Gary. 'That's your lot, Terry.'

'Great job, everybody. Fascinating. Can't remember a meeting as fun as this. So, first up, who's going to write the Chalky story?'

'I've started it,' said Sam. 'Katie, want to help?'

'Are you serious? Of course. In the house style?'

'No, broadsheet. Frank's not having it.'

'Why on earth not?' said Caroline.

'I'm still going to get him Burke. I don't know how, but I'm going to try.'

They all started to pack up. Terry said, 'Before you go, the major outstanding action point is somebody needs to find Miss Whiplash and visit that kinky Coco shop.'

Nobody answered.

'Why are you all looking at me?'

# CHAPTER 26

## WEDNESDAY

Standing in the mews behind the house Terry pressed the key fob and the garage door eased up. He handed Joseph the car keys.

'Just be gentle with her, and that's a 6.3 litre V8 so bring it back full.'

'This the 300SEL?'

'Best car Mercedes ever made. 1971, done just thirty thousand miles, had it since new, bought it when I was at Reuters.'

'Hardly run in. Beautiful.'

Joseph drove Sam and Goodman fairly sensibly to the lawyer's office on the Strand. They waited opposite until they saw Donald go in, gave him a couple of minutes and got out of the car. Joseph said, 'I'll collect Chalky and meet you at Heathrow.' Goodman pulled a suit bag out of the boot and slung it across his arm.

'Something good in there, I hope?' asked Sam.

'Oh, yes. Me up against Donald? Got the smoke machine. Tonight, Matthew, I shall be... Elvis Presley.'

From reception, Paul went off to change, and as he went Sam said, 'On my signal.'

'Unleash hell? Sure.'

This had seemed a good idea when they concocted it. Sam now realised how much could go wrong. He had to get Donald on side and Frank to stick to the script, not go off-piste as he usually did. He'd asked Francis Kenyon for the biggest meeting room they had, and he'd delivered. He looked as dull as you'd expect an employment lawyer to be. They all shook hands, and Francis dispensed tea and water then said, 'All the execution copies are here. The small colour-coded tabs indicate where you each have to sign.'

'Very good,' said Frank. 'Our heads on a plate, eh, Donald?'

Sam gave Frank a filthy look. Donald was too long in the tooth to rise to it. 'These are good deals, trust me. Shall we?'

Sam drop-called Goodman as they sat down to start. Ten seconds later he burst in, a vision in white and gold. 'Sorry I'm late, team.'

Francis stood up. 'You know where I am if you need me, gentlemen.' He said it deadpan and shuffled out backwards, like a butler, closing the door behind him.

'Nice whistle,' said Sam.

Goodman unbuttoned his white suit jacket to show the lining, pink with gold dollar signs.

'Close your mouth, Donald, you look like one of those bloody salmon you can't catch,' said Frank.

'You two met?' said Sam.

Goodman moved round to Donald and shook his hand. 'Of course, loads, how are you, Donald?' and went back to sit between Frank and Sam who said, 'Donald, are you going to speak?'

'Is somebody going to tell me what the hell is going on?'

Sam said, 'He's my, our, lawyer. Felt we needed a bit more, what's the word, oomph.'

Donald sat down and put his pen away.

Goodman took a folder from his file, pulled out a handful of black and white blow-ups and slid them across the table.

Donald looked at the villa photos and said, 'I don't understand.'

'Gary was watching our back.'

Donald picked them up and studied them. 'What's he doing?'

'Your so-called driver is bugging me and planting surveillance equipment in Frank's villa.'

'You don't think I had anything to do with it?'

Goodman slid a sheet across the table. 'Jean-Luc Lavelle is an employee of Canada Media Holdings BVI. Of which you,' he slid across another sheet, 'are a Director and COO.'

Donald threw them on the table. 'Guys, you have got to be joking?'

'I don't see anybody laughing,' said Goodman. 'So, where to begin, Don? For a start, two jurisdictions, Spain and the UK. Breaking and entering. Trespass. But the phone taps, well, you don't need me to tell you the law.'

Sam could see Donald was worried. He pushed his chair back and put up his hands. 'Come on, I had no idea what he was doing. He doesn't work for me.'

'So why did you turn up with him and get me out by the pool, keeping me busy and giving him free run of the house?'

'I did not.'

'Doesn't look good, Donald. At the least you'd be taken in for questioning, but given the current climate they'd probably go for a high-profile arrest, plenty of photos, *News at Ten*.'

Donald said, 'You really are a lowlife sleazebag.'

'That's a new one. Pretty confident I can get you disbarred and banned from being a Director.'

'So you're telling me about the fucking law?'

'Looks like it.'

'Listen. All I've tried to do is help you. I can't help it if Jay Lomax is on a mission. He wanted to be tougher. I fought for these deals for you. You can't tie the Lavelle thing to me.'

'Whose idea was it you for you to go see Sam at my villa? Jay's?'

'It was the fair thing to do, come on.'

'And who offered the jet and the driver?'

'I had to get there somehow.'

'So it was all Jay's idea?'

'Exactly. Case dismissed.'

They all just sat there. It wasn't going well. Donald was getting his confidence back. 'This is bullshit.' He laughed. 'I've seen your tag-team bullyboy tactics a thousand times. Jay's right, you two have lost it. You think you and this Elvis can outwit me? Really, is that the best you've got? I think we should forget these deals.' He got up, and started gathering his papers.

Sam looked at his watch. He didn't have time to play games. 'Barcelona.'

Donald stopped. 'What?'

'Conference – law and the media. March last year. Arts Hotel.' Sam took a folded sheet of A4 from his inside pocket and gave it to him. 'I've got more.'

Donald unfolded it and looked at it. He sat down. 'You fucking bastard.'

'What sort of idiot brings a knife to a gunfight?' He said it more to Frank, who smiled and shook his head.

'You fucking bastard.'

'You already said that.'

'Why would you do this?'

'You're the one who always tells us we're in the insurance business. I guess I just submitted a claim.'

Donald put his head in his hands, then looked at the sheet again. 'How did you?'

'Same way we got Burke. Gary got some good stuff.'

'You wouldn't dare show this to my wife.'

Sam went over and bent over him until their faces nearly touched. 'Try me.'

'So what's the deal?' said Frank.

Sam could see the fight had gone out of him, and he turned away. 'For God's sake, Donald, this is us. Don't play that game. You've struck a deal with Jay, what is it?'

Donald folded his arms. 'Group Managing Editor.'

'Big job. Go on then, who's Editor?' said Sam.

'You know.'

'That's a sick joke. Julian Mortlock stands for everything you hate as much as we do.'

'He's flavour of the month right now, had some great stories over the last year, flying high on your rapid decline.'

'So all you have to do is make sure Frank and I sign these deals and it's all done. Neat and tidy. Everybody happy.'

'Well, you're clearly not signing now.'

'Actually we are.'

Donald looked genuinely perplexed. 'Why?'

Goodman gave him two sheets of A4 which Donald read and put down. 'Side letters, you each have unilateral right to terminate within thirty days, like a cooling off period. Clever.'

'We sign now, you can show Jay we have, everybody calms down. We hold the side letters. If we like the deal, we tear them up. Otherwise we have an exit.'

'Don't really have a choice, do I?'

'Not really. Has Mortlock signed yet?'

'Soon as you guys do.'

'Just make sure Jay thinks everything's under control.'

'Another thing,' Sam said. 'We need to find Justine Walker.'

'Why?'

It was clear to them that Donald didn't know. So Jay had only told him what he needed to know.

'It's not important, I just do. And that's not her real name. You do realise he sent you to Canada to get you out of the way while they got the Burke story away?'

'I did wonder about that. She was fine but hardly qualified.'

Sam looked at his watch. 'I have to go. Let's do it.'

He finished and Goodman said, 'Get going, we'll wrap up.'

As Sam headed to the door, Donald said, 'What do I do now?'

'Act as if everything is on track. And don't do anything stupid.'

'And where do I stand?'

'I'd suggest in the corner, with your dunce's hat on.'

*

Frank followed Sam out into the corridor. 'Sam, I don't need this.' He tore the side letter in two and gave it to him.

'What the hell are you doing?'

'I'm taking the deal.'

'What? Why? This gives us time, we're nearly there.'

'I promised Louise I would sign. I never see the kids, or her, we never get to the villa. The deal was I'd stick by you on this one, but then that's it.'

'But this morning you wanted us to keep going.'

'No, I want *you* to keep going. You'll get there, you always do.'

'You'll be bored.'

'No, I've got a book deal to ghost Harry's autobiography – I'm going to write it by the pool.'

'You sure?'

'I am. Get out of here.'

*

Sam jogged across the ground floor reception. He couldn't believe they'd make it. Outside Gary was at the kerb astride his Honda XL. Maybe they could. Gary gave Sam a helmet and jacket.

'I looked at those names on that list, nothing special, couple of policemen, civil servants, nothing jumped out.'

'OK, let's go.'

'Relax. More importantly, you dodged a bullet.'

He handed him the *Evening Standard*.

The headline said DOWN AND OUT. They'd cropped the photo – all it showed was Sam on the bench with his beer and the tramp on the other end. Chalky had been left out.

'I don't believe it. What a story and they missed it, staring them in the face.'

Without ever seeming to ride that fast or recklessly, and avoiding attracting attention, thirty minutes later Gary rode up the ramp at Terminal 5 to Meet and Greet on Level 2 where Joseph was parked up in Terry's Mercedes. Sam took his bag from Joseph and they went up in the lift to departures on Level 5. Chalky had his baseball cap on but took the sunglasses off once inside. Sam looked at the luggage Chalky was wheeling and said, 'We'll need to go to Bag Drop, that's too big.'

'Shit, I didn't think.'

'Don't worry, it'll be OK.'

At the desk, the guy in front was taking forever. The BA lady finally said, 'Are you together?' and took their passports and boarding passes, asking Chalky to take off his hat. Sam felt nervous now. He had never before noticed just how many cameras were pointing at you or how bright the lights were. He normally sailed through with his BA Platinum Card; it felt like the last scene in *Argo* now. She took her time.

'Is there a problem?' said Sam.

'Just trying to seat you together, Mr Plummer.'

'We're fine, really.'

'Nearly done.'

She handed Chalky's back. 'There you go, I've given you a Fast Track sticker, Mr Mortimer. Have a good trip.'

Chalky put his cap back on. 'Thanks.'

Sam watched her tapping away, wondering if he was going to be OK. It seemed to take forever.

'There you go.'

Sam took it and turned round. Two policemen were in front of them, with their Heckler & Koch carbines slung across their chests. The taller of them put out his hand and said, 'May I?'

They handed over their passports and boarding passes.

'Wait here.'

He stepped away to talk on his radio.

Sam felt sweat running down his back.

He saw Chalky look across at Gary, who gave him the 'OK' sign, his thumb and index finger forming a circle. 'What the fuck?'

Chalky leaned into him. 'You don't think Gary would put me in this situation without an extraction plan, do you?'

'Are you mad? They've got OUR passports.'

'I've got another one. Joseph's at the kerb on the bike.'

'It's official. You are mad.'

The policeman came back and picked up Chalky's bag. 'Please, come with us.'

As they followed them across the concourse Sam said, 'If I don't see you again, I'm so sorry mate.'

'It wasn't your fault. You tried.'

Sam got out his mobile and speed-dialled Fox, but it went to voicemail. They followed them outside where a police Range Rover was parked. As the policeman put the bag in the boot, Chalky looked across at Joseph, astride the Honda, engine running, holding the spare helmet. He stood there for a moment, then got in the back with Sam. 'For better, for worse. Let's go Sundance.'

They heard the child locks clunk as they pulled away. So that was it, game over. He could see the headlines. This wasn't a slap on the wrist from the PCC, this was time at Her Majesty's pleasure. Aiding and abetting. Perverting the course of justice. Humiliation.

He heard the policeman talk into his radio. 'Yes, we've got them both. With you in five minutes.'

He felt bile in his throat. At least he'd signed his deal.

The policeman turned round. 'You guys cause us real headaches when you do this.'

'Do what?' said Chalky.

'Just walk in like that.'

'Like what?'

'You have diplomatic clearance, why don't you come straight to the right place? We can't guarantee your safety in there, and it's not fair on the other passengers.'

Sam and Chalky looked at each other. They were at an automatic gate now that led on to the airfield.

'I'm sorry, I've been based abroad for a while.'

'Well, Mr Mortimer, next time come straight here to VIP, it's the Windsor Suite.'

They stopped under cover where another policeman put their bags through a scanner. They drove to the plane and got out. The policeman handed them over to a BA stewardess who put them on board and upgraded them to Business. 'I'm sorry there will be a short delay while we get everybody else on board. Always nice to welcome our Platinum Card holders, Mr Plummer. Champagne?

# CHAPTER 27

## WEDNESDAY

Terry doubted he could find the femme fatale, but he had to try.

He took a cab to Seven Dials and strolled up Monmouth Street looking for number 23. When he got to Coco de Mer he looked through the window past the two mannequins dressed in what he now knew were some of their tamer products. The only girl he could see was busy, but as the sign told him they didn't close until eight, he repaired to the bar of the Covent Garden Hotel opposite and ordered a large Bombay Sapphire and tonic, if nothing else for Dutch courage. He did know you always needed to have your story ready. What could his possibly be? A present for my granddaughter? A joke present for a friend? He couldn't think of one. Maybe they just left old guys alone.

Towards the front of the shop was a lot of black and red, interspersed with leopard print. There were twelve frames on the wall, each with a pair of knickers or a garter belt. The entire place was magenta, with a dark wooden floor. He realised it was not unlike the website, or the products themselves, getting naughtier and darker nearer the back. There seemed to be an awful lot of silk and leather. And latex.

The girl approached him. He guessed she was perfect for the role, tall and slim, in a simple black dress and super high heels that only made him wonder which outfit she had on underneath.

'Just looking, thank you, dear.'

She smiled, having heard it before. 'I'm Yolande, let me know if you need help with sizes.'

In the middle of the floor was a gold life-size statue of a woman, naked except for high heels, bending over and holding her ankles. It had the feel of a very risqué Paris establishment he remembered visiting in the fifties. Glass-fronted cabinets and shelves had various smaller items, which to his eye looked like sex toys. He did wonder what on earth Pin Up Bombshell Orgasm Balm Mint was.

As he put it back down, Yolande appeared next to him. 'That's fabulous. It's got almond oil, beeswax, avocado, everything.'

'What does one actually do with it, my dear?'

'Just a dab, directly onto the clitoris.'

'Righto,' said Terry.

He wandered round some more then came back to the girl, not having to feign his embarrassment. 'Do you have the Persephone Playsuit in stock? Daughter of Zeus you know. In red.'

She looked as if old boys in handmade linen suits asked her this every day and said, 'Absolutely, one of my favourites. Do you know what size?' as she led him over to the rail.

He pulled out the photos of Justine.

'Do you remember selling one to her?'

The girl's body language changed, stiffening and stepping back, she looked round to check the door. 'Are you a policeman?'

'Journalist, retired. Don't worry, she's not in trouble.'

He could see her weighing this up. 'I recognise her, used to come in quite a lot.'

'Do you have any details?'

'I can't.'

'I can pay you.'

'It's not that. I don't have the records here. Maybe head office?'

'Well, I'm sorry to bother you, Yolande.'

She said, 'Hold on,' and reached under the counter, producing a tin of the Pin Up Bombshell Orgasm Balm Mint. 'Present for you. Don't overdo it.'

Terry thanked her, and as she opened the door for him she said, 'Anyway, those girls get twenty per cent off and usually pay cash.'

'What girls?'

*

Her hands were on his shoulders, pushing him back on to the sofa. She was astride his thighs, already down to just a G-string, her hair falling forward over his face. Her lips were right next to his ear.

'What's your name?' she said, fighting the music.

'Henry. Terence. Terry.' He wasn't used to shouted conversations.

'Don't worry, I won't tell.'

'Yours?'

'Tinkerbell.'

Terry could feel the sweat running down his back.

'Pleased to meet you, Tinkerbell. I like your knickers. Coco?'

She stopped grinding. 'You want cocoa?'

'Your thong thing, Coco de Mer?'

She laughed. 'No, Intimissimi, these.'

Then she turned round and the G-string came off. He'd never been to Stringfellows. It looked like the basement of Coco de Mer, except the mannequins were alive, it was louder, and the lighting much lower. And it was hotter. Her hands were on his knees now and she was backing up towards him, bottom first, swaying side to side in time with the thumping music. He looked around to see if there was any acceptable behaviour at this stage, but having already been made aware of the 'no touching' rule, he just kept his hands by his side.

She had got awfully close, but now she was back face-to-face and it was clearly the end of his dance. She had one hand placed on his thigh, a long way up.

'How was that, Terry?'

He thought 'top hole' wouldn't work so just said, 'Excellent, what's the form, my dear? How much?'

'First time?'

'Here. Yes.'

'Up to you, Terry, but the rate is twenty.'

As she put her G-string and bra back on, he took out fifty, folded it, and slipped it into her garter belt, his hand shaking, realising that was the only reason they wore them.

She kissed him on the cheek and said, 'Thanks, pops.'

He dabbed the sweat off his brow, took a deep breath, and said to himself, 'Steady, Trigger. Calm down.'

He turned down a couple of dances while he regrouped. The Coco line had been crass. He had about five hundred pounds on him, and his cards, so plenty of ammunition. He just needed a plan now that he knew roughly how it worked. He moved tables so he could watch more of the girls pole dancing.

When the next Angel came by he said, 'Can we go somewhere quieter?' and she led him by the hand through the bacchanalia to a quieter alcove towards the back. They all looked much the same, but this one was taller.

As she started he said, 'Can we just talk?'

She dismounted and squeezed in next to him. 'Still costs, I'm afraid.'

'Drink?'

Another Angel appeared and they ordered.

'I'm Terry, by the way'

'Desdemona.' She had a strong cockney accent.

'Ah. Look to her, Moor, if thou hast eyes to see. She hath deceived her father and may thee.'

'What?'

'Shakespeare. Desdemona was Othello's bit on the side.'

'My mum wanted a boy, to call Des after Des O'Connor. She

still calls me Dessy for short.'

'So how does it work back here, moneywise?'

'Still twenty basic, but the clock's running if you're just nattering away like this. Two hundred for a private dance if you want. But no hand or blow jobs, I'm afraid.'

Terry pulled out the photos and said, 'I need to find this girl. I think she worked here.'

'Put that away, Christ.'

'Sorry.'

'She used to work here. Her name's Bambi.'

'I need her real name.'

'I don't know. I'll have to get it. What's it worth?'

'Two hundred and fifty pounds, but I need it now.'

'Let's make it four hundred and I'll throw in the best dance you'll get tonight.'

'Deal.'

She wasn't kidding. When she finished she said, 'Her best friend is on second shift. I'll get it at the changeover. Can you meet me in the bar of the St Martin's Lane Hotel at ten-fifteen?'

'It's a date.'

'No, it's not.'

He'd had enough. Out on the street in the fresh air and bright light he reflected on what he'd just done and seen. He felt proud that he had actually made some real progress... if she turned up with a name anyway. He had an hour to kill so he bought *Private Eye* and installed himself at a table in the hotel bar.

She slumped down in front of him, looking very different, with little make-up and a simple black dress. The waitress came over and Terry said, 'More champagne, Des?'

She gave him a withering look, and in a cut glass accent said to the waitress, 'Manhattan please, on the rocks, lowball glass,' and to Terry, 'My noble father, I do perceive here a divided duty.'

Terry looked puzzled.

'Desdemona explaining that she owes a duty to her father and her new husband, Othello. Key scene.' She put out her hand and said, 'Cordelia.'

'Charmed. And confused,' said Terry, taking it.

She handed over a piece of paper. 'Maxine Glover. There's her mobile and email. She hasn't got an address. They used to share a flat, but she moved away.'

Terry reached for the cash but she said, 'Not here, don't want people to get the wrong idea.'

'So what do you do?'

'I'm an actress. My mother was too.'

'Hence Cordelia.'

'Exactly. The worst bit is our surname's Smith so I have to stop people calling me Delia. If I had a pound for every "Cor! Delia Smith" I'd be rich. Anyway, I'm resting, as we say. I need to make a living, so I trudge round castings all day, and I'm in there at night. When I do get a job they're fine about it.'

'And the accent?'

'Just for variety I do loads. Change my name and accents – Swedish, French, Scottish, Russian, South African. Sometimes I do very posh; we all work out pretty quickly what they'll pay most for. City boys like a bit of rough, think it's their best chance to meet you outside the club. Get caught out sometimes but the punters just think it's funny. Frankly, if they get an eyeful you can talk Swahili. Did you enjoy it?'

'It was delightful. But, I didn't have my reading glasses, so frankly it was all a bit of a blur.'

She looked him in the eye. 'Well, that's a shame.'

He blushed. 'To be honest, I think that might have tipped me over the edge. Or they would have steamed up.'

She laughed. 'Next time. Look, I'm 36, been married twice, no kids, I'm the oldest girl in there.'

'Well, you don't look it.'

'That's because you didn't have your glasses on. But, thank you.'

Outside he offered her the money.

'Are you really sure?'

'I insist.'

She took it and kissed him on the cheek. He gave her his card.

'I'll email you.' She waved and walked away.

*

As they flew over the Channel, Sam wondered if leaving British airspace meant he was safe, and maybe Chalky too. Could BA be forced to turn back?

When Chalky woke up Sam asked him, 'Do they have the power to arrest us when we get there?'

'I don't think so, we're on Spanish soil.'

'Come on, you must be the living expert on this.'

'On extradition, yes. Letting us in is another matter.'

'So we could end up in limbo on the plane or sent back.'

'Well, we'll soon find out.'

As they got off the plane, Sam rang Fox but there was no answer. They split up at passport control, Sam hanging back to give Chalky a better chance. He watched him get through without any trouble. As the line edged forward, the woman next to him said, 'Are you that bloke in the papers?'

'No.'

She turned to her husband. 'Dave, it's that bloke from the papers, the one causing all the trouble.'

He went to the loo, waited for five minutes and rejoined the queue at the back. He found Chalky at the baggage carousel.

'I need a drink, badly,' said Sam.

Sam read his texts. 'Bingo. Gary says Terry got her name. Maxine Glover.'

'Good old Terry.'

He tried Terry but his phone was off, so he rang Gary. 'How did he do it?'

'Ended up in Stringfellows, she used to work there.'

'Bloody hell.'

'I'm working on her. Only got a Gmail account and a defunct mobile, the number you had. I'll find her.'

Sam's mind wandered. It explained so much – the body, the lack of inhibition, the way she moved. Was it just a coincidence that the two women he'd had the best sex with both danced naked for a living?

'Are you still there?'

'Sorry, Gary. Did you make any progress on the safe stuff?'

'Damir says the letters are pretty dull. Protocol stuff. List of names, all look British. Few on Google. Nothing interesting. Policemen, civil servants it looks like.'

'You and Joseph OK?'

'We're fine.'

*

Nacho was there to meet them. They rang ahead and checked there was nobody outside the front gate. Sam went straight to the guest house, had a shower, watched some TV with an Estrella, and kept an eye out for anything breaking online while he did a few emails and texts. He sent one to Clare to say he'd signed his deal, and she replied, 'Thank God. Well done. xx'

# CHAPTER 28

## THURSDAY 10th July – DAY 13

***Daily Express*: HOW YOU CAN LIVE ANOTHER TEN YEARS**

***Daily Mirror*: GREEDY STARS TARGETTED OVER £5 BILLION TAX DODGE**

Sam's phone woke him up. 'Jesus.' He fumbled for it and saw it was 3.37 but didn't recognise the UK number.

'Hello?'

'Sam, it's Leonard Fox. We've got a problem.'

'Hold on.' He sat up, and turned on the light. 'OK.'

'The *Guardian* are running the full photo of you and Chalky on the front page, uncropped. Bit smarter than the *Standard*. It'll break about five online, we're told.'

'Shit.'

'And they've got Chalky off the CCTV at Heathrow without the sunglasses and his passport scan. You were lucky to get out.'

'Shit.'

'The police are issuing a warrant for your arrest but they know you've both gone and where. It'll be a lawyer-fest with the Spaniards so they won't turn up yet, but the media will be on their way. The fact that the police drove Chalky to the plane has made them a laughing stock. You need to go into lockdown. Don't say shit again.'

'Bollocks.'

'They ID'd Joseph driving and know the car is registered to Gary. They want to question them. They need to sign up with Goodman now. Can you warn them?'

'Sure. How do you know all this?'

'Technically I finished two weeks ago and start on Monday, so I'm in limbo, but when Chalky popped up they dragged me back in. So I'm involved.'

'Could this affect your new job?'

'If my name comes out it's not happening. They know I gave the clearance to get him through Heathrow. Bit of a solo effort, I'm afraid. Police have gone ballistic, and the Foreign Office. You can imagine, PM on one of those law and order crime-fighting drives and we let Chalky walk in and then we escort him out.'

'Is the PM involved?'

'Sam, everybody's involved. I'm in first thing at Number Ten. See what happens.'

'Blimey. Why are you doing this?'

'You have no idea what Chalky means to me. I can't explain now, but just remember, he was one of us. Well, he still is. Forget all this other stuff, I have to help him. Yes.'

Sam admired his commitment. The more he saw of Chalky, the more he understood why Fox inspired the loyalty he did.

'What should we do?'

'Stay there and stay in touch with me. The mobile I gave you is secure. You found the mother?'

'She's there. Damir's on his way. Thanks for that.'

'Just remember we like her. We just can't control who she sleeps with. Listen, Sam, there's only one way this works.'

'Which is?'

'You know your world, I know mine. We have to manage this.'

'We need the Firm to admit they, you, ran Chalky, that's all.'

'That's all. That's all? Jesus. I know. You're just going to have to leave that with me, it's not easy.'

'I understood what you said. But I need to use Gary's stuff from the villa if I'm going to get Burke.'

'You can't. It'll cause us huge problems.'

'Then I won't. Chalky is a bigger story and more important.'

'Well, I'm with you on that. You guys never give up, do you? Anything else I can get you? Winning lottery numbers?'

Sam could hear another phone ringing in the background.

Fox said, 'Have to go, keep your phone on.'

This changed everything. He couldn't go home, and he was in the same boat as Chalky now, the one he was rocking.

*

He couldn't believe he could sleep, but he did. When he woke up he had so many messages in every digital form, he just tossed his phone on the bed and went outside. Chalky was coming towards him and said, 'You've seen it all?'

'Fox rang me about four.' It took Sam five minutes to bring him up to date.

'Sofia's gone ballistic.'

'I bet she has. No idea why, but Fox seems to be treating you as his priority.'

'All that wonga in the Caymans.'

Sam didn't believe it for one minute. This wasn't about money.

'Chalky, do I sense that you're quite enjoying this?'

'Watching you go through what I've put up with for over twenty years? A bit, yes.'

'Maybe we should move. Fox said we should stay put but… '

'Then we do what he says. I'm not going anywhere. This is your first day on the set of *The Fugitive*; I've been doing this for a long time. Relax.'

Sam looked at him and said, 'Feels more like *Assault on Precinct 13.*'

They went over to the house and into the kitchen where Sofia was having breakfast and watching TV. She didn't even look at him. On the screen was the shot of them on the bench, which then switched to headshots of Chalky and Sam.

He sat down and Maria brought him a coffee.

Sofia gave Sam a filthy look. 'So now you know what it feels like, eh?'

Sam said, 'Sort of.'

'Why did you persuade him to go back? It was so stupid.'

Sofia switched to Spanish and went into a tirade, with Chalky doing the best he could to fight back.

'I should go,' said Sam.

'Stay where you are,' said Chalky. 'Sofia. Shut up.'

She slammed her mug on the table, spilling her coffee. 'How dare you?'

'Sit. Down.' Sam hadn't seen this side of Chalky. He pulled a chair up in front of her and took both her hands.

'I know this will be tough, but give me one word answers. Do you love me?'

'Of course... yes.'

'Do you trust me?'

'Yes.'

'You remember the marriage vows, the bit in English about love, honour and obey?'

'Yes.'

'Then just for one day, will you please do exactly what I say?'

She took her hands away and sat back. 'Just one day?'

She got up to fetch a cloth and wipe up the coffee. 'OK. Until midnight.'

'Thank you. Are the kids here?'

'Alex is. Nacho's gone into town.'

'Get him back. Everybody stays here today. Nobody talks to anybody. Get the guys to lock all the gates and put somebody on each one. Put Jorge full-time watching the CCTV, and tell him to get two guys to ride the perimeter all day. No guns.'

BBC News 24 was still rolling on. Chalky turned up the volume. 'If you're joining us for the first time today, our main story... ' Tim Willcox was holding up the front page now to another camera. The headline read CHALKY WHITE ESCAPES – AGAIN. Underneath it said, 'Bungling police help him leave.' There were two big pictures, one of Sam and Chalky enjoying their Doom Bars, the other a CCTV grab of them being escorted through Heathrow Terminal 5 by the armed police. '...that the fugitive Chalky White has been in London for at least two days, and that he fled to Spain last night. This story is developing by the minute, but the most remarkable element is that it seems the police escorted him to the British Airways plane. The police have declined to comment but they have issued an arrest warrant for the man with him in the pictures, Mr Sam Plummer, the journalist.'

The coverage cut to a wide shot of the studio: two men were sitting at the desk.

Sam said, 'Look. It's my mate Phil.'

'With us are Ryan O'Rourke, a criminal lawyer, and from the *Sunday Times* Insight team, Phil Nagle.'

It then dawned on Sam that Phil might turn against him – some NewsCorp corporate line from up on high to dump on him. If the Lomaxes had gone down without a fight, why would anybody connected to Murdoch help him?

'Mr O'Rourke, let me start with you. How could this have happened?'

'Thank you, good morning. We understand that White travelled under a false passport,' they put up a shot of Chalky's passport, 'in the name of Dennis Mortimer.'

'But why was he escorted to the plane?'

'According to the BAA who run Heathrow, they had diplomatic clearance or status.'

Willcox said, 'But we do know he arrived on a private jet on Tuesday and first went to visit his terminally ill father.'

Chalky said, 'Bloody hell. What's this got to do with my dad?'

Sam saw that Sofia had her hand over her mouth and tears in her eyes. She got up and left.

'It makes the police look incredibly foolish,' continued O'Rourke, 'and the entire security services. They're trying to restore public confidence but this looks farcical. MI5 say the current UK threat level for international terrorism is officially "substantial" – this means that an attack is a strong possibility. And Chalky White just walked in and out.'

'And Mr Nagle,' said Willcox, 'tell us about Mr Plummer, who's clearly involved in this.'

'We don't know that.'

'I know we have to be careful here, but he's in both photos. It's been widely reported this morning that he was in Spain last week and he fled the country with him.'

'I worked with Sam for over ten years, he's one of the best journalists I've ever worked with.'

Under his breath Sam said, 'Good boy.'

'I admire your loyalty, but he is the man who was fired in the aftermath of the Lord Burke story, which smeared a highly respected national figure and appeared to endanger the lives of two young women.'

Phil shifted on his seat. 'I'm not sure we know that. Look, all I'm saying is that we need to find out the facts... '

'Which he's obviously not very good at doing,' said O'Rourke.

'He left the paper by mutual consent, and he's not been charged with anything.'

Willcox said, 'Now we know the police also want to question these two men.' Up on screen came two very serious mugshots of Gary and Joseph, clearly from some time ago.

Chalky said, 'Blimey. Look like the guys from *Bravo Two Zero*.'

'On the left is Gareth Lake, and on the right, Joseph Kelly. The police have advised that these men should not be approached by members of the public.'

Phil laughed.

'What's funny, Mr Nagle?'

'Joseph took my kids to Alton Towers last month. He's not dangerous. They were both in the army, fought in Iraq with distinction. They're well known in our industry, good guys.'

'We can now go over to Downing Street live and join Michael Leonard,' said Willcox. 'What's happening, Mike?'

He was in the classic position across the road, the black front door behind him, guarded by a solitary policeman. A black Range Rover was pulling up.

'Well, you can't see them but there is an enormous number of TV crews here. We've just seen Britain's most senior police officer, Commissioner Jack Burgess, arrive. You may recall that, as Inspector, Burgess was the policeman who waged war on the Costa del Crime in the nineties with mixed results. We also believe that Sir Christopher Lines, the recently appointed Head of MI6, otherwise known as C, is in there.'

'Is the Prime Minister attending?'

'We can only assume so. Embarrassingly, he is supposed to be announcing crime figures today.'

Chalky muted it. 'Excellent. If that's not rocking the fucking boat, I don't know what is.'

*

Sam went back to his room. Checking his emails, he read the one from Cheche in Miami first, then looked to see if his phone still had a number for Pete Bolwell. He went outside – he only needed to drop in one word to know.

'Pete, it's Sam Plummer.'

'Christ, Sam, what the hell are you up to?'

'I'm at Chalky's now. Look, he told me about Ojén.'

There was a long pause. 'Did he?'

'I don't want you to talk about it.'

'Well, I'm not going to. It was a really tough time for me. I've never said one word about it to anybody. In my line, you know when to keep your mouth shut.'

'Yeah, Pete, keeping your trousers on was your problem.'

Bolwell laughed. 'Bit rich coming from you.'

'Fair point. How are the books going?'

'My alter ego PJ knocks out one a year. Jason Statham's bought the film rights, money for old rope.'

'What happened with you added to the legend of Chalky locally as a villain, scared us all off, but didn't get reported. Brilliant.'

'You going to expose it?'

'Well, you're going to see them in a different light on Sunday.'

'Them?'

'The two guys from the barn, in Ojén.'

Bolwell was too good not to know this was fishing, but he let it go. If Chalky wanted to tell him, that was his call. He had saved his life. 'Where?'

'In the papers.'

'And you're keeping me out of it?'

'And the other guy.'

'I don't know who he was. Honestly.'

He read Cheche's email again. One Spanish, two Colombian. Their two bodies had been flown home to Bogotá. A professional hit, with none of the trademark signs of a gang kill.

*

They were in a windowless meeting room. The PM was late. Sir Christopher Lines had Len Fox off in one corner. 'I've hardly got my feet under the table, Len, and you're fucking about with Chalky White.'

'I wasn't the one that reneged on his deal.'

'There was no deal to bring him back. We set him free and we made him rich. Period.'

'We'll agree to differ on that.'

'And I've just seen the logs – you signed them out of the country. I hope you know what you're bloody doing.'

Fergus Loughran walked in, unrecognisable from the scruffy

but brilliant hack who had worked for Sam all those years ago. Now he was a fully fledged Number Ten insider, another Whitehall mandarin. His hair was short, his suit sharp. He addressed the room. 'The PM apologises. He's asked me to chair the meeting. Shall we?'

At the other end of the table alone, in uniform, sat Jack Burgess, the Police Commissioner, the man always referred to in the tabloids as Britain's Top Cop. He didn't look any happier than Lines. He had a shock of grey hair and trimmed beard to match.

Before they sat down, Lines pulled Fox close and said, 'You dealt with Burgess?'

'A little.'

'Limited. And Loughran's a bloody journo by trade.'

Lines didn't look happy as Fergus continued, 'You all know the PM's supposed to announce the crime figures this week. As you also know they are very good but would be completely overshadowed by this. So, Sir Christopher, a quick overview would be good.'

Lines turned to Fox and gave him the hospital pass. 'Leonard?'

Fox addressed Britain's Top Cop. 'Jack, I take full responsibility for this decision. I know it's made you look bad.'

'Weren't you the guy trying to catch him for years?' said Loughran.

Burgess put his hand up. 'I was. And looking bad I deal with every day. Just stop. Listen, I'm not George Smiley or Sherlock Holmes, but let me try this. Len, you knew he flew in?'

'Correct, we did,' said Fox.

'You gave the diplomatic clearance for White and Plummer to leave.'

'Yes, sorry.'

Lines tapped his pencil, clearly unhappy with Fox being so open.

'You knew the papers had the photo of them outside the pub so you had to get them out, and you made a decision.'

'Correct. He was going anyway, and I couldn't guarantee he wouldn't get arrested by you lot.'

Fox sensed Burgess was not as thick as advertised. Burgess carried on. 'So, try this. Two things. When I was trying to arrest him for all those years I was actually up against you.'

Lines said, 'Yes. Right thing to do.'

'No problem. It fits why he was always one step ahead, sometimes uncannily. And two, you therefore had a reason to keep him out there. Either he did something for you, or he has something you need or something you don't want to come out.'

Fox said, 'All three. He did the original break-in for us. We got him out. He works for us.'

'Jesus,' said Loughran, clearly shocked by the revelation. 'Still?'

'More of a sleeper now, but it's not really a club you can resign from.'

'Does the PM know?'

Fox looked at Lines who shrugged and said, 'Not that I'm aware of. This is a standard operation, we can't tell him everything.'

After a moment to reflect, Burgess said, 'I know this case better than anybody. When he was arrested he had nothing on him. But he was a safe-breaker, so you wanted him to open the safe.'

'And photograph the contents. But he got caught first.'

Loughran felt like he was back as a journalist now. 'And what was in the safe?'

Fox had played this game his whole life. Disinformation, holding back. Sometimes just one fact changed everything, the whole dynamic. He decided he had to tell them; any longer and he was actually misleading them, and he technically hadn't even started his new job. He was going to be running the Joint, not the Solo, Intelligence Committee. 'As I'm sure you've noticed, Chalky White's pretty smart. I've just discovered he did get into the safe.'

Lines couldn't admit he didn't know this, but he kicked Fox under the table.

'He was so angry we let him down, he wanted insurance.'

'Why didn't he tell you then?'

'We'd have taken them off him, by fair means or foul. If it's still what we think, it could be embarrassing to us, and more so the Russians or even Americans.'

'Oh great. The PM really needs that right now.'

'And he won't hand them over,' said Burgess. 'Because he wants to come back, on his terms. He needs you to tell the truth.'

Loughran looked around the table. 'That's not exactly our specialty, is it?'

Burgess carried on. 'So White linked up with Plummer to manage his story and put pressure on you. He's tired of being known as another Ronnie Biggs. He wants to come home.'

'Very good, Mr Holmes,' said Fox.

'And Chalky turned out to be a great asset, a good investment.'

'One of our best. Christ, his wife doesn't even know. If it's any consolation, loads of the guys you did arrest and get back, the really bad guys, were down to him. He helped make your career.'

Lines didn't like the way this was going. 'He just did his job. A lot of people sacrificed more, even their lives. They didn't come out or come home.'

Burgess ignored this. 'And finally, you're up the creek because you haven't made a deal.'

Fergus Loughran wanted to laugh. The best guy he'd ever worked for was now branded a disgraced former hack, wanted by the police and on the run, but he was somehow sitting on the scoop of the century. It could only happen to Sam.

Fox said, 'Plummer is very smart. We can go into full denial and say Chalky's a fantasist, but he's got me with him, in photos, then Cobbold, the stuff from the safe. Plummer will get other witnesses, but it'll take him time. The longer White is out there, the more stupid we all look.'

Burgess said, 'But if it all comes out, every villain he helped shop, or their sons, will go after him.'

'They'll think he grassed them,' said Fergus.

Sir Christopher Lines had now decided he really didn't care what happened to Chalky, or if Fox didn't start on Monday. 'We're far more worried about offending every country we spied on down there, particularly the Saudis, Russians, the Americans.'

Fox said, 'Let's be clear. Funded and taught by us, Chalky White has spied on everybody. He owns the local photo agency. He was connected to every criminal and drug dealer. There isn't a celebrity, policeman, diplomat or media person who's had an exotic cheroot or a shag south of Madrid in the last twenty years that he hasn't got on file. And I know for a fact he kept a log and diary in the form we would expect.'

Fergus couldn't resist it. 'You, Sir Christopher?'

'What?'

'Shagged anybody interesting in Spain?'

Fox caught Fergus' eye and winked.

'I shan't dignify that with an answer.'

Fergus continued, 'Have we got any leverage?'

Burgess said, 'Sure, until the charges are dropped he can't come back. We'd have to arrest both of them now.'

Fox wrote 'thick plod???' on his pad so Lines could see it.

'The PM's asked me to make it very clear he needs Len here, ASAP, running the JIC, squeaky clean. I know it's a cliché, but I need to give him solutions, not problems. Have you got one?'

Lines said, 'Our advice is to leave White out there. It'll calm down. Plummer will have to come back and give himself up.'

'But we look stupid,' said Burgess.

'Worse for the PM, he looks stupid and weak.'

Fox said, 'May I? I have a suggestion.'

Fifteen minutes later, Fergus had heard it, gone out and reported, and returned. 'The PM says that sounds good. I'll leave you guys to sort out the details. We may cancel the crime figures announcement or let somebody else do it.'

As they all stood up, Fox said, 'Do you have a minute, Fergus?'

They went to the garden, each knowing they were both dying for a cigarette. Fergus said, 'You don't like Sir Christopher, do you?'

'Not my favourite.'

'That's why you got the job. PM doesn't want the Firm stitching us up.'

'You're old mates with Sam, aren't you?'

'We are; I worked for him. Great operator, straight guy.'

'Yes, I'm learning that.'

'So?'

'The PM's at this media lunch today. Is he going to mention Burke in his speech?'

'Planning to. We're a bit short on good news.'

'May not all be quite as it seems,' said Fox.

'Really? Trouble is, it's Brits yomping all over Ukraine, their PM and his lot arriving. It's embarrassing.'

'I gave Gary a rocket. When's the delegation leaving?'

'After lunch at Chequers on Sunday.'

'If this plays out, we'll have something before then. I think Sam needs our help, and he might help us.'

'That would help me no end. When are you and Burgess off to see Butch Cassidy and the Sundance Kid?'

'We're going straight to Northolt from here. Might I suggest the PM still does the crime numbers, but on Monday?'

*

Chalky was making bacon and eggs. Sam was at the coffee machine and did the voice: 'It's day two in the Big Brother House. Sam and Chalky are in the kitchen.'

'What?'

'Sorry. How long could we stay here?'

'You mean like a medieval siege? Indefinitely. We've got water, livestock, fruit. Sky.'

'I was thinking more like Rorke's Drift.'

'As I recall the Royal Engineers didn't have 15,000 bottles of Tempranillo.'

'That's true. What if I got appendicitis?'

'Sofia could whip that out on the kitchen table. But you might find she's out of anaesthetic.'

Sam was amazed how philosophical Chalky remained.

'How did they get me at my dad's?'

Sam said, 'As soon as any paper knows you've been in the UK, they find out where all your relatives are and send a reporter to as many as they can with the photo. Download shots off the CCTV, easy.'

*

Fox picked up Burgess from Scotland Yard in his Range Rover, with the blue lights embedded in the grill on but no siren. Burgess was still in his uniform, and a marked police car followed them.

As they set off for Northolt, Fox said, 'I'm looking forward to working together, Jack.'

Burgess loosened his tie. 'Likewise, Len.'

'So cards on the table, how long ago did you work it out?'

'Can we talk in front of your driver?'

'He's fine, don't you recognise him?'

They were stopped at traffic lights, so Gary turned round. 'Hello, Commissioner.'

'Jesus guys, what are you trying to do to me? I can't be seen with you. Good headline – Commissioner escorts another fugitive out of UK.'

Gary pulled away. 'I'm turning myself in, Sir.'

'Let me think. OK, that could work. You're in custody. I'm questioning you, and if I like what you say I'll release you under caution. That should do it.'

'You want to cuff me?'

'Not while you're driving, no.'

Burgess took a sheet from his briefcase. 'Start with the date.'

Fox took it. '26th October 2004.'

'It's the letter I wrote to my personal lawyer, nobody else.'

Fox was shocked. 'You worked it out ten years ago? How?'

'I met you at some security conference organised by the Home Office. You looked very familiar. I went back through the archives and there you were, Wilkins the Marbella playboy, with all your hair and the Magnum moustache.'

'It was a bit.'

'I was almost full-time on the Costa del Crime. The real targets were people like Colin Nobes and that paedophile Michael McCartney, and all the hard drug dealers, but Chalky was the headline act, even though he'd never done anybody any harm. We were doing really well, mostly off amazing intel that you guys were gathering down there. But every time I got near Chalky, we missed; it was like he had a sixth sense.'

'And then you found out about the business.'

'I knew he had it, but he sold it two years later and wasn't so central. But when we connected you, it all made sense.'

'So why didn't you tell anybody?'

'Knowledge is power. My then boss, Jackson, was a dickhead with an ego. Why make him the hero? If I spooked you, the information might dry up. Chalky was harmless. I kept a file going with my lawyer so nobody could say I was smart after the event, and if I got killed there was a record. I kept my mouth shut.'

'Well, Chalky made my career too,' said Fox.

'But I didn't know he got in the safe. Clever bastard.'

'It's the last card Chalky can play. He's going to keep that close to his chest.'

# CHAPTER 29

## THURSDAY

Julian Mortlock thought it was time to make his first visit to the office, but still went up the back stairs. He would sail in through the front when the time was right. He really wanted to see Sam and Frank's offices, so he could make his choice, but that would have to wait a couple more days. Jay Lomax topped up his champagne glass as they watched Sky News still milking the story. Mortlock lounged on the sofa, letting it all sink in.

Jay raised his glass. 'I just can't believe how well this has worked out. Nice play, Julian.'

'Stick with me, kid. This is just the beginning.'

'Love it.'

Mortlock looked at him. In North America he'd be known as playing in the Little Leagues. He couldn't see the big picture.

'This must all breach Plummer's termination deal. Can't we just tear up the contract? Get rid of him, save the money.'

Mortlock was glad to see Donald Whelan arrive; he would see sense. 'Champagne?' said Jay.

'No thanks, I'm OK.'

Jay pointed at the muted TV showing shots of Sam and Chalky.

'Can you believe how stupid these guys are?'

'Yes, I am a little surprised,' said Donald.

'Surprised? Can we terminate the deal?'

Mortlock knew the trick was to let guys like Jay think they were in charge, when in reality they had no fucking clue.

'Correct me if I'm wrong, Donald,' said Mortlock, 'but while the answer is probably yes, and you would of course save some money, if we enforce it he does have to keep quiet and go on gardening leave. We have all our ducks in a row.'

Donald gave Jay a file and said, 'I agree. That's copies of their deals, all done.'

Jay said, 'Nice job.'

Mortlock looked at them both, checking the signature pages, then topping up his glass.

'I think you're right, Julian, let's see how it plays out first, with the police. No rush.'

'Still fascinated how he got to Chalky White, and why,' said Mortlock.

'Well, we sent him down there to get him out of the way,' said Jay.

'Did you really? I'm mystified. He goes off on a wild goose chase, fine, but then they come back here together, and then back to Spain. What the hell's that all about?'

'No idea,' said Donald.

Mortlock tossed the file on the desk. 'Well, he and Frank have signed, they're history. So who gives a toss?' He picked up his glass. 'To infinity and beyond.'

'I'll drink to that,' said Donald. 'Talking about loose ends, have you got the lawyer signed off?'

Jay picked a file up off his desk. 'Justine? She's signed too. I'm glad we used her.'

'We certainly did that,' said Mortlock.

Jay got up, went over to the small safe built into his bookshelves and put the files away.

'That's those three done. And how are your two deals?'

Donald said, 'Nearly there, it's always the tax stuff. Ready to sign Monday morning.'

'I love it when a plan comes together,' said Jay.

Mortlock wanted to say, 'I love it when I'm dealing with a pliable dickhead.'

*

On his way back to his office, Donald called Sam. 'I've stalled Mortlock signing until Monday.'

'Good man. Thanks.'

'Hold on, Sam. Listen. Jay's got a file on Justine, it's in his office.'

Sam knew that this might finally lead her to him. 'Really? Can you get it?'

'Of course I can't. I saw him put it in his safe.'

'Shit. Might have to send Chalky in.'

'I assume that's a joke.'

Sam couldn't think of anything else.

*

All the Whites were at one end of the terrace having lunch. Chalky was sitting with Nacho and Alex. Sofia was drifting in and out. Sam wondered if this was what it was like as a fugitive. Calm but with underlying tension, knowing one day a storm was coming, in one form or another. Sam was at the other end, on the phone. He ended the call and waved Chalky over. 'Sorry to interrupt. Can you help me break into a safe?'

'Why?'

'Donald says Jay's got a file on Maxine in his office safe.'

'Get him to take a photo of it and write down any serial numbers he can see.'

'OK.' Sam rang Donald back and passed on the message.

'You are fucking kidding.'

'Please.'

'I'll try,' said Donald.

Sam could sense it was subdued and wondered what the day would bring. He saw Chalky checking his watch. It felt like high noon. He stood up and said, 'I know I've put you all in a terrible position, but I want you to know that over the years I did everything for one reason only, and that's all of you.'

Sam could see him fighting to stay composed.

'By involving Sam and going home, I put us all at risk, but I decided I couldn't go on like this, living a lie. The truth is going to come out, one way or another. It's very possible you are going to think less of me after this, but I will have to live with that.'

'What's the truth?' said Nacho.

'Wait and see.'

Sofia shook her head.

Sam heard the faintest of noises far off. They could hear the horses getting agitated in the stables. The sound grew but was coming from behind them. Nacho ran to the side of the house to get a look. 'Helicopter.'

'Photographers, everybody inside,' said Sofia, standing up.

Nacho was back. 'Not in this one, Mama. Jesus. Papa, you and Mama hide. I'll get the guys.'

'No, stay where you are. All of you,' said Chalky.

The pilot told Sam later that he did do it for effect, the RAF Chinook CH-47 thundering straight overhead at no more than a hundred feet, the twin rotors smacking the air, nose down, at the no-payload limit of 200mph. Once past them, he put it into a steep turn, came back at them and landed on the open ground between the house and the stables, at the last minute turning away so the tail faced the house. They were lost in the dust cloud. As he powered down, the ramp lowered and four fully kitted soldiers jumped down and fanned out as the dust settled. Then out of the darkness behind them, the two men appeared.

Sofia crossed herself and pulled Alex to her. They walked towards the house, both in sunglasses, one in a white shirt with epaulettes but no jacket, the other in a suit.

'Don't recognise him?' asked Chalky.

'My God,' said Sofia. 'Is that Wilkins?'

'And my erstwhile nemesis, Burgess of the Yard.'

They walked slowly towards the terrace. To Sam's eye it looked like Wyatt Earp and Doc Holliday walking up Main Street in Tombstone on their way to destiny and the OK Corral.

When Fox reached the shade, he took off his sunglasses. 'Hello Sofia, long time.'

Sofia just looked at him, then said, 'I don't understand.' Chalky put his arm round her shoulders.

'Mama, who is this?'

'This man is Jonathan Wilkins, he was your father's business partner. He ran away.'

'And I'm Jack Burgess, from Scotland Yard. Hello.'

'The bastard who tried to get your father home for twenty years.'

'Hello, Inspector,' said Chalky, and held out his hand.

'Hard to believe I know, but the bastard Commissioner now.'

Sam wondered who was going to move first.

Sofia turned to Chalky with tears in her eyes. 'So is this it?'

'Well, sort of.' He looked at the others. 'Shall I?'

They all just looked at him.

'Sofia, boys. This is Sir Leonard Fox.'

Sofia said, 'Not Wilkins?'

'No, I work for the British Government, for MI6.'

'You're a spy?' said Sofia.

'I am. Well, I was.'

She looked completely confused and shocked. She was trying to figure out what it meant.

Chalky solved the riddle. 'Now don't get mad, Sofia. So am I.'

Nobody wanted to speak, they all knew it was her moment. She said, 'You're fucking crazy. You're all crazy. This is a sick joke.'

She turned to leave and Chalky grabbed her. As she tried to break free, Burgess stood up. 'Mrs White. It's all true.'

She stopped fighting and turned to face Chalky, slapping him as hard as she could. 'Hijo de puta.'

'I couldn't tell you.'

'I'm your wife.'

'That's why it was so hard. I didn't want you to carry the burden.'

'So I lived a lie.'

'I'm sorry.'

He pulled her to him and they embraced. When they finally moved apart, Chalky said, 'You said I had until midnight.'

She hit him again, this time not so hard, laughing.

They all sat down on the sofas while Chalky explained it all. Through the laughter and tears, all Sofia could manage was to keep saying 'coño' to all of them.

When he got to the bit about the security business, Fox said, 'Ah, I have some news on that. I know you think that I was building my own pension fund in the Caymans, but we don't actually work like that. We put it all in a nominee name, and when you sold up we put the proceeds on deposit.'

He pulled a sheet from his inside pocket. 'We put it in your joint names. Did particularly well on the exchange rate.'

'But the Firm funded the start up. It's their money, not mine.'

Fox laughed. 'Fair point, but it's not on our balance sheet. We reckon Sofia's your partner more than me; you both earned it.'

'OK, well I think Sofia should have it then.'

Fox gave her the statement. She looked at it, covered in figures. She handed it back to Fox. 'I don't understand it.'

'Well, it's just over nine million. US dollars.'

'Oh my God.'

Sofia could see the four soldiers moving around, watching. One talked into his radio and broke away, coming over. Sofia and the boys watched him arrive and loom over them. Nacho liked guns and recognised the 9mm Browning on his hip and the HK MP5 he was carrying, the world's most famous counter-terrorist machine gun.

He said, 'The boys and I would kill for a cold beer.'

Sam laughed. 'Gary, you are a twat.'

'Hey boss. We thought you might need some snaps.'

Fox stood up and said, 'I'll find some beers. Let's leave the family to it for a bit. Gary, do your stuff.'

As they walked away, Chalky called after Burgess, who went back. 'Come on Jack, you've waited twenty years. You have to.'

'Are you sure?'

'Gary, you have to get this.'

'John Stanley White, I'm arresting you in connection with, well loads of things. You do not have to say anything. However, it may harm your defence if you do not mention when questioned something which you later rely on in court. Anything you do say may be given in evidence.'

Chalky held his hands out for him.

'And sold to a Sunday newspaper.'

'No handcuffs?' said Chalky.

'Forgot them.'

'I could taser him,' said Gary.

Back with the group, Burgess turned to Sam and said, 'I do actually have to arrest you, Sam, and take you back.'

'For show?'

'Yes. I haven't arrested anybody for twenty years, now I've done two today.'

'Well I haven't written a story for twenty years. Welcome to the club.'

'In fact, I can't arrest you here. We'll do it at Heathrow.'

'I'm sorry, I'm sitting on the story of the year and you want me to come back so you can lock me up? I don't think so.'

Fox lit a cigarette. 'OK, here's the offer. I'll give you Hardy Cobbold instead of me, on the record, and he's really Mick Allott.'

'He's fucking dead, for Christ's sake, you told me. I know I'm good, but even I can't interview dead people.'

'I'll give you the quotes. But you don't use the stuff from the safe now, and then not unless we clear it, and you give it all to us.'

Sam looked at Fox, amazed that he wanted to believe him. 'You guys lie for a living.'

'That really is true.'

'But for some bizarre reason I want to believe you.'

Fox stubbed out his cigarette. 'Well, Houdini, if you've got a better plan I'm sure we'd all like to hear it.'

They went back to join Chalky.

Fox kept going. 'What we're going to do, Chalky, is give you two or three other jobs we did in the UK ourselves. You can take the credit for those.'

'OK. But how do I cover my arse for the rest of the time here?'

'We'll agree some things you can say you did, dull stuff like Gibraltar. You just say we held back on the money to make sure you kept your mouth shut, and we fell out, not least because we told you to lie low but you went off partying. We'll deny you did anything serious for us down here.'

'Don't worry,' Sam said. 'We can polish that.'

'Sam, you get the story out this Sunday, no later. We approve the text. We liaise on our response, and Jack here fronts up and says the police knew all along. Everybody looks good.'

Sam looked at Burgess. 'Did you know?'

'2004. Recognised Len from the file.'

Chalky and Sam looked at each other and nodded. Sam said, 'If the stuff from the safe leads to a story, you give it to me.'

'I can't promise, but yes. But in the story this weekend, he got caught before he opened the safe. Chalky, you stay here. I'm leaving two of the guys, but they have to be plain clothes, without weapons. You should think about coming back overnight on Saturday. I'll sort a passport and a jet.'

'So when does my arrest warrant get cancelled?'

'I'm guessing just before you fly would suit.'

Sofia looked at them all. 'I know I should hate you all, for lots of reasons, but this is the happiest day of my life. He was always a good man, you know. You taught him so much, Wilko.' She went over and hugged him.

'And him me.'

Sam took Chalky to one side and showed him a photo.

'Good old Donald. Safewell. SW-23EQ, hotels mostly.'

'Can you do it?'

'We can try. Email it to me.'

*

Two of the soldiers stayed behind without their weapons. Sofia kissed Sam goodbye with real affection for the first time. The boys both embraced him.

The hold of the Chinook was uncomfortable and noisy. On the short flight to Gibraltar to connect with the plane, Fox said to Sam through the headset, 'I've done the PM a big favour. He was going out on a limb to support Burke at some lunch today, but he's holding back. With Ukraine it would really help if we could nail Burke on Sunday too.'

'Well, great, but you're the one stopping me. Why?'

'Where shall I start? Law and order's top of his agenda; right now with Chalky he looks like an idiot. With Burke, if the Ukrainians could see we weren't farting about for no reason in their back garden, that would be good. And these things leak. You don't need me to tell you that. Can you?'

'I need it done more than you. I need to use the stuff from the villa. The only other chance is we find Justine or Maxine or whatever the hell her name is.'

'Is using Gary's stuff from the Villa really critical?'

'Absolutely. Maybe enough to stall Mortlock, but that's personal. I have to be absolutely certain that Burke was in on it and sleeping with the mother. I need the girl, I need Burke on the record, Mortlock to confess, and Jay really.'

'Not much then.'

'And I need it all now. After last week I just can't risk it. This needs to be more watertight than a duck's arse.'

*

On the BA flight the four of them had the front row, Sam across the aisle from Burgess. Before they took off, Sam rang his mate Harry, the fixer at Heathrow. After he thanked him for helping Felix and calling Katie, he asked him a favour. 'Sam. For you, anything.'

Sam took him through it. 'Remember, the more the merrier.'

In the air, Sam worked through his bag sorting his papers. Burgess said, 'What's that?'

He handed him the crumpled A4 print-out of Mortlock's mystery woman, now covered in scribbles and notes.

'Who are they?'

'That's Julian Mortlock. Her, we never figured out; they were spotted having dinner by an old mate of mine, in Nottingham.'

Burgess gave it back. 'I know who she is.'

'You're kidding me. Who?'

'You first. Tell me what you know, and I might tell you.'

Gary and Fox were listening. 'All we discovered was that she had been seen with a man, maybe having an affair. Doug Slateford, made his fortune in the US, tech business called PSN.'

'I know them,' said Gary. 'The army uses their encryption software. So do the Americans.'

'That it?' said Burgess.

'We lost interest. So, who is she?'

'She might be the smartest woman I've ever met. Or employed.'

'What? She's a policewoman?'

'Not exactly. She rebuilt the National Crime Database and designed how it talks to other programmes, like Witness Protection.'

'And let me guess, the NSA and Interpol,' said Fox.

'Yes. Her name's Jane Gower, recognised as one of the best cryptographers in the world. She now has a consultancy in Derby. We retain her.'

Sam looked at the photo. 'Bloody hell. More questions than answers.'

'Indeed. That is slightly worrying, to say the least,' said Fox.

Burgess looked very uncomfortable. 'Guys, this could explain a lot, in fact everything. Might I suggest nobody says anything about this to anyone just yet?'

Sam turned to Chalky and said, 'I'm not sure I can handle three stories just now.'

*

They landed late at Heathrow. Fox and Gary slipped away first in a car that met the plane. Burgess and Sam let the other passengers get off, which took forever. As they sat there waiting, Burgess said, 'Do you want us to look for the girl too?'

'Maxine, could you?'

'Why not, I could come up with a reason. I'm not sure about honeytraps.'

'That's because you've had undercover policemen having babies with women, you guys are on another level.'

As they took their bags from the overhead locker, Sam said, 'You're enjoying this, aren't you?'

'You are too, aren't you?'

'Bit out of the frying pan to be honest.'

'Come on, let's do it. Showtime.'

The same two police officers were there to meet them at the gate. One said, 'Mind if we cuff you, Mr Plummer?'

As they walked through the airport, Sam saw a shot on a TV of a reporter, clearly live, waiting at Terminal 5. They bypassed passport control and emerged to a wall of TV cameras and lights. They fought their way through. The rolling media maul reached the pavement where Sam was bundled into the back of a police car. Burgess shut the door behind him and the car drove away at speed. He turned to face the media.

'Mr Plummer voluntarily agreed to return to the UK with me. Once here I formally arrested him, and he will be questioned in custody. I am not taking questions, but it is our intention to make a statement later this evening. Thank you.'

The policeman undid the handcuffs as Sam was driven into the Heathrow police compound where he was transferred to Fox's Range Rover. Joseph was driving, with Gary next to him up front.

Fox said, 'Home, James. Maybe we could stop for a couple of pints?'

'Not funny, Len,' said Sam. 'Any news, Joseph?'

'I've been working with Len's guys. We've run Maxine Glover

across all databases and used the facial recognition software. Nothing, I'm sorry.'

'Jesus, she's not Osama bin Laden. So, Len, the combined forces of British Intelligence can't find a lap dancer?'

'We haven't developed the software for recognising arses yet.'

They drove on through Kingston in silence.

Finally Gary said, 'So, the only option now is to get into Jay's safe.'

*

Back in Wimbledon, Gary set up in the kitchen.

Sam rang Chalky. 'We need to get in that safe.'

'OK, my guys in Spain install these all the time. I've got the code sequences.'

'We just need somebody to do it.'

'And hope they haven't changed the factory settings, but it's very unlikely. Easiest is whoever's doing it I talk them through it.'

'OK, we'll call you back.'

Sam took a sandwich and opened a Heineken. 'Right, it's dead simple. Chalky thinks he can talk somebody through it. We just need somebody who knows the layout. Someone unflappable, reliable, smart, can avoid getting caught. Any ideas?'

'Tom Cruise?' said Gary.

'How about Katie?'

'You can't ask your daughter to break into the Chief Exec's office,' said Fox.

'No, you're right.' Sam picked up his phone. 'There's only one person.' They all looked at him. 'Frank, where are you?'

Gary put his head in his hands. Fox ran his finger across his throat. Sam put him on the speaker.

'Just leaving the Café Royal. Boring awards thing. I took some real stick; you too. And I probably drank too much. They put the live feed from Heathrow up. Am I your one call?'

'I'm not calling you from prison. I'm in Wimbledon. I told Burgess I'd stay here, scout's honour.'

He brought him up to date and explained what needed doing. 'I know it's a lot to ask. Say no if you want to.'

Sam thought the line had gone dead.

'Fuck it. I'm close. In for a penny. The seventh floor is usually closed down now, any idea how I do that?'

Gary took over. 'Don't worry. You have seen Mission Impossible, haven't you?'

'I'm in black tie. Bit more Cadbury's Milk Tray really. I'll call you when I'm there.'

Len lit a cigarette. 'Is this really such a good idea?'

'We can't wait,' said Sam. 'And there might be more.'

'And what about your golden rule about not breaking the law?'

'You can't steal from your own office.'

*

Sam had four missed calls from Clare and knew he couldn't put it off any longer. He went out into the garden and called her.

'Sam, what the hell are you doing? Explain how you being frog-marched in handcuffs on national television equates to you, as you put it, having everything under control?'

'Well, it is.'

'You told me you signed your deal.'

'I did.'

'I thought you were in Spain all that time.'

'I had to pop back.'

'Pop back? It was on the front page of the bloody *Guardian*. You're an idiot.'

'Clare, you're absolutely right, I am. But I haven't got time for this. What do you want?'

'You know what I want, what do you want?'

He thought about it and said, 'I'll tell you what, a divorce.'

He hung up. They'd talked about it so many times and never bothered, but now he knew they both meant it. Oddly it felt good, no more compromises.

He then rang Hodgy.

'Hi Sam, still no luck I'm afraid, we don't know who she is.'

'Well, I do. Her name's Jane Gower. Based in Derby.'

Sam gave him what little he could of the story and said, 'Huge favour to ask… can you remember how to run full cover?'

Hodgy laughed. 'Sam, as I think you've just found out, we never lose it.'

'You got some guys?'

'Might have to get one or two of the old dogs off the golf course.'

'Usual rates.'

'If you're going to get Julian Mortlock, we'll pay you.'

*

Frank walked in through the front door and had a short chat with the two security guys. 'Left something in my office.'

'Want us to come up, Frank?'

'No, I'm fine.' As he walked to the lift he turned back and looked at their bank of monitors, then took the lift to the fifth floor and went to his office. The open plan office was almost deserted.

Back in Wimbledon Len looked at Gary, who had three laptops going on the kitchen table, the landline, and two mobiles. 'Looks like the ops room at Legoland.'

Gary leaned back. 'I've got the CCTV system on these two, Joseph's looking at the feed the guards see, we'll get Chalky on the landline, I'll do Frank on speaker on a mobile.'

'How does he open the safe?'

'Chalky said hotel guests are always forgetting their codes or getting pissed and making too many wrong attempts, so there's always a factory set master code.'

'Unless they change it.'

'In which case we're buggered.'

Sam looked at the screens, worried about Frank. This was a

big ask. But there was no point in telling Frank to back down now. They were both committed.

In his desk drawer Frank found the earpiece for his phone and plugged it in. He hung his dinner jacket on the back of his chair.

He rang Gary. 'I'm at my desk.'

'Phone on vibrate?'

'Check Red Leader.'

Sam smiled and shook his head. Only Frank.

'OK, go to the loo, the one by the stairs.'

Gary was looking at the screen. 'I'm watching the CCTV, they're on the standard rotation, they'll only save the recordings if there's an incident. Get automatically wiped.'

Fox moved close to Sam and whispered, 'Great idea to take his dinner jacket off, easier to spot.'

'Open the door to the back stairs and wedge one of your shoes in it so it stays open, you'll need the other when you get in upstairs. The door code up there is 1991.'

Frank did it and said, 'I'm ready.'

On the screen, the stairwell CCTV images kept changing, counting up from floors one to ten, then starting again.

Joseph had a stopwatch. 'On our mark, you've got twenty seconds to get up and in.'

'I'm sixteen stone, I only use these stairs to go out for a fag.'

Joseph said, 'Three, two, one, GO.'

They could hear Frank breathing heavily from the off. When he got to the door he was almost done.

'Five seconds, 1991.'

Frank fumbled with the keypad and fell through the door, collapsing in a heap on the floor, panting, his foot wedged in the door.

Gary looked at the screens. 'Stay there, that's a blind spot.'

Frank put his other shoe in the door. The CCTV moved round on Gary's screen. The low level night lighting was on, the floor deserted.

'You OK, Frank?' said Gary.

'Never better.'

'Pretty simple now, you just need to go to Jay's office. He's on a touch pad, but you're cleared for all of them. There's no CCTV in his office, it's just the one outside that looks through the glass wall. So when you're in, get behind the sofa.'

Halfway there Frank put his foot in a wastepaper basket and went down hard. 'Fuck, shit. I'm down.'

'Get under a desk.'

As the cameras panned round, Sam said, 'Where is he?'

'Don't know. Frank, you OK?'

'No I fucking am not. I'm under a desk with my foot in a wastepaper basket, feels like I've broken my toe.'

'I need to know where you are. Wave.'

As the cameras changed Gary said, 'OK, I've got you.'

A minute later Frank was behind the sofa.

On one screen Joseph watched a guard get up and head to the lifts. There was no point spooking Frank. They got Chalky on the line. 'Hey, everybody.'

Frank, down behind the sofa, said, 'I hope everybody appreciates the irony of me breaking into a safe under the instruction of Britain's most wanted man, a safebreaker, who completely cocked up his last effort.'

'Well, you say that,' said Chalky. 'Frank, put in hash 4321 hash, then read me whatever comes up on the display. My guys will give you another number.'

Frank had one attempt. 'It's so dark. I forgot my sodding glasses, I can't see the numbers.'

Gary said, 'OK. Use your phone as a torch.'

Frank was back. '6767.'

They heard Chalky talking in Spanish to somebody, then came back. 'Factory setting, 0000 hash. 6767 is his code.'

Gary told him when to go again, then Frank was back behind the sofa. 'OK, got it, bunch of files.' Using his phone light he went through them. 'Bloody hard to read. Mortlock, Burke, Numbers, Wedding, Maxine... '

'Wedding?' said Gary and Sam at the same time.

Frank opened the file. 'Draft announcement, I think. Miss Angelina DeLorenzo. November 14th.'

Blimey,' said Sam. 'Do Maxine.'

'Right, contract between blah blah blah and Lily Jean Maxwell-Glover – double-barrelled, no wonder you couldn't find her – of 27 Vera Road, SW6 4UJ.' Then he gave them her mobile number which was written on the inside flap. 'What next?'

Joseph held up his stopwatch and tapped it.

'Forget it,' said Gary. 'The guard's on the third, moving up, you have to go. Put everything back. Now.'

'Hold on.'

'No Frank, now,' said Sam. 'Please.' Frank followed Gary's instructions, closing the safe. When he got to the stair door, Gary said, 'He's on five now, far end. Going to be close. Go.'

Frank got back down and in, sweating heavily, recovered his shoes and went into the gents. As he stood panting over the sink, the security guard came in. 'You OK, Frank?'

'Hey Steve, prawns tonight. Been throwing up for ten minutes. I'll be OK.'

After the guard had gone, Frank took his earpiece out and splashed his face with cold water.

When he got back to his office, Fox said, 'Frank, just to let you know you've passed the MI6 induction test.'

'What about the dry martini and the birds?'

'That's phase two.'

Gary closed his laptops and said, 'Thanks Chalky, great job,' and ended the call.

Joseph said, 'Guards are back down, Frank's having a beer. Normal service resumed.'

'Love to know what's in that Burke file,' said Sam.

Fox said, 'Very impressed, you might have another career, Gary. I'll get my guys to stop looking for Maxine Glover then.'

'Let's go, guys,' said Sam, standing up.

'Hang on, I gave Burgess my word I'd keep you all here.'

Sam faced him. 'And?'

'Oh for God's sake. Just don't let anybody see you.'

Joseph said, 'There's a police car out front.'

'Good point,' said Len, who went to the hall and made a call, then took them to the back of the garden. 'Hop over this wall. It's my neighbour, Chris, he's a film producer. Let's just say he owes me a favour. He'll lend you his car. Come back the same way.'

*

Joseph and Gary had to help him up and over. They all set off in Chris's Volvo Estate.

Gary said, 'I'm sorry to tell you this, Sam, but you know she probably won't be there.'

He knew this was true. 'I know, if I was Mortlock I'd have got her out of the country the next day. France maybe, get somebody to babysit her in the middle of nowhere.'

They were going north over Putney Bridge.

'We'll do one drive-by then make a plan,' said Gary.

'You realise what Jay being engaged means?' said Sam.

'Mortlock has him by the balls,' said Gary.

'Exactly. All the stuff of Jay with Maxine is now real currency.'

Sam realised now that it was even more likely Mortlock had got her to do a number on Jay too. God, how low would she go?

'Blackmail him whenever he likes.'

'No, I'd just pull the same stunt, tell him he can bury it.'

'Would anybody really fall for that twice?'

'Only Jay,' said Sam.

'But Mortlock will use Jay shagging that so-called model in Paris first, much cleaner.'

'No question. He's relentless.'

They turned left off the Munster Road and cruised along Vera Road. Now that meeting her was a real possibility, not some dream, he wasn't sure how he felt or what he would say. He'd been craving this confrontation for days but still didn't know how to play it.

Gary was counting down the house numbers 'Lights are on.' At the end of the road Joseph turned round and parked. 'Only saw one guy, in a black Jaguar.'

Sam said, 'That's what Barry and Luke were driving.'

'I know, you gave me the reg. It's facing away from us, left-hand side, opposite the house.'

As Gary opened the door he said, 'Wait here. She might be on the clock.'

'Jesus. You mean with a client?'

'Lighten up, Sam. No.'

# CHAPTER 30

## THURSDAY

Gary made his way up the street, making sure he stayed in the blind spot. He got into the passenger seat. 'Hello, Luke.'

'Oh shit, not you.' He looked genuinely terrified.

Joseph rolled up behind.

'Aren't you wanted by the police?'

'Why don't you ring up and claim the reward? Don't believe what you read in the papers.'

'It was on TV.'

'She on her own?'

'Yes.'

'You on all night?'

'Yes.'

'Get in the car behind us.'

Sam got out when he saw Gary coming back. 'She's alone. It's our friend Luke, he's on all night so no rush.'

'OK, thanks. Call me if anybody appears.'

He wanted to see if he could catch sight of her, but all the curtains were drawn. He had a knot in his stomach. He pressed the bell a couple of times before she came to the door. 'Who is it?'

In that moment his instinct kicked in. He had to be neutral, see how it played.

'It's the plumber, I hear you've got a blockage.'

'Go away.'

'No.'

She slipped the chain and opened the door. She was pulling a silk dressing gown tight around her, over grey track suit bottoms and a rugby shirt. She had no make-up on. She looked like she hadn't slept in days and had been crying for about the same.

'This is a new look for you.'

'Fuck off.'

She turned her back and walked to the kitchen. He closed the front door and followed her. He looked round at the mess. A week's worth of newspapers were piled in the corner. Dirty dishes were stacked up, a tabby cat licking the top one. There was a pile of dirty clothes in front of the washing machine.

'Not as minimalist as your other place.'

She lit a Marlboro Light and exhaled towards the ceiling.

'Peter Stringfellow once told me the blondes always make more.'

She pushed her hair away from her face and just looked at him.

'But they tend to wash it. And brush it.'

She poured herself a glass of white wine and drank half.

'Not for me, thanks.'

'How did you get past Luke?'

'Gary.'

'Ah yes, always Gary. How did you find me?'

'The bondage underwear. Stringfellows via Coco de Mer. Terry, bless him.'

'That didn't get you here.'

'That got us to Maxine Glover. Not even the spooks could make the quantum leap to Lily Maxwell-Glover.'

'Lily was my aunt's name.'

'And Maxine?'

'I was always Max or Maxi at school. MI5 are looking for me?'

'Six actually. Not any more.'

'Maxwell-Glover is too pretentious. I don't really use it.'

He looked at her, acting cool but looking completely

stressed out. She was a mess. He poured a glass of wine to fill the silence.

'Was I the first guy you fucked for money?'

She dropped her cigarette in a mug, poured some more wine, and lit another. 'How many girls, like Caroline, have you paid over the years to fuck guys?'

He didn't bite. 'She wasn't that sort of girl.'

'Whatever.'

He could see this wasn't going anywhere. 'Right, shall we go from the beginning?'

'Why should I tell you anything?'

'First rule of holes?'

'No idea, enlighten me.'

'If you're in one, stop digging. You are in one unholy mess, and the guy you're dealing with, Mortlock, is the prince of darkness. Oddly, I'm your only hope.'

'Why should I trust you?'

'I think that's my line,' said Sam.

He sensed she'd been waiting for this conversation too. This wasn't the same girl he'd been in bed with.

'Under your skin, you and Mortlock are the same. We're just the female currency in some macho face-off. You don't give a shit about collateral damage. It's all about your ego and the next story.'

'You shouldn't be here.'

'What do you mean?'

'The way it works is that at this point you should be in hiding. You've done your job, got the photos and video, given all the details. I'd have you somewhere like France, with Luke babysitting you. Sipping piña coladas on the beach. And you should be happy.'

He could see he'd finally got her attention.

'I'm listening.'

'Let's get it out of the way. Are you a prostitute?'

'What do you think?'

'I don't think so.'

'Great, thanks.'

'OK, have you worked any other honeytraps?'

'Yes, but never where I slept with anybody.'

'You were the bait.'

He could see her thinking about whether she should keep her mouth shut. 'I used to dance at another place. Mortlock had a few girls like me that he paid for gossip. One of his guys recruited me. The trick was with celebs. We'd ask if they wanted to meet outside the club or away from the party. If they said yes, I called the guy, then I'd turn up with another girl – she would be a hooker, usually with some drugs. I'd make my excuses and leave.'

'Standard practice, we invented it really.'

'Jay was in one night and he told me to get close to him. Funny thing is I really liked Jay. He's a fun guy, he just asked me for lunch.'

'Fun? Jay Lomax is a prick.'

'You see, that's your problem, Sam. You see him as the young kid upstairs making your life hell. Look at him. He's rich, good looking and, away from the office, he's good company.'

'And he had all the toys.'

'Exactly. Cool job, athletic, Ferrari, penthouse, use of the jet and the boats. What's not to like?'

'You said you never slept with anybody for money.'

'Mortlock didn't pay me to sleep with Jay. I'd have gone out with him anyway, probably. It was never super-serious.'

'Did you know about the girlfriend in the States?'

'He said it was on and off, more off now he was over here.'

'Angelina DeLorenzo. College sweetheart.'

'Really?'

'Well it's more on than off now. They're engaged.'

'No shit.' She was warming up.

'Wedding in November. Carson's on her dad's board, and old man DeLorenzo's on his.'

She leaned forward. 'So Mortlock got me close to Jay so he could use it as leverage?'

'Blackmail, even.'

'But he's holding it back, like cards in a game.'

'Correct. As you said it's what we do. Go on.'

'Jay was OK, but you know Americans, no sense of irony. Bit too controlling. Not that keen on me working nights and people sticking their noses in my business. Mortlock was always hanging out at his place.'

'Of course he was. He's an opportunist.'

'Jay used him as a sounding board. Said Frank and you in particular treated him like a child, never explained anything. Anyway I was deep in debt, and I'd lost my day job as a legal secretary.'

'Did you ever really qualify?'

'Failed my law degree at Leeds, big student loan, spent all my time partying. Mortlock put me on retainer. He's very charming, persuasive.'

Sam could imagine Mortlock recruiting her, using the very same words he had used over the years.

'Tell me. The party circuit gig.'

'Exactly. Got me on the list for every event and night club. He'd give me the names of guys at parties to talk to. I had a big clothes budget, jewellers lent me stuff. He got me a gym membership at all the big hotels, that was the easiest way to meet the foreigners. And on the side I got a kickback from shops I sent them to.'

'That must have been nice.'

'Sam, don't patronise me. I've made a living getting thirty quid from drunks having their faces six inches from my fanny. I just gave the info to him or his guy. He'd then put one of his kiss-and-tell girls or dealers or whatever on to it.'

'You lined them up. If you ended up in the papers, you'd have been done, damaged goods. Like Henry Higgins and Eliza Doolittle, he invested time and money in you. You're too good to waste.'

'But he's wasting me now.'

'I'm afraid it does look like it. He was grooming you for the main event.'

'Sad, eh? I said you wouldn't go for it.'

He let that go. He was sitting opposite her to get Burke and Mortlock. To get one piece in that jigsaw that he could use legally to get the story on their front page on Sunday.

'But Mortlock would never tell you the whole plot with Burke.'

'I knew about the Burke story itself from the start. Mortlock orchestrated the anonymous tip, told Jay so he could send Donald to Canada, and installed me to ensure it didn't get bogged down in legal.'

'You were credible.'

'He made me do a crash course on libel, and this IT whizz called Josh Akers trained all of us, so I was really good with phones, laptops. I worked bloody hard.'

'With the libel you had to clear the way for the story so Jay could use it against me and Frank.'

'You don't remember at the Ivy when he called me Maxine?'

'My God, he did.'

'I could have killed him. After all that work he nearly blew it.'

Sam could have kicked himself. How could he have forgotten?

She got some more wine from the fridge.

'But you didn't know about the Burke scam, the twins angle, you still thought it was a real story?'

Sam knew that this was the key question. If she knew nothing about the plot she was of little use.

'Of course not. I never figured out the daughters bit.'

'That's a real shame.'

Sam wasn't sure where to go next.

'Well, not until Jay told me.'

Bingo. 'Pillow talk?'

'You won't believe it.'

'Try me.'

'You and I heard on the Monday, at the lawyers, and we slept together that night.'

'I remember that.'

'Mortlock's tech guru Akers I told you about had set me up

the day before with the equipment to film you – lighting, sound. Even position in the room, on the bed.'

'But at your place.'

'Well, that flat, yes.'

'Sorry. Time out. So why did we go to mine?'

'Because I wanted to fuck you.'

She looked at him like he was an idiot, and he was starting to think he might be.

'I texted Luke to doorstep us so you'd leave me there. I knew I'd get you to my place in the next day or two so I set up a technical rehearsal, just me. I had it all lined up and Jay appeared that afternoon.'

'For a quickie.'

'That's what he used to do, and to be honest that was his problem.'

He laughed. Maxine laughed too. For a moment he felt they were heading back towards the way they were, but he realised he was about to hear about how she was still fucking Jay Lomax, sort of.

'Anyway he did what he always did, straight in the bedroom and dropped his trousers. Josh had set it up so I could press one button, and we were rolling. I got down to my underwear but told him I couldn't do it, said I had my period.'

Sam was relieved.

'He was in a great mood, saying it was all falling into place, started talking about Burke.'

'So he told you?'

'I kept him going with a hand job, I reckoned it might be the most expensive one of all time.'

Sam wasn't sure if he felt so relieved now. She was a piece of work. But hey, a hand job was a small price for the story.

'Now he's engaged, I'd say the price just went up.'

'He said Mortlock wanted me to hear the twins thing first with you, at the lawyers' office, so I'd be genuinely shocked.'

'But Jay couldn't resist telling you?'

'He told me the lot. Mortlock fed you the tip-off, stage-managed the photos, made sure you ran the story. Agreed the libel settlement in advance with Burke, and got him to commit to provide more.'

'Did the audio work?'

'Oh yes, and the video. Bit odd giving him one left-handed but it kept him in shot. Jay Lomax spilling the beans, in every sense.'

'I'll remember that. Was all the recording connected outside or all self-contained?'

'Just all got recorded in the flat. I'm not stupid.'

'Where is it?'

'The Jay stuff? Safety deposit box.'

'You mean you didn't tell Mortlock?'

'Are you crazy? Think what it's worth now we know he's engaged.'

Was she in some way protecting him as well as herself?

Sam was still not there. 'So you didn't film us, the first night at my flat?'

'Sam, you nearly had me in the hall. No.'

'You haven't really grasped the honeytrap, have you?'

'In what way?'

'You're not supposed to like the person.'

'You don't have to like somebody to want to fuck them.'

If he looked back over his life between the sheets, he knew that was true.

'And you were supposed to get me to your place, where you had it all worked out and wired. But you took some files from my place.'

She got up and went to a kitchen cupboard.

'There you go.'

He looked at the bag full of old magazines he recognised as his. She took them back and threw them on the pile of newspapers in the corner.

'I assumed they were still watching, I had to walk out with something.'

'Does Mortlock know?'

'It was part of our ongoing dispute.'

Sam knew he was getting closer to the truth, but could he trust her?

She fetched another wine glass and poured him one.

'Thanks.' He left it, he needed to stay focused.

'I was in a bad place, I had nobody to talk to. I was so far out of my depth.'

'And?'

'I worked out a plan. What did he really want? Leverage. If I gave him our sex shots, he'd be happy. I knew the financial stuff you told me was very thin and nobody would use it.'

'People in glass houses.'

'He can humiliate you, but what he and Jay really wanted was for you to sign your deals and clear off.'

'So the second time was to film us?'

'Yes, he put me under a lot of pressure.'

'He's got what he wants but he can't resist the icing on the cake.'

'And I'm sorry but I need the money.'

'And what about me?'

'I looked at it from your point of view. You're not really married, so shagging me just adds to the urban myth. What harm have I really done? I might have faked it but you were definitely having a good time.'

She was right on that.

'I controlled the photos of you that came out. You signed a great deal. And, the truth about Burke will come out, sooner or later. It must do, and you'll be vindicated and Mortlock will get his comeuppance. Does that make sense?'

Sam looked at her and thought about it. 'Actually it does.'

If nothing else, he had to admire Mortlock's talent-spotting. She was very smart.

'So the ongoing dispute was that you held out until I signed my deal?'

'Yes.'

'Thank you.'

She said nothing and lit another cigarette.

'But now he has got the pictures and video from your place, and we're going to be front page on Sunday.'

She smiled. 'Oh no he hasn't.'

Just when Sam thought he had worked it all out, she was off again. 'I don't understand?'

'We've had a disagreement. It seemed the best way to stall him. I told him all your files were locked away and that the video didn't work. He wasn't happy but he's OK with stills.'

Sam laughed. 'You're telling me he hasn't got any pictures of us together?'

'Only the other shots through the window you've seen.'

He wanted to kiss her. 'That's genius.'

'Sam, it was very graphic. It's not my ambition to be immortalised on PornHub.'

'Nor mine. So that's why we weren't in last Sunday, he had no more pictures.'

'Exactly.'

Sam couldn't believe his luck. 'So the disagreement must be about money. What's your deal?'

'I've been on retainer with Julian for over a year, then Jay paid me on top. For this, sixty. Twenty up front, ten for the proof of your fraud, thirty for photos and video.'

'Sixty? Christ. So, he claims you're editing and wants a discount for no video or fraud?'

'Yes. I deleted some photos too. You'll survive it but I'm in real trouble when he runs this. Look at that.'

She pointed at the fridge door. Stuck to it was a page torn from a local newspaper, showing a vicar standing in front of a church. Next to him was one of those large thermometers. The target for the roof repair was £75,000 but they were hardly out of the bulb at the bottom.

'So your dad's not in Melbourne with BP.'

'No, sorry. It would kill him. I'm an only child. My mother died when I was young. I bet you already know the headline.'

'TART AND VICAR. You should have thought about that before you got started.'

'I really don't know what to do, Sam.'

'Where are the photos?'

'A full set in the same deposit box. The ones I'm planning to give him on a stick, here.'

'How much does he owe you?'

'We agreed today on fifty grand, all cash. So he's coming tomorrow morning at ten with the thirty he owes. Would take him some time to get it, he said. And you're right, I'm flying tomorrow with Luke. Don't know where, he's got my passport.'

Sam got up. 'Clean yourself up, and this place. When he comes you need to look strong and in control. Give me the house phone number, I've got your mobile.'

'And when are you going to tell me exactly what I should do?'

'Soon. I need to work out the exact details.'

'Are you coming back?'

'Might just be Gary.'

'Will I see you again?'

It sounded like she wanted him to say yes, and he wasn't sure, but he said, 'Of course.' Whatever she said, and whatever he felt, she'd taken money to seduce him, to use him.

'I'm scared, Sam.'

'You don't need to be.'

In reality he knew she should be. And she'd need all her skills to play it out, but he could now see a way. She stayed sitting at the table.

'I'll let myself out. Put the chain on.'

*

He stopped at the pavement and looked back at the front door. He wondered if he really would ever see her again. Gary got out of the car to meet him and they walked down towards Luke.

'Kiss and make up?'

'That's not happening.'

'Any good news?'

'You won't believe it. She's got Jay on tape telling her about the Burke scam. And she hasn't given Mortlock my photos yet.'

'You're kidding me. Explains everything.'

'Exactly.'

'That's a result. But you still need Burke to admit the scam.'

Sam stopped. 'Gary, telling me things I already know doesn't really help, does it?'

'Pardon me for talking.'

'And I know I have to do it all by Saturday.'

'Which is tomorrow now, or maybe you knew that already too?'

They got to Joseph's car. Gary said to Luke, 'There's two ways to do this, kid. One you walk away, or two you probably go to prison.'

'This is my gap year. I'm just on work experience.'

'What are you going to read?' asked Sam.

'Psychology, at Oxford.'

'So what do you reckon on Mortlock, a sociopath or a psychopath?'

'Well obviously I'm no expert, yet, but he seems like a real scumbag to me.'

They both laughed. 'Good answer,' said Sam. 'How about I give you a way out, completely clean?'

'Whatever you say, he's only paying my expenses.'

'Starting now, you're on a grand a day until Monday. All you have to do is exactly what Mortlock wants and what we say. Any problems, you call Gary, and you take all his calls. OK?'

'Deal, thanks Mr Plummer.'

'Call me Sam. Do you have Mortlock's schedule for Burke and the Cheeky Girls?'

'Yep.' He had his bag on his lap.

'You got Maxine's passport?'

He handed it over. Sam turned on the interior light and looked at it. Lily Jean Maxwell-Glover. Gary was scanning the schedule. 'Is the Piers Morgan interview thing confirmed?'

'I think Burke's on his way to New York now, doing it tonight.'

'And flies straight back with Piers on Saturday for Caroline's fashion show,' said Gary.

'Where are you taking Maxine tomorrow?'

'Menorca, on EasyJet.'

Gary gave Luke back his keys. 'Good boy.'

As they set off Sam said, 'Mortlock's turning up at ten tomorrow morning with thirty grand.'

'So what's the plan?'

'I rather hoped you would tell me.'

# CHAPTER 31

**FRIDAY 11th July – DAY 14**

***The Independent*: CAMERON PLOTS TO BRING BACK SNOOPERS' CHARTER**

***Evening Standard*: MAKE YOUR MIND UP ON SEAT BORIS**

***Daily Star*: BRIT TOFFS SHOCK OUTDOOR SEX ROMP**

They were all up early at Fox's in Wimbledon. In the kitchen with Fox they watched Sky News.

'Overnight we understand the journalist Sam Plummer has been released, having surrendered his passport. Reports suggest that the fugitive from British justice, Chalky White, is back at his house in Spain. The other two men wanted by the police, Gareth Lake and Joseph Kelly, presented themselves to the police and have been released under caution.'

*

Damir was having breakfast by the pool of the Hotel Candille just outside Mougins. He'd dressed the part to fit in, pretending to read *l'Equipe* while a waiter topped up his coffee. Then, making it look like he was doing emails, he'd taken a couple of photos. He called Sam.

'Plumski.'

'Damski, how is it?'

'Beautiful place, very secluded, classy.'

'Is she there?'

'I'm looking at her.'

'Does she look ill?'

'I've lost count but I think she's done about sixty lengths.'

Damir had watched her crawling up and down, breathing alternate sides every three strokes, and gliding into tumble turns. But this time she swam to the steps and climbed out, took off her goggles and then her cap, letting her hair fall down. She was in a bikini, the bottom black and white stripes, the top pink.

'If she's had chemo, her hair grows quickly. You can tell where her daughters get their looks, great looking woman.'

She moved her sunbed so it faced the sun, took off her top, and lit a Marlboro Red before she lay down.

'If she's trying to avoid cancer, she's on the wrong programme. What shall I do?'

'Send the photos. And stay close.'

When they came through Sam showed them to Fox who said, 'You know the significance of her bikini?'

'It's very small?'

'They're Burke's racing colours.'

*

Gary took a cab to Fulham. He went over to Luke who got out.

'Present.' Gary gave him a Costa coffee and a Danish.

'Wow, thanks Gary.'

'All quiet?'

'Yep, confirmed still coming at ten.'

Maxine let Gary in. The place was spotless and she looked good. She was ready to fly, her jacket on top of her suitcase in the hall. That was clever. She was in tight jeans and a tighter white T-shirt.

'Nice to see you again.' He put down the bag of pastries.

'You, too.'

'I need the stick with the photos.'

She took it out of her jeans pocket. 'Can I leave you to it?'

She went upstairs while Gary worked on them. When she came down he said, 'For what it's worth, you did a good job.'

'If you mean technically, I'll take it as a compliment.'

He gave her another memory stick. 'Will he want to check them?'

'I'm sure.'

'Will he bring a laptop?'

'He never has.'

'Well, it works either way. Very simple, the file opens and you can see the photos. It needs a password – just tell him it's Maxine, all upper case. When he gets home, it'll work once but they'll automatically delete and it'll come up as a software problem.'

'That sounds clever.'

'Not really. He'll see it all again, but that's it.'

'What happens when he finds out?'

'You'll be long gone. He'll think it's his IT cock-up.'

As he worked away on it he said, 'By the way, if you're OK with it, I'm going to bug the room. That's legal, it's your house.'

'Sure.'

'Don't try and get anything out of them, it'll sound false. Just do it as quick as possible. Money, pictures, done.'

'Where will you be?'

'Is there a loo downstairs?'

'Yes.'

'Then I'll go upstairs so I can listen.'

Gary went out and told Luke he was staying inside but not to call him, just text. He was walking back to the house and just about to put his phone on silent when Joseph called. 'They're early, behind you.'

He ducked down as the Mercedes cruised past, looking for a

space, then stayed low as he ran back to the house. He kept his finger on the bell. As she let him in he said, 'They're here.'

'Oh, God.'

He stopped and looked at her, putting his hands on her shoulders. 'You can do this.'

'OK. I can do this.'

'And if you can't I'm going to come down and beat the shit out of them.'

He went up the stairs two at a time. The doorbell rang as he got to the top.

Mortlock walked in with Harrison in tow.

'Photos?'

'Nice to see you too, Julian.'

He walked straight past her. 'We're in a rush.'

'Money first,' she said.

Harrison put a black Nike holdall on the table. She sat down and started to count it.

'Come on, it's all there,' said Mortlock.

'Are you going to check the photos?'

'Of course.'

'Then I'll check the money.'

Mortlock sat down. 'For fuck's sake.'

She went wrong twice on purpose just to annoy him. After ten minutes she said, 'I think it's fifty over,' and held out a note.

'Stick it in your knickers.'

She took the stick out. 'Got a laptop?'

'Use yours.' Harrison sat at her laptop and she gave him the file password, then took the bag upstairs. Gary gave her a thumbs up and she smiled. She stopped on the stairs, listening to them absorbed in the photos, Mortlock seeing them for the first time.

'Forty-two images. Crackers,' said Harrison.

'Let's go,' said Mortlock, and started scrolling through. 'They're brilliant.' He tilted his head. 'Love that one, mirror's good.'

'She has got a body to die for.'

'Sam's a dirty bastard. Blimey – zoom on that.'

She felt sick, but walked in and said, 'What do you need?'

Mortlock took the stick and stood up. 'Not bad. Seen better, but they'll do. Video would have helped. As agreed, fly today with Luke, he'll babysit you. Don't speak to anybody. Take your SIM out.'

He looked at the fridge. 'Look on the bright side – it'll pay for the church roof.'

And with that, they were gone.

Gary called Sam to say it was done and went down. She seemed remarkably calm.

'You did really well. I trust you now see what Mortlock is really like.' He started recovering the bug he'd planted in the kitchen.

'Gary, can I say something?'

He stopped. 'Sure.'

'You don't like me, do you?'

'This is not just about you and Sam. A lot of people are going down with the ship here – this is the end of an era, the team. Frank. Terry's out.'

'I understand that.'

'Sam is our leader. I know you think it's a joke but he also has a family. They also rely on him. You took the money. You didn't need to take your knickers off to screw the rest of us.'

'I'm sorry.'

'Whatever. We need to go.'

They went out after he'd checked with Luke. Gary got in the back with the bag of money, using it as a pillow. 'I'd better keep my head down. Luke, trip's off, sorry. Wimbledon please. Harrison's going to call you, just say it's all fine, pretend you're at Gatwick. If he asks to speak to Maxine say she's in the loo or something. You'll turn it off at the time you were due to fly, two hours after that I'll lend you a Spanish mobile, you can say it's a pay as you go from the airport.'

Luke said. 'You've done this before, haven't you?'

'Once or twice.'

*

Sam hadn't typed like this for twenty years and had to keep stopping to stretch his fingers. He kept emailing sections to Katie and Terry, while Katie sent hers to him.

Fox came in to see him. 'How's it going?'

Sam kept typing, clearly in mid-flow, then paused. He had two laptops going, one to write and the other for search. The printer was churning out sheets.

'Struggling. I used to do this in my sleep. Now I have to think about how I write it. You've probably forgotten how to torture people.'

'No, you never lose that.'

Sam laughed. 'And I have to write in the style of a serious newspaper. Long words, proper sentences. Pronouns, adverbs, that sort of stuff. And no exclamation marks.'

'How much?'

'This'll be 800 words front page. 3,000 double-page spread. Two or three other items – one on history, one on Burgess, another on events of the last week. Maybe 5,000 total.'

'When do we see it?'

'You can look at it in an hour or so. I'll run the Allott and other quotes past you. When I sell it I'll tell them it has to be verbatim. No edits.'

'Your byline?'

'That's the plan, if I can nail Burke, otherwise Terry. If it all goes wrong, I might still need my deal.'

'Haven't you got enough on Burke now?'

'No. He has to go on the record, with witnesses, saying he was part of the scam.'

'That all?'

'Oh yes, by tomorrow night, and he doesn't get back from the States until early evening.'

'How the hell are you going to do that?'

'I'm working on a plan. What would you guys do?'

Fox thought about it. 'Probably the same. And if nothing else, torture him.'

Sam looked at Fox. He liked him but couldn't figure him out.

*

Terry took the 8.31 Eurostar which got to Gare du Nord bang on time at 11.47. First class put him at the front so there was no taxi queue, and forty minutes later he walked into le Meurice. As he crossed the lobby he heard a voice behind him. 'Dear chap.'

Terry turned round and said, 'Vivian,' as they shook hands. At well over six feet, Sir Vivian Mayther looked every inch the French aristocrat he wasn't. Tasseled suede loafers, cream linen suit.

'Terry, what an absolute delight to see you, thank you so much for coming. I want to hear it all.'

'Well, all I can tell you is it's an awful lot.'

'I thought you'd enjoy Alain Ducasse.'

Vivian had always had a bit of Fred Astaire about him. The maître d' took them to what Terry thought was the best table, with an uninterrupted view of the Jardin des Tuileries. Mayther chatted away to him in French as Terry looked round. The vast gold chandeliers, the oval murals, the space between the tables you could drive a bus through.

'Alain's still got his three Michelin stars, quite rightly in my view. If you're fine, I've taken the liberty of ordering.'

'Of course. Extraordinary place.'

'It's what happens when you let loose a genius, in my view, like Philippe Starck and he thinks he can enhance Louis XVI. It's based on the Salon de la Paix at the Château de Versailles. Right, shall we do business first?'

'Yes. Are you up to date?'

'They tell me the odd bit, not much really.'

Terry knew this was laughable. Sir Vivian Mayther KCMG OBE joined MI6 in 1954, aged just 21, and was Chief from 1987 to 1992. Even though he was now in his mid-eighties, he had a range of interests including Oxford University and the board of Ergo, the global intelligence firm. He'd been based around the world, including Moscow, Prague and Delhi, where they'd first met, and was Director of Operations for the five years before he took over. Chalky was small fry, but it was on his watch.

Mayther laid his napkin on his lap. 'What's so urgent? Lord Nigel Burke?'

While Terry knew that Mayther was a three hour, three bottle lunch man, at least, he always cut to the chase.

'No, but I'm happy to talk about him first. After the libel money, says he couldn't deny the story, hiding behind needing to get the girls out, last minute visas.'

'Poppycock. They could easily travel with their stepfather's connections and Nicky Pavlovich. I know them, good chaps.'

'We now know Julian Mortlock planned the whole thing.'

'Of course. So what's the problem?'

'The proof we need was at the villa in Odessa. We stole it, sort of.'

'Ah.'

'Diplomatic incident if we use it. Fox says we can't and that he won't help Chalky if we do.'

Mayther took some bread from the basket the waiter offered.

'Julian Mortlock had a brief flirtation with my god-daughter Stephanie.'

'I trust Stephanie saw the light.'

'Well, he certainly did. I explained one or two things to him.'

Terry was just about to speak when the sommelier glided over. 'Bonjour, Sir Vivian.'

Terry listened to an interminable debate in French. They finally agreed on something.

'You know who the SBU is?'

'Ukraine's answer to the KGB.'

'Run by Valentyn Nalyvaichenko. Obviously we were once on opposite sides. We now, shall we say, have a dialogue.'

'A common adversary.'

'Something like that.' Mayther produced a sheet from his inside pocket. 'This might help you along.'

Terry looked at it.

'Memo from the head of the visa section in Kiev. Instructing the visas be granted for the twins and the mother.'

'We know that already. I don't see how it helps.'

'It's dated two months ago but says the visas should be dated the day before their date of travel. It had to look last minute.'

Terry put it in his pocket. 'So that was all pre-planned too?'

'Indeed.'

The sommelier arrived with the white wine.

Mayther said, 'Vouvray Sec. 2007. I think you'll like it.'

'Domaine Huet,' said the sommelier.

'Good. Now, El Blanco. I assume Chalky is the urgent element.' Mayther picked up his glass. 'Santé, lovely to see you.'

'All just coming to a head, maybe even this Sunday.'

'Which paper?'

'*Sunday Times*, we hope.'

'Well, it's all fallen nicely into place really. Divided opinion at the Firm. Some think he should take it on the chin. Others, including me, have a more enlightened point of view. Times are changing. The timing with Plummer was perfect.'

'So, why now?'

'You're the media man, you tell me.'

'Len's new job, I assume.'

The waiters arrived with the first course. 'That's the foie gras and shiso, with seaweed jam, fabulous. Bit rich for me. This is the asparagus with anchovy béchamel. Terry, you're right, of course. Len is going to be high profile chairing the JIC. Huge job, very sensitive. We have to do due diligence, tidy up loose ends.'

'And Chalky talking about his high life with Fox aka Wilko would constitute a loose end.'

'That would be an understatement. I think Len may have taken method acting a little too far. It appears he stayed in character for over two years.'

'Was there a Plan B if Sam wasn't available?'

'I suspect so. Him getting fired was a bonus, perfect timing. They would have pressed harder.'

'How?'

'I'm speculating obviously, but it probably made it clear to Chalky the Firm weren't going to support him.'

Terry said, 'Well, that was happening, but it has to be managed. Chalky going solo and exposing Fox would be very bad all round.'

'Exactly.'

'What made you think he'd move now?'

'Fox reappearing is a typical catalyst. We also knew Chalky was using that fake Dennis Mortimer passport more and more, his dying father couldn't travel. Those things all add up.'

'What I've never understood... what did you think Chalky was going to find in that safe?'

'Kubashov was definitely involved in spying on the West, buying industrial secrets, that sort of stuff. We wanted to know who he was paying. Look, it wasn't going to be another Cambridge spy ring, but it could have been valuable information.'

'Have you talked to Len?'

'No. But it's all academic, we'll never know. It remains one of the great mysteries.'

Terry reached down to his bag and pulled out a folder. He handed it to Mayther. 'Until now.'

'Are you pulling my leg, Terry?'

'No, he did the job, but when he got caught and you left him stewing in prison he got scared.'

Mayther took his half-moon glasses from his top pocket, put them on and said, 'So Chalky kept this, as insurance.'

'Exactly.'

'And Chalky won't show the Firm, that's his best leverage.'

Terry could see why nothing got past him.

'Good old Chalky. So you want me to tell you it's the crown jewels so he can force them to back his story.'

'You've got it.'

'Gosh, how exciting, let's see.' Mayther opened the file and started reading, picking at his asparagus, sipping the Vouvray. He flicked through it quickly then started again. Terry enjoyed watching him do it, wondering how many intelligence reports and state secrets he'd pored over down the years. After ten minutes he put his glasses away.

'This is a bit like the chaps on the *Antiques Roadshow*, or Fiona Bruce, telling you if your painting really is a Chagall.'

'The suspense is killing me.'

'Well, as always, you see it's not what's here, but what the Russians and Americans, in this case, think might be.'

'Explain.'

'Kubashov was a Russian businessman. Hugely wealthy, armaments mostly. His daughter Anna Slack is now in the UN, long way up, big ally of ours. What we always believed was that he was paying off government officials in the UK, and probably the US, with Russian money. Even now if that came out it would be very embarrassing, here and there.'

Mayther put down the file but kept one sheet. 'This list of names is interesting.'

'It is, isn't it? We did some quick research online – as far as we can see, civil servants mostly, two police officers, one now very high ranking, two from the RAF.'

'We'll have a break before the main course. I hope you like veal.'

'I do,' said Terry, wanting to get on.

'They call it la Blanquette.'

'Excellent. Do you recognise any names?'

'Angus McWear, he was a really tricky bugger. Out-and-out left-winger.'

'Communist?'

'No, a left-winger. Little intelligence test for you. How many names on the list?'

Terry counted them. 'Eleven.'

'How many women?'

'Alex?'

'Alex Wakefield. Man.'

Terry looked at it. Nobody had come on up on search as that interesting. Eleven men. The penny dropped.

'You're not going to tell me it's a cricket team.'

'Football. And I was Arsène Wenger. I picked it.'

Terry looked at it and laughed. 'Well, I'm blowed.'

'Yanks were getting into it, soccer – it was a PR initiative. Reagan had a pitch at Camp David. We were 4-0 up at half-time but Mrs T wouldn't let me tell them to ease up. We won 7-0.'

'What a hoot.'

'It was a three-way love-in, Gorbachev was there, he brought a team. They stuffed us, and when we checked them out, turned out half of them played for Moscow Dynamo.'

'Why was it in his safe?'

'No idea. Anatoly Kubashov might well have been at the game, can't remember, he was big mates with Gorbachev.'

'Any value at all?'

Mayther handed back the papers. 'None.'

'Could you expand on that?'

'How about none whatsoever?'

Terry sat there in shock. He looked at Mayther who didn't seem even surprised. 'Disappointed?'

'Not at all. Happens all the time as you know.'

'Chalky will be mortified.'

'Don't tell him then.'

'His life's work.'

'Come on Terry, he did thirty-odd years of really great work, this was just a catalyst.'

'Fair point.'

'And correct me if I'm wrong, you're going to do exactly what we did. You're going to let the Firm and the Government think you've got something of great value here.'

'Are you happy to go along with that?'

'I think you know where I stand with Chalky, and that I'm not exactly Chairman of the Sir Christopher Lines fan club.'

Terry had always loved the way these men's minds worked.

'Chalky's wealthy and happy, that's all most of us can ask for. He's been infamous, and on Sunday he's going to be famous – and a free man.'

'That's also true.'

'Lovely to see you again, Terry.'

'You too, Vivian, as always.'

'Good. Now we can gossip. Shall we try the 2004 Château Giscours?'

'The Margaux? Be rude not to.'

*

Gary drove Sam up to town in Fox's Range Rover and parked on the top floor of an NCP two streets away from the office. Frank arrived ten minutes later and got in, breathing heavily. 'What is it with you guys and making me go up fucking stairs?'

'Sorry,' said Sam.

'Be quick, I've got a meeting.'

'Think we might run Chalky this weekend. I'm going to sell it.'

'So we're too down market for it?'

'You won't have room on the front page. I'm getting you Burke on a plate.'

'When will I know?'

'If it goes to plan, about ten tomorrow night.'

Frank laughed. 'If it goes to plan?'

'It'll be tight.'

'Tight? So just to clarify, you want me to keep it clear until the very last minute, with no legals and without me seeing the copy or any photos?'

'Yes.'

'On the one subject over which we've effectively been fired?'

'Correct.'

Frank was still laughing as he got out. 'So it's a sort of corporate suicide note really?'

'Exactly.'

As he walked away he gave them two fingers, without looking back.

*

They left Frank and went on to Battersea Park, pulling up outside the Revolution, a huge semi-permanent marquee used for big events like art exhibitions and trade fairs. The car park was full of trucks being unloaded. Caroline came out to meet him.

'Come and have a look.'

They went inside where they were building the runway and rigging the lights. 'Are you OK, Sam?'

'Bit confused why everybody keeps asking me. I'm fine.'

'You clearly aren't, come over here.'

She steered him to a table and poured some water.

'It's Justine, isn't it?'

'Maxine.'

He told her what he'd discovered. She drummed her fingers on the table which usually meant he was about to get some home truths.

'So, she was paid to entrap you, and you did it six times?'

'Seven actually. OK, six and a half.'

'You and I finished with a half.'

'Don't remind me.'

'Then she refuses to give Mortlock any information, she deletes the video, and she holds out as long as she can so you can sign your deal.'

Sam took a drink, not wanting to hear it.

'That girl stood up to that shit Julian, and she's prepared to stick it to Jay Lomax. We all make mistakes, Sam.'

He wanted to agree but finally he said, 'She still did it for the money.'

'And you, Mr Clean, are not sure if you want to give her a second chance? Please.'

'Maybe.'

'Like you maybe wanted to with me? So are you going to screw up twice?'

He didn't know the answer. It looked like it.

'Look, I need to get on. So what's so urgent?'

'Tell me how this show is going to work.'

'You're obviously interested because the Burkes are all coming.'

'He's coming straight from the airport.'

'So that's the only time you can get him, and you fancy one of your famous set-piece stings.'

'I can't see any other way to pressure him. I have to get him on the record tomorrow night. I can't fuck this one up.'

'Well, the twins are in it, and they're brilliant. They rehearsed earlier today. And he's playing the proud dad. He's even doing a speech about some charity he supports, something connected to foreign aid. We're giving him some of the proceeds.'

'Unbelievable.'

'I offered to step down when Burke broke, but nobody minded, and Carson said it would show weakness.'

'Is he coming?'

'Yes, he's hosting a table.'

'What's the format?'

'Drinks reception, fashion show emceed by Chris Evans, then dinner plus Johnnie Gould auction. Not going to be a late one.'

'What's the theme?'

'Best of British – means you can wear anything you like – I've got loads of designers involved.'

'Models?'

'Of course, and a mix of A and B-listers and footballers.'

Sam looked around. It could work. 'Do you have a running order?'

She pulled one from the back of her clipboard.

'Caroline, I need a table next to Carson and a big favour.'

*

When he got back to the car Gary said, 'Fox called, we've got to meet him. Says it's urgent, can't wait.'

'We got time?'

'It's on the way.'

They drove east along the south side of the river. As they got close to Vauxhall, Sam said, 'Bloody hell, are we going in?'

'Don't know.'

Sam looked at the ugly green and gold headquarters of the Intelligence Services and could see why they called it Legoland and Babylon-on-Thames. An eyesore that, in his view, they should have blown up properly, not just with CGI in *Skyfall*.

Gary parked the car. 'He told me to wait right here.'

They were at the back, stopped in the no-parking zone. Two CCTV cameras moved to watch them. An armed policeman nodded at Gary. After five minutes Len came out of the gate with an older man, thick set, in a dark suit. Sam said, 'Who the hell is that?'

'Wild guess but an angry Ukrainian?'

They came over and got in the back.

'Hi guys. Sam, meet Nikolay Pavlovich.'

Sam turned round and shook hands awkwardly. 'Hello, Mr Pavlovich.'

Before they could go on, Pavlovich's phone rang, and an animated exchange in Ukrainian or Russian followed. Sam assumed he was about to get the same treatment. The call ended. 'Call me Nicky, everybody else does,' he said, in a flawless American accent.

'We're in a rush,' said Fox. 'Nicky needs to rejoin their PM's delegation.'

Fox handed Sam a sheaf of papers. 'Before we go on, I need you to sign this.'

'The Official Secrets Act? I can't sign that.'

'Why not?'

'I'm a journalist.'

'You won't be the first, or the last. Kim Philby did.'

'And look what happened to him.'

'I've already told you too much, and if I'm going to do what I do next, I really do need it.'

Sam turned to Gary for support. 'Just do it. I did, years ago.'

'Christ, where do I sign?'

After he passed it back, Pavlovich said, 'I didn't know anything about what was going on at my villa. I'm pretty pissed.'

'I'm sorry,' said Sam. 'It really wasn't my intention to embarrass you.'

'No, it's not you, it's that douchebag Mortlock. Your Lord Burke's been an idiot, but he's a patsy.'

'We agree on that.'

'That's why I'm so glad I hired you.'

'Excuse me?' said Sam, confused.

'When I originally became suspicious about Burke and Mortlock. Len here recommended Gary – hi Gary, by the way.'

Gary said, 'Hi Nicky.'

'Recommended Gary to watch what they were doing in my villa.'

The penny dropped. Fox had persuaded Pavlovich to rewrite history, but that's what they did all the time in the Eastern Bloc.

'A pleasure.'

'And I'm not happy about Mortlock coercing my staff. My lawyer will be in touch.'

'Thanks,' said Sam.

'Oh and Gary, Ivan says hello.'

Fox opened the door and they got out.

As they walked away, Gary said, 'Did that really just happen?'

'Len just made everything we did legal. Albeit backdated. But it works.'

Fox ushered Pavlovich across the road then came back. Sam lowered the window.

'Guys, at some point I'd like my car back.'

'Len, you are a genius, how did you do that?'

'Don't even ask. You bloody owe me.'

As they drove away Sam said, 'This changes everything.'

*

Gary had booked a meeting room at the Tower Hotel. Sam and Goodman were sat at the table eating sandwiches. Goodman looked at his watch. 'Ten minutes late, what if he's been told not to come?'

'Phil Nagle has never ever let me down. He'll be here.'

'You got any other buyers lined up?'

'No, and he doesn't know that.'

'Pretty bloody high risk.'

Phil walked in. 'So sorry I'm late. Hey Gary, what a pleasant surprise.'

Gary shook his hand. 'Phil, lovely to see you. Thanks for sticking up for me and Joseph on TV.'

He then embraced Sam.

'And thanks for sticking up for me, too.'

'No problem, you'd have done the same. You out on bail?'

'No, and my passport's at home. You know Paul.'

Phil looked at Goodman, not looking thrilled to see him. 'Who are you here for?'

'I act for both Sam and, well, you'll see.'

He looked at Sam, who nodded.

'OK, I'm intrigued.' He sat down and took a sandwich and a small bottle of Evian. 'Want me to sign an NDA?'

'I think we can skip that. You know what this is about?'

'If it was Burke you'd be running it in your paper. Must be Chalky.'

Sam put a small envelope on the table. 'Correct. In that envelope is the best offer I have for his story. I'm not running an auction. If you beat that number, it's yours.'

'Why no auction?'

'Look, we all know there were four hundred news organisations chasing Paul Burrell; we haven't got time for that.'

'OK. Conditions?'

'Run it this Sunday, front page lead, main paper, you can't change one word. Byline me or Terry.'

'Buy up all rights, worldwide?'

'Of course.'

'OK. Let's play.'

Sam gave him the first two stapled sheets of A4. 'Front page.'

Phil started reading. Without looking up he said, 'It's not April the first, is it?'

Nobody answered.

'Jesus. This is unbelievable.'

He just kept reading, shaking his head as Sam gave him more. Finally he stopped. 'Pictures?'

Gary sat next to him with his laptop. Each photo was captioned and dated, going back to Hardy Cobbold, through the farm and up to Burgess 'arresting' him.

Sam said, 'And you get his photos and usual stuff when he comes back.'

Phil sat there surveying the story and the photos, and after what seemed like an eternity smiled and said, 'Lazarus eat your heart out. I'm speechless. Amazing.'

'I'll take that as an expression of interest.'

'Can you guys give me five minutes?'

'I know you can sign this off, Phil.'

'I really have to speak to the boss on this one.'

They went out into the corridor.

'Who's he calling?' said Goodman.

'Could go all the way to New York. Most likely they'll want to stall for a week, check it all.'

'That would be bad news. Has to be now.'

Sam said, 'I always used to make people wait, string it out.'

Phil called them back in.

'He wants a book deal too.'

'He?'

'They.'

Sam pointed at the envelope. 'That doesn't include the book, you'll have to give me two numbers.'

Phil said, 'Look, I trust you, but I need to check at least one source, and the quotes.'

'Thought you would. You know Fergus at Number Ten?'

Phil dialed and they listened to his end of the conversation. 'Hey Fergus. Oh you do. OK. Can you read me the PM's quote? Good. Yes, it is. I hope so. Thanks.' He hung up and said, 'Fair enough. What about the Firm?'

'Not on the record, they said if we made a deal you'd know who to speak to.'

Phil laughed and asked for one more minute, went out, and came back in.

'This is like one of Frank's poker nights.'

'You in?' said Sam.

'We're all in.'

'So how much for the book?'

'Three hundred, plus usual upside.'

Sam looked at the others. It wasn't about the money, that was just the score. It was accepting the terms. His story. This Sunday. He stood up. 'My turn now, talk amongst yourselves.'

Outside he rang Chalky. 'They want to do a book too. Three hundred advance, includes serialisation.'

'You closed on the story?'

'Not yet.'

'Is that good for the book?'

'It is.'

'Would you write it?'

'With Terry probably, yes.'

'Go for it.'

Sam took a deep breath and went back into the room.

He sat down. 'OK Phil, show me what you've got.'

Phil wrote his number on a sheet of paper, hidden by his hand.

Sam said, 'I call.'

Phil showed him: £700,000.

Sam opened the envelope; it was empty.

'You idiot,' said Phil, laughing.

Sam smiled. 'You don't seriously think I'd have sold it to anybody else? And you got the book. Paul will do the paperwork; Gary will sort the photos.'

'Paul, can you run the process for us? I need to sort out our other little problem.'

Phil left with his story. Sam got some beers from the fridge and rang Chalky. 'We're on and you're just over a million richer.'

'Blimey. Less commission?'

'For discussion.'

'Bit of a week, this. Be ironic if they let me back in and I have to leave for tax reasons.'

'You'll be able to buy Villa soon. You got a passport?'

'Fox said it's being delivered today, and he's sorting a plane. I'll chase him. When should I get there?'

'Saturday night. If all goes to plan, a big showdown.'

*

Back in Wimbledon Dixon told Sam that Maxine had mostly stayed in her room. He wasn't sure they should have included her in the plan. She was perfect but anybody could do it, if they had the hair and the body. He sat with all the others round the huge, solid kitchen table. Terry was back from Paris. Dixon shuttled back and forth from the oven with pizzas.

*

After a while Sam went into the garden and sat alone on the terrace, nursing his glass of red. Through the window he saw Maxine come down, and he watched Terry use all his charm to break the ice and introduce her. Katie said something that made her laugh. Then he watched the conversation get animated.

Maxine came out and sat with him.

'Terry says we need his friend Cordelia. What's that about?'

'I've made a mistake, we can't ask you to do it, it's not fair. Gary has her on standby.'

'Hang on, you told me the plan, I said I'd do it, I've sorted the outfit. And it won't fit Cordelia.'

'I'm just not sure.'

'She's got much bigger tits.'

'You know that's not what I meant.'

Her tone changed. 'Oh, so you're happy to trust another stripper, who you've never met, but not me, who you do know?'

'Sorry.'

'Sam, we had sex, the earth moved. I didn't fake it. You're on the verge of two of the greatest stories of all time. Move on.'

He looked away.

'And for your information, Jay Lomax is a dreadful shag.'

'And what about Mortlock?'

'Oh, I see. For God's sake. Give me some credit.'

Sam was relieved. He looked at her and wondered if they could reset the clock on their relationship.

'Why don't we just get through this weekend?'

'Agreed.'

'So we stick with the plan, Sam.'

'We do.'

'Good, I like a man with a plan.'

She kissed him quickly on the lips and went back inside.

*

Terry and Fox came out to join him, followed by Katie with some pizza. Fox was lighting a cigar. 'Terry's going to update us on Mayther. Le Meurice for lunch, I assume.'

'Spectacular.'

'Who's he?' asked Sam.

Katie interrupted. 'You don't know? Vivian Mayther was the head of operations at MI6 when Chalky escaped, then he made C.'

'Correct. Old contact,' said Terry. 'The guy who tipped me off, actually, told me to pressure Frank to tell you to look for Chalky.'

Sam looked at him. 'Hang on. The tip-off came from C? You never told me that?'

'Well, retired now. Does it matter?'

Sam looked at Len, who was clearly impatient. 'You want to know about the stuff in the safe, don't you?'

'Slightly.'

'Stop taunting me.'

Terry looked at his wine. 'Bandol. Lovely, only wine dominated by the Mourvèdre grape.'

'Terry.'

He took a sip. 'Worthless, I'm afraid.'

'You're kidding.'

Fox just laughed.

'But we can't tell Chalky, it'll kill him,' said Sam.

'That's what Mayther said.'

Katie had a bag with her and said, 'While we're here, do you all mind if I run something past you?'

They all sat there waiting.

'I've done lots of research on Chalky, like you asked me, Dad.'

'You did, and I speak for us all, brilliantly.'

She turned to Terry and smiled. 'Terry, the other day we talked about the Mumtaz.'

'We did, Chalky's Indian restaurant in Puerto Banus.'

'You said the food was rubbish.'

'It was. Appalling tourist Indian.'

'It only lasted a year, then they relaunched. It took a while but I trawled through your expenses. It can't have been that bad, you ate there nine times in 1997, the year before you retired.'

'I used to play golf there, the other boys liked it.'

'Gary said when they collected you in Seville, you had a BA lady looking after you. Only Platinum cardholders get that, and you've got the tag on your bag. You get those for doing millions of miles.'

'Well, I used to. They let me keep it. They're discretionary.'

She took some photocopied A4 sheets from her file. 'Sorry, Terry, when I was at your house I looked at your passport, it was on your study desk.'

Terry and Fox exchanged a look.

Sam said, 'Hang on. Katie, you can't go through people's private things. This is inadmissible as evidence.'

'Overruled,' said Terry. 'Go on.'

She flicked through it. 'When you say you like golf, you mean you're obsessed. Last five years: Pakistan, multiple entry business visa; India, multiple entry; Bangladesh; Afghanistan twice last year; Sri Lanka tourist visa. Hardly any pages left.'

Sam looked at Terry, who shrugged his shoulders.

'I also looked at the books on the shelves in your library. Wonderful collection, but there were six new copies of one.'

She reached into her bag and pulled out a book. '*A Firm Hand* by John Cooper. I quote – "A brilliant analysis of the relationship between the media and the Intelligence Services in Britain during the twentieth century".'

'I've read it, it's very good,' said Fox.

She turned to the inside flap. 'No picture, naturally. I quote – "John Cooper worked extensively as a journalist for several news organisations and for the intelligence services, both at home and abroad. He is now retired and lives in Barnes, West London."'

'And your point is?' said Sam.

'1973. *The Heroes*. Shocking Italian war film, a comedy of sorts. The English officer, John Cooper is played by?'

Fox laughed and said, 'Is that where it came from, Terry?'

'Maybe,' said Terry, joining in.

Sam looked confused 'I'm sorry, you've all lost me.'

Katie said, 'John Cooper was played by *the* Terry-Thomas, who died in Barnes. It's you, Terry, you wrote this book.'

'Bravo, Katie.'

'Oh I see. Very funny,' said Sam. 'Terry, the secret author.'

'For God's sake, Dad, he's not a secret author, he's a secret agent.'

Sam looked at the three of them. 'Don't be daft.'

None of them spoke. Terry and Fox stopped laughing.

'You're not joking, are you?'

'It all makes sense.' Gary said. 'How long ago, Terry?'

'Actually forty years now.'

'Forty years?' said Sam. 'That's simply not possible. You were my boss.'

'I'm aware of that. They recruited me while I was at Reuters back in Delhi in '73.'

'All that time?' said Sam.

'Yes, and you've known me, what, thirty years, and you never had a sniff. Your daughter's known me for ten days and she worked it out.'

'At the same time I feel equally proud and stupid.'

'Maybe you should be the one on work experience?' said Fox.

'How did I miss it?'

'Lot of journalists work for us. Terry was perfect, fluent in Urdu and Hindi, great contacts. They loved the eccentric act. His father was in Imperial Tobacco. Our guys didn't want him to come back. All the politicians and billionaires running India now are his vintage, so fifteen years ago he came back to work.'

'I said you couldn't retire.'

'Of course not, how boring would that be?'

'Genius,' said Gary.

Sam took one of Len's cigarettes and lit it, so much falling into place. 'So the media guru behind the scenes was you, Terry?'

Katie looked at him and said, 'That's how I worked it out. It was always too clever. I could see somebody like you, Dad, was doing it. It had to be Terry.'

'Yes. But Chalky doesn't know it was me,' said Terry.

'So this was an MI6 plot from the start?'

'Not entirely,' replied Fox. 'Bit of a difference of opinion inside the Firm about Chalky and others like him. One school of thought is hard luck – this isn't like marriage, this is a lifetime commitment. Vivian Mayther and I, amongst others, have a more liberal view. So we needed a little shove.'

Sam laughed, 'Oh I know what the little shove was. The phone call to Chalky with the message about rocking the boat, Archie Hunter, that was you, Terry.'

'Yes, we needed to get Chalky off his arse.'

'You were boat-rocker-in-chief.'

'I was. But you had the relationship with Chalky from years ago, we needed somebody we, and he, could trust. Your Burke problems were just good timing; I'd have just got Chalky to call you and you'd have bitten anyway.'

'Mayther and I just couldn't be seen to be the architects of it,' said Fox. 'It had to look like Chalky breaking ranks.'

'So just how active were you, Terry?'

'As and when they needed me. Ask Len.'

'Well, with us you can't be slightly pregnant,' said Fox. 'His role was really more as a consultant on media matters. And journalism is a great cover story – the Russians are the best; we always assumed that every Russian journalist was working for the KGB or GRU.'

'So I've been fooled again?' said Sam. 'But this time by people I know and trust. Everything I stand for I learned from you, Terry. Honesty, integrity, independence, holding the government to account.'

'I'm proud of that.'

'And the whole time it was all a bloody fraud, a charade. You were one of them.'

Terry raised his glass. 'As my namesake would say, it's a mad, mad world.'

# CHAPTER 32

**SATURDAY 12th July – DAY 15.**

***The Independent*: PM TRIES TO SOLVE 'WOMEN PROBLEM' WITH RESHUFFLE**

***Daily Mail*: CAREY: I'VE CHANGED MY MIND ON RIGHT TO DIE**

***Daily Mirror*: BRIT PILOT DIES AFTER CROC ESCAPES ON PLANE**

Sam, Terry, Goodman and Gary walked across reception in step looking like the Reservoir Dogs. They could sense everybody staring at them. As they arrived at the desk the security guard picked up his phone. Gary only had to look at him to make him put it down.

One of the girls on the desk said, 'Who are you meeting, gentlemen?'

Gary looked at the security guy again. 'Hey, Fitz.'

'They're good.' He buzzed them in.

As they walked through Gary looked back to see the girl picking up her phone. In the lift Sam pressed five.

'He's on seven,' said Gary. 'You forgotten already?'

'I want an audience. How are we on time?'

Gary had an earpiece in. 'Jay's five minutes away.'

They got out and walked across the editorial floor, bringing the entire place to a halt before the buzz picked up. Sam could see Frank wave from his office.

Sam shook a few hands as he went through – he wanted people to know they were there. Terry seemed to know everybody. Sam saw Katie and said, 'Come on, you need to see this.'

'I'm not supposed to know you.'

'Bit late now.'

At the back stairs they retraced Frank's breathless steps up to the seventh and went in. At Jay's office Sam said to his PA, 'What time's he due, Liz?'

'I don't know.'

Gary whispered in his ear. 'He's getting in the lift.'

'Thanks, we'll wait.'

Confused, she said, 'But you can't...'

Sam had barely got his feet on the desk when Jay arrived, trailed by Fitzgerald and two more security guards. 'Get out of my fucking chair and my fucking office.'

'Sit down, kid.'

'No I fucking won't. Get out.' He turned to the guard. 'Whatever your name is, throw them out, now.'

Gary went over and stood in front of the guard, who was trying to look as tough as he could.

'Right Fitz, throw me out, I'm ready.'

Fitzgerald looked past Gary at Sam, who just shook his head, then back at Jay. 'Mr Lomax, sorry, we're going to leave you to it.'

Jay watched them leave and saw there were more people than usual on the executive floor looking through the glass wall. He picked up the phone on the desk and dialled. 'Donald, get up here, now.'

'Good call. You know everybody? Gary, Terry, Paul? All people you've paid at one time or another,' said Sam, gesturing round the room. 'Oh, and this is Katie, she's an intern.' Katie smiled. 'Congratulations are in order, I hear.'

'For what?'

'Your engagement to Angelina. Long Island, very classy.'

'It's not announced yet. How do you know?'

Terry was using Jay's Scotty Cameron to putt into one of those machines that popped the ball back. 'Shinnecock's a good course, long though.'

'Where's the stag party?' asked Sam.

'None of your business.'

'How about Paris?'

Sam lobbed a photo on the desk of Jay coming out of the Buddha Bar, hand in hand with a brunette.

'Where did you get this?'

Nobody said anything.

'She's a friend, a model.'

Everybody laughed.

'Jay. You really need to sit down for the next one. To be fair, I fell for it too.' He gave him another photo.

'What's this?' said Jay, sitting down, knowing exactly what it was, and showing it as he reddened. Sam took it back.

'Do you play poker, kid?'

'Not really.'

'Good, you're useless. That's a date and time-stamped picture of you in the bedroom of the girl you hired twice, once here and once to frame me. Justine, Maxine. I have more.'

'Jesus H. Christ.'

Sam had him on the line and was playing him now.

'So, I had one stupid moment, with an ex. And hidden cameras are illegal. Aren't they?'

'Unless I lost count, that was two stupid moments,' said Goodman.

'Did I mention the video worked, too, and the audio?' said Sam. 'So we've got you blabbing all about Burke and Mortlock, and I believe what they call in that industry, the cum shot.'

Sam thought the kid was about to burst into tears. 'So you think you recruited Maxine?'

'I did.'

Terry laughed. 'Out of the mouths of babes.'

'No, you didn't. She was already on Mortlock's books. She found you.'

'Oh, God.'

'And Paris. She might be a model on some days, but that night she was a thousand euro hooker.'

'He won't have photos, will he?'

'You went back to her place?'

'Oh, God.'

'And you're CEO and you don't know the law? It's her flat, she can do what she likes. It's when you do it like this you're in trouble.' Sam gave him a photo of Jean-Luc Lavelle bugging the villa.

Jay put his hand over his mouth. Katie thought he was going to be physically sick. Red a minute ago, he was now white. It was almost a party trick. 'Where did you get this?'

'I took them,' said Gary.

'Your dad's plane and car. Lavelle works for you. Donald went on your instructions.'

Jay now appeared to be in shock.

'Paul, could you explain?'

'I'm obviously not acting for you, Jay, but that's what six people were just on trial for at the Old Bailey.'

'Lavelle does stuff for my dad, I thought it was insurance.'

'Your father is implicated in the felony.'

'Oh shit.'

'I'm guessing Mortlock doesn't know about this?' asked Sam.

Jay shook his head.

'No, he'd never sanction it,' said Goodman. 'He's smart enough to know this would mean go straight to jail, do not pass go. But hey, you are allowed to get married in prison these days.'

Sam turned to Katie. 'Would you do the honours?'

'Sure, Dad.'

'Dad? What the fuck?' said Jay.

She went over to the safe and opened it, bringing all the files back to Sam.

'How did you... ?' Sam almost felt sorry for him.

'That's interns for you,' said Sam, smiling as he leafed through the files. 'What have we here? Mortlock. Caroline. Burke. Lavelle. Wedding. Justine.'

Sam tossed the wedding file to him. 'That's yours,' he said. 'So I'm guessing the rest were paid for with Group funds somehow? What happened to that speech the other day about cutting costs?'

Jay just sat there.

'So tell me if I'm wrong, Paul, but they're company property.'

'That would be correct, Sam, yes.'

'Mortlock said you two would be pushovers.'

Sam laughed. 'Did he now? And you believed him. Did that Untouchables thing go over your head?'

'Fuck you, Plummer.'

Sam spread his arms out and leaned back.

Terry went over and opened the door. 'Liz dear, could you get Frank to pop up?'

'Yes, Mr Thomas.'

'Oh, and cancel all Jay's meetings today.'

Jay regained his composure. 'OK, well how about I know you've been screwing my stepmother?'

They all said 'Ooooh' together; it was like panto.

'Big talk. You spoken to her yet?'

'No.'

'Keeping the photos as leverage against her and to impress your dad if you fuck up.'

'Exactly.' He seemed proud of his logic.

'You stupid boy.'

'Oh, God, you're not sleeping with her, are you?'

'Of course I'm not. Ask her. How much did you pay Mortlock for them?'

'Well, the guy who took them, one fifty.'

'On the money,' said Terry. 'Exactly what I said. Jay, he didn't buy those. They're his pictures, you twit. His guys took them. Do you really think any editor would take on your dad? And those shots of you and Justine. He didn't buy those either. How much, old boy?'

'One hundred.'

'He's holding them and the Paris ones back to blackmail you nearer the wedding if you mess about on your deal.'

'What deal?'

'You really do think I'm stupid, don't you? To make him editor,' said Sam.

'How the hell do you know about that?'

'As somebody once said, nearly, your friend Donald is actually my friend Donald. Speak of the devil.'

At that point Donald and Frank came in.

Jay turned to Donald. 'Thank God you're here. They've signed their deals, haven't they? They're in that file.'

'Yes and no. They have an escape.'

'Why would you do that?'

'Because you made me part of your stupid plan at the villa. I could go to prison.'

Jay said, 'Ah. So what happens to me now? You all going to tell my dad?'

'That depends.'

Sam got up and walked over to the window. He looked down and across London thinking about it all. He was enjoying the moment, just letting Jay sit there. He turned back.

'I'm only really interested in nailing Mortlock and Burke. So I need you to cooperate.'

'Do I have a choice?'

Sam told him exactly what to do, amazed he had to repeat it about four times and coach him. One thing for certain, he was doing Carson a huge favour. The kid was hopeless.

Jay made the call. 'Hi Julian, I've got something important for you. No, I think it's a positive. I can't discuss it now. No, I've got a lunch in South Ken, I'll come to you. In an hour, say eleven-thirty. Bye.'

'There, that wasn't so hard, was it? Now give me your phone. Gary's going to take you. Stairs or lift? Sorry, elevator.'

'Will this be the last time I walk out of this office?'

'We'll send your stuff on. Take the wedding file and your putter.'

Jay followed Gary across the open plan office, carrying his wedding file and his Scotty Cameron, everybody looking at him. As the door closed behind him applause broke out.

Sam stuck his head out of the door. 'Back to work, you lazy bastards.'

Gary held Jay's arm as they crossed the pavement. Joseph opened the rear door of his Escalade for him. Jay got in and slid across to open the other side and run. Joseph and Gary just looked at each other.

'Don't fuck about, Jay. Child locks,' said Gary. 'Which is pretty appropriate really if you think about it.' Joseph laughed. Jay slammed his hand against the window in frustration.

'Reinforced.'

Jay held his wrist. Gary stuck his head in the car. 'Joseph will look after you. You're basically under house arrest. He's very good on seating plans, and he has lovely ideas on flowers and canapés.'

*

They sat at Jay's meeting table.

'Dad, why exactly are we playing this game with Burke?'

'You mean the fashion show?'

'Yes.'

'Given the timing it's actually the only place we can get him.'

'And Mortlock?'

'He's the one who set out to destroy us. We just have to get that exactly right, no room for error.'

'But we want the best story out of it we can. Our story,' said Frank.

'And there is the small matter that you've promised the Prime Minister and the Head of MI6 that you'll have the whole thing wrapped up by midnight, Cinderella,' said Terry.

'No pressure then,' said Sam. 'Come on. Let's go.'

Sam had shared everything with Frank from the first day. But he couldn't know the truth about Terry. It was Katie's discovery, her source, and Terry had made it very clear.

Terry produced some sheets from his inside pocket and handed them out. 'I've written most of it, Frank.'

'So I'm editing what you've written? This is bizarre.' He started to read it. 'Well Terry, you haven't lost your common touch.'

'Thanks. Gary's got more Burke photos. Damir's got shots of the mother in France.'

'So let's be clear, you're going to run this without telling Carson?' said Donald.

'Apparently,' said Frank. 'But what do I know, I'm only the editor.'

Sam said, 'The only way this works is nobody outside this room knows about it. This has to hit the streets while the others are still promoting Burke as Mother Teresa. Only shame is it won't quite be the biggest story tomorrow.'

Katie said, 'I don't want to change the subject, but why don't you just give the case to the police? Mortlock and Burke would both go to prison?'

'And both Lomaxes maybe,' said Goodman

'Good question,' said Sam. 'If the police get involved, it goes to trial. They hire lawyers like Paul here and conduct a forensic examination of the evidence.'

'The way stuff was gathered here, in Ukraine, France,' said Goodman.

'Then everybody's involved. You'd all be witnesses, the paper's involved. It would drag on for years. Cost millions.'

'Basically, we'd end up washing all our dirty linen in public. And plenty of others are doing that for us right now.'

'And currently there's no real victim, it's not like phone hacking,' said Goodman. 'No harm has actually been done – everybody who's been libelled is in the game.'

'And Burke's the golden goose, the present that never stops

giving,' said Frank. 'He's no use to us out of a job and in jail. He becomes an annuity if we get him.'

'So Dad, when push comes to shove, would you rather get Mortlock or Burke?'

'Not sure. The evil of two lessers. Frank, what's the absolute drop dead time for me to get Burke on the record?' said Sam.

'Ten-thirty, not a minute later, Cinders.'

*

Joseph drove in silence, watching Jay in the rear-view mirror trying to figure out where they were.

'You know this is kidnapping?'

'No shit.'

Half an hour later they pulled up outside an ugly concrete council block.

Joseph followed Jay as they climbed the outside stairs. 'Lift's broken.'

On the tenth floor they went along the outside corridor, past bagged rubbish, washing and smoking kids. Jay scanned the skyline, all he could see was the Olympic Stadium.

'Where are we?' said Jay.

Joseph took out a bunch of keys. 'Dalston.'

'What a shithole.'

'My family are from here.'

Jay looked around the flat, with just a TV and one armchair.

'Christ, it stinks.'

'We had the last guy here for a month.'

'It's filthy.'

'Can't get the staff. Sky, no pay channels. Carlsberg in the fridge. All the windows are barred, the door's reinforced. If you scream, the neighbours will just ring me. I'll see you later.'

'When?'

'Later.' He shut the door behind him, double-locking it.

Jay tried the TV and then the lights, but there was no power.

He ran across the room and smashed the TV screen with his putter. As he did it the lights came on.

He screamed, 'Fuck.'

*

They got to the block on Sloane Avenue in Chelsea where Mortlock lived. The entry phone had no video so Gary pressed twelve.

'Yes?'

'Hi, I've got a delivery for number eleven, needs a signature. They're not in, can I leave it with you?'

'Come up.' They were buzzed in.

'Sounded like my mate Barry Harrison.' They went in and took the lift to the top floor.

Harrison opened the door slightly. Gary hit it with his shoulder, sending him sliding back across the wooden floor.

Sam followed and said, 'Morning, Julian.'

Mortlock was at a big refectory table in the open plan loft space, in jeans and a T-shirt, on his laptop. It was very cool, acres of wooden floors and rugs, with exposed steel beams. Gary lifted Harrison up and sat him down.

'Doesn't this violate the terms of your bail?' said Mortlock, not moving.

'Jay sent us.'

'No he didn't.'

'I was there when he said 11.30, and it is. We're the positive he mentioned.'

'You were in the room?' Mortlock looked confused now.

Sam still so wanted to hit him but sat down at the table. He produced the picture of Jay in Paris. 'How do you think Carson is going to react to you getting off his plane and setting his son up?'

Mortlock glanced at it. 'Do you really want to do this, Drainman? I've got a lunch in an hour.'

'She's a hooker.'

'Odette's a model. That the best you've got? That's pathetic.'

'And doing the same with Justine?' He held back her real name for effect.

'Young bachelor shags lap dancer? Not exactly a splash. But old married man shags same lap dancer, with pictures, that is.'

'And selling Jay stories you actually already owned, and following his dad's wife. Me and Caroline, you sold that to Jay too.'

'More fool him, he's just naive.' Mortlock stood up. 'Really, is that it?'

Sam was enjoying just hanging it all out there, holding back, letting Mortlock think he was on top. It was like rope-a-dope.

Sam showed him the photos of Lavelle bugging the villa. 'Look at these.'

Mortlock took them. 'What is this, the last five minutes of *Poirot*?'

'Bugging Frank's villa.'

Mortlock said, 'Christ.' Then, 'Well that proves it's nothing to do with me, I wouldn't do anything so stupid.' He tossed them back on the table.

'Jay. The boy wonder.'

'What an idiot. Not guilty. No points on the board yet. Next.'

Sam wanted Mortlock to be enjoying it, and he was. It was time to throw a punch. 'Maxine. We know. I've got her and Luke.'

Harrison joined in. 'No you haven't. I just spoke to him in Spain.'

'On Gary's Spanish mobile, in Wimbledon. They didn't fly. Gary was in the house, the black Nike bag. The bad jokes about the church roof.'

'Want to hear it?' asked Gary.

Mortlock thought about it. 'So? Your deals are done, I've got the photos, it doesn't matter.'

'Check the file,' said Gary.

Mortlock tapped away and watched the file delete itself. 'Barry, come and check this.'

Harrison came over and worked on the keyboard. 'It's gone, Julian, looks like some sort of bug.'

'It can't have just disappeared.'

'Technology, eh?' said Gary.

For the first time Mortlock looked confused.

'Tell him, Gary,' said Sam.

'The no-refund policy?'

'The villa.'

'I went back to the villa in Odessa. I had cameras inside.'

'I don't believe you.'

'Why would I make that up?'

'Ah, so Mr Clean plays dirty when he wants to. Even if you found anything you can't use it. The golden boy and his golden rules. Theft and trespass.'

Sam pulled out a copy of the faxed pool shot. 'Your handwritten notes and, I'm afraid, your fax number. Dated a month ago.'

'Inadmissible.'

'Not in the court of Carson Lomax. You're not editor yet.'

Mortlock looked worried.

'Sorry, but Nikolay Pavlovich who owns the house, Nicky to me now, is pretty pissed off that you ran the scam in his villa,' said Sam, 'and that you coerced his housekeeper into lying.'

'So?'

'His lawyers have given us confirmation that we acted on his behalf. Now looks like he was in control, not being duped. The housekeeper Oksana has given us a statement, said the last one was given under duress. We can use it all.'

Mortlock sat down. 'How could you possibly get Pavlovich to do that?'

'Friends in high and low places.'

Mortlock thought about it. 'OK, just say we made a deal, what would it be?'

Sam stood up, circling for the kill. 'There is no deal, Julian.'

'We've both got good cards, Sam, there's always a deal.'

'Tuesday last week, the day of Burke's press conference.'

'Wonderful day, remember that.'

'You went out for dinner.'

'Often do.'

'In Nottingham.'

Sam watched the blood drain from his face. He had never seen Mortlock look scared before.

'Must have been a very special lady to go all that way.'

He waited, he wanted to see him crumble. 'Right now you're wondering if we tracked her down, what do you reckon?'

Mortlock wasn't going to answer, then finally said, 'Fucking Hodgy, and his daughter taking that photo.'

'Indeed, let's get him on the line and you can tell him.' Sam called him and put his phone on speaker. 'You all set, Hodgy?'

'We are.'

'Now Julian, the next voice you will hear is… hello?'

'Hello.'

'Caller, could you identify yourself? I'm with Mr Julian Mortlock.'

'It's Jane Gower. I'm sorry, Julian.' She sounded scared too.

There was a long silence. Sam finally said, 'Thanks Jane, talk very soon. Bye Hodgy, great job.'

'Who the fuck was that?' said Harrison.

'Effectively the cleverest policewoman in Britain. Or she was,' said Sam. 'Explains why Julian is where he is today.'

Harrison sniggered. 'You mean the best at what he does?'

'No, up the creek.'

'Shut up, Barry,' said Julian.

Sam sat back down. 'Funny, isn't it? We bang on about the relationship between us, the police and the Government being deeply flawed.'

'So Burgess wasn't arresting you in Spain? You were in on it together?' said Mortlock.

'You might say that. I couldn't possibly comment.'

'You bloody hypocrite.'

'Burgess uncovers your mole in the Met. He's the hero.'

Sam looked at Mortlock, at the look of resignation on his face. 'Julian, this is the bit where the referee stops the fight. How many of your stories now link directly to Jane Gower?' Sam reckoned dozens. He wondered how Burgess and the Met would play it. Gower was finished.

'Sticking to the facts on Burke,' said Sam, 'this was a planned scam, a fraud. Criminal.'

'May I?' said Gary who took Mortlock's laptop without resistance. Gary attached a hard drive to the laptop, pressed a few keys, and sat back. 'Always a good idea to back everything up.'

Mortlock sat there for two minutes watching his working life slip through his fingers. Gary unplugged the drive and said, 'Right, just delete a few things.'

After another couple of minutes he said, 'There. All done.'

'Who do you bank with?' asked Sam.

'Go fuck yourself.'

'There's a NatWest log in on his favourites bar,' said Gary.

'So you got one fifty for Caroline, a hundred for Jay and Maxine, and how much for Burke?'

Mortlock said nothing.

'You want to do this the hard way?'

'Retainer, plus outgoings.'

'Pin and password?' asked Gary.

Mortlock said, 'You bastards,' and told him.

Gary tapped away. 'We'll need to set up a new payee. Oh no, Maxine's already here. Now then, current account a bit low, but your short term deposit's looking very healthy at, wow, just under four hundred and fifty grand. Look at this.'

'You can't...' said Harrison, but before the next word was out, Gary hit him, sending him across the floor.

'I can't what?'

He got to his knees, holding his bleeding nose. 'Nothing.'

Gary picked up his rucksack and went over to him. He grabbed his shirt front and dragged him to one of the pillars supporting the rafters. Harrison managed to get 'I'm sorry' out before Gary zip-locked him to the pillar. He took Harrison's laptop from the table and put it in the microwave with his phone. 'Two minutes should do it.'

'You can't do that,' said Mortlock.

He pressed start. 'You going to stop me?'

Gary sat back down and Sam went round and looked at all the credits on both accounts for the last two months. 'Shall we call it three fifty, nice round number?'

Mortlock folded his arms.

Gary tapped away. 'That's confirmed, and just to keep things neat and tidy I'm changing your pin and password – you can't be too careful these days. Oh and I've emailed myself all your statements from the last three years.'

'Inland Revenue love all that stuff,' said Sam.

Gary was about to slide the laptop back but Sam stopped him. 'Search Theadora or Thea in his contacts and email.'

'Don't bother,' said Mortlock. 'Her real name's Lula, Tallulah Connell, half American.'

'And you put her on to Clare.'

Gary was surprised Sam stayed so calm, but he pushed his chair back just in case he needed to intervene. The microwave pinged.

'I've also got the contents of the safe in Jay's office.'

'Nicked that too?'

'He gave it to us, in front of a lawyer. Donald. That lot will get you in the star chamber with the others, and a custodial sentence. Last time your case collapsed, this one won't. You've got no chance with public opinion here.'

'You don't want a trial any more than me.'

'True. So you never work for Lomax again.'

'So, we are talking about a deal here?'

'Everything on Caroline and Maxine you hand over. You stay here for 24 hours. Break the curfew and the fine is... how much, Gary?'

'Close to one fifty, we can have.'

'If you play we'll also send you your new pin and password.'

The huge figure of Paul Goodman's doorman appeared in the doorway. Sam was amazed how anybody in a Hawaiian shirt could look so intimidating.

'Ah,' said Gary. 'We can go, the babysitter's here. Hi, Django'

'Gentlemen.'

Gary gave him Mortlock's mobile and laptop. 'They can do anything, but no communication with the outside world.'

'You got it.'

Sam went over to Mortlock and put his hand out. 'So, deal or no deal?'

He put his hand out. 'Deal.'

Sam held on to it and patted Mortlock's cheek with his left hand. 'Good boy. Oh and, Julian, I nearly forgot... Gotcha.'

# CHAPTER 33

## SATURDAY

Gary parked on a double yellow line in Bruton Place in Mayfair.

Sam said, 'Won't we get towed?'

'This is Fox's car. They don't even get tickets. What was the "Gotcha" bit?'

'Catchphrase. And what he said when he caught me with Caroline.'

They were in Tim Everest trying on suits. Gary came out of the changing room. 'What do you think?'

'Prince of Wales check, I love it.'

'Well the theme is Best of British.'

Sam said, 'Fits you perfectly. Given we've had a good week, and we want to look sharp, this is my treat.' He turned to the assistant. 'He'll need a shirt and tie too.'

As they walked back to the car his phone rang. He wasn't sure how he felt when he saw it was Maxine. 'Are you OK?'

'I'm not sure, something very odd's happened.'

She sounded worried. 'Tell me.'

'Mortlock just transferred me three hundred and fifty thousand pounds.'

He laughed. 'Ah yes, should have told you. Well whatever you do, don't send it back or spend it… yet.'

'I wasn't going to. What does it mean?'

'I'll explain later. Everything still OK for tonight?'

'You bet.' She sounded upbeat, like the girl he had first met.

'Tell Luke they know he's not in Menorca, and that he's clear. You sorted your outfit?'

'Oh yes, talk later. Thanks for trusting me, Sam.'

Sam hung up. He didn't trust her quite yet.

'She sounds calm; it's all coming together.'

Gary pulled out into Berkeley Square. 'Well, don't count your chickens. And don't turn round – we've got company.'

Sam glanced in the second rear-view mirror that was standard in these cars. 'Police?'

'Don't think so, and I'm just guessing, but don't think they're paps or Fox's guys either. Man and a woman. Pretty certain I know them. Guy in his mid-thirties, buzz cut. Good-looking woman.'

'Shit. Not now.'

Gary made two more turns and they were still there, two back, so he turned right into Clarges Street which was one way. When the lights turned green he got out as people started hooting. He walked to the black cab between them. Before the driver could say anything, Gary offered him two fifty-pound notes. 'A ton if you just sit here for two minutes and take some shit. Ignore the yanks behind.'

'Done, mate.' He shouted after him. 'Need a receipt?'

Gary waved and drove off, turning left on to Piccadilly, tucking in past a parked UPS truck.

'Probably makes sense to find out what they want, agreed?'

Sam wasn't sure.

Gary saw them in the wing mirror and pulled out as they went past. The Americans stopped at the lights in front of them. They too had two rear view mirrors. Gary could see the girl eyeing him. He checked Sam had his seat belt on.

'Sorry Len, but I still don't think it's really yours anyway,' said Gary. As he put his foot down, Sam shouted, 'What the fuck?'

Gary drove the Range Rover into the back of the Chrysler, hard enough to pop the boot and shove them out to the middle of the junction. A policeman at the bottom of Dover Street turned round while a coach full of Japanese tourists started snapping away.

Gary opened his door. 'Stay here. And in case you're wondering, they disarm the airbags on these.'

The Americans got out.

'What the hell are you doing, Gary?' said the guy.

'You started it.'

The policeman strode over to them. 'Anybody hurt?'

'No, officer,' said the girl and handed her ID to him. 'We're with the US Embassy.'

'OK, well let me just write down your name,' said Gary as he took the ID. 'Barbara Gleasure. But she wasn't driving, officer.'

The guy got his out and gave it to the policeman. 'Tommy Ayres, sir. Can we go, please?'

The policeman was in no hurry. 'Insurance, please.'

'Look, we've got diplomatic plates. We're covered.'

'Well you say that, Tommy,' said Gary, enjoying himself.

'Look, he rear-ended us, it's his fault.'

Sam got out and started taking pictures with his phone.

'Will you please not do that, sir?' said Tommy, raising his voice.

'Their brake lights weren't working,' said Gary.

'Yes they were,' said Barbara.

The policeman smiled. 'Well, they're not now, Mrs Gleasure.'

'It's Miss.'

'Right, Madam.'

'Officer, I'm happy to get the cars off this junction and sort it out with them, if they're OK with that.' said Gary.

'We are, officer, thank you,' said Barbara.

Gary noticed the Range Rover was virtually unmarked, he'd just cracked the number plate. They turned left into Albemarle Street and parked, with the Americans behind, their boot still open and their smoking exhaust trailing on the ground. Gary let them get in the back.

'Hi Barbara, hey Tommy,' said Sam. 'I just picked up so many followers this week, understandably, so I'm just going to tweet this picture of you two. Hashtag CIA, I suppose. Just imagine, with the wonders of modern technology, this'll be on every screen in Langley in thirty seconds.'

'We'd rather you didn't, Mr Plummer.'

Sam turned round and stopped joking. 'And how would you two kids make that worth my while?'

Barbara was listening to her earpiece and said, 'Our boss would like to talk to you.'

'Why didn't you just say that in the first place? Does everything have to be so complicated?'

'We were just supposed to follow you for now.'

'They like to gather intelligence first, it's what they do,' explained Gary.

Sam opened the door. 'Give us one minute. Come on, Gary.'

On the pavement he called Fox and it went to voicemail. 'Shit. What do you think?'

'In the US Embassy we're on American soil, could be anything.'

'They could arrest us?'

'In theory. Must be to do with Chalky.'

Sam wasn't sure. Tonight was huge; he couldn't afford to be distracted, let alone detained. Were they really going to put him in an orange boiler suit and spirit him out of the country? He was intrigued.

'Let's go.'

Gary drove them all through Grosvenor Square and into Blackburne's Mews at the back of the US Embassy. They drove in, and the massive gates slid closed behind them.

'Welcome to the United States of America,' said Tommy.

*

They went through security and took a lift down two floors to a huge, windowless, open plan office. Every wall had screens showing animated data and maps. At every work station young people sat in headphones drinking Coke Zero looking at more screens, most with two, some with three. Tommy took them across the floor to the only office, a glass-walled one in the corner. He let them in and closed the door behind him as he left.

The guy behind the desk was on the phone and waved them to sit at the meeting table. Sam looked around. There was an American flag in the corner, two screens on his desk and two massive ones on the far wall. One showed what looked like a satellite shot of somewhere in the desert, the other was covered in data, changing and scrolling all the time.

He was talking. Sam turned to Gary who mouthed 'Turkish.' He looked like CIA central casting, the white button-down Brooks Brothers shirt, the loose red tie. He finally signed off with, 'Bye Ferit, talk later,' and came over, shaking their hands.

'Sorry, I'm Mike Reichel. Hi Sam, hey Gary.'

He went to the fridge and came back with three small bottles of Mountain Valley water. He pointed at the two big screens.

'You know what that is, Gary?'

Gary got up and walked over to the two screens.

'From the coordinates I'd say that's Northern Iraq.'

'Keep going.'

'IS?'

Reichel turned to Sam. 'You heard of them, Sam?'

'Islamic State, not much.'

'Trust me, they're going to be big news very soon.'

Sam wondered why he was clearly demonstrating that he worked on another level, the power he had.

Gary was looking at the data now. 'MQ1 means it's a Predator. A drone, Sam. It's already in position, could stay there for hours.'

'Very good, surprised you're wasting your time shooting birds.'

Reichel killed the screens. 'Going to be another hour.'

Sam drank some water. 'Mike, are you the UK head of the CIA?'

'Hell no, I'm head of the CIA in Europe and the Middle East.'

Sam was leaning towards Ukraine; this had to be something to do with Nicky Pavlovich. He wondered what Reichel had in the blue folder in front of him.

'Why exactly are we here?'

'Well, I've pencilled you both in for a day of sensory deprivation, then some waterboarding.'

Sam didn't want to banter but said, 'I'm sorry, we're busy tonight.'

Reichel opened the folder, all trace of humour gone. 'John White. El Blanco.'

Sam was shocked to see a stapled A4 copy of his article, which Reichel started flicking through. 'We have a problem with this.'

'Where did you get that?'

'A mutual friend.'

'What do you mean, you have a problem with it?'

Reichel ignored the question. 'We know all about Chalky White.'

'All?'

'Sure, he worked for you guys the whole time. He got us great stuff too via Len.'

Sam looked at his mobile on the table; he had no bars.

'You won't get a signal in here.'

'How did you work it out?'

'The house he broke into in Ascot belonged to Anatoly Kubashov, you know that. Republican sympathiser. We were all over him. We had to check properly at the time of the break-in, but Chalky looked clean to us – he was holding down two jobs, studying at night school; as far as we could tell, he'd done nothing in the three years he'd been out of jail. His MO had been offices and factories, then he popped up in a big country house two hundred miles from home. Didn't compute.'

'Makes sense.'

'As you know, once Len had house-trained Chalky in Spain he became a truly great asset and started to get more involved, so we told them our suspicions and Len confirmed it.'

'So did Chalky know you knew?'

'Shit no. He trusted the Firm. If he thought then, or over the last few years, that we or your police knew, he'd have probably made his move earlier. The Firm would never let Chalky's name come out, but I can't speak for the NSA or another Snowden fucking it up.'

Sam was getting impatient. 'Are you telling me that you can stop the *Sunday Times* publishing my article? I have a contract.'

Reichel laughed. 'Oh really? American newspaper?'

'No, it's not.'

'American citizen.'

'You can't do this to me.'

'Try me.'

Sam could see it all falling apart. Gary put his hand on Sam's arm. 'Can I suggest we just listen to what Mike's got to say?'

Sam leaned back, trying not to look stressed.

'You look stressed,' said Reichel.

'I don't understand what the problem is?'

'Len has sign-off on this, doesn't he?'

'He does and he already has. I've sold it as that.'

'Well, I'm part of that deal, and I haven't signed it off.'

'Jesus.'

Sam saw he had the photos in the file. He slid one across the table. 'You know the guy on the right?' Sam looked at it. The tennis match. Chalky at the net with Vitas and Speedy González.

'Hector González, Mexican mate of Chalky's. Costa del Crime's number one coke dealer, hence forever known as Speedy.'

'And he's in the story tomorrow?'

'Yes, Chalky used him to get close to the right people. We've got good photos of him, and he's dead.'

'Why's that so good?'

'Can't libel him. In a rush, dead people are good.'

Gary leaned forward. 'So he was one of yours?'

'Yep,' said Reichel.

Sam looked at Gary, confused, then turned back to Reichel. 'Oh, so you put him in and used drug dealing as his cover?'

'No,' said Gary. 'He really was a drug dealer, they recruited him. That's his real name.'

Reichel said, 'That's right again. Then he has the best back story you can have; well, as good as Chalky's. We caught him and turned him. He didn't have much choice. You only find out how good they are once they're in the field. It's like Zig-Zag and those double agents in the war – career criminals can end up doing heroic stuff.'

'Cometh the hour.'

'Exactly. And how do you become the most popular man in Marbella?'

'Have the best drugs?'

'And girls. Who has access to the best drugs?'

'The agency,' Gary said.

'Check. But the Spanish would be mightily pissed if they thought we'd cultivated their next generation of dealers and cokeheads, even though we used the information to put so many people out of business and behind bars.'

Sam was playing catch up. 'So you'd like us to keep Speedy out of the story?'

'He may be dead, but it would be hugely embarrassing.'

Reichel's desk phone rang. They listened to his end of the conversation. 'Hi. Yes, great. Think so. Not really. We're getting there.' He then held out the handset. 'Sam, it's for you.'

He knew it could only be one person.

'You OK, Sam?' said Len Fox.

'Fright of my life.'

'Sorry I couldn't warn you, at number ten, well done for going. Mike likes to mess with people. But you can trust him. Call me later.'

Reichel came back from the fridge, this time with three Budweisers. 'There's a girl in your office been researching the hell out of Walid Khalifa, lot of chatter, calls to Egypt.'

He was astonished; the CIA were monitoring his daughter.

'My daughter Katie, she's sort of an intern.'

'We know. She's been putting two and two together on three continents and coming up with a lot of fives.'

'To be honest she's a very fast learner.'

'You ain't kidding. How did she do it?'

'Date on his death certificate the same as Speedy disappeared.'

'Smart girl. He's Egyptian, and that's a mess too right now.'

Sam said, 'Does Chalky know about Speedy?'

'No, and it really needs to stay like that for now.'

Sam looked at the photo again. 'Are you telling me that you want me to cut Speedy out?'

Reichel slid the whole file across. 'And the line in the article.'

'That's it? One line?'

'Yep. You should take Gary to all your meetings, Sam.'

Reichel stepped out to let Sam use his phone to ring Phil at the *Sunday Times*. He came back in and heard the end of it. 'Thanks.'

'Couldn't we have just done this on the phone in five minutes?'

'I wanted to meet you both. And, connected to this, can you make a deal with Jez Clifton, buy out all photos of Speedy? We've managed to keep him out of it for years. We'll pay.'

'I'll try.'

'You're keeping Len out of it too, I see.'

'Yes, Mick Allott is our guy. Hardy Cobbold as was. Dead too.'

'Good, we're very keen that Len stays running JIC. So the stuff in the safe was a Maguffin?'

Gary said, 'What's that?

Sam laughed. 'It's a plot device. It's usually something tangible. You a movie man, Mike?'

'I am. Alfred Hitchcock said that in thrillers it's the necklace, in spy movies it's the papers. So here it's the stuff in the safe.'

'But the point of a Maguffin is that while it's central to the plot, like the Maltese Falcon, it doesn't actually necessarily mean anything.'

'The Firm thought it important enough, then spent thirty years protecting Chalky and telling us it was far too sensitive for us to see. So we've been crapping ourselves that it's something like photos of Roosevelt and members of the Royal Family, or it's some list of double agents.'

Sam had warmed to Reichel who added, 'In this business you never build your hopes up; you just cover your ass. But you didn't.'

'What do you mean?'

'The girl with the great ass, the honeytrap.'

'Yes, I missed that.'

'Listen, in the old days in Eastern Europe, it was a national sport. They tried it so many times we had an apartment just to take the girls they sent. Some of the guys had the best sex of their lives. We turned a couple into double agents; one guy even married one.'

'Really?'

'Of course. Hell, you got laid. Forget about it.'

# CHAPTER 34

## SATURDAY

They all got ready at Fox's, then left in a minibus with Dixon driving. Fox was in the front and turned round. 'Feels like the old days, going on a mission.'

Sam said, 'Seriously, listen up. For obvious reasons I haven't been out on a Saturday night for about twenty years so can we please make it special? I just heard Chalky's in the air. We'll see him at the Ivy after the show, with the Dozen – see them grovel.'

*

They came up from Queen's Circus, and as they turned left into Battersea Park Fox said, 'Let me out here, I need to swerve the red carpet.'

'You're not a spy now,' said Sam.

'No but you're on bail, sort of. And I'm not with my wife. You girls look amazing, but I don't think so. Old habits die hard.'

Maxine and Cordelia had slightly overdone the brief on looking sexy. Sam was trying to figure out if Cordelia was actually in a dress or had just been body-painted. 'Trust me, you two are going to get stopped, so just milk it, enjoy yourselves. Katie, I know I've failed spectacularly but if you are thinking about journalism as a career, try and stay low-profile.'

Sam and Fox got out, hopping over a small picket fence and heading for the back entrance, sticking to the shadows.

'Done this much before?' said Sam.

'You and me both, I suspect.'

When they got close Fox said, 'Weird, lots of security here.'

'I can't see any.'

'That's the whole point. Trust me, there are. Top boys.'

Cars were pulling up and dropping off guests.

'Christ, look,' said Fox. 'Get down.'

Burke was getting out of his car. He walked to the red carpet, loving the spotlight.

'Thank God he's here,' said Sam. 'Come on, Mr Bond.'

Fox took out his cigarettes. 'Let's give him five to get to the VIP party. So what are you going to do after all this?'

'Well, I've always wanted to write a novel.'

'Got an idea?'

'Sort of, try this. Journalist goes to Spain on the trail of an expat villain, gets mixed up with some real villains, all comes to a climax when they kidnap him.'

Fox was deadpan. 'Sounds good, then what?'

'He's rescued by the man he was pursuing, there's a face-off, the three kidnappers are shot.'

Fox looked down as he stubbed out the cigarette underfoot, then held Sam's gaze. Fox was looking straight through him. Was this really a man who could host a karaoke evening in a white suit, knock out Elvis covers, curl his top lip, and then the next day walk in and shoot three men in cold blood?

'That's fiction. I know why you think it – Pete Bolwell. But it simply didn't happen.'

Sam, for once, believed him. He was disappointed.

'We should go.'

'Relax. I didn't shoot three men. The Spanish guy was on lookout; I killed him with my bare hands. Quietly.'

'Bloody hell.'

'Calzada was on America's Ten Most Wanted list. I shot him and his Colombian mate.'

'Did you have to?'

'That's an impossible question to answer. Put it this way, nobody complained. But you can't tell anybody. Not just because you've signed the Act, but because it would endanger Bolwell and Chalky.'

'And you.'

'I can look after myself. Come on, let's go.'

They walked to the rear trade entrance which was guarded by a policeman who said, 'You can't come in this way.'

Sam showed their invitations.

'Front door, mate.'

'I want to surprise my wife.'

He smirked. 'You can do that later when you get home.'

Fox clearly didn't want to do it but pulled out his ID. The guy looked at it and said, 'Sorry sir, didn't mean to be facetious.'

'Forget it. Who's coming?'

'I believe a few of the Ukraine delegation that's over, some Yanks and a couple of Ministers.'

'Names?'

'Don't know, sir.'

Out front it went to plan. Katie slipped in with Gary and Terry milked it on the red carpet between Maxine and Cordelia. Maxine scanned the wall of photographers, wondering how many were on Mortlock's roster and if any would recognise her.

Somebody shouted, 'Get out the shot, Terry.'

Maxine felt strange. For months she'd been living in the shadows – a false name, no trails – living a lie. Now she was on the red carpet, flaunting it.

Terry walked on with Maxine. 'Stage fright?'

'I don't want to let Sam down.'

'You won't. Nerves are good.'

Inside, Terry got the three girls together.

'Now Angels, listen to Charlie. Everybody set? Maxine?'

'I fooled Sam, I can definitely handle Burke.'

'That's the spirit. Break a leg.'

Sam met them backstage. 'We won't see Burke, he's in the VIP drinks thing already.'

Caroline was rushing round, clearly in charge, trailed by her assistant with a clipboard and a headset.

'My turn to ask. You OK?'

'Not great, few men short. That Ukrainian who plays for Fulham said he'd come but he hasn't. We'll manage.'

Outside he could hear Chris Evans introducing the guests. 'My Lords, Ladies, gentlemen, have we got a show for you!?'

Gary scanned the room as he always did, probably spending a little more time on all the girls in various states of undress, and said to Caroline, 'You look OK for girls. I see the twins are here.'

'Thought Julian would show, with them and Burke here.'

'He's tied up.'

'I can imagine.' She turned to Sam. 'Your seats are marked, where you wanted. Afterwards table two, next to ours.'

*

Sam walked behind the rows of seats with Gary. They saw the CIA's Mike Reichel chatting with Fox and a guy they didn't recognise.

Reichel said, 'Colleague of mine, Eduardo Sánchez, Eddy.'

The guy was big and sleazy-looking, with a shaved head.

'All looking good, Sam. Not exactly a covert op.'

Sam wondered what the stranger knew. 'Thanks.'

'Gary, you met Eddy?'

'Sort of feel I know him.'

Reichel laughed. 'Gary, you're very good.'

'When we were in your office, you said, "Speedy *may* be dead... " which I got.'

Sam looked at him, shocked. 'You're the late Speedy González?'

'Long story. I got a tennis scholarship to the States. To make ends meet I dealt a bit of drugs, got caught, and the CIA recruited me. I had perfect cover – I played tennis, I dealt drugs, I spoke Spanish. Had to change my name.'

'You worked for the CIA, all that time?'

'Sure, but Chalky doesn't know. I'm on my way to your face-off later.'

'That's going to make his day.'

*

Sam waited until the lights were lowered. As the dry ice started and they pumped up Lenny Kravitz, he squeezed along the front row, holding hands with Maxine. They'd put place names for Mr Sam Plummer and Mrs Clare Plummer, so the photographers knew where he would be.

It felt strange, surrounded by A-listers and everybody looking at him. He could see people pointing and explaining who he was to their partners. Piers Morgan was on the other side of Maxine. He shook her hand and said, 'You look good, Clare, you must give me the name of your doctor,' then leaned across and said, 'You didn't tell me you were dating Rene Zellweger.'

'It's complicated, Piers.'

'Your whole bloody life's complicated, Sam. Good to see you.'

'You too. This is Maxine.'

'Hi Maxine. Have we met?'

'Not professionally.'

Piers said, 'Let's get a selfie,' and took one of the three of them, leaning into Sam. 'I'll tweet that and four million people will know you're here. Chalky coming?'

'No. Do me a favour. Give it an hour, would you?'

'Sure. Christ, you're up to something, aren't you? Is this a Plummer special?'

'Wait and see. Did you do Burke live in the States?'

'Sure. Ironic, eh?'

'You might need another slot.'

Sam scanned the audience, looking for familiar faces. He saw Fox in the back row, next to Nicky Pavlovich, who just nodded at him. Facing Sam, as planned, separated only by the runway was Nigel Burke. He was next to Liz Hurley, who smiled and mouthed, 'Hi, Sam.' Lomax was down the other end, as far from Burke as he could be. Sam gave Burke a little wave. It was odd, this was the closest Sam had ever been to him. Burke looked confused, as if to say, 'Who, me?'

He watched Burke make a call and hang up, knowing that every time he tried Mortlock it would go to voicemail and annoy him. He imagined him in his flat with Harrison and Django. He hoped they were watching the live stream.

The music switched to The Doors' 'Break on Through.' First up was a juggling unicyclist and then out came the twins, both in sequined hot pants – Tatiana in a tight England football shirt, cropped to show her midriff, Irina in a Ukrainian one – and carrying large national flags they twirled above their heads.

Backstage, Cordelia was about to head to her seat but Caroline grabbed her and said, 'Those two won't go out,' pointing at an arguing couple she thought might be from *TOWIE*. 'I can't have a gap. It'll be a disaster.'

Cordelia turned to Terry. 'What do you think?'

'I'm not really one for the limelight, darlings.'

She took his hand. 'We'll take that as a yes.' At the exit a girl with a clipboard said to Terry, 'What you wearing?'

'I'm sorry, dear?'

'We need to know, for the photos.'

'Oh I see. Well, from the ground up. Shoes, Lobbs. Suit, Doug Hayward. Boxers, New & Lingwood. Shirt, Turnbull & Asser. Tie... ' he had to look. 'Oh dear, not very British, Ferragamo.'

Cordelia said, 'Shoes, Louboutin. Dress, what there is of it, McQueen.'

'Is that it?'

'Does it look like I'm wearing anything else?'

Behind Terry, Caroline said, 'Can you take Bertie?'

They hit the runway to a huge cheer, a cameraman with a Steadicam walking backwards in front of them. Bertie was a British bulldog in a Union Jack waistcoat. Every photographer knew Terry and starting calling his name. Cordelia was clearly born for it. Sam and Maxine whistled and clapped.

As she went past Sam shouted, 'Cor Delia,' and she laughed.

When Terry came back he gave Sam the thumbs up.

Tatiana came back out to 'Starship Trooper' in the outfit she'd been told was for the cover of *New Scientist*. Her hair up, Clark Kent glasses, a white laboratory coat. They'd persuaded some poor sod to wear a full cosmonaut suit and he lumbered alongside. At the end of the runway she twirled and unbuttoned the coat to reveal what, to Sam's newly trained eye, looked like something from the lingerie section of Coco de Mer.

Despite the chaos backstage, as far as Sam could see it was running pretty smoothly. He noticed Burke was watching him and the audience more than the show. Maxine gave him a running commentary – 'Paul Smith, Burberry, Galliano.'

'Isn't he French?'

'No – Richmond, Westwood.' She stood up. 'Right, show time. Wish me luck.'

He watched her go, moving past the outstretched legs, much the way she'd walked across the office two weeks ago to the day. Terry slipped into the empty seat.

Sam had no idea how he managed it, but Paul Goodman was up next. Later Caroline would tell him, 'Kelly's his client and nobody else would wear the suit.' The pair were billed as 'Cool Hand Luke'. Kelly Brook was dressed as Boss, in a black Stetson and mirrored Ray-Bans, albeit also in hot pants and Jimmy Choos, and Paul was in a comedy prison suit, in broad horizontal black and white stripes. As he went past, he winked at Sam, who thought dragging the black football on a fake gold chain was the best touch.

Backstage, Caroline looked at Maxine. 'Perfect.'

'Thank you.'

'Don't blow it.'

'Once I get out there, I'll be fine.'

'I meant with Sam.'

'Oh, I see.'

The music changed to Matt Monro singing 'From Russia with Love' and Terry laughed.

Sam said, 'We couldn't think of a song with Ukraine in the title.'

'Bit insensitive at the moment?'

Sam looked round to see how many photographers were there and saw young Luke with his camera, smiling. The mood changed with the music, the lights going down.

Maxine came out and she had the runway to herself, a spotlight picking her out. Her hair was up under a Panama. As she got level with Burke she stopped, put down the briefcase and kept going. At the far end she did a turn, taking off her raincoat and kicking away the shoes. Then she carried on in the white suit. It was uncanny. Sam just watched Burke, his eyes moving back and forth between Maxine and him. She'd done a great job – she looked exactly like Katia on Gary's video.

When Maxine came back, she stopped in front of Burke. The spotlight was wide enough to pick out Burke's face. She took off the Panama and let her hair tumble down, tossing him the hat.

Somebody shouted, 'Put it on.'

He threw it on the floor.

Then the jacket came off to reveal the top half of a swimsuit, in Burke's racing colours. The crowd cheered.

Burke was on his feet.

Then Maxine grabbed the waist of the trousers, specially designed for 'Full Monty' quick release and removal, and pulled them off in one movement.

The place went wild, cameras flashed, and Burke was off. Sam went after him.

# CHAPTER 35

## SATURDAY

Burke stumbled out of the Evolution front door and looked around. He already knew he shouldn't have run, but sitting there watching Sam Plummer just staring him down had freaked him out. Who the hell was that girl dressed as Katia? Where the fuck was Mortlock?

He turned left which took him to the Thames in fifty yards. He was on the south bank. He looked both ways and decided to head west towards the lights of Albert Bridge. Seriously out of shape, he lumbered along. Sam caught up with him without breaking a sweat. Burke was doubled over, gasping, sitting on the steps of the Peace Pagoda with his hands on his knees. Sam stood there looking down at him. He sat there wheezing while Sam made a call and said, 'Meet us at the pagoda in ten.'

'No fucking comment,' said Burke, taking out his phone.

'Put that away, Mortlock won't answer,' he said, and sat down next to him. 'Nigel, listen to me. It's over. I know what you did and it's going to be in the papers tomorrow.'

'No comment.'

'It's just a question of how bad it is, Nigel. And I'm the one who's going to decide.'

Burke put his phone away and folded his arms, defiant.

'It's pretty simple,' said Sam. 'You've already destroyed your marriage, but if you don't play ball we're going to ruin your career and your reputation. Your world is full of womanisers and people who made mistakes; so is the government. But nobody likes a liar and a fraud. Particularly the Serious Fraud Office.'

Sam waited. Burke leaned back and looked up at Sam.

'You can't prove anything.' He fumbled for a cigarette and lit it.

Sam's phone rang and he stepped away. It was Frank. 'You're cutting this really fine, I'm holding three pages and I'm not running it unless you get it.'

'I'm on it.'

'You've got exactly, er, twenty-seven minutes.'

'Well, actually, we can.' Sam took out a letter from his jacket pocket and gave it to Burke. 'Exhibit A.'

'I can't read it.'

'You can read the date.'

'28th April. So what?'

'It's from the head of the visa section in Kiev, granting the visas over two months ago, but saying to post-date them.'

Burke gave it back to him. 'So you say.'

'Three visas, not two.'

'And your point is?'

Sam looked at his watch and realised he didn't have time to go through all the evidence he had. He rang Django and said, 'Put Mortlock on the phone.'

Sam put him on speaker. 'Julian, I'm with Nigel, he wants some more of your fabulous advice.'

'Julian?' said Burke. 'Where the fuck have you been?'

'Nigel, it really would be best all round if you did what he says.'

'Sorry, if I do what *he* says?'

'He knows everything.'

'You said you had it all under control, you little shit.'

'Sorry Nigel, you win some... '

Sam ended the call.

Burke got up and kicked at nothing. 'Bastard.' He took a long drag of his cigarette. 'Give me a minute.'

He walked away from Sam, trying to pull himself together.

He'd seen it a thousand times in the old days, the moment when they realise they have to confess – that the truth will come out. He came back and sat down. Sam sat next to him.

'OK. I've known him for years. A few years ago he had the story about me and a woman, high up in the Civil Service, married. He was very friendly and buried it and we both owed him one. Me getting the girls out of Ukraine was a good story, worth something, but it was good for me.'

'Logical – but Mortlock took it to Jay so they could both get me. You all win.'

'That's it,' said Burke.

'You do realise this wasn't about you, it was about him and me. They just needed me to fuck up something big.'

'You have to believe me, I really didn't like the sound of it, but he had me by the balls.'

'He got photos of you with this woman?'

'Yes. Actually a lot more than that.'

'OK, let me spell it out for you. I have Mortlock's hard drive.'

'That's theft.'

'No, he gave it to me. Part of the deal.'

'You're lying.'

'You want me to ring him back?'

Burke looked resigned.

'And I have pictures from inside the villa.'

Burke turned to face him. 'You can't have.'

'You saw the fashion show. We didn't think the kaftan really worked. You and Katia.'

Sam showed him a video clip on his phone. 'Exhibit B.'

'That's illegal, you can't use that.'

'Pavlovich gave us permission. He's in there at the show,' said Sam. 'And we have all the photos that were taken in what I'd call the "rehearsals" – Mortlock art-directing. Exhibit C.' He pulled out the faxed photo and explained it. 'All taken the week before. They prove the whole conspiracy.'

Sam scrolled through his pictures. 'This one's from yesterday,

Katia doing chemo in Kiev. It may just be a trick of the light but to me she looks like she's smoking a fag by a pool in Antibes.'

Burke put his head in his hands. 'Oh, God.'

Terry strolled up to them, whistling 'Colonel Bogey'. 'Evening gentlemen.'

'You two know each other, I believe,' said Sam.

'Yes, we do have some previous, old boy.'

Terry offered his hand but Burke wouldn't take it. 'Et tu Brute?'

'Don't be an arse, Nigel. I wasn't your friend then, and I'm not now. You've brought this entirely on yourself.'

Sam said, 'We're running the story tomorrow. Your affair with Katia restarted a few years ago as your marriage fell apart. She is alive – we have pictures. The line is you were a fool not to deny it, and then to pursue the libel case.'

Burke's mood lightened. 'I don't understand – so not the whole plot, the fraud?'

'Not yet. Maybe never. It's "there's no fool like an old fool". That's the story.'

'Mortlock just kept cranking it up.'

'It'll take me ten minutes to figure out the woman at Ofcom.'

'I know.'

'Pressure, that's what we do. So we get Katia's story too, and the twins. I'm sorry this is going to hurt your family.'

'No you're not.'

'OK. Well, as sorry as you were about getting me and Frank fired and hurting ours.'

'That bit wasn't my plan.'

'I know. Mortlock is over. I own you now, all media. Think of it like a free transfer.'

Sam looked at his watch, took out his phone and put it down next to Burke. 'You're going on the record, with witnesses. Let's go.'

He called Frank, and put him on speaker.

'Frank, record this. The next voice you will hear is Lord Nigel Burke's. In attendance, Terry Thomas.'

'Christ,' said Frank. 'The good old days. I'm typing. Go.'

Sam said, 'Whole truth, nothing but, please. When did the affair start again with Katia?'

'It never stopped, except when she was in jail, and hospital briefly. She's an amazing woman.'

Sam shrugged, looking impressed. 'Is she alive?'

'You know that.'

'I need you to say it.'

'Yes, and fully recovered, well, in full remission.'

Sam and Terry went on like this for twenty minutes, with Frank lobbing in a couple of questions.

When they finished, Frank said, 'Bye Nigel, looking forward to working together. Sam, I love you mate,' and hung up.

Sam said, 'I need a photo of you and Katia together. What have you got on your phone?'

Burke scrolled through his pictures, Sam looking over his shoulder. 'That one, and that, email them to me.' He gave Burke his card and called Frank to say more photos were on their way.

He looked at his watch, it was 10.28. 'Gotcha.'

Terry laughed. 'Indeed.'

'What now?' said Burke.

'More of the same. We need to keep you, her and the girls in a safe place. Interviews, more photos. TV. Why don't we put you in France with Katia?'

They started to walk back, leaving Terry back on the phone to Frank. As they walked Burke said, 'Do you actually enjoy destroying people's lives for a living?'

Sam stopped. 'Let's get this straight, Nigel. You are the architect of these ridiculous rules to give the government more control of the media. And here you are manipulating the media in the worst possible way.'

'They're not all my ideas.'

'Bullshit. You're a hypocrite. What we've done here is absolutely in the public interest.'

'My career's over, thanks to you.'

'And so was mine, nearly. Come on.'

'Isn't Mortlock going to come after me?'

'Trust me, you're going to have no trouble from him. You know, handled right, you could come out of this OK. You did a good thing to support those girls and Katia. You stuck by your family.'

'Thank you.'

'You'll be seen as naive; you'll just have to get everybody on side that you were never going to take the libel money.'

'Who the hell's going to do that for me?'

'You're looking at him.'

'Really?'

'Not because I like you; because I own you.'

# CHAPTER 36

## SATURDAY

Jay had been on the loo mid-afternoon when somebody, he guessed the kids, put a McDonald's through the cat flap.

Now it was dark outside and he'd got fed up reading the wedding file. At one point he was sure he heard gunfire. He was starting to wonder if he was there for the rest of the night when Joseph opened the door, which he easily filled, and said, 'You're out of here, man.'

Jay followed him out towards the stairwell. 'You can't just leave me here. It's not safe.'

'Get a cab.'

'I haven't got any money or cards. Can you lend me some?'

Joseph just ignored him until they were down and reached his black Escalade, which two kids were minding. Jay could see a gang of youths in the shadows.

'Give you fifty for the Daytona.'

'This watch is worth six grand for Christ's sake.'

'Fair enough, a hundred.'

Joseph produced a huge roll and peeled off a fifty each for the two kids, then two more and said, 'Take it or leave it.'

Jay looked around, then gave Joseph his Rolex and took the money. 'Where do I find a cab?'

'No cabs round here. Jump in, I'll give you a lift.'

'Jesus, and how much will that be?'

'On me, kid.'

They set off and merged into the Saturday night traffic heading south along Kingsmead Road.

'What about my phone?'

'When we get there.'

'Where's there?'

Joseph patted Jay's thigh and said, 'Chill man,' putting on some Jay-Z and turning it right up. Jay wondered if it was one of those cars that bounced.

*

As he walked back Terry wondered if he'd ever be able to tell Frank about his double life. It felt very odd, Sam and Katie now knowing.

He reached the car park in front of the Evolution where Gary was with Burke and Sam, who said, 'We're just waiting for Joseph. You go in and look after the girls. Table two.'

As he walked away Sam said to his back, 'Your Cordelia's a star.' Terry waved without looking round.

'He's not, is he?' said Gary.

'It's a lovely idea, but no.'

Joseph arrived and gave Jay his watch and phone, taking his hundred back. Jay glanced their way as he went inside.

Sam turned to Burke. 'Joseph's going to take you.'

'Where am I going?'

'I'd go home.' Sam looked at his watch. 'You've got about ninety minutes. Tell your wife to pack a bag and go to a friend's. You'll go to a safe house. Joseph knows.'

As Sam waved him off, Chalky called, 'The eagle has landed.'

Sam was really pleased to hear his voice. 'Fantastic. Feel good?'

'Very strange. Can't stop at the pub I suppose, can I? How's it going?'

'Burke's done. I'm at the show, the final piece of the jigsaw.'

'Good luck with that. See you at the showdown.'

# CHAPTER 37

## SATURDAY

Sam went back inside and found their table. He could see Katie and Maxine leaning into each other, giggling at something on Katie's phone like two schoolgirls. In that moment he realised that Maxine probably made no sense.

As he sat down he looked around. He knew there had been over five hundred people, paying ten thousand for a table. He looked across at Lomax's, recognising some guests, and watched a waiter squeeze in another place for Jay. He listened to the emcee apologise for Burke's early departure.

When Carson Lomax went to the loo towards the end of the auction, just after he'd paid eighty thousand for a day's shooting, Sam followed and intercepted him on the way back. 'We need to talk.'

Lomax kept walking. 'No, we don't, Sam. I have guests.'

'You won't regret it.'

'Let's do this on Monday.'

'Funny, isn't it? Always the same with guys like you, always something bigger on your agenda.'

'That's true.'

Sam stopped walking and said to his back, 'Two years, we reckon. You'll probably only serve one if you behave.'

Lomax stopped and turned round.

'A good lawyer and you could go to that nice place Conrad Black went to.'

'What the hell are you talking about?'

Sam walked towards the bar area and sat on a sofa. Lomax followed and stood opposite him.

'Did you really think you could put the kid in charge of the sweet shop without consequences?'

'You've signed your deal. You don't work for us anymore.'

'Not quite true. He fucked that up too.'

'Why don't you just give me the headlines?'

It took Sam just a few minutes. When he finished he knew exactly what Lomax would be thinking.

'I don't give a crap about the money. How does it play out?'

'Well, Mortlock's also been following Caroline for months, maybe years. He's peddling that she and I are having an affair. Which we're not.'

Lomax waved that away. 'She told me – that's not a story. I'm talking about legal.'

'I have the evidence that Jay was in on Burke too. It's fraud. Criminal.'

Lomax sat down. 'OK. You've got my full attention.'

'Mortlock orchestrated the whole thing, duped your son the whole way. He's also planning to blackmail him.'

'Why am I not surprised? Paris?'

'Yes. But Jay went solo and thought getting Jean-Luc Lavelle to bug Frank's villa was a good idea. He works for you.'

'Jesus. When will it all come out?'

Sam looked at his watch. 'In about an hour, front page lead.'

'Fuck. Not me?'

'No, Carson, not you or Jay. I've neutralised Mortlock.'

'Which paper?'

'Yours. We're exposing Burke.'

It was going perfectly, the man realising just how much was at stake. 'So that's why you got Jay out of the way. But what's the Burke story?'

'Simple. The mother's alive, Katia, the affair never stopped. The marriage is a sham – Burke wants to set up home with her. And she's fine now – we've got her by the pool in Antibes yesterday, them together, and we've got her story. This is huge.'

'You got him on the record?'

'You think I would risk it if I hadn't? My guys have him.'

'True. Are we paying him?'

'Burke? You terminated Terry, if you remember, so you're paying him. Two hundred. He got the story and sold it to Frank.'

'Jesus.'

'You've saved more on the libel – think of it like you're ahead.'

'So what's the rest of it tomorrow?'

'Burke saying he was just stupid, that he never went along with any fraud.'

'And Mortlock with egg on his face all over Fleet Street.'

'Correct. He's finished.'

'You're saying Jay and Burke are collateral damage. You're after Mortlock.'

'Being rational, getting rid of Burke and undermining his position of influence is actually the bigger picture. You're going to be very popular again.'

'Guess I can keep the case of Petrus now.'

Sam still had no idea exactly what that meant.

'Sam, you're a smart guy, let's cut to the chase. This is about a deal. What do you want?'

'Jay goes now. Frank stays, as Managing Editor. Full control, including hires and fires.'

'OK.'

He wasn't going to tell him Frank was off; they needed to sort a replacement first.

'You honour my termination deal in full and you pay me my salary as a consulting fee, but I go freelance now.'

'We get first look?'

'Not tomorrow. Chalky White, in the *Sunday Times*.'

'You serious?'

'Yes. And Jay never sets foot in the building again.'

Lomax laughed. 'Think that might be one of *my* conditions. You crack me up. You kidnap my son, you compromise my wife, you take me for a million bucks, you sell the story of the year to my arch-enemy, but I still kinda like you.'

'I'll take that as a compliment.'

'Look, between you and me, I'm probably going to sell up. The UK's not for me, and I'm not sure about papers – while you're consulting can you just help Frank get the paper in good shape? If you've got any shares, hang on to them.'

'I'll do what I can.'

'I guess you can hang that Untouchables poster back up.'

*

Sam went back in and sat with his gang, keeping a straight face, his back to Lomax. Lowering his voice, he said, 'Nobody show any emotion now, and don't look over, but he went for it.'

'Everything?' said Terry.

Maxine put her hand on his thigh and squeezed it.

'The lot. Two hundred for the Burke story too. Right, it's all in hand, get to the Ivy. Chalky's on time. We've got both front pages. It should be a full show from the Dozen.'

Maxine moved her hand higher.

Raising his voice, he said, 'Right, let's go. It's going to be a huge night everybody.'

As they got up she whispered in his ear, 'It certainly is.'

Katie took him to one side. 'Oh Daddy, I'm so proud of you.'

'Well, I feel the same.'

'I was wrong.'

He put his arm around her shoulder. 'No. You just changed your mind, we both did. I'm proud of you.'

'Phil Nagle's offered me a job.'

'I thought you hated journalism'

'Maybe. Anyway, I took it.' She hugged him. 'You coming?'

'Of course, I'll see you there. I need to talk to Caroline.'

He watched her catch up with Maxine and walk away, linking arms, then just smiled and shook his head.

*

He found Caroline in the back alone at a table and sat down. 'That was a great night.'

'The auction raised just over two million. I really enjoyed it.'

'Do you realise it was exactly two weeks ago that you and I were in the Ivy?'

'And Mortlock came over. And you were falling in love.'

'Don't go there. To me it looked like all your friends were doing the bidding.'

'They were. So it went well with Carson?'

'All done, perfect.' He held her hand. 'Thank you.'

'I didn't do anything.'

'Sounds like Carson's moving out.'

'I know, I think I will too.'

'Back to Toronto then?'

'Him not me, yes.' She looked him in the eye.

'Wow. Really?'

'Look, we're not Frank and Clare Underwood. It's just not for me.'

'I didn't see that coming.'

'Sam, I have unfinished business.' She took her hand away and stood up.

He didn't know what he wanted that to mean, but before he could ask her she said, 'You go on. I need to finish up first.'

*

Outside he looked at his watch again – he was cutting it fine. 'Estocada,' he said out loud. He'd remembered what the last part of the bullfight was called, from the time Chalky had explained the structure and the rituals. Estocada was in the third act, when the matador finally pierces the bull's heart. It was rarely done perfectly, but when it was, the crowd would stand and wave their white handkerchiefs. Is that what he really needed, the undiluted adulation of every man and woman?

He walked across the car park to the embankment. A hundred yards to his right was Queenstown Road, where he could see empty black cabs streaming north towards Chelsea Bridge.

At the river he leaned on the smooth granite wall. He texted Gary. 'It's your show. Pull the trigger,' then turned it off. He thought about Frank in the office, about Caroline somehow back in his life, and about Maxine, who wanted him back in her bed. He watched a couple of party boats slide past, then just looked at the London skyline, before he turned his back and walked the other way, towards the lights of Albert Bridge.

*

As he got close to the pagoda a voice well behind him said, 'I may be wrong but I think you're going in the wrong direction.'

He stopped and turned to face Fox. 'Hi Len, you may be right.'

Fox closed the gap and offered him a cigarette. 'No thanks.'

'I can understand you not going.' He lit one. 'Come on.'

Sam sat down next to him on the pagoda steps. 'Why?'

'Deep down you're actually more interested in the result than your day in the sun. It's the same way we work.'

'Like Terry?'

'I sense that's upset you.'

'What I can't understand is that he was always evangelical about our independence, but it was all a lie. The whole time he was working for you guys. And Gary?'

'Not exactly. And you couldn't do that?'

Sam thought about it. 'I don't think so, no.'

'Why don't we find out?'

Sam looked at him. 'Are you saying what I think you are?'

'Sure. Despite what he says, Terry needs to wind down, and we need good people.'

'Christ, I don't know.'

'Isn't today your last day?'

'And tomorrow's my first.'

'Do you actually think that we still invite people round for a cup of Earl Grey and ask them to solve the *Times* crossword?'

'Don't tell me that was all a test?'

'Think of it more like an audition.'

Sam stood up and said, 'I'll call you next week,' before turning and walking away, having no idea if he would. In fact, he had no idea about anything.

# THE BACK PAGE

### *The Guardian* 25th June:

### COULSON: THE CRIMINAL WHO HAD CAMERON'S CONFIDENCE

### *The Sun* 25th June:

### GREAT DAY FOR RED TOPS. REBEKAH BROOKS NOT GUILTY

While entirely a work of fiction, it was always my plan to set the story over fifteen days immediately after the English legal system had finally decided who was actually guilty of phone hacking. Well, sort of.

In reality it turned out to be two quiet news weeks, dominated by a heat wave and a great World Cup, albeit without England by then. Exactly the sort of silly season when stories like Burke, Sam and Chalky could have hogged the headlines.

A matter of days later, 'normal' service was resumed when Russian-backed rebels shot down flight MH317 and Israel embarked on its civilian bombing campaign.

### *The Guardian* 22nd July:

### TULISA DRUG TRIAL COLLAPSES

The story was neatly book-ended when, a week later, the drugs case against Tulisa Contostavlos collapsed.

*The Sun on Sunday*'s 'fake sheikh', Mazher Mahmood, had allegedly tried to get Tulisa to have sex with him for £3.5 million in exchange for a part in a Hollywood film. Judge Alistair McCreath's view was that there were 'strong grounds' that Mahmood had 'lied' at a pre-trial hearing.

*The Sun on Sunday* then suspended Mahmood.

# SUPPORTERS

Unbound is a new kind of publishing house. Our books are funded directly by readers. This was a very popular idea during the late eighteenth and early nineteenth centuries. Now we have revived it for the internet age. It allows authors to write the books they really want to write and readers to support the writing they would most like to see published.

The names listed below are of readers who have pledged their support and made this book happen. If you'd like to join them, visit: www.unbound.co.uk.

Benjamin Abbott
Chris Akers
Nick Allott
Christine Asbury
Andrew Ashenden
Liz Ayto
Jason Ballinger
Robert Barclay
Charlotte Barnes
Charlie Beauchamp
Rhys Beer
Roger Bennett
Michael Berkeley
Alberto Billato
Adam Black
Jane Blanco
Sandra Blatter
Nathan Bloomfield
Paul Bolwell
Luiz Eduardo Borges
Marc Boughton
John Boulter
Laurence Boyd
Edward Breeze
Richard Brooke
Phil Brown
Simon Brydon
Rhod Burgess
Wayne Burt
Buzz Hornett

Gareth Capon
Debby Carr
Steve Carter
Henry Chappell
Matthew Charles
Sean Chettleborough
Humphrey Cobbold
Neil Colligan
Matt Collings
Alex Conlin-Oakley
Joshua Connell
Aidan Cooney
John Cooney
Jeremy Cowdrey
Laura Cowen
Joanna Croker
Kathy Croker
Ted Croker
Hardy Cubasch
Stefano D'Anna
Andrew Dart
Greg Davies
Harrison Davies
Luke Davies
Andrew de Gruchy
David Dein
Simon Denyer
Matt Di Giorgio
Antony di Lorenzo
Lee Dixon
Richard Dorfman
Connor Doyle
Ray Dulieu
Elaine Dye
Trevor East
Clare Edwards
Chris Ellis
Guy-Laurent Epstein
Lottie Eyre
Richard FitzGerald
Adam Fox
Tom Fox
Isobel Frankish
Mark Gamble
John Gleasure
Frank Golding
Julian Goodman
Alex Gough
Lizie Gower
Fiona Green
Simon Greenberg
Marek Gumienny
Patric Hadzsinicsev
Ross Hair
Thomas Harding
Charlie Harrison
Nick Harrison
Victoria Haslam
Dominic Hayes
Chris Haynes
Lars Heidenreich
Matt Heiman
James Heneghan
Christopher Hodgson
Harry Horsley
Rupert Howell
Peter Hutton
Richard Hyatt
Johari Ismail
Sonya Jasinski

Tony Kelly
Peter Kenyon
Dan Kieran
Mun Wai Kong
Gareth Lake
Crispin Latymer
Michael Lavelle
Micky Lawler
Guy Le Grew
Jimmy Leach
Jonathan Licht
Simon Lillistone
Philip Lines
Mark Loosemore
Jochen Lösch
Angus Loughran
Gary Love
Timo Lumme
Ross MacEacharn
Daniel Markham
Isaac Martin
Graham Maunder
Paul McGrath
Randal McLister
Alec Meadows
Mike Mellor
Peter Milburn
John Mitchinson
James Moakes
Jörg Mohaupt
Simon Monk
Chris Moody
Simon Mottram
Elisabeth Murdoch
Peter Nagle
Carlo Navato
Will Neale
Stephen Nuttall
Jon Owen
Warren Palk
Peter Parmenter
David Pearson
Alex Peebles
Ian Penrose
Jean Percy
Justin Pollard
Louise Quinn
Peter Michael Reichel
Richard Relton
Duncan Revie
Jhansi Ridgeon
Andy Roberts
Michelle Roberts
Jonathan Rogers
Michael O'Rourke
Nigel Rushman
Annalie Salisbury
Ben Saunders
John Scales
Ola Scholander
Juliet Scriven
Jefferson Slack
Neal Slateford
Hazel Slavin
Oliver Slipper
Harvey Smyth
Kate Smyth
Germain Souquet
Ingrid Southorn
Lisa Stevens

Paul Stimpson
John Stoddart
Chris Sumner-Smith
Gabrielle Tana
Gül Tatlı
Simon Thomas
Leo Thompson
Mike Scott Thomson
Paddy Thornton
Jacopo Tonoli
James Tree
Ahmet Unuvar
Paul Vaughan
Charles Vollum
Paul Walker
Justin Walkey
Malcolm Wall
Ben Warn
Tom Watt
Simon Wear
Ben Wells
Andrew Wessels
Mark Whitehead
Jeremy Wilkins
Peter Williams
Derek Wilson